KISSING THE PRINCE

Viktor and Regina touched flutes and sipped champagne. They sat on the settee and drank their champagne in companionable silence.

"What did you think of our reception tonight?"

"I expected worse." Regina giggled. "These bubbles tickle my nose."

Gently, Viktor turned her face toward him and planted a chaste kiss on her mouth. "You taste sweet."

Regina felt suddenly shy, sitting alone with the prince. Yes, they had stood alone in the gazebo at the duke's, but so much had happened since then. They were no longer polite strangers. Intimate strangers, more accurately.

Viktor lifted the empty champagne flute out of her hand and set it on the table beside him. "What are you thinking?"

Regina gave him a nervous smile. "I was wondering if Constable Black will ever catch the murderer."

"We will not speak or even think of murder tonight."

"What shall we discuss?" Regina lifted her gaze to his, but he had focused on her lips.

"This." Viktor inched closer until his mouth covered hers in a lingering kiss . . .

Books by Patricia Grasso

TO TAME A DUKE

TO TEMPT AN ANGEL

TO CHARM A PRINCE

TO CATCH A COUNTESS

TO LOVE A PRINCESS

SEDUCING THE PRINCE

Published by Zebra Books

SEDUCING THE PRINCE

Patricia Grasso

ZEBRA BOOKS
Kensington Publishing Corp.
http://www.kensingtonbooks.com

Chapter 1

London, 1821

> *"I forbade you to write that book."*
> *The petite redhead stood to confront her husband.*
> *"I do not take orders from you."*
> *Bertram Merlot, the Earl of Brentwood, scowled at*
> *his wife and marched across the study. He stopped*
> *short when the Great Dane beside her growled.*
> *"Good boy, Horatio." Dementia patted her dog's*
> *head and gave her husband a challenging smile.*
> *"Well, Bertie—"*

Regina Bradford, the Countess of Langley, lifted her gaze from the paper. Tapping the quill against her lips, she let the warm breeze from the open window glide across her face.

A solitary bird serenaded the world from a branch in the silver birch tree. The perfume of roses, bluebells, and iris wafted into the study and mingled with the scent of ink.

After dipping her quill in the ink, Regina resumed writing. The quill scratched across the paper, an oddly comforting sound, more soothing than rhythmic pattering of rain against a window. Lying beside her chair, a Great Dane snored and twitched in sleep.

Regina stared out the window again. The singing bird winged away from the silver birch tree and glided through the air past her window.

A yearning swelled within her. Regina longed to soar like an eagle, a hawk, or a merlin. She would settle for the smaller wings of a wren, a dove, or a sparrow. Even a butterfly. Whenever she felt trapped, she could fly away to freedom.

"Are you writing again?"

Regina ignored her husband's question, but a spark of irritation flickered to life inside her. The Great Dane lifted its head and growled low in its throat, bringing a smile to her lips.

"I forbade you to write that book."

Regina stared at what she had written. Apparently, she was writing what she knew.

"We have had this conversation a hundred times." Regina stood to confront her husband. "I do not take orders from you, Chuck."

"Do not call me that," Charles Bradford ordered. "I dislike nicknames."

"Yes, I know. *Chuck.*"

The Earl of Langley marched across the study toward his wife. He stopped short when the Great Dane sat up and growled again.

"Good boy, Hamlet." Regina stroked her dog's head and gave her husband a challenging smile.

"I'll shoot that dog some day," Charles said.

"You will be signing your own death warrant," Regina said, her tone and expression pleasant.

Anger mottled her husband's complexion. "Are you threatening me?"

"Take it as you like it."

"I don't like *it* at all with you," Charles said. "That grotesque mane of red curls gives you a clownish appearance."

"I know you prefer blondes, especially named Adele," Regina said. "And I thank the Lord every night for His blessing."

Charles ignored her insult. "Be prepared to leave in the morning for the Duke of Inverary's estate. Remember, mingle with the other guests but do not argue with your betters."

"I told you I would not accompany you to the duke's," she reminded him.

"I cannot attend His Grace's party without my wife," he said. "Besides, I have already accepted for both of us."

Regina felt her irritation growing. Why did his wishes hold more importance than hers? She loathed venturing into society, where she was an unwelcome intruder.

"Once we arrive," Regina complained, "you and your mistress will disappear, and I will be alone for four days. I prefer staying home with my son."

"Your inability to conduct yourself properly in society does concern me," Charles said. "People will tolerate your presence if you keep your thoughts to yourself."

Regina felt like screaming, her irritation mixing with angry frustration. Not surprisingly, her husband refused to understand her feelings.

"I am *not* going anywhere."

"You will accompany me," he threatened, stepping closer, "or you will be sorry."

The Great Dane's growls drew their attention. Hamlet stood beside his mistress and bared his fangs.

Regina placed her hand on the dog's head. "Slowly back away, or you will be the sorry one."

Charles inched backwards, his gaze never leaving the dog. "Wipe the damn drool."

Regina looked at Hamlet. Great globs of drool flowed from both sides of his muzzle. She took a handkerchief from her pocket and crouched beside the dog to wipe the drool.

Then she stood and faced her husband. "Very well, I'll bring my writing."

"My wife will *not* publish a book."

Regina smiled sweetly, her green eyes sparkling with amusement. "One word to Hamlet, and your widow will be publishing a book."

"Are you threatening me again?" Charles stepped forward, glanced at the dog, and thought better of it.

"You married a wealthy merchant's daughter for money," Regina said. "My father forced me to the altar to secure a title for the family. Now I intend to get what I want."

"Which is?"

"Independence."

Her husband laughed without humor. He walked toward the door where Louis, his valet, waited for him.

"Charles?"

He turned around. "What?"

"If Hamlet dies before old age," Regina warned, her hands clenched into fists at her sides, "you will soon follow him into the hereafter."

Depleted of energy, Regina dropped into the chair and stared out the window. She hated Charles Bradford and others of his ilk, high society and low morals.

She had married the earl to please her father. Another futile attempt to win his love. Her father blamed her for not being the son he wanted.

"Just like your mother," her father would say before shaking his head in disapproval.

If he felt that way about her mother, why had he

married her? Or had he been unable to forgive her for dying without giving him a son?

In her mind's eye, Regina conjured her mother's image, a woman she had known only from a portrait. Riotous red curls, like her own. Green eyes sparkling with humor, like her own. Ambiguous smile on full lips, like her own.

She wished her mother had lived. Life would have been different.

Two birds flew past the open window. She had never felt like soaring more than she did at this moment.

"Reggie?"

She looked over her shoulder.

Ginger Evans stood there, a worried expression on her face.

Regina did not know how she would have survived if the other woman had not agreed to live there after the death of her father. More like sisters than friends, the two women had known each other since childhood.

"You heard our latest argument?" Regina asked.

Ginger nodded and stroked the Great Dane's head. Hamlet returned the affection by licking her hand.

"Louis won't forget you insulted His Lordship," Ginger said.

"What can my husband's valet do to me?"

Ginger shrugged, always more cautious than her friend. "I will take good care of Austen and Hamlet while you are gone."

"Are the household accounts finished?" Regina asked.

"Completed and balanced," Ginger answered, her pride in her mathematical abilities apparent.

Like her late father, she was a genius with numbers.

"Did you manage to squirrel anything away for our escape fund?"

"We don't need to do that anymore," Ginger said. "Our distillery investments are producing incredible profits. I took part of our gin profits and invested in Kazanov Brothers vodka and Campbell Whisky. I needed to use a business agent, of course."

"Is there any risk?"

"I diversified our investments. If one fails, we don't lose everything." Ginger smiled at her friend. "Do you believe our fellow Englishmen will suddenly find temperance more attractive than drunkeness?"

"More people drink ale and beer," Regina said, her thoughts on increasing their profits.

"I am investigating other possibilities."

"I'm glad you agreed to live here when your father"—Regina paused for a fraction of a moment—"when your father passed away."

"My father did *not* commit suicide. Someone murdered him."

"I believe you," Regina said. "I sent a note to that constable and asked him to call upon me the day after tomorrow. I didn't want Charles around."

"Thank you, Reggie. I don't know who would hurt my father," Ginger said, "but he would never have done that." Tears welled up in her eyes. "I want him buried in hallowed ground."

"Persuade Amadeus Black to investigate further."

"My lady?" The Bradford majordomo stood in the doorway.

"Yes, Pickles?"

"Your father is waiting in the drawing room."

Regina rolled her eyes and grimaced. She did not want another argument today.

"Your sentiments match mine," Pickles drawled, making the women smile.

"Tell my father I will be along shortly."

"Yes, my lady."

"You must admit Reginald has been less critical since Austen arrived," Ginger said. "He only wants to visit his grandson."

"I wish he would visit from a distance."

Ginger smiled. "You can't have everything."

"Given a choice," Regina said, "I prefer my father to blond hair."

Damn her. She had gone too far this time.

Prince Viktor Kazanov climbed the stairs to his wife's bedchamber and fought to control his fury. If he failed to suppress his anger, he would probably strangle her. Going to the gallows for murdering his wife meant his daughter would be orphaned, and he would not allow that to happen.

Viktor paused outside the bedchamber, his black gaze fixing on the closed portal. Willing his temper to cool, he counted to one hundred and then added another hundred for good measure.

After taking a deep breath, Viktor barged into the bedchamber and slammed the door shut. The heady scent of gardenia, her favorite perfume, hit him with the force of a slap. His wife was preening in front of the cheval mirror, unable to part with her own image. She was a beauty—blond hair, blue eyes, long legs—but so too were the most venomous snakes.

"I prefer you knock before entering," Adele said, watching him in the mirror.

"I do not give a damn what you prefer." Viktor closed the distance between them.

Adele ignored him. She held an emerald and diamond choker in one hand and several long ropes of pearls in the other. Holding the priceless choker against her bosom, Adele studied her reflection and then did the same with the pearls.

"What do you think?" Adele asked, her gaze meeting his in the mirror. She turned to face him. "I was thinking the green emeralds seem more in keeping with a country house party. You know, all that springtime green landscape."

"We are not leaving until tomorrow. Why are you packing now?"

"I am preparing, not packing."

"That gown is cut too low for a country house party," Viktor said, inspecting her. "Or are you planning to wet-nurse your lover of the moment?"

"You are crude."

"And you are an embarrassment." His tone mirrored his scorn. "How dare you wangle an invitation for your lover."

"Are you jealous?" Adele arched a brow at him. "Really, Viktor, you haven't reached for me in four years."

"I prefer a cup that has not been passed around the tavern."

Adele reached to slap him, but Viktor grabbed her wrist. "Do not provoke me to rash action."

"Spare me your empty threats."

"Revoke Bradford's invitation," Viktor ordered. "I do not want you whoring in front of my family."

"Enjoying a liaison is not whoring," Adele told him. "Charles's wife will be accompanying him. Why don't you try her? The prince and the merchant's daughter coupling in the woods. What irony that would be."

"You disgust me."

"That is your problem."

"I want us to take Sally away for the summer," Viktor said, knowing his suggestion would be rejected. "We could summer in the Cotswalds or take her to Scotland. Maybe even Paris."

Adele stared at him for a long moment. "I think not. Besides, why would you pass the summer with a woman you despise?"

"Sally needs her mother," Viktor said. "You have scarcely glanced in her direction since her birth. *Five years ago.*"

Adele gave him a feline smile. "*My* daughter will understand when she's older."

Viktor raised his brows at her. "What do you mean by that?"

"I was pregnant when we married," Adele answered. "Perhaps Sally isn't yours."

"*Liar.* You would never have done anything to ruin your chances of marrying a prince, and saying otherwise could harm our daughter." Viktor shoved his hands in his trouser pockets to keep from shaking some sense into her. "I would kill you, Adele, but you are not worth the trip to the gallows."

"You are hardly celibate," she said. "I've heard naughty rumors about you and Vanessa Stanton."

"We have an agreement," Viktor admitted. "Which was made *after* your lovers crowded our marriage bed."

Adele shrugged. "I am a lady who likes variety."

"You are no lady." Viktor lifted her left hand, slipped the jeweled wedding ring off her finger, and pocketed it. "I do not want you wearing a token of my former love while you service men."

His insult hit its mark. "I do *not* service men."

"What do you call a woman who spreads her legs for any man who asks? When I divorce you, I will keep Sally as English law states. You, my dear, will become a social outcast as English custom dictates."

At that, Viktor walked to the door.

"You would not dare create a scandal," Adele called, alarmed.

Viktor paused, contempt etched across his expression. "I wish you were married to your grave."

Regina carried her one-year-old son into the drawing room. Ginger walked behind her, followed by Hamlet.

"Good afternoon," Regina greeted her father and Forest Fredericks, her father's business associate.

"I didn't come here to visit the dog," Reginald Smith snapped.

"I'll take him," Ginger said, and turned to leave. "Come, Hamlet. I'll give you a treat."

The large well-lit family parlor exuded a cosy, bookish informality, which Regina loved almost as much as the study. With bookcases built into the walls, the parlor had been decorated in red with touches of black and ochre walls. Richly patterned kilims, paisley upholstery, Persian rugs, patterned drapes, and leather-bound books warmed the room. Of course, her father preferred—

"The Countess of Langley should entertain in the formal drawing room, not the family parlor," her father said.

"I prefer this room to the formal coldness of the other," Regina said, determined to avoid an argument. At least, she would try. "I only entertain people I like in this room."

"We're flattered," Reginald said, his tone sarcastic. "Aren't we, Forest?"

Thinking an argument seemed imminent, Regina

looked at Forest Fredericks, who winked at her. She smiled at the man whom she had always considered an uncle. If not for Forest and Ginger's father, she would have felt completely unloved.

Short and slight, Uncle Forest had a receding hairline and the beginnings of a potbelly. He wore thick spectacles that slipped constantly, which he pushed up with an index finger. Behind those spectacles, Forest had the warmest brown eyes and kindly expression.

In fact, Forest Fredericks was the opposite of Reginald Smith in looks, bearing, and personality. Her father was reasonably tall, just under six feet, and had black hair tinged with silver. The attractive widower had refused to remarry, though, certain that women wanted his money.

"How are you, Uncle Forest?"

"Quite well." He pushed his slipping spectacles up.

"Give me my grandson," her father ordered.

Regina passed him the boy. Austen stared at his grandfather's somber expression and reached to touch his face.

"Gapa," Austen said.

"He knows me," Reginald said, his dark eyes gleaming with pleasure.

How many years had it been since pleasure had registered on her father's face? She had no memory of his ever smiling at her with approval.

"The boy bears a remarkable resemblance to you," Forest said.

Regina covered her mouth to hide her smile. She looked at her father's business associate and wondered how he could say that without laughing. She supposed Uncle Forest was merely flattering her father. Many people did that to deflect his sarcastic gruffness.

Except for the black hair and brown eyes, Austen looked nothing like his grandfather. He was the image of her husband, who also had dark hair and eyes.

"I am glad you decided to visit today," Regina said. "Charles and I are leaving tomorrow for the Duke of Inverary's country house."

"You are traveling in the highest circles," Reginald said, seeming pleased. "Mind your manners, missy."

Regina felt the familiar spark of irritation. She was a grown woman of twenty-two. Did her father believe she could not conduct herself properly, or was he trying to start an argument?

"You aren't taking Austen?"

"Austen will remain in London with Nanny Sprig and Ginger."

"Then visiting my grandson today or tomorrow matters little," Reginald said, his gaze on the boy.

Seeing his daughter matters little to him.

Regina flinched at his sentiment but steeled herself against the pain. After a lifetime of callous disregard, Reginald Smith still possessed the power to hurt her.

"Well, I am happy to visit both Regina and Austen," Forest interjected.

Regina managed a faint smile. "Thank you, Uncle Forest."

"How is Ginger feeling these days?" Forest pushed his spectacles up with his index finger.

"She still believes someone murdered her father," Regina answered. "Bartholomew Evans loved his daughter too much to commit suicide."

"Bart hanged himself," Reginald said bluntly.

"There was no evidence of foul play. None whatsoever."

"I find this subject distasteful," Regina said, glad that her friend had not heard her father.

"The subject or my opinion?"

"Both." Her father was the most insensitive man she had ever met. Except for her husband.

"You will certainly enjoy yourself at the duke's party," Forest said into the lengthening silence.

"I will not enjoy myself," Regina said. "Upon arrival, Charles will disappear with his mistress."

Forest Fredericks blushed with embarrassment and pushed his spectacles up.

Reginald chuckled, drawing her attention. "Men will always be men and take what is offered. That's the way the world wags."

"Not my world." Regina lost her temper. "How can my own father condone such immoral behavior? You disgust me almost as much as my husband."

"I should have known that red hair would give you a fiery temper." Reginald shook his head in disapproval. "You remind me of your mother."

"Those famous last words," Regina said. "If you wanted a title so badly, you should have married Bradford and left me in peace."

"Watch your mouth, missy," Reginald warned. "You're not too old—"

"Spare me the fatherly discipline," Regina interrupted. "If you cannot show me respect, then expect none in return. Do not bother visiting me again."

"Charles will have something to say about that," Reginald said.

"Chuck cares only about drinking, gambling, and whoring," Regina told him. "Stop blushing, Uncle

Forest." She looked at her father again, adding, "My husband doesn't care if you never see Austen."

"He does if he wants my money."

"When you die," Regina said, "Charles will inherit all your money through me. I guarantee nothing will be left for Austen. All will have been wasted on cards, gin, and whores."

"You always did think you knew more than your father."

"Perhaps I do."

"I have taken precautions against your husband's spending habits," her father informed her.

"What do you mean?"

"Forest is the executor of my estate," Reginald answered. "Charles and you will receive generous allowances, but Forest will control my assets until Austen reaches his majority. Hopefully, your husband will have drunk himself into the grave by then."

"With all due respect to Uncle Forest, I am capable of handling my husband and my finances," Regina said, fuming at his high-handedness. "Ginger Evans has inherited her father's genius with numbers. If I cannot control my own money with her assistance, give it to charity."

"The money is *mine,* not yours," Reginald reminded her. "You ungrateful wretch. I found you an earl to marry, and your son will be an earl."

"You chose yourself a son-in-law," Regina said. "You traded me for a title."

"You will thank me—"

"—for dying and leaving me in peace."

"You will regret those words some day."

"I can manage the regret, if not my own finances."

"Regina, perhaps we could have a private word," Forest said, ending the all-too-familiar bickering.

"I don't need her permission to do what I want," Reginald insisted.

"You do, if you don't want her to give Austen's inheritance to charity." Forest pushed his spectacles up and gave him a pointed look. Her father nodded in reluctant agreement.

Regina followed Forest into the corridor. "Both Ginger and I adore you," she said, "but we can take care of ourselves."

"I understand your feelings on the matter," Forest told her. "Reginald does not comprehend that women are different these days. Your father can be inflexible." He smiled to soften his next words. "Inflexibility is a quality you have inherited from him. Once he's gone, I will relinquish full control of the money to you. Of course, I will expect to advise you for a period of time."

Regina knew that was the best she could do. Her father had never had any faith in her abilities because she could never be the son he had wanted. In his eyes, his daughter was *only* a woman.

Regina inclined her head. "I will accept his inheritance."

They returned to the drawing room.

"Regina agrees to accept the inheritance and your plans for it," Forest told her father.

"Should I thank her for agreeing to take my money?" Reginald grumbled. "How did you manage that, Forest?"

"Regina is an intelligent young woman." He pushed his spectacles up. "Though, you refuse to recognize her worth."

Reginald stood, kissed his grandson's pudgy cheeks, and passed him to her. "Do not worry overmuch about your husband's mistress," he said in an awkward attempt to soothe her.

"I pray each night for Adele Kazanov's continued good health," Regina said, her green eyes sparkling with amusement.

Reginald gave her a decidedly unamused look and then followed Forest to the door.

"Father?"

He paused and turned around.

"Resembling my mother makes me proud."

Chapter 2

"You cannot hibernate in this chamber."
Dementia looked up from her writing. Bertram
sauntered across the room toward her.
"You need to mingle with the other guests."
Dementia arched a copper brow at her husband.
"I prefer eating dirt."

Muted voices and the mingling scents of lilacs, wisteria, and roses drifted up from the Duke of Inverary's garden. Regina tried to concentrate on her writing, but the sight outside her window appealed to her senses. The landscaped gardens and the countryside's myriad hues of green contrasted sharply with London, where she had lived her entire life. Indeed, this could be paradise if she wasn't married to—

"Get out there and mingle."

The sound of her husband's voice grated on her nerves. She had traveled over bumpy roads for several hours to a place she did not want to go in order to mingle with people who did not want her there.

Regina knew she could not pass the next forty years with this man. She needed to free herself. Somehow.

He raised his voice. "Did you hear me?"

"The people in the garden heard you." Regina

set the quill aside and stood to face him. "I prefer writing until dinner."

"I don't care what you prefer." Charles marched across the bedchamber and stood close, trying to intimidate her with his size, his face mere inches from hers. "Remember, wife, your dog isn't here to protect you."

Regina gave him an ambiguous smile. "Hamlet is awaiting your return to London, Chuck."

Her husband ignored the detested nickname. "Good manners requires you to greet your hostess."

Regina knew he was right about that. Remaining in her chamber was rude, but inflicting her unwelcome presence on others was also rude.

"You bring more attention on yourself by hiding in your chamber," Charles said. "Mingle for thirty minutes, and then I don't care what you do."

Regina did not wish to bring more attention on herself. She smoothed an imaginary wrinkle from her pale yellow gown and inclined her head.

"I will mingle for thirty minutes each afternoon and evening."

"Hopefully, you won't do much damage in thirty minutes."

Suppressing a smile, Regina stared him straight in the eye. "I promised to mingle. Embarrassing you is quite another matter."

Charles gestured to the door, muttering, "I wish your hair was a different color."

Regina felt like a woman on her way to the gallows. Her heartbeat quickened with each step closer to the garden. Pasting an indifferent expression on her face, she hid her trembling hands in the folds of her gown's skirt. She knew she should not care what these aristocrats thought of her, but she did. Her emotions were not as easily controlled as her thoughts.

Stepping into the garden, Regina pressed the clammy palms of her hands against the skirt of her gown. She hoped no one wanted to shake her hand.

The Duke of Inverary's garden was an earthly paradise. A rectangular expanse of lawn, shrubs, and flowers lay nearest the manor. Small groups of attractively garbed aristocrats spoke in quiet voices, the ladies' scents mingling with the perfume of primary- and pastel-hued flowers. An Elizabethan maze created from clipped hedges stood beyond, and manicured lawns carpeted the grounds in the distance.

Without touching her, Charles escorted Regina in the direction of three women. Regina felt a dozen gazes following their progress.

How dare these shallow, indolent people judge her. In that instant, Regina decided to adopt an attitude that would live down to their low expectations of her. If she embarrassed him, her husband would leave her home next time.

Auburn-haired and dimpled, the Duchess of Inverary appeared more youthful than approaching midlife. The other two women were much younger than the duchess. The dark-haired woman smiled, seemingly approachable and pleasant. The pouting blonde had overdressed, her low cut gown and emerald and diamond necklace more suited for an evening at the opera.

"Your Highnesses and Your Grace, I present my wife," Charles introduced them. "Regina, these ladies are the Duchess of Inverary, Princess Samantha, Her Grace's niece, and Princess Adele."

"I am pleased to make your acquaintances,"

Regina said, giving the duchess and her niece a nervous smile.

"Charles?"

Regina glanced over her shoulder. Cedric Barrows and Vanessa Stanton, her husband's cousins, were strolling toward them.

"If you will excuse me," Charles said, looking at Princess Adele, "I will return in a moment."

Regina looked at the blonde. "Princess Adele, I have heard so much about you."

The other woman flushed. "Really?"

"Indeed, Chuck cannot say enough good things about you," Regina told her.

Adele looked confused. "Chuck?"

"My husband, the man with whom you are having an affair?" Regina ignored the smothered chuckles from the duchess and the princess.

"Charles despises nicknames," Adele said.

"Yes, I know."

Adele gave her a feline smile. "You aren't jealous, are you?"

"I did not walk down that aisle voluntarily," Regina said. "I love your necklace. A tad ornate for an afternoon in the country, don't you think?"

Princess Adele inspected her from the top of her red hair to the tips of her shoes. "What could *you* possibly know about taste?"

"I know that you have none," Regina said. "If you did, you would not be having an affair with Chuck."

Charles returned at that moment. "Would you care to walk with me, Princess Adele?"

Regina realized that many of the guests were watching her and the departing couple. "I apologize for making you uncomfortable," she said to the duchess and her niece.

"On the contrary, darling, I am enjoying every

minute," the duchess drawled. "You could not have handled that any better if *I* had raised you."

"I pray each night for Princess Adele's good health," Regina said, making them smile. "The Lord is more apt to answer that prayer than a request for my husband's early demise."

The Duchess of Inverary chuckled throatily and touched her arm. "I am pleased you accompanied *Chuck*. If you will excuse me, darlings, I need to greet my other guests."

Alone with the princess, Regina felt uncomfortable. She had no idea what to say and thought to return to her chamber.

"I enjoyed meeting you, Your Highness." Regina turned to leave.

Princess Samantha touched her arm. "Please don't leave. Stay and talk to me."

Her request surprised Regina. "You want *my* company?"

Samantha nodded. "I always feel uncomfortable in a large group."

"You do?"

"My aunt adores entertaining the alleged elite," Samantha answered, "but I prefer less shallow people. Like you." She gestured toward the other guests. "I feel inferior with them, though I know most of what they say are lies."

The princess suffered the same insecurities as she did? Perhaps not all aristocrats were the same.

"You are a princess."

"By marriage only. You are a countess."

Regina smiled. "By marriage only. Call me Reggie."

"You may call me Samantha."

Regina shifted her gaze to the children sitting at a table on one side of the lawn area. "Are those your children?"

"Those are mine along with a few nieces and nephews," Samantha answered. "Do you have any children?"

"I have a one-year-old son, Austen," Regina answered. "I named him in honor of my favorite author, Jane Austen. Have you read any of her books?"

"I have read all of them."

"Her stories have inspired me to write my own."

"How exciting. I have never met an author," Samantha said. "Tell me about your story."

"I would like to meet your children first."

Smanatha inclined her head. "Come along, then."

The youngest, a three-year-old boy, saw them approaching and escaped his nanny. He ran across the lawns, calling, "Mummy."

"Magnus is named for my uncle," Samantha said.

Regina crouched down to be eye level with the boy. "I am pleased to meet you."

Magnus pointed at her hair. "Red."

Regina laughed and held a fiery curl out to him. "Do you want to touch?"

He did.

"Is it hot?"

The boy shook his head.

Suddenly, Regina found herself surrounded by the princess's other children. All wanted to touch her curls, to kiss her cheek, or to bow over her hand.

"Usually, guests pay no attention to children," Samantha said. "I suppose that's the reason your attention excited them."

"I wish I had brought Austen," Regina said. "All these children would amaze him."

"Austen and you must visit us in London," Samantha invited her.

Regina smiled. "We would love to visit."

* * *

"Vodka?"

Prince Viktor Kazanov lifted the glass of vodka from his brother's hand. He raised the glass in salute to the Duke of Inverary, sitting on the opposite side of the desk, and then gulped the vodka in one healthy swig.

Muted voices drifted through the open windows from the garden, drawing his attention. Viktor knew the next few days would be embarrassing because his wife's lover was in attendance. It was past time to rid himself of his whoring wife.

"Pass me the vodka."

"Are you planning to get drunk?" Prince Rudolf asked, handing him the vodka bottle.

"I never indulge in drunkness." Viktor gave his brother a sidelong glance. "Are Mikhail and Stepan expected this weekend?"

"Our baby brothers will arrive tomorrow."

"Robert and Angelica will also arrive tomorrow," the Duke of Inverary said, referring to his son and daughter-in-law.

"If I had known your children would be here," Viktor said, "I would have brought Sally."

"Samantha sent Adele a note," Rudolf told him.

Viktor shook his head in disgust. How typical of his wife to refuse to be bothered by their daughter's presence. He cursed the day he had wed Adele, his daughter the only good coming from their union.

"I think a problem is brewing," Rudolf said into the silence. "We offered a ten percent share in Kazanov Brothers vodka to the public, assuming several people would invest. However, one person purchased the whole ten percent."

"The same thing happened with the ten percent

of Campbell Whisky offered for sale," the duke said.

"Who bought the shares?" Viktor asked.

"Mr. Warrens, a business agent, acted on behalf of Mr. Evans Smith," Rudolf answered. He looked at the duke. "Have you ever heard of Evans Smith?"

The Duke of Inverary shook his head. "The same Evans Smith scooped up the shares in Campbell Whisky."

Prince Viktor poured himself another vodka but didn't drink it. "Did you ask Warrens about Smith?"

"He refused to divulge anything except the man's name," Rudolf answered. "Smith prefers to remain anonymous and deal with us through Warrens who, by the way, has an impeccable reputation."

"I'll have my agents investigate this Evans Smith," the duke said.

"In the meantime, we should dangle another five or ten percent to draw the mysterious Evans Smith out of hiding," Rudolf suggested. "I prefer to deal directly with the man."

"If he bites," Viktor replied, "Smith will own twenty percent of Kazanov Brothers."

"We will own eighty percent," Rudolf argued.

"Do not make any moves until we discuss this with Mikhail and Stepan." Viktor gulped the vodka and set the empty glass on the duke's desk. "I have decided to divorce Adele and will be meeting with my barrister upon return to London. Sally will be better off without her whoring mother setting a bad example, and I will be free to marry again and sire an heir."

"Are you considering Vanessa Stanton?" the duke asked.

"No."

"Forget the divorce," Rudolf joked. "Kill Adele off and save an unsuspecting mankind."

"Adele is not worth my hanging for her murder." Viktor stood and sauntered across the room to stare out the window. He let his gaze drift across the guests until his attention fixed on a woman with his sister-in-law.

The unknown woman seemed to be enjoying the company of his nieces and nephews. They touched her fabulously red riot of curls, kissed her cheek, and practiced their curtseys and bows.

"Who is the redhead?" Viktor asked, gesturing toward the garden.

Rudolf crossed the room and smiled at the sight of his children surrounding a young woman. "That is the merchant's daughter."

"Who?"

"Bradford's wife."

The petite redhead stood and spoke to Samantha. Even from this distance, she appeared a beauty and modestly gowned. Unlike his own wife.

"Bradford married her for her father's money," Rudolf said. "Everyone refers to her as the merchant's daughter. I heard she is a bluestocking of sorts."

"That sounds like a marriage made in hell." Viktor smiled. "The bluestocking and the reprobate seems like a Jane Austen novel. She married him for the title?"

"Her father forced her down the aisle for the title," Rudolf answered.

"I've had dealings with Reginald Smith," the Duke of Inverary said, standing beside them. "Her father seemed like he could be a tyrant."

"Any relation to Evans Smith?" Rudolf asked.

"I have no idea."

"Any children?" Viktor asked.

"Lady Bradford has a one-year-old son." Rudolf grinned. "The lady also owns a ferocious Great Dane to protect her from her husband."

The Duke of Inverary chuckled. "Smart girl."

"How do you know this?" Viktor asked his brother.

"Servants do gossip."

Why don't you try her? Viktor recalled his wife's words. *The prince and the merchant's daughter coupling . . .*

Perhaps Charles Bradford should worry about his own wife's fidelity. The Earl of Langley needed to learn a hard lesson.

Viktor had no intention of dishonoring the woman to teach her husband a lesson, but outrageous flirting and stolen kisses did not fall into the category of unfaithfulness. The Countess of Langley was attractive enough so that would not be a hardship.

"Come along, Brother." Viktor turned away from the window. "I want an introduction to Bradford's wife."

Leaving the manor, the two Russian princes strolled across the garden. Prince Viktor kept his dark gaze fixed on the red-haired woman with his sister-in-law.

Three-year-old Magnus Kazanov dashed across the lawn and offered the Countess of Langley a handful of flowers. Accepting his gift, she kissed his cheek and said something. His nephew pointed at one of the flower beds and the countess laughed, a sweetly melodious sound carried on the gentle breeze.

"Daddy," Magnus called, seeing their approach.

Rudolf scooped his son into his arms. "Magnus, you are entirely too young for the ladies."

The Countess of Langley turned around. Her smile surprised Viktor, catching him off guard, hooking his interest.

The countess had a lovely, heart-shaped face, framed by long, fiery curls that cascaded to the middle of her back. Her lips were invitingly full and her chin stubborn. A fine sprinkling of freckles topped the bridge of her small nose. Her disarming green eyes gazed straight back at him.

Flirting with the countess would be no hardship. The woman was too fine for Charles Bradford.

Regina stared, almost mesmerized, into the prince's dark gaze. The world around her faded until only he and she remained.

Disturbingly attractive, Prince Viktor Kazanov reeked of masculinity. Two or three inches over six feet, the prince was a foot taller than she, overwhelming her with his presence. His broad shoulders, shown to best advantage in simple but expensive clothing, tapered to a muscularly lean body and long legs.

Easily the most handsome man she had ever seen, the prince had black hair and even blacker eyes that held her gaze in thrall. Angularly chiseled, his face had high cheekbones and a strong jaw.

"Red," Magnus said, pointing at her, making everyone smile.

"Rudolf and Viktor, I present Regina Bradford, the Countess of Langley," Samantha introduced them. "Regina, my husband and brother-in-law, Princes Rudolf and Viktor Kazanov."

"I am pleased to make your acquaintances," Regina said, shifting her gaze to include the other brother in her greeting.

"The pleasure is mine," Viktor said, bowing over her hand in courtly manner.

Regina gave him an ambiguous smile, her green eyes gleaming with intelligence and humor. "Your Highness, we do have something in common."

He gave her a puzzled smile. "We do?"

"Our spouses are engaged in an illicit affair."

Her announcement surprised him. Her honesty was brutal, outrageous, and wonderfully refreshing.

Viktor did not know how to respond. Beside him, his brother coughed and his sister-in-law covered her mouth to keep from laughing.

"I apologize for the hurt my wife has caused you," Viktor said, finding his voice.

"*I* apologize to *you*," Regina replied. "I pray each night for Princess Adele's continued good health."

Viktor shouted with laughter, drawing curious gazes from the other guests. "Lady Bradford—"

"Call me Reggie."

"Reggie, then." Viktor inclined his head. "I believe our prayers are at cross purposes. Would you care to walk with me and discuss a solution for canceling out each other's prayers?"

Her heartbeat quickened with unexpected excitement. Regina could not forget that he was a prince and she a mere commoner. "Are you certain you want to be seen with a merchant's daughter?"

"I cannot think of anyone else's company I would prefer." Viktor escorted her away from his family.

"I *am* sorry for my husband's behavior," Regina apologized.

"Charles and Adele are adults who must answer for their own actions."

Regina walked beside him in silence and searched her mind for something to say. She had no experience making small talk with gentlemen, her father having diligently guarded her for her entire life. The past two years had given her no experience, either. She hardly ever accompanied her husband anywhere.

The faint scent of the prince's sandalwood cologne assailed her, and her knees wobbled at the frightening thought of being virtually alone with him and expected to make interesting conversation. Almost as bad, she could feel the curious looks of the guests they passed.

Regina peeked at the prince. He was looking at her. She blushed and wished he would say something.

"The weather has held surprisingly well," Regina ventured, pouncing on an innocuous topic.

"Yes, it has."

"Her Grace could not have asked for a more perfect day."

"That is true."

"Brilliant sunshine, blue sky, and gentle breezes make for an idyllic setting." Regina knew she was rambling, but the damn prince was no conversationalist.

She gave him a sidelong glance. He was smiling at her.

"What do you find so amusing?"

"You." Viktor could not believe how nervous she seemed. The lady appeared to have no experience with gentlemen. He stopped walking and looked at her. "Is there anything else you would like to say about the weather?"

Regina felt her cheeks heat with an embarrassed blush. "I believe I have said it all."

"Good." Viktor slipped her hand through the loop of his arm and resumed walking. "Have you seen the gazebo?"

Regina felt his muscled arms and wondered how those arms would feel wrapped around her. Oh, damn. She was having impure thoughts about her husband's lover's husband.

"Reggie?"

She fixed her gaze on his lips. His wonderfully, sensuously full lips. She dragged her gaze from his lips to his eyes. "I beg your pardon?"

"Shall we walk to the gazebo?"

Regina hesitated. She needed to escape his overwhelming nearness. She needed to throw herself in his arms and kiss him with passion. She needed more experience with gentlemen.

"I do not bite," Viktor said.

Regina gave him an unconsciously flirtatious smile. "Promise?"

"Yes, I promise."

"Do you keep your promises?"

"Always."

Regina inclined her head. "I will live on tenterhooks until we inspect the gazebo."

He smiled at her. She smiled at him.

Viktor and Regina left the rectangular expanse of lawn and flower beds behind. They passed the maze and strolled in the gazebo's direction.

"Tell me, Your Highness—"

"Call me Viktor."

"Viktor, then." Regina wondered if Ginger would believe she was on a first name basis with royalty, albeit Russian. "What exactly does a prince do all day?"

Viktor grinned. "I do as other gentlemen do. My brothers and I keep busy with our various business interests."

"Brothers? How many Russian princes are running around London?"

"Rudolf, Mikhail, and Stepan live in London," Viktor told her. "Vladimir makes his home in Moscow."

"How fortunate you are. I always wanted brothers and sisters," Regina said, "but my father never remarried after my mother passed away."

"Your father must have loved her very much," Viktor said. "He could not set her memory aside."

"I suspect no other woman would have him," Regina said. "Living with Reginald would be difficult in the extreme."

"Many women overlook a wealthy man's quirks."

They reached the gazebo and climbed the three steps. Regina sat on a bench, looked toward the manor where the guests were gathered, and sighed at the perfection of the scenery. The manor, the grounds, and the guests looked like an artist's idea of gentility.

Viktor sat beside her, close enough to catch her delicate scent of jasmine and vanilla. He stared at her, entranced by her profile. "Did you get that glorious mane of red from your mother?"

Regina looked at him in surprise. "You think red hair is glorious?"

He lifted a hand to touch a fiery curl. "Glorious, yes. The color of molten copper."

"Chuck hates my red hair," she told him. "He says I look clownish."

"Who is Chuck?"

"My husband." Regina gave him a mischievous smile. "Chuck despises nicknames, too."

Viktor grinned. "So you torment him with that nickname?"

"Guilty."

"Why did you marry Bradford?"

"My father forced me down the aisle." Regina met his dark gaze. "What is your excuse?"

"I thought I loved Adele. Now I know better."

"Look." Regina pointed to a hawk gliding across the azure-blue sky. "I wish I could soar like that."

"I think you want your spirit to soar," Viktor said. "A pretty butterfly perched on the wings of an eagle would be more appropriate."

Regina stared at him. Without explanation, the prince had known exactly what she meant.

"You find Bradford oppressive." It was a statement, not a question.

"I find marriage oppressive," she corrected him.

"Marriage to the right person allows the spirit to soar," he told her.

"Unfortunately, I will never know if you are correct. Chuck is disgustingly healthy."

"Illness is not the only cause of death," Viktor reminded her. "One can never know what the future holds."

"My husband is not worth my hanging."

"Neither is Adele." Viktor looked at her for a long moment. "Rudolf told me you are considered a bluestocking of sorts."

"I never met your brother before today. How could he—?"

"Gossip." He fixed his gaze on her lips.

His attention flustered her. "I am writing a book," she announced, expecting his disdain. According to her father, women were meant to keep the homefires burning and to bear sons for their men. "My husband does not approve, needless to say, and considers my efforts an affront to his manhood."

"What kind of book are you writing?" His expression and tone seemed sincere and nonjudgmental.

She gave him a long look. "Not my favorite recipes."

He smiled. "You have not answered my question."

"I am writing a novel, the kind of story Jane Austen would write."

"I would like to read this story."

"Are you patronizing me?"

"My name is Viktor, not Chuck."

Regina gave him a rueful smile. "I will send you an autopgraphed copy if it is published."

"Of course, your book will be published," Viktor said.

"A publisher may not wish to purchase and print it."

"Then *I* will publish this book," the prince told her.

"Do you have publishing investments?"

"I will need to purchase a publishing house first," Viktor said, "and then I will publish it."

Regina knew he was flirting with her. Outrageously.

"What did Bradford say when he learned you were writing a book?" Viktor asked.

"He forbade me to finish it," Regina answered, "but Hamlet insures I can do what I want. Hamlet is my Great Dane and despises Chuck."

Viktor laughed, and then his expression became serious. He held her hand, his dark gaze holding hers captive. "You are wonderfully, artlessly delightful. Will you honor me by sitting by my side at dinner?"

"I—I . . ." Regina blushed furiously. "I would like that very much."

"I have not seen a woman's sincere blush in years," Viktor said. "Today you have gifted me with three."

Her blush deepened into a vivid scarlet. Regina felt her spirit about to soar.

He stood then and offered a hand. Without hesitation, she placed her hand in his.

"Regina?"

"Yes?"

"Thank you for blush number four."

Chapter 3

"Your Grace, I present my wife, Dementia,"
Bertram introduced them.

"A pleasure to meet you, Your Grace." Dementia
dropped the duke a throne room curtsey.

"The pleasure is mine."

The Duke of Charming was the most ruggedly
handsome man she had ever seen. If only her father
had given her in marriage . . .

"Lady Merlot?"

"Please, Your Grace, call me Dementia."

The Duke of Charming smiled and held his hand
out. "Come, Dementia. I want to show you my
gazebo."

A shy smile touched her lips. "I would love to see
your gazebo, Your Grace."

Regina touched her pulse points with her spe-
cially mixed perfume, a delicate blending of night-
blooming jasmine and soft vanilla, the only luxury
she ever allowed herself. She did not wear the fragrance to attract any man. Heaven forbid. No, she
wore the jasmine and vanilla fragrance because she
liked its scent. If she didn't like the way she smelled,
no one else would like her scent either.

Humming a waltz, Regina danced across the bedchamber to inspect her image in the cheval mirror.

She eyed herself critically, trying to see herself as the prince would.

Her azure-blue silk gown had a fitted bodice and squared neckline with a hint of cleavage. Spanish slashing decorated the short sleeves, and the hemline showed her ankles. She wore sheer silk stockings, embroidered with tiny butterflies, and gold kid sandals. She had swept her hair up for the evening, but fiery curls escaped the coiffeur to frame her face and linger on the delicate nape of her neck.

Regina decided she would pass inspection but never turn any heads with her beauty. For the first time in her life, she desperately wanted to be beautiful. For the prince.

She felt lighthearted as she conjured the prince's image in her mind's eye. A weight had lifted from her heart, leaving her spirit buoyant, like a butterfly floating on a gentle breeze. That thought reminded her of her mother's ring, given to her on her eighteenth birthday.

Regina always kept the ring close but rarely wore it. Her father and her husband did not inspire lighthearted moods. She crossed the chamber and rummaged through her belongings for the tiny velvet box containing the ring.

That her blustering father had given her mother such a romantic piece amazed Regina. It was a ring a man gave to the love of his life, and her father had proved himself incapable of that emotion.

Two delicately sculptured butterflies—created in gold, diamonds, and rubies—lay on both sides of the band. A radiant, marquise-shaped emerald topped the ring, appearing to attract the butterflies.

All Regina had of her mother were the ring, a

journal, and a letter to her. She wished she could have known the woman who had given her life.

"I hope you are ready for dinner," Charles said, walking into her bedchamber.

Regina slipped the ring onto the third finger of her right hand and looked at her husband. "Quite prepared."

Charles inspected her from the top of her head to the tips of her sandals. "You have taken special care with your appearance," he remarked. "Do not embarrass me by throwing yourself at Prince Viktor."

Regina paused in the doorway and turned around. "I beg your pardon?"

"The Countess of Tewksbury informed me of your disreputable behavior this afternoon in the garden."

Vanessa Stanton. She should have known her husband's cousin would keep him informed of her every move.

Regina arched a copper brow at him. "You did order me to mingle."

"Leave my cousin's lover alone."

"What?"

Charles smiled with immense satisfaction, having managed to shake her frigid exterior for the first time in two years. "Vanessa is Prince Viktor's mistress and does not appreciate your trying to move into her territory."

Regina gave him a feline smile. "Does she now?"

"Leave Viktor alone. You cannot give him what he wants."

Charles abandoned her at the door of the drawing room. Without another word, he walked away and headed straight for Adele.

Touching her butterfly ring for courage, Regina poised inside the entrance and tried to get her bearings. She felt awkward and out of place, her buoyancy dissipating like fog beneath the noonday sun. Self-consciousness blinded her to the richly decorated drawing room and the rainbow of colors of the women's gowns. She even missed the sweet scent of the fresh-cut lilacs placed in vases scattered around the room.

Regina dare not inflict her insignificant, merchant-class self on these allegedly important people. She would rather stand aloof than risk getting the cut direct.

Standing at the far end of the drawing room, Princess Samantha would probably speak with her. Prince Viktor did not count, though, because well-bred ladies should never approach a gentleman. At least, that was what her father had told her. She refused to make conversation with her husband's cousins since those two snobs had taught her a hard lesson on the cut direct one embarrassing evening at the opera.

Regina hesitated for another agonizingly long moment. Crossing the drawing room required that she reach the other side without a humiliating incident. She could kill her father for marrying her to Charles Bradford and placing her in this uncomfortable position.

A glass of sherry materialized in front of her face. "Good evening, Reggie," said a familiar voice.

Relief surged through her. Regina smiled at the prince. He appeared breathtakingly handsome in his black formal evening attire.

"You look beautiful in blue," Viktor said, his dark gaze caressing the swell of her bosom in the gown's fitted bodice and hint of cleavage. He offered her the sherry again.

"I don't drink spirits."

"Two drops of sherry," he coaxed. "You need only hold the glass and pretend to sip. No one will notice you are not drinking."

Regina smiled at his logic. She took the glass from him and lifted it to her lips.

"I never thought I would ever be jealous of a glass," he murmured.

Regina blushed.

Viktor grinned. "I do believe that is blush number five."

Her emerald eyes sparkled with merriment. "Shall we gamble on the amount of times you make me blush?"

"I would love to see your whole body blush," Viktor whispered, against her ear.

"Your Highness, that remark is improper."

"Ah, blush six." Viktor gave her a long look. "I command you to call me Viktor."

"Very well, Viktor."

"Have you met the Duke of Inverary?"

Regina shook her head.

"Come with me. I will introduce you to our host."

"Won't your lady be upset if you ignore her?"

Viktor flicked a glance across the drawing room. "Adele and Charles are involved in their own conversation."

"I meant your other lady."

Viktor snapped his dark brows together. "Explain yourself."

"Vanessa Stanton, your mistress? Charles ordered me to keep my distance from you lest his precious cousin feel hurt."

"Have you considered Charles said that to keep you away from me?"

Regina had not thought of that possibility. "Was

Vanessa your lover?" she asked, and then regretted it.

"You should not have asked that. Unless"—he gave her a wicked grin—"unless, you are applying for the position?"

Viktor watched her reaction to his question, a vibrant blush. Any other sophisticated woman of his acquaintance would have remarked on the double entendre of the word *position*. Not the beauty by his side, though. Could she really be that innocent? Or was she too much of a lady to give him a witty, albeit naughty, reply?

Regina gazed into his eyes, darker than a moonless midnight. She had no experience with flirting and did not know what to say.

"That makes seven blushes," Viktor teased her. "Come, I will introduce you to His Grace."

Viktor led Regina across the drawing room, pausing along the way to introduce her to several aristocratic acquaintances. Without the prince beside her, Regina knew most would have given her the cut direct.

"Your Grace, I present Regina Bradford, the Countess of Langley," Viktor made the introduction. "Regina, you have met his duchess."

"I am pleased to make your acquaintance, Your Grace," Regina said, and then nodded at the duchess.

"The pleasure is mine," the Duke of Inverary said. "I heard about your dog."

"Hamlet?" Regina echoed, surprised.

"How big is the Great Dane?"

Regina gave the duke a mischievous smile. "Hamlet is big enough to frighten Charles."

Everyone laughed.

"I would love to see that," Viktor said.

"You don't think your husband's fear would provoke him to harm your pet?" the Duchess of Inverary asked.

"Charles understands that his fate is linked with Hamlet's."

"Darling, your panache leads me to believe we could be distantly related," the duchess drawled.

"I would consider that a great honor, Your Grace."

Regina could not understand how she had ever considered all socialites anathema. Judging all aristocrats by her husband's measure had been wrong.

"Viktor, darling, Lady Regina is a treasure," the duchess said. "If you know what I mean."

"I understand completely."

Regina could not credit what the duchess was implying. She dropped her gaze in embarrassment.

"You are blushing again."

She smiled at him. "You are incorrigible."

Regina lost her smile when she spied Vanessa Stanton and Cedric Barrows approaching. She disliked her husband's cousins who did not hide the fact that they considered her dirt beneath their feet.

Ignoring Regina, Vanessa sidled up to the prince. "I hope you plan to sit with me at dinner," she purred.

"I have already invited Lady Bradford to sit with me."

"You do have two sides," Vanessa reminded him.

"Don't worry about Regina," Cedric said to the prince. "I'll sit with her. Regina realizes her betters dislike the idea of breaking bread with the lower classes."

Mortified and angry, Regina lifted her glass and pretended to sip the sherry. Now she understood the reason one needed a glass of spirits in hand.

With her hand occupied, she could not slap the obnoxious boor.

"I said—" Viktor started to reply, but his brother
and sister-in-law joined the group.

"You have made a conquest of my son," Prince
Rudolf told Regina.

"Magnus keeps asking where the red lady went,"
Samantha added, making her smile.

Vanessa leaned closer to the prince, saying in a
loud whisper, "I need to speak privately with you."

"Another time, Vanessa."

"Apparently, you prefer slumming with the lower
classes," Vanessa said. "Come, Cedric."

Watching them walk away, Viktor suffered the
urge to slap Vanessa and her brother. He felt
strangely protective of the merchant's daughter, a
woman he had met only this afternoon. Regina had
done nothing to deserve such a personal attack.

"I apologize," Viktor said, gazing into her eyes.

"Vanessa told the truth," Regina said. "I am a
merchant's daughter." She gestured to the duke's
guests. "These aristocrats inherited their money
and estates from long-forgotten ancestors who pillaged and plundered. At least, I know what my
father did to earn his riches."

"The higher the title," Samantha teased her husband, "the more that ancestor pillaged and
plundered."

Prince Rudolf planted a chaste kiss on his wife's
cheek. "You know I love plundering you."

Regina smiled at their byplay. The prince and the
princess enjoyed a loving marriage. Once upon a
time, she had wished the same for herself. Unfortunately, her father had forced her into marriage
with one of the most obnoxious snobs in London.

Drawing her attention, Viktor lifted the untouched glass of sherry out of her hand and set it on a nearby table. He offered her his arm, saying, "We are going down to dinner."

In the dining room, Viktor assisted Regina into the seat beside his. He noted the name card on the place setting beside Regina. Cedric Barrows. He gave his brother a pointed look and shifted his gaze to the name card.

"I need to speak with my brother." Prince Rudolf slipped onto the chair before Cedric. He smiled at Regina, saying, "I cannot think of anyone with whom I would prefer to dine. Excepting my wife, of course."

Princess Samantha sat on the chair beside her brother-in-law's. "Vanessa, darling," she drawled, sounding like her aunt. "Sit over there with your brother."

Beneath the majordomo's supervision, the duke's footmen poured wine. Then they began serving dinner's first course, oyster soup.

"Napoleon passed away last week," the Duke of Inverary said. "The *Times* reported it this morning."

"What wonderful news," Vanessa said. "He won't be returning again."

"I agree with you," Princess Adele said. "I know I will sleep more soundly at night."

Regina glanced at the prince. "John Keats died last week, too."

Viktor gave her a blank look. "Who?"

"John Keats," Regina repeated. "The poet wrote *Ode to a Nightingale.*"

"The bluestocking shows her true colors," Vanessa sneered.

"I have read and enjoyed Keats," Viktor lied. "His passing saddens me."

"I found his poetry thought-provoking," Prince Rudolf added.

Footmen cleared their plates while others served dinner's second course. Regina sent both princes a smile of thanks but thought she should keep quiet for the remainder of the dinner. Only, Cedric and Vanessa irritated her to the point where she could not control her tongue.

"The coronation is less than two months away," Cedric remarked. "I wonder when invitations will be sent."

"Do you think Queen Caroline will be invited?" Vanessa asked.

"Caroline is an adulteress," Cedric said. "I have never considered her my queen."

"I hadn't realized the Prince of Pleasure was a model of marital fidelity," Regina said, her voice laced with sarcasm.

Viktor snapped his gaze to her. He could tell the lady did not suffer fools, but giving voice to such thoughts in this company would certainly provoke an argument. He gave her hand a gentle, warning squeeze.

Cedric Barrows looked apoplectic, his face reddened with anger. Charles Bradford glared at his wife.

A surge of fierce protectiveness for the lady swept through Viktor, surprising him. If Bradford dared touch her—

"Men and women are different," Cedric announced, finding his voice through his anger.

"Thank you for enlightening me about that," Regina said. "If I remember the marriage ceremony correctly, men take a vow of fidelity, too."

Cedric glared at her. "The king is a man with a

man's needs. A woman of your lowly station speaking disparagingly about my king offends me."

"I agree with my brother," Vanessa said.

"Noble is as noble does," Viktor told the other man, feeling the need to defend the lady.

"Do not concern yourself with Cedric's rudeness," Regina said to the prince. "Some families carry the gout, others inherit red hair. The Bradford-Barrows clan suffers from obnoxious snobbery. Unless, of course, they are strapped for money. In that case, the Bradford men lower themselves by marrying daughters of wealthy merchants."

Viktor swallowed his laughter. Giving voice to her thoughts was foolhardy. He could not protect her indefinitely. She was married to Bradford, not him.

Viktor glanced down the table at Charles Bradford. He appeared ready to pounce on his wife, but Adele and the footmen serving the third course drew his attention. For once he was grateful to his faithless wife.

The remainder of the meal passed in relative peace. Cedric and Vanessa spoke together but threw sour looks at Regina. Viktor caught Charles Bradford's occasional glare at his wife, and that worried him.

The Duchess of Inverary stood at dinner's end. "Ladies, let's retire to the drawing room and leave the gentlemen to their cigars."

"I will see you soon," Viktor whispered.

Regina felt heartened by the prince's words. For once, she would not be sitting alone when the gentlemen joined the ladies.

Princess Samantha and she left the dining room together. They followed the other ladies down the corridor toward the foyer.

"Regina."

She paused, recognizing her husband's voice, and turned around. He looked annoyed.

"I will see you upstairs," Regina told the princess.

Surprising her, Charles grabbed her face by the chin and yanked her toward him. Then he slapped her hard.

"I warned you about embarrassing me," Charles snarled, raising his hand to strike her again.

"*Stop!*"

Prince Viktor grabbed his hand to thwart the strike. Charles swore and released her chin.

"How dare you interfere with my wife and me."

Towering over the other man, Viktor stepped dangerously closer. "If you touch her again, I will make you regret it."

"My wife will never give you what you want," Charles sneered.

"Swine like you have no idea what I want." Viktor stared at him a moment longer and then ordered, "Return to the dining room. Now, Chuck."

"We are not finished, Regina." Muttering to himself, Charles Bradford marched down the corridor toward the dining room.

Regina looked at the prince, the only man she'd ever known to offer her protection. "Thank you."

Viktor turned her face one way and then the other, inspecting for bruises. There were none, only a slight flush where she'd been struck.

"Are you well?"

Regina managed a faint smile, embarrassed that he had witnessed her husband's cruelty to her. "I will be fine."

"I will see you upstairs."

When she walked into the drawing room, Princess Samantha beckoned her to sit on the couch. "Tell me about your son."

"Austen is one year old and the most delightful baby," Regina said.

Vanessa Stanton and Princess Adele sat together on a nearby settee. "Did you name him for that writer?" Vanessa asked.

"Jane Austen is my inspiration," Regina answered.

"Charles doesn't want you to write a book," Adele said.

"Chuck is much too busy spending my father's money to care about me," Regina told her.

"You are correct about that. Charles does not care for you."

"Our feelings are mutual," Regina said, fingering her mother's ring. "You are welcome to him."

"You are *not* welcome to my husband."

Regina gave her a feline smile. "I will ignore Viktor if you will ignore Chuck."

"How dare you speak disrespectfully to a princess. *Low-class cow.*"

Regina looked her straight in the eye. *"Whore."*

There was a collective gasp in the drawing room and then silence. All gazes fixed on the two women.

"How exceedingly entertaining," the Duchess of Inverary drawled. "This could prove an interesting few days, a weekend party the gossips will recount for years."

Princes Rudolf and Viktor, the first of the gentlemen, walked into the drawing room. Both men stopped short and stared at the silent women. Tension hung like a cloud in the room.

"I have never seen speechless women," Prince Rudolf said, his voice sounding loud in the silence.

"Neither have I." Viktor crossed the room to sit beside Regina on the couch.

She arched a brow at the blonde. The blonde curled her lip at her.

"We were enjoying a discussion about husbands," the duchess told the men. "I asked if any lady could say something positive about husbands. Hence, the silence."

By two's and three's, the other gentlemen trickled into the drawing room. Charles beckoned Adele, who rushed to his side.

"Would you like coffee, tea, or something stronger?" Viktor asked.

"I don't want anything."

"Neither do I." Viktor stood and offered her his hand. "Let us walk outside."

Regina accepted the prince's hand and rose from the settee. She could feel dozens of interested gazes on them as they left the drawing room.

Thousands of stars glittered in a moonless black sky. The trees rustled softly in a gentle evening breeze, and the scents of myriad flowers perfumed the air. Adding to the romantic atmosphere, several torches had been lit in the section of the garden nearest the manor for any guest wanting to venture outside.

"Let us walk to the gazebo," Viktor said, and took her hand in his.

Regina felt nervous and excited. She had never been alone with a man excepting her father and her husband. Sadness tinged her thoughts. This flirtation had no future. Both were married to other people.

"Thank you for defending me," Regina said.

"Rescuing damsels in distress is my specialty," Viktor said, a smile lurking in his voice. "Why were the ladies silent in the drawing room?"

"Adele and I had words."

"What words?"

"Adele called me a low-class cow," Regina answered. "I returned the compliment by calling her a whore. I'm sorry."

"You spoke truthfully."

Regina said nothing. What could she say? Princess Adele did not bother to hide her infidelity. She could not understand why the other woman preferred Charles Bradford to Viktor Kazanov. Chuck was a dish cloth when compared to the prince.

Viktor gave her hand a gentle squeeze. "I should have married a woman like you."

Regina felt uncomfortable where their conversation was leading. Though attracted to the prince, she could never engage in an affair with him. She glanced at the night sky, seeking divine guidance for a suitable topic to distract the prince.

"Look there." Regina pointed toward the northern sky. "Polaris."

Viktor looked up. "The constant north star, one of man's most dependable guides."

"Polaris will be waiting for us there when we are old and have experienced a lifetime of joys and regrets," Regina said, a wistful note in her voice. "That fact makes me feel like one of God's most insignificant creatures."

Viktor released her hand and put his arm around her shoulders, drawing her against the side of his body. His warmth seeped through her thin gown, the intimacy of it confusing and exciting her.

"I have never met a woman who thought about stars, joys, and regrets," Viktor told her. "Most women of my acquaintance think about jewels, gowns, and furs. A few, like Samantha, think about their children and their husbands. You are a sensitive observer of life, my lady, and that makes you a good writer."

"My lack of talent may surprise you," Regina said. His compliment pleased her, though. Criticism was a closer friend than flattery.

Viktor tightened his hold and leaned closer. "I doubt that."

His proximity was beginning to panic her. She wanted his kiss, yet the idea of it frightened her. "Look toward the east. Arcturus is the brightest star in the spring sky."

Viktor slanted a smile at her. Regina realized he knew she was avoiding his kiss.

"I ache for poor Galileo each time I look at the night sky," Regina said. "Imagine his frustration at knowing a universal truth but disbelieved."

"Only you would ache for a long-dead astronomer."

They walked in silence across the lawn beyond the maze toward the gazebo. The prince kept his arm around her shoulders and her body pressed against his side.

Needing to fill the silence, Regina gave voice to the first thought that popped into her mind. "What do you think about dew?"

"I beg your pardon?"

"The grass is dry," she said, "but in the morning dew will cover it. How does dew get there?"

Viktor kept walking but dropped a chaste kiss on the crown of her head. This woman delighted him as no other ever had, his having reached an age that appreciated sensitivity and kindness and innocence.

"While the world sleeps," he answered, "the fairies sprinkle dew on each blade of grass and flower petal."

"Ah, you sound like a poet." Regina climbed the three steps into the gazebo.

"I must make a confession," Viktor said. "I never read John Keats and neither did my brother."

Regina smiled. "I won't tell a soul."

"I also asked Her Grace to sit us together at meals."

Her heartbeat quickened at his admission. Did the prince really like her or— "Are you flirting with me to revenge yourself on my husband?"

"I would never use anyone for my own purposes." The prince sounded offended.

"I apologize."

"I forgive you." Viktor traced one long finger down the side of her face. "Does Charles abuse you?"

"He took advantage of Hamlet's absence."

"You will tell me if he touches you in anger?"

"I will if you want."

"I want."

Regina knew he was going to kiss her. She watched his face inching toward hers and closed her eyes. One kiss would not compromise her. She caught his arousing sandalwood scent. Their breaths mingled and their lips touched.

Wrapping his arms around her, Viktor claimed her mouth in a gentle first kiss which drifted into another. His lips were warm and firm, their touch sending a delicious shiver down her spine, enticing her to surrender to the incredible sensations.

Regina answered his subtle invitation, giving herself into his keeping. Viktor deepened the kiss and tightened his arms around her, one hand holding the back of her head and the other sliding down to cup her buttocks to pull her against his powerful frame.

She sighed in surrender to his sensual persuasion. He slashed his mouth across hers, encouraging her to follow his lead.

He flicked his tongue across the crease of her lips, which parted for him, beckoning him to explore the sweetness of her mouth. Their kiss was long and langorous, creating a melting sensation in her lower regions, surprising her.

Desire surged through her, urging her to take what he offered. The world faded away, only the man and incredible sensations existing in her universe.

His powerful masculinity surrounded her without threatening. He led her where he wanted with gentle encouragement, not domination.

And then Viktor drew back, breaking the kiss, his lips hovering above hers. Regina stared in a sensual daze at him, reminding him of an innocent maiden taken by surprise by her first kiss.

He placed the palm of his hand against her cheek. "You are blushing again."

"Yes."

"I feel I have known you forever." Viktor held her close, pressing her against him, cradling her head against his chest. "Will you ride to the village with me tomorrow afternoon?"

"Yes."

"Is *yes* all you can say?"

"No."

Viktor chuckled and set her back a pace. "We should return to the manor or risk creating gossip. Go directly to your chamber and lock the door. I will return to the drawing room alone to discourage the birth of gossip."

Regina wanted to remain in his arms forever. She looked at him through emerald eyes that shone with budding love. She would savor these few days with her first, her only, admirer but knew they would never make love.

How could she explain being a wife, a mother, and a virgin?

Chapter 4

"I will protect you from your husband."

She gazed at him through eyes shining with love and trust.

"Kiss me, sweet lady," the Duke of Charming murmured.

Dementia wrapped her arms around his neck, pressing her body against his, and drew his handsome face toward hers.

Their lips touched, his kiss promising love everlasting.

He would arrive any minute now.

Ginger Evans sat in the countess's study and wondered for the hundredth time how to persuade the constable to investigate her father's death. Nervously, she smoothed the skirt of her white morning gown and glanced at the desk.

In her haste to leave, Regina had left part of her manuscript on the desk and Ginger read the first page to distract herself. Her lips twitched when she saw the heroine's name. Ginger would bet her quarterly profits that Regina was the heroine and Charles the dissipated husband.

"You miss her when she's gone," Ginger said, patting the dog lying on the floor beside her chair. "I'm sure she misses you, too."

Her mind wandered to the constable. Amadeus Black was a legend in London. Part private investigator and part public servant, the man had a fierce reputation for catching the most cunning criminals.

Rumor said that instinct and logic blended perfectly in Amadeus Black. Society's elite paid a fortune for his services when needed. The City of London paid him somewhat less when officials faced a particularly difficult or gruesome crime.

Ginger had heard nothing of a personal nature, not even his age or appearance. She envisioned a middle-aged man with a shrewd mind and a potbelly.

Amadeus Black could prove her father had been murdered. Would he take her case, though? Money was no object. She had her share of profits from the Evans Smith investments.

Pickles walked into the study. "Mr. Amadeus Black has arrived."

"Please escort him here. Then serve us tea and cookies."

Ginger rose from her chair, as much from surprise as courtesy, when Amadeus Black appeared. He was definitely not what she expected.

Dressed conservatively in black, Amadeus Black stood several inches over six feet and filled the doorway. Broad-shouldered, the man possessed a warrior's body with narrow waist and lean hips. He wore his black hair long and shaggy, as if he had no time to spare for a proper haircut. His eyes were a striking blue, his nose straight, his jaw strong.

He was shockingly young, probably no older than thirty. He needed to be absolutely ruthless to have earned his reputation in so few years.

Not middle-aged. Ginger smiled at him. *No potbelly.*

"Lady Bradford?"

"Please sit here, sir."

He crossed the study and sat in the chair beside the desk. His piercing blue gaze never left her, and she suffered the uncanny feeling that he had already analyzed and judged her.

A soft, rhythmic banging on the carpet drew their attention. Hamlet lay on the floor, his tail wagging, thumping the carpet.

"A Danish dog." Amadeus Black reached down to scratch behind the dog's ears.

"He likes you," Ginger said. "Hamlet is a good judge of character."

"What would Hamlet have done if he didn't like me?"

The corners of her lips curved into a smile. "I shudder to think about that."

Pickles returned to the study. The majordomo set the tray on the desk.

"Thank you, Pickles. I will serve the constable." Ginger poured tea into a bone china cup. "How do you take it?"

"Naked."

"I beg your pardon?" She heard the surprised squeak in her voice.

"Nothing added."

The tray held a mixture of lemon and ginger cookies. She placed a couple of each on a bone china plate that matched the teacup.

"Help yourself." Ginger noted how delicate the cup appeared in his massive hand. "I made the cookies."

A baking countess? That surprised him.

Amadeus studied her while she poured her own tea. The countess had dressed simply in a white morning gown. Dark brown hair framed a delicate face. Long, thick lashes accentuated enormous brown velvet eyes.

She was not wearing the earl's wedding band.

The countess crumbled a few cookies on a plate. Then she set the plate on the carpet for the dog.

Amadeus swallowed a chuckle. He would bet his last shilling she never did that in the earl's presence.

"Shall we discuss business, my lady?"

"I am not my lady," Ginger admitted, her smile apologetic.

His black brows snapped together. "I don't understand."

"The countess is my dearest friend," Ginger told him. "We felt you would respond more readily to a countess than a mere miss."

Amadeus stared at her for a long moment. "I commend your logic. Who are you?"

"I am Ginger Evans and need your help."

"Explain your problem."

"Someone murdered my father, Bartholomew Evans," Ginger began. "Authorities called his death a suicide because the murderer's method was hanging. My father would never take his own life. Will you help me find his murderer? I can pay handsomely for your skills."

Amadeus said nothing. Stalling for time, he reached for another cookie and let his gaze wander across the desk. "What is that?" he asked, pointing to the pile of papers.

"Reggie's manuscript."

"Explain."

"Regina is writing a novel. What has this to do with my father?"

"Nothing." The chit should have been a barrister, telling him to stick to the facts. "Most men commit suicide with a pistol, but accidental and homicidal hangings are rare. If the authorities said suicide, then it was."

"My father would *not* take his own life."

Amadeus took another cookie and stretched his long legs out. "Tell me about his death."

"My father was a business associate of Reginald Smith, the countess's father," Ginger told him. "Regina and I awaited my father for dinner one evening. When he failed to arrive, we went to the Smith offices—" Her voice cracked with emotion.

"I know this is upsetting." Without thinking, Amadeus patted her hand. "Take your time."

"We found him hanging from a ceiling beam."

"What did you do after discovering the body?"

"Uncle Forest cut him down," Ginger answered. "Then he sent for the authorities and Reggie's father."

"Who is Uncle Forest?"

"Forest Fredericks is another business associate. He had forgotten something and returned to the office a moment after we arrived."

"I see." Amadeus sat up straight and reached for her hand, boldly offering comfort. "I need to ask certain difficult questions."

Ginger nodded. "I understand, sir."

"Call me Amadeus."

"Thank you. Call me Ginger."

Amadeus inclined his head. "Was the office door locked or unlocked?"

"Unlocked."

"Was the bruise on his neck an inverted *V* or a straight line?"

Ginger closed her eyes and tried to picture her father in death. "An inverted *V.*"

"A straight bruise indicates homicide," Amadeus told her. "An inverted *V* means suicide."

An avid reader of mysteries, Ginger recalled the story where a murderer made his victims appear as suicides. "Isn't it possible to make a homicide look like a suicide?"

Amadeus smiled at her. Ginger Evans was nobody's fool. She had been blessed with a remarkably logical mind. Amazing in a woman, since the fairer sex tended to feel rather than think.

"A murderer could make a hanging appear a suicide if his victim was unconscious when hanged," Amadeus admitted. "Unfortunately, proving the murder is almost impossible—"

Ginger moaned in disappointment. "Please help me."

"I am an investigator, not a magician," Amadeus said. "The only way to prove this a murder is to find the murderer and force a confession."

"You will help me?"

"I want you to take a couple of days to write down all you remember about the crime scene and anything you know about your father's personal and business life," Amadeus instructed, evading her question. "Meanwhile, I will review the magistrate's report. By the way, what were your father's duties?"

"He did the accounting. Is that important?"

"Everything is important." Amadeus smiled. "Would you care to luncheon with me in two days?"

An answering smile lit her expression. "I would love to luncheon with you."

Amadeus stood. Why had he asked her to lunch? He had felt no inclination to resume socializing with the fairer sex since his late wife's passing. And yet—the invitation had slipped out before he could swallow the words.

"Are you ready?"
"Quite."

Seated on the phaeton, Prince Viktor gave Regina a sidelong smile and urged the horse into a leisurely pace. He had the whole afternoon to enjoy her company.

Regina Bradford was perfection in a white gown with petal-pink roses embroidered around the scooped neckline and hem. Matching the dress, she wore a white hat with streaming, petal-pink ribbons.

The real treasure lay beneath her pretty packaging. She was kind, candid, and caring.

"What a beautiful afternoon."

"Are we discussing the weather again?" Viktor teased her.

She felt her cheeks heating.

"Another blush?"

Regina smiled. "You are incorrigible, Your Highness."

They rode into a picturesque village a short time later. The prince halted the phaeton in front of one of the small shops lining the main street.

"A sweet shop," Regina exclaimed.

"I thought you would like it." Viktor helped her down.

Most women of his acquaintance would have preferred a jewelery shop. Somehow he had known the merchant's daughter would love a sweet shop.

Viktor opened the door and ushered her inside. Her emerald eyes sparkled at the sight that greeted her.

Rows of gleaming glass jars, filled with tempting jewel-like sweets, packed the shelves. There were lollipops, glittering twists of barley sugar, gob stoppers that changed color as they were sucked, nougats, creamed violets, and walnut creams along with a huge variety of other sweets.

"I thought we would buy sweets," Viktor said,

"and then we could ride to a peaceful place along the stream near the duke's."

Regina kept her gaze fixed on the candy. "Choosing what I want will be difficult."

"We can buy two of everything," he suggested.

"If we did that, you would need to roll me back to His Grace's." Regina tore her gaze from the sweets and smiled at him. "When I was a little girl, I begged my father to buy a sweet shop and promised to work there without salary. He said I would eat all the profits."

Viktor smiled.

"I was devastated."

"Shall I choose for you?"

"No." Regina inspected every item like a general before her troops. "I want nougats, walnut creams, lemon creams, and creamed violets."

Viktor nodded at the proprietor. The shopkeeper grabbed a sheaf of paper, twisted it into a holder, and began filling it with candy.

"Wouldn't you care for a Wellington stick?" Viktor whispered against her ear. "How about a couple of Nelson's balls. Are you blushing again?"

Regina laughed. "You should not make suggestive remarks."

With their purchase, Viktor and Regina left the shop and rode away from the village. Instead of returning to the manor, he turned the phaeton onto a small road. Several minutes later, a stream appeared in the distance.

Viktor halted the phaeton and climbed down. With her bag of sweets clutched in her hand, Regina let him lift her down, their bodies mere inches apart when he set her on the ground. Then he reached behind the seat and produced a blanket.

Regina stared at the blanket for a long moment. Then she raised her gaze to his.

"My intentions are honorable," Viktor promised.

Regina inclined her head and walked beside him down the path to the stream. The scents of wildflowers and moss wafted through the air on a breeze, birds chirped from their hiding places in the trees, and the stream's running water gurgled.

Nature's glory surrounded Regina. Only the man and his arousing sandalwood scent won her attention.

Viktor placed the blanket beneath the sweeping branches of a willow tree. Regina sat on it and patted the spot beside her in invitation.

"Which sweet do you want?" she asked, gazing into the twist of paper.

"You."

Regina gave him a feigned disgruntled look.

"Blushing again, my dear?" he teased her. "I will have a lemon cream."

Regina passed him two lemon creams and chose a nougat for herself. "Nougats taste like French sunshine."

"I am glad you like them. Will you ride with me tomorrow?"

"I don't know how."

"I will teach you," he said. "Later, we will play croquet. If it rains, I will challenge you to a game of chess."

She passed him a creamed violet. "That sounds like fun."

"Your ring interests me," Viktor said, the gold and jeweled butterfly ring catching his attention.

"It belonged to my mother." Regina held her hand out for his inspection. "I can hardly believe my father bought her this romantic piece."

"Legend says that rubies, emeralds, and diamonds bring the wearer protection, peace, and joy," Viktor told her. "You remind me of these exotic butterflies."

"Thank you, I think."

"You are welcome. Tell me about your parents."

"My mother died when I was very young, but my father never remarried," Regina said. "My father and I have always been at odds. What about your parents?"

"My father lives in Moscow, and my English mother lives at Rudolf's estate on Sark Island." Viktor stared into her green eyes. "My father locked my mother in an insane asylum when she passed her childbearing days. She remained there for fifteen years before my brother could rescue her."

Regina dropped her mouth open in surprise. She had always thought ill of Reginald for blustering, but her father appeared saintly when compared with the prince's father.

"I plan to divorce Adele," Viktor told her. "Naturally, Sally will remain in my custody. Her mother certainly never took an interest in her."

"I will leave Charles some day," Regina said, "and he will give me custody of Austen if he wants to maintain his style of living. My father cannot complain because I will not need his money."

"Are you independently wealthy?"

"My friend Ginger is a mathematical genius like her late father," Regina answered. "We formed our own company and made some profitable investments. Of course, we needed to use a business agent."

Viktor smiled in pleased surprise, never having met any woman who refused to be a man's accessory. Or victim. Yet, here was this slip of a girl and her friend planning for financial independence, never to be placed at the mercy of a husband's whim. What a novel idea. If only his own mother had been able to do that.

"Tell me about your company."

Regina gave him an ambiguous smile. "We named our venture the Evans Smith Company. We purchased—"

Viktor shouted with laughter. "You purchased a ten percent share in Kazanov Brothers and a ten percent share in Campbell Whisky. On behalf of my brothers, I thank you for your confidence. Why did you choose us?"

"Ginger said that spirits was a sound investment because our fellow Englishmen would never quit drinking," she answered, making him smile. "You won't tell Charles, will you?"

"I promise." Viktor planted a chaste kiss on her lips. "That seals our partnership in Kazanov Brothers."

"Will all your brothers kiss me?"

"Absolutely not, but I am willing to relay their kisses to you. Perhaps tonight?"

Regina blushed and looked away.

Viktor reached out and, with one long finger, gently turned her face toward him. He leaned close and gave her another chaste kiss. "I want you to come to His Grace's office before sherry is served in the drawing room."

"Is this a social or business meeting?"

"Both."

Regina had intended to work on her novel for an hour or two, but the lure of primping for the evening proved too much to resist. Now she understood the reason most women wasted hours on their appearance instead of productive work. Though she had always considered herself practical by nature, even she succumbed to the frivolous temptation of trying to look perfect for the man she loved.

She loved the prince?

That shocking thought nearly felled her. She sat on the edge of the bed to steady herself.

How could she have let this happen? The prince and she had no future together. Even if he divorced his wife, she was bound to her husband. Divorcing him for the prince would be a selfish move that could only hurt her son beyond repair.

With a deep sigh for what might have been, Regina decided to enjoy tonight and tomorrow to the fullest. Once she returned to London, her royal flirtation would end. She would live unhappily ever after.

If only Charles would die young. No, even thinking that was wrong. Perhaps killing Bertie off in her novel would give her a measure of satisfaction. At least, Dementia could live happily ever after with her duke.

Regina chose an iced-blue silk gown with a high waist and scooped neckline. She wore no jewels except her butterfly ring and her wedding band.

Leaving her chamber, Regina walked down one flight to the duke's office. She hesitated outside the closed door, touched her fiery curls, and then tapped on the door.

Viktor opened it and smiled. Taking her hand in his, the prince drew her inside. "You look ravishing."

Regina blushed at his extravagant compliment. She would regret returning to London. To her surpise, three other men sat in the office with the Duke of Inverary and Prince Rudolf.

Viktor escorted her across the chamber. "Regina, I present Princes Mikhail and Stepan, my brothers, and Robert Campbell, the Marquess of Argyll, His Grace's son."

All five men greeted her with warm smiles but seemed confused by her presence. She did not know what she was doing here either.

Viktor grinned and placed his arm around her waist to draw her forward. "Gentlemen, I present the co-owner of the Evans Smith Company."

Prince Rudolf stared at her, as did the others. From their expressions, Regina knew they would have been less surprised if Hamlet had spoken.

"Sit here," Viktor said, guiding her to a chair. "Tell them about the Evans Smith Company."

Regina looked at each aristocrat in turn. "Your obvious surprise offends me."

"We apologize," Prince Rudolf said, fighting a smile. "We mean no insult."

"You don't sound sorry," Regina said, but inclined her head accepting his apology like a queen granting a favor. "My dearest friend Ginger Evans is a mathematical genius and has lived with me since her father's passing. She persuaded me that we could make money by investing in other people's companies. We invested in Kazanov Brothers and Campbell Whisky because there is no chance of Englishmen quitting their drinking."

"I would like to meet this Ginger Evans," Rudolf said.

"Charles knows nothing," Regina said. "I hope none of you will tell him."

"We will keep your confidence," Rudolf said. "Where did you get the money to invest with us?"

"From the profits we made investing in gin."

All the men smiled.

"If you do not mind my asking," Rudolf said, "where did you get the money to invest in gin?"

Regina gave him an ambiguous smile. "Ah, but I do mind your asking."

"Then I will not press you."

"Tell me, Your Highness, will you still be offering another ten percent in your company?" she asked. "If not, we will be forced into beer and ale."

The men laughed.

"Miss Evans and you may call upon me to discuss the possibility," Prince Rudolf told her.

"You may also call upon me and my son," the Duke of Inverary said.

"Why would a woman want her own business?" Prince Stepan asked.

"I want my independence."

"Whatever for?" This question came from Prince Mikhail.

"You would not ask that if you had married Charles Bradford," Regina answered, making them smile.

A short time later, Viktor and Regina walked into the drawing room together. The three Kazanov princes, the Marquess of Argyll, and the Duke of Inverary followed behind. Regina spotted Charles, standing with his entourage, on the opposite side of the room.

"Here comes trouble." Viktor passed her a glass of sherry. "Lift the glass to your lips and pretend to drink."

Regina watched Charles, Adele, Vanessa, and Cedric advancing on them. "Charles looks ready for battle."

Viktor leaned close to whisper against her ear. "I will protect you."

And then Charles stood in front of her. "What do you think you're doing?" he demanded.

"I don't understand," she said.

"My hounds do not hunt for their own pleasure," Charles sneered, "and my merchant-class wife will not mingle with her betters for her own entertainment."

"Lady Regina was with me," Viktor said, throwing the other man a challenging look.

Charles ignored the prince, his lapse in etiquette surprising even his own supporters. "I forbid you to socialize with foreigners."

Viktor growled low in his throat and stepped toward him. Regina held up her hand in a gesture that she could take care of herself.

"You will refrain from giving me orders." The glint in her emerald eyes boded ill for her husband. "If I leave you, *Chuck*, my father will cease funding your"—she flicked a glance at Adele—"your hobbies."

"What is yours is mine, dear wife."

"That is not precisely true."

"What do you mean?"

"The Duke of Inverary's drawing room is hardly—"

"I demand an answer."

"Simply this, dear husband. Reginald does not trust you. When he passes away, Forest Fredericks will control the inheritance, and you will receive an allowance."

"Was this your idea?"

Regina smiled. "Yes, of course."

Charles raised his hand to slap her. Viktor blocked the strike, grabbed the other man's neck, and lifted him off the floor.

"If you touch her again, I will kill you." Viktor's voice sounded overly loud in the silent chamber.

In an instant, the three Kazanov princes disengaged their brother's hand and stepped between the two men. Cedric Barrows and Robert Campbell drew Charles Bradford away.

Regina glanced in her husband's direction and then made a public choice. She touched the prince's arm and smiled when he looked at her.

"Let's go down to dinner, Viktor." Ignoring his brothers' surprised expressions, Regina placed her hand in his and led him out of the drawing room.

Protected by Viktor and Rudolf, Regina sat between them at the dining table. Samantha, Mikhail, and Stepan sat across from them. Other members of the duke's extended family insulated them from Charles.

Regina ate little, upset at being the cause of the scene. She knew in growing dread that she'd created a scandal by taking the prince's side and leaving the drawing room with him.

Viktor drank more than he ate. Even the other guests remained unusually subdued.

"You will tell me if he hurts you when we return to London," Viktor said. "That is a command, not a request."

"Hamlet lives to protect me." Regina cast her husband a dangerous look. "If he harms my dog, I will kill him myself."

"Brothers, I want to play golf with you in the morning," Prince Rudolf said into the tense silence.

"I have made plans to give Regina a riding lesson," Viktor refused.

"Teaching a commoner to sit a horse is like teaching swine to fly," Charles said, his voice intentionally loud.

Regina glanced down the table at him. "Have you sprouted wings, *Chuck*?"

The Kazanov brothers roared with laughter, as did most of the other guests. Charles Bradford stood, tossed his napkin down, and left the room. Princess Adele gave her husband a venomous look and followed her lover.

The remainder of the dinner passed peacefully. Only Vanessa Stanton and Cedric Barrows seemed sullen.

"Ladies, let's leave the gentlemen to their brandy," the Duchess of Inverary said at dinner's end.

Viktor stood when Regina did. She gave him a questioning look, but he grasped her hand and escorted her out of the dining room.

"Let us walk outside."

"Won't we create gossip?"

Viktor smiled in genuine amusement. "My lady, we have already given the gossips enough to make them hoarse."

Viktor and Regina stepped into the torchlit garden. Created for lovers, the night was dark, no moon shining overhead. Thousands of stars dotted the infinite blackness. A gentle evening breeze caressed them, and mingling scents seduced their senses.

By unspoken agreement, Viktor and Regina strolled across the lawn to the gazebo. They held hands like young lovers, wanting intimate seclusion.

"I thank you for protecting me," Regina said, "but threatening Chuck's life—"

"I meant what I said," Viktor interrupted. "I will protect you, and you must promise to tell me if he raises a hand to you."

"I promise." Regina felt certain that only the night's romantic mood inspired his sentiment.

Viktor lifted her hand to his lips. "My lady, will you dance with me?"

Regina smiled. "Your Highness, we have no orchestra."

"We will make our own music."

"In that case . . ." Regina placed her hand in his.

Viktor drew her closer into his arms. Humming a waltz, he swirled her around and around the gazebo.

The prince stopped suddenly and pulled her against the hard planes of his body. He dipped his head, his mouth covering hers in a kiss filled with passion.

Viktor drew back and gazed into her hauntingly lovely face. "I lo—"

Preventing his words, Regina placed a finger across his lips. Her heart ached when she whispered, "We are still married to other people."

Chapter 5

"You should not have come, Your Grace."

"Sweet, sweet Dementia." The Duke of Charming gave her a smoldering look. "How could I stay away?"

Dementia stared into his love-filled gaze. "I do admit your visit makes me happy."

"Lady Merlot?" Constable Green walked into the drawing room and looked from her to the duke. "My lady, Lord Merlot is dead."

"Dead? Has Bertie suffered an accident?"

"Yes, an accident." The constable stared hard at her. "Your husband walked into a bullet . . ."

Regina left her bedchamber the next morning and hurried down the corridor to the stairs. She had owned the forest green riding habit for two years but had never worn it until today. Her father had insisted that a countess should own a riding habit. It didn't matter that she had never sat on a horse. The riding habit itself was lovely, the forest green complementing her hair. She had dispensed with the matching hat and its absurd feather.

Regina had expected to see Charles either last night or this morning. Thankfully, her husband had kept his distance from her, probably too busy making love with Adele Kazanov. She dreaded the thought of the coach ride to London the next day.

Prince Viktor was waiting in the foyer. Except for his boots, he was not dressed for riding.

Regina hid her disappointment behind a smile. "Have your plans changed?"

"No." Viktor lifted her hand to his lips. "How do you manage to look so beautiful in the morning?"

She ignored his compliment. "You aren't dressed for riding."

"Today I am teaching you the basics."

"Wouldn't you prefer a brisk ride?"

"I prefer being with you." Viktor led her down the path to the stables.

Regina breathed deeply of the clean country air, the day another rarity of blue sky and sunshine. Leather and oil and hay scented the air inside the stable. Walking beside the prince, Regina thought even the horse droppings smelled good. Well, almost.

"Saddle one of the New Forest ponies," Viktor instructed a groom. "We will wait outside."

"You don't trust me on a horse?"

"Learning on a pony is easier."

"I expected a visit from Charles," Regina said, "but I haven't seen him since he left the dining room last night."

"I have not seen Adele, either."

The groom appeared then, leading the pony out of the stable. At five feet tall, the dark brown New Forest pony looked like a small horse and suitable for riding. It had a black mane and white diamond markings on its broad forehead.

"What is its name?" Regina asked, stroking the pony's forehead.

"Cosmo," the groom answered.

"Good morning, Cosmo." Regina looked from the pony to the prince. "What is that?"

"A saddle."

"A *side* saddle," she corrected him. "I want to ride astride."

"Ladies always ride side saddle."

"Not this lady."

"Riding astride is considered risqué."

"Then consider me risqué."

Viktor inclined his head. "As you wish, my lady."

He gestured to the groom, who led the pony into the stable. A few minutes later, the groom reappeared with the pony resaddled.

"These are the reins," Viktor said, holding them up.

Regina rolled her eyes. "I know what they are."

"Do you know how to use them?"

"No."

"Hold the reins loosely but firmly across the palm of your hand," Viktor instructed her. "Tug on the left rein to turn left and the right rein to turn right. Tug on both to stop. Come, I will help you up." He gave her a lift onto the saddle and then, holding the reins, led the pony around the penned exercise yard.

Regina looked down. "Cosmo didn't look tall until you put me up here."

"Do you fear heights?"

"I would never consider heights my favorite place."

Viktor led the pony around the exercise yard several times, giving her time to accustom herself to sitting on the pony. He stopped finally, passed her the reins, and said, "Walk him around the yard. When I tell you to turn left or right, use the reins. If you perform well, we will ride together next time."

"I'm returning to London tomorrow."

Viktor caught her gaze. "Do you believe our friendship will end when we return to London?"

Regina did not know what to say. She knew what he was asking, but men and women did not usually become friends. How could she be his friend when she was in danger of losing her heart?

"I am a virtuous woman."

"I am an honorable man. Do you doubt me?"

Regina shook her head. Perhaps they could enjoy a friendship.

After she had circled the exercise yard several times, Viktor put her through her paces. "Turn left. Turn right. Stop. Start."

"That will do for today." Viktor lifted her off the saddle, his hands lingering on her waist longer than necessary.

Regina stared into his eyes. Their dark intensity held her captive.

Viktor gazed into eyes so green he could drown in their fathomless depths. Unable to stop himself, he inched his face closer and closer.

"Don't kiss me here," she whispered in an embarrassed panic.

He grinned. "Then I will kiss you in private."

Hand in hand, Viktor and Regina walked down the path to the mansion. Reluctant to part, they wandered around the manor to the rear gardens. Princes Rudolf, Mikhail, and Stepan were practicing their golf swings on the expanse of lawn beyond the maze.

"Have you ever played golf?" Viktor asked.

"No."

"I will show you how it is done."

His brothers halted their play when they approached. All three princes greeted them with a good morning.

"I am demonstrating golf to Reggie." Viktor lifted the ash driving club and a leather-covered ball out of Rudolf's hands. He set the ball on top of the wooden tee and, after a moment, swung the club.

Wham! The ball sailed through the air and landed near the trees separating parkland from woodland.

Regina applauded his effort, inciting his three brothers to laughter. Her green eyes gleamed with excitement when Viktor winked and passed her the golf club.

Stepping up to the tee, Regina tried to hold the club the way the prince had done. Viktor set the ball on the tee and backed away.

Regina lifted the club, swung hard, and tried to locate where the ball had flown. She heard the princes laughing.

"Look down," Viktor said.

Regina looked down and laughed. The ball still sat on top of the tee. "This game is not as easy as you make it look."

"I will guide you." Viktor stepped behind her, his arms circling her body. "Are you blushing?"

"Yes." She could feel the warmth of his breath on the side of her neck, the heat of his body pressed against hers.

Viktor smiled at her honesty, positioned her hands on the club, and kept his hands on hers. "Grip the shaft like this, and spread your legs."

Blissfully innocent, Regina asked, "Is that wide enough?"

"Perfect." Viktor glanced at his smiling brothers and grinned. "Keep your head down and your eyes on the ball. We will swing in an arc and follow through until the club is over your left shoulder."

Viktor inhaled her vanilla and jasmine scent and wondered why he was tormenting himself. With his hands covering hers, he swung the club. The ball flew toward the distant trees.

"I did it." Regina whirled around, her body still pressing his from breast to thigh. She blushed and stepped back a pace, mumbling in embarrassment, "I'm sorry."

"I am not sorry." Viktor lifted her hand to his lips. "Will you luncheon with me?"

"Yes." No hesitation there.

"What will you do until lunch?"

"I will work on my novel. Perhaps my heroine will learn to play golf."

Viktor watched her walk toward the mansion. When she disappeared inside, he turned around and surprised his brothers. "I plan to marry Lady Bradford."

Regina passed the next three hours writing about the Duke of Charming teaching Dementia to ride a horse and to swing a golf club. She made the scene as seductive as possible, stopping short of vulgarity, and then set the quill on the writing table. If only her own life could be as wonderfully romantic as her heroine's.

She was tormenting herself. Nothing could ever come from her friendship with the prince. Not even if Charles met an untimely end. She enjoyed the prince's stimulating company and felt freer with him than she had in her whole life.

The reality of her life was she had grown from childhood to womanhood stifled by an overbearing father. The man, who supposedly loved her, had forced her down the aisle to marry an obnoxious swine.

Regina stood and stretched, her muscles protesting the hours sitting at the table. She inspected her appearance in the cheval mirror and decided that the pale yellow of her gown complemented her red hair.

Regina sighed, knowing that tomorrow she would be returning to London and leaving the prince's friendship behind. She intended to savor this final day of his royal attention.

Since the unusually fine weather had held, the Duchess of Inverary planned an outdoor luncheon at tables set on the lawn nearest the manor. Regina stepped outside and inhaled the perfume of lilacs growing near the mansion. She stood there a long moment without the awkward feeling she had experienced the first evening in the drawing room. Scanning the crowd, Regina noted Charles's and Adele's absence. Her husband and his lover seemed to have fallen off the edge of the world.

Prince Viktor stood a short distance away. Regina smiled when he caught her attention and winked at her. Then she noticed the sultry brunette clinging to his arm. Vanessa Stanton.

Regina didn't know what to do, but the prince had invited her to luncheon with him. She started across the lawn toward him and recognized the approval in his gaze.

"Regina."

She stopped at the sound of her name and then regretted it. Cedric Barrows stood beside her, his hand on her arm. To prevent her escape? She suffered the urge to pull away from his touch but thought the other guests would gossip about her rudeness.

"Good afternoon, Cedric." Regina sent the prince a silent plea for help.

"Come, cousin. Let us sit together." Cedric pulled out a chair for her.

Regina forced herself to smile at him. Cedric sat beside her, his gaze on her breasts.

"I should not refer to you as my cousin," he said. "Lucky for us, in-laws are not blood relatives. We can become as familiar as we desire."

"I have no desire to become familiar with you." Regina heard a deep rumble of laughter.

Prince Viktor stood beside the table, Vanessa still clinging to his arm. The prince assisted the brunette into a chair and then sat between the two women.

"Would you prefer wine or lemon barley water?" he asked her.

"Lemon barley water." Regina helped herself to a filet of sole, several thin slices of roasted beef, and a spoonful of vegetable medley.

Cedric leaned close. "Drinking wine will relax you."

"Move back, Cedric, or I will skewer you with my knife."

"You don't mean that."

Regina stared into his brown eyes. "I have never been more serious in my life."

"Viktor, darling, what night are we attending the opera?" Vanessa asked, leaning close to the man.

The prince looked nonplussed. "I will send you a note."

Regina felt her heart sinking to her stomach, and her newfound confidence waned. Unfamiliar jealousy surged through her, constricting her chest, making breathing difficult. She had let the prince kiss her and believed he considered her special. What a damn fool. She had neither the experience nor the inclination to play these sophisticated games.

"Viktor has one of the most expensive boxes at the opera house," Vanessa told her.

"How nice for Viktor." Regina managed a ghost of a smile. She wondered how long she needed to endure the present company before escaping.

Viktor watched in irritation as she slid back into her shell. He could have kicked himself and Vanessa from here to London.

"I would like to read your novel," he said, hoping to block her emotional retreat.

Regina gave him a stiff smile. "My work is far from complete."

"You'll never finish it," Vanessa said.

"Even if you do finish," Cedric added, "no one will publish it."

"I will ask my father to buy a publishing company for me." Regina set her napkin on the table and moved to stand. "I have developed a headache."

"Do not leave." Viktor covered her hand with his. "I was hoping for a game of croquet."

"I don't play croquet."

"I will teach you." Their gazes clashed. "Please."

She sat down again, and when the meal ended, Viktor offered her his hand. "The game of croquet awaits us, my lady." Leaving sister and brother to follow behind, he escorted her across the lawn where footmen had set wickets and pegs. "I am sorry for our spoiled luncheon."

"You do not need to apologize," she said. "You belong to Adele, not me."

"I do not belong to Adele. Nor do you belong to Chuck."

Regina smiled at his use of her husband's nickname. He winked and passed her a mallet. When she set her red ball down on the start line, he stepped behind her to position her body into the proper stance.

"With your left hand, hold the top of the mallet close to your body," Viktor said. "Grasp the shaft lower with your right hand."

Regina thought she would swoon with his arousing nearness. She longed to lean back against the muscular planes of his body, to close her eyes and feel his strength pressed against her.

"Lady Bradford?" The duke's majordomo approached. "Excuse me, my lady. Your man needs to speak with you."

Regina shifted her gaze toward the manor. Artie, her husband's coachman, stood at a discreet distance from the duke's guests.

"Thank you, Tinker." Regina handed Viktor the mallet and walked in her coachman's direction.

"My lady, the earl and the princess have gone and will not be returning," Artie told her. "They took the prince's coach, and His Lordship said he would see you in London tomorrow."

Regina glanced in the prince's direction and knew she could not remain as the duke's guest now. "Artie, prepare to leave for London in two hours."

"Yes, my lady."

Regina started back to the others, but Viktor met her halfway across the lawn. "Charles and Adele took your coach. I will be leaving for London in two hours."

"May I ride with you?"

"Yes, of course."

Viktor grasped her arm, and they walked toward the mansion. "Do not look back," he warned, "or Vanessa will follow us."

Regina laughed.

"Your laughter warms my heart," Viktor said. *And your body will soon warm my bed.*

Dusk had aged into night by the time their coach reached the outskirts of London. The hours in the prince's company had passed pleasantly, and Regina wanted to prolong their time together.

"Would you care to sup with me?" Regina invited him. "Austen will be sleeping, but you could meet Ginger and Hamlet."

Prince Viktor rested his arm on the leather seat behind her. He smiled, igniting a hot melting sensation in her lower regions. "I would love to sup with you."

The coach halted in front of the Bradford residence. "The prince won't be leaving until later," Regina told Artie. "Get yourself supper."

"Thank you, my lady."

The front door opened. "Welcome home, my lady," the majordomo greeted her.

"Thank you." Regina turned to the prince. "Your Highness, I present my friend, Pickles."

"A pleasure to meet Your Highness," Pickles greeted him.

Viktor felt confused. Apparently, Pickles was not the earl's majordomo as he had thought.

"Serve us a light supper in the parlor," Regina instructed the man. "Then ask Ginger to join us there."

"Yes, my lady."

Viktor touched her arm. "Is Pickles your majordomo?"

Regina gave him a blank smile. "Yes, he is."

"Reggie, you are an Original." Viktor grinned. "I

know no one who would even consider introducing me to their servants."

"Pickles is my friend, too."

Hamlet bounded down the stairs and darted past her. The Great Dane leaped at the prince and tried to lick his face. Viktor laughed so hard he couldn't summon the strength to push the dog down.

"Hamlet, sit." The dog obeyed, but his tail swished back and forth across the floor. "He likes you."

"So I assumed. I cannot believe Chuck is afraid of this big baby."

"Hamlet growls when he sees Chuck."

Viktor patted the dog's enormous head. "Good boy, Hamlet."

Regina and Viktor climbed the stairs to the parlor. She led him across the chamber to the settee in front of the hearth.

Viktor looked around. "This feels comfortable."

"I love this room, too."

Pickles arrived with a tray of sandwiches and pastries. A footman followed with the tea tray.

Hamlet sat at attention beside Viktor. He glanced at the dog and then reached for a sandwich. Refusing to be ignored, the Great Dane placed a paw on the prince's leg.

"Do not feed that beggar. Hamlet, lie down." The dog ignored her.

"Down," Viktor ordered, his deep voice stern. The dog whined and then lay down. The prince looked at her. "You need to be more forceful."

"I suppose my forcefulness will improve once my voice changes. Sopranos get no respect."

Ginger Evans rushed into the parlor before he could reply. "Your Highness, I present Ginger

Evans. Ginger, this is Prince Viktor Kazanov of Kazanov Brothers."

"A pleasure to meet you." Ginger started to curtsey, but the prince stopped her.

"I always shake hands with business associates." Viktor offered his hand. Ginger smiled and shook his hand.

"Is Austen sleeping?" Regina asked.

"Nanny Sprig put him down hours ago."

"Please join us," the prince said.

Ginger opened her mouth to refuse, but Regina spoke first. "His Highness has exciting news for us."

"I understand you are a mathematical genius," Viktor said. "Rudolf, my oldest brother, insists on speaking with you when he returns to London. Something about another investment."

"The Duke of Inverary will meet with us, too," Regina said, "and no one will tell Chuck."

"Tell me, Ginger," Viktor said, "what other investments are you considering?"

"If I divulged that, Your Highness, we would never make any money."

"You have the instincts of a shark."

Ginger smiled. "Thank you for the high praise, Your Highness."

"Did the constable call?" Regina asked, changing the subject.

Ginger nodded. "We are lunching together tomorrow."

Regina looked at the prince. "Ginger's father passed away."

"I am sorry for your loss."

Without embarrassment, Ginger looked him straight in the eye. "The authorities called it suicide."

"Ginger believes her father's death was a homicide disguised as a suicide," Regina told him. "I sent for Amadeus Black, hoping she could convince him to reopen the investigation."

"And what did the constable say?" Viktor asked.

"He wasn't encouraging but did promise to review the findings," Ginger answered. "We will discuss my father's case at lunch. I read a story once—*The Butler's Dilemma*, I believe—"

"Ginger loves mysteries," Regina interrupted. "She's very good at unraveling them before the ending."

"What kind of man is this Amadeus Black?" Viktor asked.

Ginger sighed, her expression becoming dreamy. "He's very tall and handsome and dark and blue-eyed and—" She broke off abruptly and blushed. "I really must be leaving. Meeting you was a pleasure, Your Highness."

Prince Viktor stood. "Rudolf and His Grace will send you notes when they return to London." He sat when the other woman slipped away. "Tell me about your book, Reggie."

"What do you want to know?"

"What is the title?"

"I don't have a title yet."

"Your heroine must have a name."

"Dementia Merlot, the Countess of—"

Viktor shouted with laughter. "You named your heroine Dementia?"

"Since there can only be one Jane Austen," Regina said, blushing, "I thought I would write a romantic comedy. That way, no one will compare my work with the formidable Miss Austen."

"That is very clever. How did you decide on your heroine's name?"

"I was considering her name one day when Charles walked into my study and started bickering about a trivial matter," Regina said. "What a demented buffoon, I thought, and the word *dementia* stuck in my mind. She's originally from France and has a long-lost sister named Vendetta. I will write Vendetta's story when I finish Dementia's."

Viktor smiled and stood. "The hour is late. I will leave so you can retire."

Regina met his gaze, her yearning for him to stay shining from her eyes. "I will walk you to the foyer."

Viktor lifted her hand to his lips. "Do not feel sad, Reggie. We will see each other again. I promise."

Downstairs, Regina sent Pickles for Artie and the coach. She waited in silence, certain she would weep if she spoke.

Viktor reached out and, with one long finger, lifted her chin. He dipped his head and covered her mouth in a gentle kiss. "Jealousy consumes me," he admitted. "I wish Charles and Adele had never been born."

"My lady," Pickles called, hurrying into the foyer. "I cannot find Artie, and the horses are down for the night."

Viktor turned to the door. "I will walk home."

"Don't leave." Regina touched his hand. "The streets are dangerous at this hour, and we have several guest chambers."

Viktor wanted to stay as much as she wanted him.

"We can breakfast together in the morning," Regina said. "Charles won't return tonight."

Viktor inclined his head. "Then I accept your invitation."

"I'll show you to your chamber. That will be all for tonight, Pickles."

Hand in hand, Viktor and Regina walked upstairs. She pretended they were married and did this every night. He decided that, somehow, they would marry and enjoy this last walk of the day before they found paradise in their bed.

Regina stopped in front of a door on the third floor. "Here you are."

"Where is your chamber?"

"At the end of the corridor."

"Lock your door, Reggie, or the temptation will prove too great to resist." Viktor lifted her hands and, turning them over, kissed her palms. "I do not want to dishonor you." He brushed a finger across her lips. "Our day will come, Reggie. I promise."

"What do you think?"

Amadeus Black looked at the man beside him and then lifted his gaze to the depressingly cloudy sky. A raw drizzle had begun at almost the same moment he had reached the crime scene, a deserted stretch of road on the outskirts of London.

"I think I hate this weather, Barney."

The other man rolled his eyes. "Everyone hates this weather. I meant, what do you think about these two?" He shifted his gaze to the corpses.

I think I will be forced to cancel my lunch with Ginger Evans, Amadeus thought. Too bad he hadn't made their luncheon for yesterday.

"I think these two are dead." Amadeus circled the corpses, his sharp gaze noting all the details.

Barney rolled his eyes again. "And?"

Amadeus sent his assistant a crooked smile. "I think this is no suicide."

Barney gave him a long-suffering look. "These two are Quality, but neither is wearing jewels or carrying money. I suppose robbery was the motive?"

Amadeus shifted his gaze to the lady and gentleman lying in pools of blood. What an ignominious ending to their lives. "Perhaps the murderer wanted us to believe the motive was robbery."

Barney grinned. "You always amaze me."

"You are easily amazed. Transport the bodies to London."

"Where are you going?"

"I need to cancel a previous appointment."

Grim-faced, Amadeus Black halted his carriage in front of the Earl of Langley's residence thirty minutes later. He banged the door knocker and walked into the foyer when the majordomo greeted him.

"Good morning, Constable Black," the man greeted him.

"I wish to speak with Miss Evans."

"I'll fetch her."

Amadeus hadn't felt this nervous since he'd courted his late wife. He hoped the young woman's disappointment would not prevent her from forgiving him.

Ginger appeared a moment later and gave him a warm smile. "Isn't the hour a bit early for our lunch?"

Amadeus regretted canceling. "I am sorry, Ginger. I will need to reschedule for later in the week."

She looked disappointed.

"An unavoidable business emergency."

She inclined her head. "I understand."

"May I speak with the countess?"

His question obviously surprised her. She gave him a puzzled smile. "Yes, of course. Come with me."

Amadeus followed her down a long corridor to the dining room. A smile touched his lips as he admired the gentle sway of her hips. He hadn't felt this way since—

Laughter reached his ears. A man and a woman.

Amadeus stepped into the dining room, drawing the couple's attention. The Countess of Langley and Prince Viktor Kazanov. How interesting.

Prince Viktor stood at his entrance. Amadeus gestured him to sit, but the prince remained standing.

"Your Highness and Regina, I present Constable Amadeus Black," Ginger introduced them.

Prince Viktor offered his hand. Amadeus shook it, feeling the gesture symbolized the long struggle beginning between them.

"Please join us," the countess invited him.

"No, thank you."

"Have you decided to reopen my father's case?" Ginger asked.

"I have not reached a decision on that yet." Amadeus looked from the prince to the countess and then back to the prince again. "I apologize for being the bearer of bad news." He hesitated a long moment. "Your spouses are dead."

"Charles and Adele are dead?" Prince Viktor echoed.

The countess stood to face him, a strange look in her eyes. "Did Charles—?" She paused and took a deep breath. "Did Charles walk into a bullet?"

Amadeus stared hard at her. "A bullet walked into him."

With a soft cry, the countess dropped into her chair. She leaned back and closed her eyes.

"Reggie, are you ill?" Prince Viktor asked, his hand cupping her cheek. "Ginger, fetch the hartshorn."

"*No.*" The countess opened her eyes. "I did not swoon."

So the husband of the deceased female victim worries about the wife of the deceased male victim. That is astonishingly interesting.

"Where were you last night?" Amadeus asked.

Both the prince and the countess gave him a horrified look. Either they were innocent or excellent actors. And the latter seemed more probable.

"How dare you," Ginger cried, rounding on him. "How dare you even suggest such a vile thing."

"Miss Evans, I am merely doing my job," Amadeus said. "I must ask these questions."

"Are we suspects?" the countess asked.

"Everyone is suspect."

"Everyone in London?" the prince asked. "Or everyone in this room?"

Amadeus gave the prince a cold smile. "I am positive Miss Evans did not commit murder."

Chapter 6

"... he that believeth in me, though he were dead, yet shall he live ..."

Dementia placed a single rose on her husband's coffin. Lord, but she would prefer the fires of hell to seeing Bertie in paradise.

"Come, Lady Merlot." The Duke of Charming escorted her away from the grave.

Constable Green stood near the ducal coach. "Where were you last night?"

Dementia met the constable's cold gaze. "Are we suspects?"

"Everyone is suspect."

"... Death is swallowed up in victory. O death, where is thy sting? O grave, where is thy victory ...?"

Prince Viktor Kazanov gave his daughter an encouraging smile. With her tiny hand in his, the prince led her to her mother's coffin to place a single rose on it.

"Well done."

Viktor lifted his daughter into his arms and walked back to his country house. Family and friends followed behind.

"Godfrey, I hope the refreshments are prepared," Viktor said.

"Quite ready, Your Highness," his majordomo assured him.

"Ah, here is Nanny Devon." Viktor set his daughter down. "Nanny Devon will get you lunch and then read you a story."

Sally held her nanny's hand and started down the corridor. She hadn't taken more than five steps when she turned around and ran back to her father. Crooking her finger at him, she beckoned him closer.

Viktor crouched down to be eye level with her. "Is there something else, poppet?"

Sally wrapped her arms around his neck and gave him a smacking kiss on the lips. "I love you, Daddy."

His dark eyes shone with unshed tears. "I love you more."

"No, Daddy, I love you more."

"I do."

Sally giggled. "Equals?"

He hugged her tightly. "Equals forever."

Viktor watched his five-year-old daughter walk away with her nanny. Before disappearing from sight, she looked over her shoulder at him and winked. He laughed at her instinctive flirting. His daughter was the blond-haired, blue-eyed image of her mother. Thankfully, the resemblance ended there. Adele on the outside and him on the inside. One day in the distant future, his princess would make some gentleman very happy.

Two hours later, the funeral guests had departed for London. Viktor stood at the window in his second-floor study and stared at the gloomy day. He shifted his gaze to watch his daughter playing with her cousins in the garden below.

"How is Sally reacting to Adele's death?" Rudolf had spoken.

Viktor sipped his vodka before turning around to face his brother, lounging in a chair. He shrugged. "Sally never saw much of her mother."

"You never should have rushed into marriage with her," Prince Mikhail said.

Prince Stepan snorted with exaggerated disgust. "Too bad, he did not learn his lesson."

Viktor gave his youngest brother his attention. "What does that mean?"

"I suggest you think long and hard before committing yourself to the merchant's daughter."

"Leave Lady Bradford out of this." Viktor sipped his vodka. "Regina Bradford is as different from Adele as day is to night."

"You cannot know that," Prince Mikhail agreed with his youngest brother. "You believed Adele was all she seemed."

Viktor gave his brother a wry smile. "I am not as young or gullible as I was." He lifted his gaze to the portrait of his late wife hanging over the hearth's mantel and raised his glass in salute. "I wanted to be rid of you, Adele, but a divorce would have sufficed."

"Do you have any idea who would want them dead?" Rudolf asked. "Besides Lady Bradford and you, that is."

Viktor shook his head. "Whoever did the deed wanted Charles dead. Adele was in the wrong place at the wrong time with the wrong man."

"You may be considered a suspect," Rudolf said. "Do you have an alibi for that night?"

"No." Viktor refused to use Regina Bradford as his alibi. Her reputation would be ruined if he announced that he had slept at the Bradford residence. No one would believe he had passed the night in a guest chamber. "I came directly home and retired for the night."

"Did anyone see you?" Mikhail asked.

"No."

"Shit, that constable has the instincts of a bloodhound," Prince Stepan said. "You are the man he will suspect first."

"I never struck my faithless wife, nor did I murder Charles and Adele."

"Constable Black does not know you as we do," Stepan replied.

"Since I am innocent of wrongdoing, there can be no proof of guilt."

"When a princess and an earl are murdered on the road to London," Rudolf said, "the authorities will want a quick arrest. Evidence or no evidence."

"Everyone heard you threaten Charles," Mikhail reminded him.

"Is it possible Regina Bradford hired an assassin?" Stepan asked.

Viktor turned a cold gaze on the youngest Kazanov. "If you were not my brother, I would call you out for daring to suggest that."

Stepan inclined his head. "I apologize, but these questions need asking if you are not to hang for a murder you did not commit."

Viktor lifted the glass of vodka to his lips but paused before downing the fiery liquid. "I plan to attend Charles Bradford's funeral tomorrow."

"Damn it." Stepan banged his fist on the arm of his chair. "You cannot do that."

"Regina may need my support."

"I suggest you keep your distance from Regina Bradford," Mikhail said.

"I repeat, Regina may need my support."

"If Viktor cannot keep his distance, brothers, then he cannot keep his distance." Rudolf looked from Mikhail to Stepan. "The four of us will attend

Bradford's funeral so Viktor may assure himself that Regina is well." He looked at Viktor. "Does that meet with your approval?"

Viktor inclined his head. "I plan to marry the lady as soon as possible without tarnishing her reputation."

Rudolf looked from his youngest brothers to Viktor. He raised his glass in salute. "Congratulations are in order. All we need to do is keep you out of the hangman's noose long enough to take your vows."

". . . we therefore commit his body to the ground; earth to earth, ashes to ashes, dust to dust . . ."

The earl is dead, Regina thought, biting her lips to keep the smile off her face. *Long live the baby earl and her independence.*

She did not wish harm, especially death, to Charles and Adele. On the other hand, death had freed her from a stifling marriage that she had not wanted. Never again would she marry, especially to win her father's approval. No matter what she did, she would never have that.

Regina dropped her gaze to her butterfly ring and struggled to maintain a properly somber expression. Relief surged though her. She would soon spread her wings and soar. Her marriage had freed her from her father, and death had freed her from her husband. God had generously answered her prayers.

Thankful for the black veil covering her face, Regina placed a rose on the coffin. She turned around and noted the four Kazanov princes in attendance.

Escorted to the coach by her father, Regina paused to speak to the princes, but her gaze fixed on Viktor. "Thank you for coming. Please join us at the house for refreshment."

"Of course, we will accompany you," Viktor accepted for his brothers.

Regina and her father shared a coach while Uncle Forest and Ginger rode in another. Behind their coaches came the funeral guests, including Cedric Barrows and Vanessa Stanton, her husband's cousins.

Settled in the seat opposite her father, Regina lifted the black veil off her face and closed her eyes. Only a few short hours until she could live in peaceful independence. No arguments with Charles. No unwanted visits from his cousins. No unwelcome forays into society.

"The noble send-off for Charles pleased me," Reginald said. "Several earls and countesses, not to mention four princes."

Regina opened her eyes and stared at him. Titles impressed her father. She could almost feel sorry for a man more concerned with superficial trivialities than truly precious things in life. Like love and loyalty and respect.

"Charles Bradford was an obnoxious boor," Regina said. "A snob of the first order."

Reginald ignored her comment. "A tad unseemly of that Russian prince to attend. Though, he did bring his brothers along."

"I don't believe his presence is unseemly," Regina said. "Princess Adele was Chuck's mistress, not Viktor."

"Don't get mouthy with me, missy."

Regina closed her eyes again and tried to ignore her father's presence. Now was not the moment to argue. They had the rest of their lives to bicker.

At Bradford House, Pickles supervised the footmen serving her guests coffee, tea, and pastries in the formal drawing room. Regina disliked the cold formality, preferring the warm color scheme and the books in the family parlor.

"Humph! We needed a death in the family to sit in this drawing room," Reginald remarked.

Sitting on the settee, Regina cast her father a warning look. Her heart sank to her stomach when Cedric Barrows sat beside her. Ignoring him, she gave her attention to the Kazanov brothers.

"Your Highnesses, I present my father, Reginald Smith, and his associate, Forest Fredericks, 'Uncle Forest' to Ginger and me," Regina made the introductions. "Father and Uncle Forest, these are Princes Rudolf, Viktor, Mikhail, and Stepan."

Both men stood to shake hands with the princes. Her father took the royal guests in stride. Uncle Forest sat down, blushed, and pushed his spectacles up with an index finger.

Carrying Austen, Ginger walked into the drawing room. Without being told, she passed the boy to his grandfather.

Only then did Reginald notice the Great Dane trot into the room and sit beside its mistress. He gave his daughter a withering look. "Regina, I and your guests did not come here to visit the dog."

Regina gave her father a warm smile and decided to soar. Ignoring the paternal scolding, she passed the dog a tiny piece of pastry.

"Regina!"

"Charles is dead," she said baldly, watching his complexion redden in anger. "I am mistress of this house. Hamlet stays."

"Dearest Regina, your father is correct." Cedric reached for her hand. "Adorable though he is, guests do not want to bother with a dog."

Regina yanked her hand back. "When I want your opinion, I will ask for it."

Vanessa Stanton gasped. "My brother is merely trying to help."

"You keep quiet, too." Regina heard the smothered chuckles coming from the princes.

"The stress of burying her husband colors the lady's judgment and manners," Viktor said into the silence.

"On the contrary," Regina said, "this day is one of the happiest of my entire life."

"Breeding does tell," Vanessa sneered. "Perhaps you hired an assassin to murder my dearest cousin."

"If I wanted Charles dead," Regina drawled, "I would not forgo the pleasure of killing him myself."

"*Regina!*" Her father sounded appalled.

Before conversation could deteriorate further, Forest Fredericks defused the situation. "Intense grief sometimes makes people behave strangely."

"Did Charles leave a will?" Cedric asked.

Regina looked at him as if he'd grown another head. "Charles had nothing of value to leave anyone. The money he squandered belongs to my father."

Reginald Smith shook his head in disapproval. "Your mother lacked tact, too."

"Shall I handle the household finances for you?" Uncle Forest asked.

"No, thank you. Ginger does the accounts."

"That is unfeminine," Reginald said, making the other girl blush.

"Addition and subtraction have nothing to do with gender," Regina informed her father. "Keep your opinions to yourself."

Reginald shook his head again in disapproval. "Just like your mother."

"Thankfully, I did not take after you."

"That is no proper way to address your father," Prince Viktor spoke up. "You must apologize at once."

Rebellion glittered from her green eyes and clashed with his dark gaze. Then she looked at her father. "I apologize for my disrespect."

Reginald Smith appeared stunned. He looked from his daughter to the prince and then back at his daughter. "I forgive you, of course." He stood then and passed his grandson to her. "Forest and I must take our leave."

"I'll walk you to the foyer." Regina rose from the settee. She sat again when he gestured her to stay where she was.

"We must be leaving, too." Viktor and his brothers followed the two men out, leaving only Cedric and Vanessa.

"Mr. Smith, I would like a word with you," Viktor said when they reached the foyer.

Reginald gestured Forest out and turned around.

Viktor hesitated. He wanted to tell the man to make no matches for his daughter, but realized his matrimonial intentions would be tasteless on the day the man buried his son-in-law.

"I want you to know I admire your daughter," Viktor said.

Reginald dropped his mouth open in surprise. "You admire my daughter?"

Viktor nodded. "Lady Regina is refreshingly candid and sincere. Few women of my acquaintance can compare with her."

"You are referring to my Regina?" the older man asked in disbelief. "She is as cantankerous as a camel."

Viktor grinned. "A gentleman will never become bored with your daughter as his wife."

"Are you asking to court her?"

"Both Regina and I are in mourning. Today is inauspicious to speak of second marriages."

Reginald Smith narrowed his gaze on him. "Did you murder Charles and Princess Adele?"

"No."

The older man nodded, accepting his word. Then he walked outside to join his associate.

Viktor knew his brothers were waiting but walked back upstairs to the drawing room. He paused in the doorway at the sight that greeted him.

Cedric Barrows clutched Regina's hand. "You must marry me," he said. "I won't take *no* for an answer. Once your mourning—"

With some difficulty, Regina managed to free her hand. "I don't want you visiting me, never mind living here."

"You need a man to care for you."

Regina arched a copper brow at her husband's cousin. "If I need a man to care for me, why would I marry you?"

Viktor laughed, drawing their attention. "Cedric and Vanessa, you are overstaying your welcome. The lady deserves peace and privacy on the day she buried her husband."

Vanessa stood. "The crass commoner never cared for Charles. How he suffered being married to a merchant's daughter." At that, she left the drawing room.

"I will return soon," Cedric promised.

"In that case, walk slowly."

Viktor crossed the drawing room. "I will call upon you soon. Perhaps I will bring Sally."

Regina smiled. "I would like that."

After the prince disappeared out the door, Regina sighed and turned to her friend. "I instructed Pickles to send me Louis and need you to witness my interview with him. Bring Austen to Nanny Sprig first."

Ginger lifted the boy out of her arms and returned to the drawing room before the valet arrived. "Are you terminating him?"

Regina smiled at her friend. "I will savor every moment."

"My presence will humiliate the man."

"I need you here."

Louis, her husband's valet, walked into the drawing room. "You sent for me?"

Regina noted he refrained from giving her the respect of calling her *my lady*. So be it. She suffered no qualms about insulting the man but could not bring herself to rudeness.

"Your services in this household are no longer required," Regina told him. "However, you may remain until you find another position."

His complexion red with angry embarrassment, Louis glanced at Ginger. He nodded once to Regina and marched out of the room.

"Louis is a vindictive man," Ginger said. "You should not have fired him in front of me."

"You worry too much. What could Chuck's former valet do to me?"

"Pleased to meet you, Mr. Black." Reginald Smith shook the constable's hand and then gestured to his associate. "This is Forest Fredericks, a trusted employee."

Amadeus shook the other man's hand, his shrewd gaze observing the differences between the two men. Still a handsome man, Reginald Smith appeared prosperous and dignified while Forest Fredericks seemed hopelessly dominated by Smith. Definitely *not* dignified.

"This is my associate, Barney." Amadeus smiled at the two businessmen. "Please do not ask if Barney is his given name or surname."

"Please sit," Reginald said. "Forest, bring us coffee."

Amadeus sat across the oak desk from Smith. The scent of ink permeated the air inside the office, and muted voices from outside drifted into the room through an open window.

"Thank you," Amadeus said, when Forest passed him a cup of steaming coffee. "Let me see your hand."

"My hand?" Wearing a surprised expression, Forest held his palm out to reveal an angry burn mark.

"That looks sore." Amadeus lifted his gaze to the man's. "However did you get that?"

Fredericks shrugged and reddened with his embarrassment. "I cannot recall, but I did ride without gloves a few days ago."

"I see." Amadeus lifted his cup to sip the coffee and then turned his attention on Smith. "I apologize for intruding on your day but do need to ask a few questions."

"I understand." Reginald Smith nodded. "A murderer runs loose, and I will help in any way possible."

"I appreciate your civic-mindedness." Amadeus gave Barney a sidelong glance when the other man slurped his coffee.

"Do you know anything about your son-in-law's private life? I mean, apart from his marriage to your daughter."

"I am sorry," Reginald answered, "but I know nothing beyond the fact that Charles enjoyed spending my money and made another man's wife his mistress."

"You did not respect your son-in-law?"

Completely relaxed, Reginald Smith leaned back in his chair. "I did not need to respect him in order to purchase his title for my family."

"Bradford was a rake," Fredericks added. "Gambling, drinking, womanizing."

"You feel strongly about the man?"

Barney slurped his coffee, drawing their attention. His face reddened with embarrassment.

"Did you have strong feelings about Bradford?" Amadeus repeated his question.

Fredericks slid his spectacles up. "I have strong feelings for Regina, whom I have always considered the daughter I never had. His treatment of her was abominable."

"Hateful enough for you to murder him?" Amadeus cocked a dark brow at the man.

Reginald Smith shouted with laughter. "Forest fears his own shadow."

"What about you, then?"

"I had no need to kill Charles. He would have drunk himself into an early grave."

Barney slurped his coffee, drawing attention from Amadeus again.

"What about your daughter?"

Reginald shifted his gaze. "What about her?"

"Apparently, you exchanged your wealth for his title via marriage to your daughter," Amadeus said. "How did she feel about being used as a pawn?"

Reginald bolted out of his chair, his gaze colder than the Thames in winter. "My daughter did *not*

murder her husband, nor did she cause his death.
Furthermore, I did not use my daughter as a pawn."

Unruffled by the older man's outburst, Amadeus
merely stared at him for another long moment.
"What is your opinion of Prince Viktor Kazanov?"

"I scarcely know the man."

"Do you believe he had anything to do with the
murders?"

"If you want to know who murdered Charles,"
Reginald said, "look at his gambling debts."

Amadeus stood and set the coffee cup on the desk.
"I thank you for your time." He turned to leave but
then paused. "What precisely was Bartholomew
Evans's job?"

"Bart was my accountant," Reginald answered.
"Why do you ask?"

"Do you think he committed suicide?"

Reginald shrugged. "Bart never seemed the suicidal type to me, but one never knows what sorrows
a heart may bear."

"I believe Bart may have been slightly depressed,"
Forest spoke up. "I assumed he suffered from the
winter doldrums."

Reginald looked at his associate. "I never noticed
anything."

Forest gave the other man an apologetic smile
and pushed his spectacles up. "Nobody would ever
accuse you of sensitivity."

Amadeus looked at his underling. "Come, we
have other stops to make."

Barney slurped his coffee a final time and set the
cup on the desk. Then he follwed Amadeus out.

"Do you think Smith is behind the murders?" he
asked, once they had left the building.

"If pressed into choice," Amadeus answered, "I

would choose Fredericks. Sometimes, one must look at the quiet ones."

"So, you think Fredericks did the deed?"

Amadeus stopped walking and looked at Barney. "I said if given a choice. However, Fredericks has no motivation to murder. I merely suggested that you need to look at all aspects before making decisions that could affect clear thinking."

Both men climbed into the coach, Amadeus taking the reins. "Oh, by the way, slurping your coffee proved a great distraction. Good job."

Barney beamed. "Thank you, Amadeus."

"What will you do at the cousin's home?"

"Pick my nose? Scratch my butt?"

Amadeus rolled his eyes. "Forget the distraction."

A short time later, Amadeus halted the coach in front of the Barrows's residence in Russell Square. "Wait here with the coach," he ordered.

Amadeus hurried up the stairs and, when the majordomo answered the door, stepped into the foyer. He flicked a glance around the foyer and noted the worn look, realizing the Earl of Dover could be in financial straits. This assumption proved true when he walked into the drawing room.

The Countess of Tewksbury sat on a settee that had seen better days. She smiled, apparently noting his gaze on the worn furniture. "You know how bachelors are about their households."

"How fortuitous that you are visiting, my lady," Amadeus said. "You were next on my list."

Cedric Barrows walked into the room. "What list?"

"I am investigating the Kazanov-Bradford murders," Amadeus said. "I need to question both of you. Separately."

"You do not suspect us?" Vanessa asked.

"No, my lady. I want to speak about the Earl of Langley."

"I'll step into my office," Cedric offered. "How long do you need with my sister?"

Amadeus shrugged. "Ten minutes."

Once they were alone, Amadeus turned to the countess. "Do you know anything about your cousin's personal life?"

"I know that he married beneath him," Vanessa answered, unable to keep her dislike of his wife out of her voice. "He did enjoy his pleasures, and pleasures cost money."

"Do you think Prince Viktor could be involved in your cousin's murder?"

"Viktor is a gentleman without a violent bone in his body," she defended the prince. "He had no need to harm Adele. I heard he planned to divorce her."

"Could Prince Viktor have conspired with Lady Bradford?"

"That common bitch hired an assassin to murder my cousin. She despised him. In fact, after his funeral today, Regina said it was the happiest day of her life."

"Thank you for your time, my lady."

"If you have more questions," the countess said, standing, "please call upon me at my residence."

Cedric Barrows returned to the drawing room a few minutes later. "I can tell you now that Prince Viktor murdered my cousin."

Amadeus raised his dark brows. "You sound certain."

"I heard the prince threaten Charles's life."

"Were there other witnesses?"

Cedric smiled. "Thirty others heard the threat at the Duke of Inverary's country house."

"I see." He would need to obtain the guest list from His Grace and question those present. "Could the earl's wife be involved?"

"Absolutely not," Cedric answered. "Regina is the sweetest, most biddable female I have ever met. Which is unusual in a commoner, I suppose."

"Thank you for your help, my lord." At that, Amadeus quit the drawing room. Outside, he climbed into the coach. "That proved almost a waste of time."

"What now?"

"You are returning to the office," Amadeus told him. "I am lunching with Miss Evans."

"Surely, you are not implying—?"

"I imply nothing." Amadeus reached across the table and touched her hand to reassure her. "Solving a murder begins with the victim. I need to learn his habits, weaknesses, and personal connections. Then I investigate those connections until I discover the guilty."

Easily the handsomest man in London, Ginger thought, staring into his blue eyes.

"Investigating Lady Bradford or Prince Viktor does not necessarily imply their guilt," Amadeus concluded. "I am gathering pieces of information to put together like a puzzle. Do you understand?"

Ginger did not want him asking questions about her friend. Regina was incapable of hurting anyone, though she did threaten realistically. She never backed down.

"Reggie did not murder the earl. Investigating her is a waste of time better used elsewhere."

Amadeus sighed, and then changed the topic of conversation. "You are playing with that beef. Do not waste my hard-earned coins by leaving food on that plate."

Ginger narrowed her gaze on him. He sounded like he was scolding a child. Perhaps Reggie had the right idea about men. No sane woman needed a man.

"What do you consider your greatest asset?" Amadeus asked.

"My intelligence." No hesitation there.

"Men are not attracted by intellect."

"Intelligence appeals to intelligent men. The problem with the world is there aren't enough of those around."

Ginger scanned the crowded Guinea, a tavern on Bruton Place frequented by servants of the wealthy. She shifted her gaze to her handsome companion. "Do not bother to ask me questions about Reggie. Discussing her is a waste of your valuable time."

Amadeus patted her hand. "I appreciate your concern."

Ginger felt like screaming in frustration. Instead, she fixed a smile on her face. Insulting the man who, she hoped, would discover her father's murderer was decidedly unwise.

"With two dead aristocrats, the authorities want a quick arrest," Amadeus told her. "I dislike quick arrests. The faster the arrest, the greater the chance for mistakes. Unfortunately, my report is due to the magistrate within a week."

"What about my father's case?"

"I cannot think about that until I make an arrest in this case," Amadeus answered. "I am sorry."

Ginger nodded, accepting his apology.

"At the time of his death, what was your father's mental state?"

"He behaved normally."

"Reginald Smith said the same," Amadeus said, "but Forest Fredericks believed otherwise. He said your father appeared depressed."

"Depressed is not suicidal." Ginger wondered why Uncle Forest would say that. Had her father suffered a secret disappointment?

"I would like to speak with the countess," Amadeus said, standing.

"Reggie is willing to cooperate."

When they returned to Bradford House, Ginger led Amadeus upstairs to the drawing room. He touched her arm before following her inside. "I enjoyed today. Would you care to join me for lunch again next week?"

"I would like that very much," she accepted, trying to keep her excitement under control. Then she led him into the drawing room where the countess sat with her son on her lap.

"Good afternoon, Lady Bradford," Amadeus greeted her. "I apologize for intruding on you, but I do have a few questions."

"Austen and I were playing the face game." Regina passed Austen to Ginger, who left the drawing room to deliver the boy to his nanny.

"I don't believe I am familiar with that game."

"We touch the parts of our faces and name them."

Amadeus smiled. "I will keep that one in mind when I have my own children. Lady Bradford, did Prince Viktor threaten your husband's life?"

Regina hesitated. "Would you like coffee or tea?"

"I would like an answer to my question."

"Viktor was protecting me from my husband's abuse," she told him. "The prince would not publicly threaten Charles if he meant to do the deed. He is not stupid."

"May I speak with your retainers?"

"All of them?"

"Well—"

"How about Pickles, the majordomo, Artie, the coachman, and Louis, the valet? Those men would have had the most contact with Charles."

"Those three will suffice for today." While the countess left to fetch the men, Amadeus paced back and forth in front of the hearth. He did not believe the prince had murdered his wife and her lover. No, the motivation behind this murder was more subtle than jealousy.

The majordomo walked into the drawing room. "Constable Black?"

"Mr. Pickles, tell me everything you know about the earl's private life," Amadeus said.

"Prone to drink and gambling, the earl fell into debt," Pickles answered. "Which was the reason he married Lady Regina, a most delightful woman."

"Theirs was no love match?"

Pickles chuckled. "Theirs was a hate match, and I do believe the lady was winning the war."

"Thank you, Mr. Pickles. Send me the coachman."

The majordomo left the room. A young, dark-haired man appeared a few minutes later.

Amadeus looked at him. "Your name?"

"Artie."

"Please tell me what happened at the Duke of Inverary's estate."

Artie stared at the carpet, the hands at his sides flexing and unflexing in a nervous motion. "I don't understand."

Amadeus wondered at the man's nervousness. Was it knowledge of the murder or something as innocuous as standing in the earl's drawing room?

"I meant, regarding the comings and goings of the Bradfords and the Kazanovs."

Artie looked at him, his expression clearing. "His Lordship and Her Highness left the party in the prince's coach," he answered. "His Lordship instructed me to tell Lady Regina he would see her at home the next day. Prince Viktor returned to London with Lady Regina in the earl's coach."

"And did you drop the prince at home?"

"His Highness and Her Ladyship came into Bradford House."

Amadeus snapped his black brows together. "You did drive the prince home later that night?"

Artie shook his head. "I never saw the prince again that night."

"Thank you, Artie. Please send me the valet."

"Yes, sir." The coachman left the room, and a slight, black-haired man entered a moment later.

"Your name?" Amadeus asked.

"I am Louis, the earl's valet." The man sounded unusually haughty for a retainer.

"Since you served the earl closely, you would know his private habits." Amadeus gave the man an encouraging smile. "Please tell me whatever you know."

"I know who killed the earl."

"And that person would be?"

"Lady Bradford murdered His Lordship. She threatened his life the day before they left for the Duke of Inverary's country estate."

"Did His Lordship tell you this?"

"I heard her with my own ears." Louis smiled with cold delight. "If you don't believe me, ask Ginger Evans. She heard the countess threaten the earl's life, too."

"Thank you, Louis." Amadeus descended the

stairs to the foyer where Ginger awaited him. "I would speak privately with you, Miss Evans."

She followed him outside. "Well?"

"You lied to me," Amadeus said, his piercing blue gaze accusing her. "You neglected to tell me that Lady Regina threatened her husband."

"Charles threatened Hamlet, and Regina returned the threat," Ginger defended herself. "I never lied to you or anyone else."

"It was a lie by omission, young lady."

Ginger narrowed her gaze on him. "That is no lie, *old man*."

Chapter 7

"What a lovely home."

"I am thrilled you accepted my dinner invitation."
The Duke of Charming smiled at her. "I know how
unsettling the death of a spouse is."

"Your thoughtfulness is appreciated." Dementia
returned the duke's smile. Her heart swelled with
love for him. What did he feel for her? What were his
intentions? She refused to be any man's mistress.

"Excuse me, Your Grace." Constable Green stood
in the drawing room's doorway. "I hold a warrant
for your arrest on suspicion of murdering the earl."

"That is ridiculous. Why would I murder Mer-
lot?"

Constable Green flicked a glance at Dementia.
"Your motive was jealousy."

Regina sat at the desk in her study and wrote the
next chapter in her book. A week had passed since
the funeral, the most peaceful week she had ever
enjoyed in her life. No longer did she expect an interruption when she worked.

Setting the quill down, Regina gazed out the window at the glorious, mid-May afternoon. Nature
had come alive this month in a riot of primary colors and shades of green. Near the silver white birch
stood an apple tree. Before month's end, breezes

would blow the last of the apple blossoms and shower the lawn with pink and white petals.

Regina closed her eyes and inhaled deeply, savoring the mingling scents. Bluebells. Iris. Lilacs. Ink.

The Duke of Charming had just been arrested for murdering Bertram Merlot. Regina wondered how Dementia could help the duke clear his name. Her determined heroine refused to lose her newfound love to the gallows.

The word *love* reminded her of Prince Viktor. She was much too fond of the prince. Where had he hidden for the past week? How many days did he consider *soon?*

Her luck had held, though. She had not seen her father or her husband's cousins, either.

Regina glanced at her butterfly ring. She was ready to soar but felt empty at the thought of soaring alone.

"You should have worn black instead of that yellow gown." The voice belonged to Ginger Evans.

Regina looked over her shoulder. Ginger stood just inside the doorway and carried Austen.

"I'm afraid to ask." Regina crossed the room and lifted Austen into her arms.

"Nose." Austen grabbed his mother's nose and pulled.

"Ouch!" Regina smiled at her son. "Very good, Austen, but point instead of pull."

"Reginald and Uncle Forest are waiting in the parlor."

Regina grimaced. "Now I'll need to listen to him complain about the parlor." Then she called over her shoulder, "Come, Hamlet."

Regina walked into the family parlor and handed her father his grandson. "Here we are." She sat in a high-backed chair, her dog sitting on the floor beside her.

Reginald fixed his gaze on the Great Dane but, surprisingly, refrained from comment. "How is my Austen today?" he asked the boy.

"Nose." Austen reached up and yanked his grandfather's nose, making the old man laugh.

"We need to practice *point* and *pull*," Regina said. "How are you, Uncle Forest?"

Fredericks pushed his spectacles up. "I am well."

Pickles walked into the parlor and set the coffee and tea service on a table. He served them and left.

Regina relaxed in the chair and enjoyed the perfumed breeze wafting through the open window. Watching her father and her son, she felt an unusual sense of peace. She could tolerate her father better without Charles to upset her. Even he seemed to have softened since the funeral. Unless—

"Father, are you ill?"

Reginald snapped his gaze to her. "Do you want me to get sick?"

"Of course not." Regina paused a moment and then said, "Your good mood surprises me."

"I feel calmer without Charles Bradford spending all my money."

Her father had disliked her husband, too. She hadn't realized that before since his criticisms had always been leveled at her, not her husband.

"My offer to handle the household accounts still stands," Fredericks said.

"Uncle Forest, I do value your knowledge and advice," Regina said, "but Ginger and I are capable of handling the household accounts."

"If you overspend your monthly allowance," Reginald warned, "I will not advance you extra funds."

"I never expected you would."

"My lady?"

Regina glanced toward the doorway where Pickles stood, but before the majordomo could continue, she heard another voice. "Don't bother to announce me." Cedric Barrows brushed past Pickles. "Regina, how good to—you aren't wearing black."

She heard the surprise in his voice. "I decided black was too somber for celebration."

"What are you celebrating?"

"My husband's untimely passing." Regina heard the muffled chuckles emanating from Reginald and Forest but could scarcely credit her hearing. Now she was positive her father was feeling under the eaves.

"What a scandalous statement." Cedric took a step closer, anger mottling his complexion.

Hamlet growled low in his throat, though he had not moved a muscle.

Cedric came to an abrupt halt and turned away to greet her company. In growing amusement, Regina watched her husband's cousin.

Ignoring Forest Fredericks, Cedric gave her father an ingratiating smile. "Mr. Smith, how good to see you again."

"Is it?"

"I always look forward to seeing you." Cedric touched her son's dark hair. "And sweet little Austen."

"Don't touch my grandson," Reginald snapped.

Cedric yanked his hand back. "Mr. Smith, I would like to speak to you."

Reginald lifted his gaze from his grandson. "Speak."

"Privately."

"Speak here or not at all."

"Very well." Cedric took a deep breath, as if fortifying himself. "Mr. Smith, I am formally requesting your daughter's hand in marriage."

How did the sniveling swine dare to walk into her home and demand marriage? *Money*. The Bradford-Barrows tribe was always short of assets.

"My daughter is in mourning despite the inappropriate color of her gown."

Cedric was not put off so easily. "I meant, marriage after her mourning period has ended."

Regina watched her father carefully. His response to this request would prove his regard for her.

"Do you love my daughter?"

Regina couldn't credit her father mentioning love.

"I love her madly."

"Are you telling me you have loved your cousin's wife these past two years?"

"No, I—"

Apparently, her father had decided one title in the family would suffice. Not that she considered Cedric Barrows husband material. In fact, she planned never to marry again.

"I meant . . . ." Cedric seemed to compose himself. "I meant I admire her greatly and believe that love could grow between us."

Reginald flicked a glance in her direction. "My daughter is a grown woman with her own household. Only she can accept a proposal of marriage."

Regina stared in surprise at her father. She had never expected that much recognition from him. It was too late to build a close relationship with him, but she was so accustomed to his critical editorializing that she didn't know what to feel or think.

Unexpectedly, Cedric whirled around and knelt

on one bended knee in front of her. "Lady Regina, will you do me the honor of becoming my wife?"

"Don't be ridiculous."

"Does that mean yes, no, or maybe?"

"That means no."

"I can be a very persistent man." Cedric stood and smiled at her. "I intend to change your mind."

"Take your persistence somewhere else," Regina ordered. "Do not visit again without an invitation."

"You don't mean that."

Regina stared him straight in the eye. "I have never been more serious in my life."

"I will leave now," Cedric said, "but I will return another day." At that, he quit the parlor.

"That was too cruel," Uncle Forest remarked.

"Sometimes cruelty is a kindness," Regina said.

"If you play your cards right," Reginald said, "you could marry royalty. Prince Viktor admires you."

So that was the reason her father had insisted she was an adult and would choose her own husband. It made sense. Why settle for an earl when his next grandson could be a prince?

"I intend never to marry again," Regina announced.

"You will marry again," Reginald told her, and stood to pass her Austen. "Either you choose your next husband, or I will choose for you. Come, Forest."

The other man stood on command. "Good day, Reggie."

"Good-bye, Uncle Forest." Regina looked at her son. "I will not marry again. I will devote my life to you and my writing."

The thought of living without a companion made Regina feel lonely, but sharing a life with Cedric

Barrows made her nauseous. She preferred loneliness to nausea.

The time to soar had arrived, and a woman could not soar within the confines of marriage. Besides, she would never jeopardize her son's inheritance by taking another husband.

A yearning for Viktor swelled within her. She was no fool, though. The prince was a man beyond her reach.

"My lady?"

"Yes, Pickles?"

"Prince Viktor is here."

"Send him up." Had her thoughts conjured the man?

Holding a young girl's hand, Prince Viktor walked into the parlor a few moments later. "Good afternoon," he said. "Lady Regina, I present my daughter, Sally."

"I am pleased to meet you," Regina said, and moved to the settee, leaving the high-backed chair for the prince.

Regina noted the five-year-old was the image of her mother. Blond curls, blue eyes, fair skin. "This is my son, Austen. Would you like to sit with us?"

Sally nodded and sat beside her. "Austen is a baby, and I am a big girl."

Regina smiled at her. "Yes, you are a big girl."

"My mummy is dead," Sally said, looking at her through enormous blue eyes.

Regina looked at the prince. She had the feeling that Sally did not really understand the meaning of *dead.*

"I am sorry for your loss. Austen's daddy is dead, too."

"Oh, I did not know that." Sally looked at her father. "Lady Regina can be my mummy and you can be Austen's daddy."

Regina felt her face flame with embarrassment. Viktor was smiling at her.

"I will consider that possibility," he told his daughter.

"I like all your books," Sally said. "Daddy is teaching me to read. Do you know any stories?"

"I know lots of stories," Regina answered. "Do you know any stories?"

Sally nodded. "Shall I tell you a story?"

"I would like that."

"Once upon a time," Sally began, "a turtle and a lizard and a rabbit grew up in the same garden and were best friends. The turtle and the lizard made lots of money and moved to a palace, but the rabbit became a merchant who sold—I forget, you know the stuff that makes grass grow.

"One day the rabbit drove to the palace to bring that stuff," Sally said. "Do you know what I mean?"

"That stuff is called manure," Regina told her.

"Thank you." Sally continued her story, "Rabbit felt happy to see his best friends, but the butler answered the door.

"Rabbit said, 'I want to see turtle and lizard.'

"Butler said, 'Mr. Tur-*tell* is in the *well* and Mr. Liz-*zard* is in the *yard*.'

"Rabbit was angry and said, 'Tell Mr. Liz-z*ard* and Mr. Tur-*tell* that Mr. Rab-*bit* has brought the *shit*.'"

Regina burst out laughing. Which made Austen giggle.

"Sally, who told you that story?" the prince asked.

"Uncle Rudolf."

Viktor shook his head. "I should have known Rudolf was the culprit."

"What is culprit?" Sally asked.

"A culprit is a person who says or does naughty things," Viktor explained. He looked at Regina. "Will you dine with me tomorrow night?"

His question caught her off guard. "I am in mourning."

Viktor gave her a wolfish smile. "Wear black."

Her first business meeting. Ginger was almost unable to contain her excitement. She loved numbers more than she loved mysteries. Actually, investing was a type of mystery; one never knew the outcome until it happened.

Ginger knew her father would be proud of her. Only a few, rare men could take a tiny amount of money and make it grow as she did. Now here she was, sitting in the earl's coach on her way to Park Lane and her first business meeting.

The coach halted in front of the fashionable mansion belonging to the Duke of Inverary. Artie appeared a moment later to open the door and help her down.

"Thank you, Artie."

He nodded. "I'll be waiting here for your return."

Ginger tried to quell the nervous butterflies winging in her stomach and knocked on the door. "I am Miss Evans," she told the majordomo. "I have an appointment with His Grace."

The majordomo stepped aside to allow her entrance. "Come with me, Miss Evans. His Grace and the others are expecting you."

Ginger followed the man upstairs to the second-floor study. She could not believe the opulence of the duke's mansion. The Bradford home seemed to house paupers in comparison.

Lord, but she felt uncomfortable and out of

place. She wished Regina had accompanied her instead of being busy deciding what to wear to the prince's dinner. Which was wholly uncharacteristic of her. Had Regina fallen in love with the prince? She hoped not, unless the prince returned her tender feelings.

All six aristocrats stood when Ginger walked into the study. There were the Duke of Inverary, his son Robert, and the four Russian princes.

Wearing a smile of greeting, Viktor stepped forward and escorted her to a chair in front of the duke's desk. The others sat when she sat.

"I thought Regina would be accompanying you," Viktor said.

"Reggie was trying to decide which gown to wear to dinner with you. Oops! I should not have said that."

"I am glad you did." Viktor grinned. "I have been puzzled about which outfit to wear myself. You may quote me on that."

"I doubt your outfit matters as long as you wear pants and a jacket," Prince Rudolf quipped. "Showing your ankles at this early stage would be scandalous."

"Shall we get down to business?" the Duke of Inverary said, and then gave Ginger his attention.

Ginger could not believe the size of the duke's oak desk. The bigger the desk, the more important the person. Or so she supposed.

"Miss Evans."

Ginger blushed and cleared her throat. "If possible, Reggie and I want to invest another five or ten percent share in each of your companies."

"I still cannot credit a woman being interested in business," Prince Stepan said.

Ginger gave him a quelling look. "Not every

woman is capable of singing the starring role in an opera," she said, referring to his publicized romance with a certain opera singer.

Stepan's older brothers did not bother to hide their amusement. Blushing with embarrassment, the youngest Kazanov prince said, "I apologize for my criticism."

Ginger inclined her head. "And so do I." She looked at each aristocrat in turn and then continued, "Reggie and I discussed several other investment options."

"Such as?" the duke asked, wearing an amused smile.

Ginger had the sudden feeling she had been invited here for their amusement, but decided to treat the duke's question seriously. "In regards to beer and ale, Reggie and I thought we could make a larger profit if we purchased our own farms for the grains and bought breweries. Thereby, we would eliminate the middle man, so to speak."

"Did Regina really discuss that with you?" Prince Viktor asked.

Ginger cast him a sidelong glance. "Reggie is more creative than practical. In terms of business, she tends to listen and follow my advice."

"Do you have any other ideas?" Prince Rudolf asked.

"Regarding money-lending, I would offer a two percent less interest rate but reduce the risk of loss by doing business with secure companies seeking expansion," Ginger told them. "Those new industrial companies is another option but only if they are kind to their workers."

All the men laughed at that, making her blush.

"I see no reason why we shouldn't offer the ladies another five percent interest in our whisky, with the stipulation that if they sell, it must be to us," said Robert Campbell, the duke's son.

"We can offer another five percent in our vodka," Prince Mikhail said.

"We would appreciate that," Ginger said.

"I am willing to act as your business agent," Prince Viktor offered.

"What will your services cost?" Ginger asked.

Again, the men laughed.

"I will accept a dinner at Bradford House each week," Viktor answered.

"That is generous of you," Ginger accepted his offer.

"If you were a man," Prince Stepan said, "Viktor would not offer his services for a mere dinner."

"I would not offer them at all," Viktor qualified.

"Precisely my point," Stepan said. "Why do you accept free services on the basis of being a woman?"

"I may be a woman but I am no fool." Ginger gave the youngest prince her most engaging smile. "A good businesswoman would never refuse free services."

"The lady is a better businessman than you," Mikhail told his younger brother.

Prince Stepan gave his brother a good-natured grin. "With three older brothers taking care of me, why would I waste my time conducting business?"

"Your idea of purchasing farms and breweries is interesting," Prince Rudolf said. "I suggest the seven of us pool our resources to experiment with it."

"If profitable, we could have a beer and ale cartel," Ginger said, excited by the idea of keeping potential loss at a minimum.

The Duke of Inverary poured six shots of whisky and then looked at Ginger. "Would you care to drink to our joint investment, Miss Evans?"

Ginger blushed. "I would prefer lemonade."

"I will tell Tinker to fetch lemonade," Prince Stepan said. He opened the door but found the majordomo standing there.

"What is it, Tinker?" the duke asked.

"Your Grace, Constable Black would speak with the gentlemen."

"Send the man here."

Ginger froze. What would Amadeus think when he saw her there? What she did was none of his business, especially after his anger of the previous day.

She turned in her chair and watched Amadeus walk into the study. He stopped short when he saw her.

"What are you doing here?" Amadeus asked, his tone gruff.

Ginger lifted her nose into the air. "I am discussing business."

"What business?"

"*My* business."

Ginger glanced at her new business associates. All six were watching with great interest.

"I apologize for intruding on your meeting," Amadeus said to the duke. "I must speak privately with Prince Viktor."

"Let us step outside." Viktor glanced at his brothers and shrugged before following the constable into the corridor. The door clicked shut behind them.

"Where did you go when you returned from His Grace's estate?" Amadeus asked.

"I supped with Lady Regina at Bradford House," Viktor answered.

"And after supper?"

Viktor stared at the constable. He refused to soil Regina's reputation with the truth. He did not murder Charles and Adele so there could be no evidence against him.

"Your Highness?"

"I walked home and went directly to bed."

"The constable stared hard at him, as if knowing he lied. "What time was that?"

"I don't recall."

"Did anyone see you?"

Viktor realized he should not say *no*. "Godfrey, my majordomo."

"You should have asked your retainer to verify your alibi." Amadeus scowled and shook his head. "You have made my position difficult to defend, Your Highness."

"What do you mean?"

"I do not believe you murdered your wife and her lover," Amadeus told him. "Unfortunately, city officials want a quick arrest and required me to present the facts so far. The magistrates issued an order for your arrest, pending the validity of your alibi. I am sorry, Your Highness, but you must come along with me."

Viktor inclined his head. "May I step inside His Grace's study to inform my brothers?" At the other man's nod, Viktor walked into the study and turned to his brothers, who took one look at his face and stood in alarm. "I am being arrested for murder."

"Shit!"

"Damn it!"

"Son of a bitch!"

Each of his brothers, from oldest to youngest, swore in turn. The Duke of Inverary and his son, the Marquess of Argyll, stared in obvious surprise at the constable.

Only Ginger took action. Furious, she bolted out

of her chair to confront the constable. "This is outrageous! Is Reggie next?"

"For what it is worth, I do not believe His Highness murdered anyone," Amadeus said, and then
shrugged. "The magistrates and the mayor have insisted on a quick arrest and have fallen prey to the
obvious motivation of revenge for adultery."

"You will escort the prince to the Tower, not Newgate," the Duke of Inverary ordered, taking charge.
"I have friends who will approve Viktor being
housed there as befitting his station." He turned to
his son. "Tell Percy Howell to meet us here as soon
as possible." Then he looked at Viktor, saying,
"Your brothers and I will accompany you to the
Tower and then confer with my barrister."

"Thank you, Your Grace." Viktor turned to Ginger. "Do not blame Constable Black for doing his
job. Tell Regina that I forbid her to worry."

Leaving the duke's mansion, Viktor climbed into
the constable's coach, as did Rudolf. The Duke of
Inverary, as well as his two younger brothers, rode
in the ducal coach. The Marquess of Argyll left to
find his father's barrister, Percy Howell.

East of London proper rose the Tower's pepper-
pot turrets and forbidding gray walls. The two
coaches halted at the Middle Tower.

The men walked through the Lieutenant's Lodging to the grassy inner courtyard. On the far side of
the green stood the Chapel of St. Peter ad Vincula
and the scaffold, where many famous men and
women had ended their lives.

The atmosphere inside the Tower Green was
hushed, the stone trapping silence within, seeming
as if time stood still there. A ghostly stillness pervaded the air.

"I want the prince housed in the Beauchamp

Tower," the Duke of Inverary was saying. "I will, of course, send a cook as well as a supply of food and drink."

The Tower constable and the Tower chaplain appeared. After greeting the duke deferentially, the two men led the way into Beauchamp Tower.

"Except in special cases, no prisoners have been housed here for many years," the Duke of Inverary told Viktor. He lowered his voice, adding, "Tradition requires wealthy prisoners lose at dice and cards to the constable and the chaplain. In return, you will get the best of everything."

Viktor followed Constable Black and the Tower officials up a flight of stairs. Kept in readiness for unfortunate aristocrats, the second-floor chamber was well-lit, airy, and clean. Built into one wall was a hearth, and a table and chairs stood in the center of the chamber. A spiral staircase led to the third-floor bedchamber.

Viktor looked around. He had expected worse. The English kept their wealthy prisoners in relative luxury.

After hugging each brother, Viktor whispered to Rudolf, "Protect Regina." He turned then to the duke and offered his hand. "Thank you for your assistance, Your Grace."

"We will start on your defense tonight," the duke assured him. "Those idiot magistrates cannot convict on a hunch."

Meanwhile, on the opposite side of London, Regina studied the contents of her dressing room and tried to decide which gown to wear. She had never realized how limited her wardrobe was.

Excitement coursed through her veins. Anticipation consumed her, making her tense.

Now she understood those female henwits and their silly behavior toward men. Perhaps she was not so different from other women in love.

Love? From where did that shocking thought come? Did she truly love the prince? She was a fool if she did.

"I need your help choosing a gown," Regina called, seeing her friend walking into the bedchamber. "How did the business meeting go?"

"Reggie, you need to sit down," Ginger told her. "I have bad news."

"We lost all our money?"

"No."

Alarm surged through her. "Is my father dead?"

"No, sit."

Regina perched on the edge of the bed. "What is it?"

"Constable Black arrested Prince Viktor on murder charges."

"What?" Regina leaped off the bed. "That is impossible! Viktor would never hurt anyone."

"The magistrates wanted a quick arrest and—" Ginger shrugged her shoulders.

"I will go to him," Regina said, heading for the door.

"You cannot visit him tonight." Ginger grabbed her arm. "The Duke of Inverary contrived to send Viktor to the Tower instead of Newgate. The prince will stay in decent quarters and will receive excellent care. He does not want you to worry."

"I can verify his alibi," Regina said. "Viktor passed the night of the murder here."

"If you testify to that," Ginger warned, "your reputation will be ruined."

"I don't give a fig about my reputation." Regina marched toward the door.

"The princes and a barrister are meeting at the Duke of Inverary's," Ginger told her.

"Thank you."

Fifteen minutes later, Regina stepped out of the coach in front of the duke's residence. "I don't know how long I will be, Artie."

"Yes, my lady." Artie added as she turned away, "Prince Viktor would not be sitting in the Tower if I hadn't disappeared that night."

Regina touched his hand. "Do not blame yourself."

She hurried up the steps and slammed the door knocker. A moment later, the duke's majordomo opened the door.

Regina brushed past him into the foyer. "Tell His Grace and the Kazanov princes that Lady Bradford must speak with them. Urgently."

"Follow me, Lady Bradford." The majordomo led her upstairs to the second-floor study. He knocked once on the door, opened it, and stepped aside.

Regina marched into the study. "I can alibi Viktor."

Standing at her entrance, the three Kazanov princes, the duke and another man looked at her in surprise. Rudolf escorted her to a chair near the desk.

"You know everyone here except Percy Howell, the duke's barrister," Rudolf said.

Regina looked at each gentleman and then willed herself to blush as if embarrassed by her revelation. "Viktor did not go home. He passed the night with me."

"Prince Viktor told the constable he walked home from your residence," Percy Howell said. "He saw no one to verify his movements."

"Viktor is lying to protect me." Regina blushed

again. "Constable Black found us breakfasting together the next morning."

"Are you willing to testify to that in open court?" Rudolf asked.

"I wouldn't be here if I wasn't."

"Your testimony will free Viktor but ruin your reputation," Percy Howell warned her. "What do you say to that?"

Regina looked at the prince's brothers and smiled. "A merchant's daughter has no reputation to lose."

Chapter 8

"State your name."

"Dementia Merlot, the Countess of Brentwood."
She peeked at her dearest love who sat at the defen-
dant's table. With his dark gaze fixed on her, the
Duke of Charming sent her an almost imperceptible
nod of encouragement.

"My lady?"
Dementia gave the duke's barrister her attention.

"Lady Merlot, please tell the court where you were
on the night of the murder."

"I stayed home that evening."

"Alone?"

"I don't think visiting the prince is a wise move."

Regina looked at Ginger but refused to be dissuaded from her purpose. Both women stood in
the foyer while Artie brought the coach around.

"I cannot wait another seven days until the court
hearing," Regina said. "I want to see Viktor today."

"Please reconsider."

Regina lowered the black widow's veil to cover her
face and walked out the door. She needed the Tower
chaplain and the Tower constable to witness the supposed love between them. Surely, the prosecutor
would ask those two who had visited the prince.

The knowledge that she had defied society by

rushing to the prince's side would make her testimony more believeable. If he contradicted her, Viktor would seem protective of the woman he loved, and no one would believe otherwise.

"To the Tower, Artie."

"Yes, my lady." Her driver closed the coach's door.

Regina leaned back against the leather seat. She had the perfect strategy set in her mind. Once she'd been ushered into the prince's presence, Regina planned to take him by surprise. She would rush into his arms and kiss him with passion. Viktor would be so surprised he would not push her away.

The ride to the Tower took longer than she expected, London's narrow streets clogging with people and vehicles on a business day. The coach halted at the Middle Tower, and a moment later Artie appeared to open the door and help her down.

"Shall I accompany you, my lady?" Artie asked.

Regina shook her head just as a Tower guard appeared. "I am Lady Bradford and wish to visit Prince Viktor Kazanov."

The guard seemed at a loss for what to do. Apparently, no one had given him instructions in the event of visitors.

Regina pressed two one-pound notes into his hand. "Please, sir."

The man nodded. "Follow me."

Regina walked through the Lieutenant's Lodging, emerging on the enclosed Tower Green. She shivered to think of the men and women who had been executed on the nearby scaffold. The Green was eerily silent, as if this place had been frozen in time and the world outside did not exist.

"Wait here," the man ordered, and entered Beauchamp Tower.

Regina stood alone, fright dancing down her spine, the hair on the nape of her neck raised like hackles. Lord, but this place gave her the creeps.

"Lady Bradford?"

Regina whirled around. A middle-aged man with a kind expression stood there.

"I am Chaplain Kingston," the man introduced himself. "I am sorry, but Prince Viktor does not want to see you."

"My business is urgent."

"Perhaps I could relay a message?"

Regina stifled a horrified giggle at the image of the chaplain giving the prince a passionate kiss. "My business is of a personal nature," she lied.

"I cannot force His Highness to see you." The chaplain gestured for her to walk with him toward the Lieutenant's Lodging. "He doesn't want you to see him imprisoned."

"Is Viktor in the dungeon?" she cried. "Are they torturing him?"

The chaplain could not suppress a smile. "The Tower has no dungeons, and the rack disappeared with the knights."

Regina paused when they reached the Lieutenant's Lodging and glanced in the direction of Beauchamp Tower. "Is Viktor being well-cared for?"

"I promise the prince remains in excellent health," the chaplain answered. "The Duke of Inverary sent the prince his cook and supplies."

"God bless His Grace." Regina turned to leave, saying, "Thank you, sir." She hurried to her coach and ordered, "Take me to Prince Rudolf's, Montague House on Russell Street."

A short time later, Regina stepped out of her

coach and rushed up the stairs of Montague House. The door opened before she knocked.

Regina brushed past the majordomo. "Please tell Prince Rudolf that Lady Bradford wants an interview."

"Yes, my lady." The majordomo hesitated and then asked, "Do you have an appointment with His Highness?"

"Do you have a brain inside your head?"

"Apparently not." The majordomo disappeared up the stairs, and when he returned, Prince Rudolf was with him.

"Lady Regina." The prince bowed over her hand. "To what do I owe this honor?"

"We must speak privately." Regina glanced at the listening majordomo. "About Viktor."

"Come along to my office." Rudolf gestured to the stairs.

Regina rounded on him as soon as the office door clicked shut behind them. "I went to the Tower, but Viktor refuses to see me."

"You care about my brother." Rudolf put his arm around her and drew her across the room to the chair in front of his desk. "Viktor does not want you to see him imprisoned."

"That is what the chaplain said. Does Viktor know I will testify at the hearing?"

"Percy Howell advised against it. He felt my brother would veto the idea."

"I want you to get me into Beauchamp Tower."

"Let Viktor save his pride."

"I have a particular reason for wanting to see him," Regina said. "If I catch Viktor by surprise and kiss him passionately, the Tower chaplain and constable will inform the prosecutor. My testimony will appear to be truthful."

Prince Rudolf narrowed his dark gaze on her, reminding her of Viktor. "Are you planning to perjure yourself."

Regina gave him her sweetest, most innocent smile. "I swear Viktor and I passed the night at Bradford House."

Prince Rudolf relaxed, and Regina felt guilt tweak her conscience. Then she told herself that she was not lying, only leading others to the wrong conclusion.

"Viktor will not thank you for forcing your way inside," Rudolf warned.

"He will thank me when he is a free man."

The following afternoon, Regina climbed the narrow staircase to the second floor of Beauchamp Tower. Her hands shook and her legs felt weak at the thought of seeing Viktor suffering.

Prince Rudolf walked in front of her. He tapped on the door, called out his name, and entered the chamber.

And then Regina stepped inside. Viktor, the chaplain, and the constable played cards at the table set in the middle of the room. A roasted chicken and an open bottle of wine sat on the table amidst the cards.

He wasn't suffering at all.

Prince Viktor rose from his chair in surprise when he saw her. Regina rushed across the room and threw herself into his arms.

Drawing his head down, Regina kissed him as if no one were watching. Instinctively, Viktor returned her kiss, and Regina felt his arousal through the thin gown she wore.

"Oh, my love, I missed you," Regina said in a loud whisper. "Have you missed me, too?"

Viktor stared into her upturned face, his puzzlement all too apparent. Covering for him, Regina pressed her soft curves against his hard muscular planes.

"My faith in true love is renewed by this heartwarming reunion," Prince Rudolf said, his tone filled with sardonic amusement. "I will sit with your cards, Brother, if you and the lady want to steal a few private moments upstairs."

"Indeed we do." Viktor smiled at Regina, but she saw the fury in his eyes. He lifted her hand to his lips, murmuring, "Come, darling." At that he led her up the spiral staircase to his bedchamber and shut the door.

"What game are you playing?" Viktor demanded.

Regina opened her mouth to explain. Then she remembered she could not tell him about her appearance at his hearing.

"The authorities believe I murdered Charles and Adele for revenge," Viktor said. "Do you want them to believe I also murdered so we could be together?"

"I never considered that."

Viktor remained unmoved, his black gaze cold on her. "Perhaps *you* had Charles and Adele assassinated and want me to pay the price."

His accusation stunned her. "How can you say that?"

"You hated Charles Bradford and never wanted to marry him," he reminded her. "I loved Adele at one point, at least."

His words of love for Adele stabbed her heart. Regina stared at the floor, her eyes and her heart downcast.

"I am sorry," she whispered. "I only wanted to see you with my own eyes."

"I am sorry, too." Viktor drew her into his embrace. "I did not want you to see me here. Knowing I cannot protect you is proving difficult."

She raised her emerald gaze to his. "Protect me from what?"

"From the person who murdered Charles and Adele." Viktor lowered his head until his mouth hovered above hers. "I want more of this." He claimed her lips in a demanding kiss that seemed to last forever, one kiss melting into another. And then another.

Without warning, the door creaked open. Still locked in an embrace, they looked toward the doorway.

"Prince Rudolf is leaving," the Tower constable said, and disappeared again.

"You will be vindicated." Regina stood on her toes and planted a kiss on his chiseled lips.

Viktor caught her against him and nuzzled her neck. "We will continue this when I am free."

The remaining five days until the court hearing were the longest of her life. Each day contained a decade's worth of worry.

Regina awakened at dawn, much too early to dress for court, and tossed and turned in her bed. Surrendering to the inevitable, she jumped out of bed.

Dressed in a black gown, Regina set a black hat on her head but lifted its veil away from her face. Then she wandered downstairs to the dining room.

Ginger, Pickles, and Artie drank coffee at the dining room table in spite of the early hour. All three started to rise, but she gestured for them to sit.

Ignoring the food on the sideboard, Regina poured herself a cup of coffee and joined them. "Is everyone ready to testify?"

All three bobbed their heads. Reluctance had etched itself across their expressions, though.

"Tell the truth," Regina advised them, "and the prince will be vindicated."

Regina glanced at Ginger, their gazes colliding in an unspoken battle of wills. Regina dropped her gaze to her coffee. Though her dearest friend believed otherwise, she knew that testifying for the prince was the right thing to do.

An hour before the court sessions opened, Princes Mikhail and Stepan arrived to escort Regina in their coach while her retainers traveled in another. The princes would stand with her in the back of the courtroom until Percy Howell called her to the witness box.

"I am ready." Regina lowered the sheer black veil that covered her face. She was glad to have the veil's protection from prying eyes. No one would expect her appearance in court or recognize the woman shrouded in black.

A crowd had gathered in front of the Old Bailey, the novelty of royalty charged with murder too exciting to ignore. The Kazanov coach halted, and Prince Mikhail climbed out first, followed by Prince Stepan and Regina.

"Here are some important ones," said someone in the crowd.

"Those could be the brothers," another said.

"Ya mean, I'm lookin' at royalty?" a third gasped.

"Who's the woman?"

"Dunno."

"We know she ain't the prince's wife." That quip earned the speaker an earful of laughter.

And then Regina stepped inside the courthouse, more crowded than the street outside. She trembled in fear, the thought of being the day's star witness nearly felling her.

"Do not speak to anyone," Prince Mikhail said, taking her hand in his. "Let Stepan and me talk if anyone approaches."

Prince Stepan leaned close. "Keep your face covered until you stand in the witness box."

Spectators and reporters jammed the courtroom. The noise of all those talking and laughing rivaled any London street fair. Which surprised Regina. She had always assumed the business of a court was serious.

Standing between the two princes, Regina looked toward the front of the room. Looking incredibly handsome, Viktor sat at a table with Percy Howell and Prince Rudolf. Across the aisle sat the prosecution, the enemy, whom she disliked instantly.

Three court justices entered the room and sat at the high bench where they could supervise all. The one in the middle banged his gavel for order.

"Mr. Lowing, you may proceed with your evidence," the Chief Justice told the prosector.

Lowing stood and faced the gallery. "I call Mary Walker to the witness box."

Who the blue blazes is Mary Walker? Regina wondered. What did this unknown woman have to do with Charles and Adele? Could she be a witness to the murder?

"Adele's former maid," Mikhail whispered.

A plain woman in her late twenties, Mary Walker stood in the witness box without sparing her former employer a single glance. Regina knew that could not be a good sign.

"Miss Walker, what was your connection to Princess Adele Kazanov?" Lowing asked.

"I served as Princess Adele's personal maid."

"Please tell the court what you overheard the day before the prince and the princess left for a country house party, a mere two days before the murder."

"I heard Prince Viktor arguing with the princess," the maid answered. "He called her a whore and threatened her life."

Regina gasped. Excited conversations erupted in the courtroom. The Chief Justice banged his gavel for silence.

"No further questions."

The Chief Justice looked toward the defense table. "Mr. Howell?"

"Thank you, my lord." Percy Howell advanced on the witness box. "So, Miss Walker, how long have you been eavesdropping on private conversations?"

The woman paled at the question. The prosecution leaped up and called, "I object."

"Sustained."

"Where were you during this conversation between the prince and the princess?" Percy Howell asked.

"I was in the dressing room preparing gowns for the Duke of Inverary's country house party."

"What request did Prince Viktor make of his wife?"

"His Highness wanted the princess to revoke her invitation for the Earl and Countess of Langley to attend the party," Mary Walker said.

"And Princess Adele refused?"

"Yes."

"What other request did the prince make?"

Mary Walker pursed her lips, seemingly reluctant to answer. "The prince asked his wife to go away for the summer with him and their daughter."

Percy Howell smiled pleasantly. "Don't you think a dead woman would be unable to go away for the summer with her family?"

Lowing bolted out of his chair. "I object."

"Sustained."

"Besides death," Howell continued, "with what did Prince Viktor threaten his wife?"

"Divorce."

Murmurs raced throught the crowd, and reporters scribbled their notes. Regina felt her heartbeat slow. A man bent on passing the summer with his wife or divorcing her did not commit murder.

"Do you know the reason Prince Viktor wanted to divorce his wife?"

"I have no idea."

"Did Princess Adele ever confide in you?"

"I—I heard . . . things."

"From the dressing room?"

The spectators burst into laughter. Regina smiled, too. Percy Howell was a supremely intelligent man.

"My lord," the prosecutor whined in complaint.

"Mr. Howell, this is not Drury Lane," the Chief Justice admonished. "Play to the bench and not the gallery."

"I apologize, my lord." Howell seemed to switch strategy and reconsider whatever he had planned to ask. "No further questions."

Mr. Lowing stood. "I call Cedric Barrows, the Earl of Dover."

Regina watched Cedric stand from where he sat with Vanessa Stanton. She wondered what he could possibly say about the murders.

"My lord, please tell the court about the altercation between the Earl of Langley and Prince Viktor."

Regina realized Viktor should never have insulted Cedric by insisting he leave Bradford House. This testimony was Cedric's revenge. She wondered how this would play to the sister, who still had designs on the prince.

"When the Earl of Langley was reprimanding his wife," Cedric said, "Prince Viktor stepped between them and threatened the earl's life."

Lowing shook his head in disapproval. "The prince seems prone to violence."

"I object!" Percy Howell called.

"Sustained." The Chief Justice gave the prosecutor a disgruntled look. "Lowing, your job is *asking* questions, not testifying."

"I apologize, my lord." Lowing gave Cedric his attention again. "Please describe the earl's friendship with Princess Adele."

"The princess and the earl were close friends," Cedric answered.

"Were they lovers?"

Silence reigned in the courtroom, the spectators and reporters straining to hear the answer to that.

"No, they were not lovers."

Regina gasped at the lie. Her husband's cousin had just perjured himself. Both princes gently squeezed her hand in a gesture for patience.

"No further questions."

Percy Howell stood and advanced on the witness box. "What form did the late earl's reprimand take?"

"I don't understand."

"Did the Earl of Langley reprimand the countess verbally or physically?"

Cedric paused a long moment. "Both."

"So, the Earl of Langley not only scolded his wife

for some infraction but also used physical force," Percy Howell said in a voice loud enough to carry to the far corners of the courtroom. "Is that correct?"

"Every man has the right to—"

"I asked if that was correct," Percy Howell interrupted.

"That is correct."

"Could Prince Viktor have been rescuing a damsel in distress?"

Lowing bolted out of his chair. "I object."

"Sustained." The Chief Justice looked at Howell. "You may rephrase your question."

"Thank you, my lord." Howell turned to Cedric. "If a husband raises his hand to strike his wife, but another man steps between them, would you say this other man is protecting the lady?"

Cedric stared the defense barrister straight in the eye. "I would say this other man was *interfering*, not protecting."

Chuckles erupted from the spectators. A few even applauded the earl's response. Encouraged by that, Cedric sat up straighter and gave the barrister a contemptuous look.

"When did you last visit Bradford House?" Howell asked.

"A week after we buried my cousin."

"Are you in debt?"

Lowing stood. "I object. This man's wealth has nothing to do with a murder charge."

"My lord, I intend to demonstrate to the court that the Earl of Dover's lack of wealth plays an important role in his testimony," Howell said.

The Chief Justice looked down at Cedric. "You may answer the question."

"Are you in debt?" Howell repeated.

"I have a habit of spending more than I can afford," Cedric answered.

Percy Howell nodded, considering that reply. "What request—concerning the countess—did you make of Reginald Smith, the countess's father?"

"I asked for Lady Bradford's hand in marriage after her mourning period ended."

"You were so upset by your cousin's murder that you asked for his widow's hand in marriage the week after you buried him," Howell said. "Is Lady Bradford her wealthy father's heiress?"

Cedric shrugged. "I suppose so."

"You know so, my lord."

"Very well, I know so."

"How did Mr. Smith reply to your request?" Howell asked.

"Smith insisted the decision to remarry belonged to his daughter," Cedric answered.

"Did you ask the lady to marry you?"

"Yes."

"What did she say?"

"She said, 'Don't be ridiculous.'"

Howls of laughter echoed within the courtroom. Regina saw the judges smiling at that. The laughter subsided finally.

"Do you consider Prince Viktor a rival for the lady's affection?"

"No."

"You have sworn to tell the truth," Howell reminded him.

"The truth is," Cedric said, "royalty would never stoop to marry a common merchant's daughter. He merely desires a dalliance."

Regina felt her cheeks heat with a humiliated blush which, thankfully, nobody saw because of the veil. Both Mikhail and Stepan squeezed her hands, offering comfort.

"Are you privy to the prince's thoughts?" Howell asked.

"No."

"No further questions."

The prosecutor stood. "Mr. Louis deVere."

Regina felt surprised. She watched her husband's valet walk to the witness box and wondered at the reason for his being summoned.

"How did you serve the Earl of Langley?" Lowing asked.

"I was his valet," Louis answered, his tone haughty.

"Did the late earl ever confide in you?"

Louis preened at the question, always ready to puff his self-importance. "The earl trusted me."

"Tell the court what the earl said about Prince Viktor."

"His Lordship confided that the prince was paying undue attention to the countess, but—"

"No further questions," the prosecutor interrupted.

Percy Howell crossed to the witness box. "What were you going to say when Mr. Lowing interrupted?"

Louis smiled with malicious glee. "I heard Lady Bradford threaten the earl's life."

The gallery erupted in loud, excited chatter. The Chief Justice banged his gavel, but the spectators refused to be quieted.

Regina froze. Was Howell's strategy to demonstrate that any number of people wanted Charles dead? She was glad she had decided to wear the black veil.

"Howell," Viktor called, standing without permission. "I told you—"

Prince Rudolf yanked Viktor into his chair. He leaned close to his brother and whispered furiously in his ear. Finally, Viktor sat back in his chair.

Percy Howell turned to the Chief Justice. "My client apologizes, my lord." He looked at the valet again. "The Earl and Countess of Langley were not in accord?"

"They despised each other."

"You had an interview with Lady Bradford after the earl's funeral," Howell said. "What was the purpose of this interview?"

"The countess terminated my employment."

"No further questions."

Regina watched Howell return to the defense table. Viktor leaned close to the barrister and began speaking in obvious complaint.

"I told you to leave Reggie out of this," Viktor snapped at his barrister, his complexion reddening with his anger.

"Calm yourself," Howell said. "The countess is in no danger of prosection. No one could ever believe her capable of shooting a bird, never mind two people."

Rudolf touched his shoulder and urged, "Listen to your barrister."

Viktor nodded. Thankfully, Regina was not in attendance to hear his barrister eliciting disparaging testimony about her. If he thought there was any real danger of her being prosecuted, he would stand up and confess to the crime he did not commit.

"Constable Amadeus Black," the prosecutor was calling.

Amadeus Black walked to the witness box and swore to tell the truth.

"Describe the crime scene," Lowing said.

"Princess Adele and the Earl of Langley were shot in the chest," Amadeus Black said. "They wore no jewels and carried no money. No witnesses observed the crime. At least, none came forward."

"Don't stolen jewels and money signify robbery?" Lowing asked.

"The perpetrator could have taken their valuables in order to make the crime look like a robbery."

"No further questions."

Percy Howell stood. "*Could* the missing valuables mean a robbery?"

"Yes, of course."

"What scene did you come upon when you went to Bradford House to inform the countess of her husband's death?" Howell asked.

"The prince and the countess were breakfasting together," Amadeus Black answered.

"What was their manner toward each other?"

"They appeared intimate."

Viktor banged his fist on the table. How dare Howell ruin a good woman's reputation! If he had wanted to ruin her reputation, he would not have prevaricated about his alibi.

Howell turned around to look at the prince and then said to the Chief Justice, "May I have a moment with my client, my lord?" At the judge's nod, he walked to the defense table.

"I told you I do not want Regina's name blackened in any way," Viktor said. "You swore you would leave her out of this."

"Do you want to hang?" Rudolf asked in a harsh whisper. "Is the lady's reputation worth your death?"

Viktor groaned and closed his eyes. He was an innocent man. There was no evidence against him.

"I assure you, Your Highness," Howell told him, "the countess approved this line of questioning."

"I could kill her," Viktor grumbled.

"Do not say that too loudly," Rudolf warned.

Viktor smiled in spite of his anger. "Do what you must," he said to his barrister.

Percy Howell addressed the justices. "No further questions."

Lowing stood. "Chaplain Kingston."

Regina watched the Tower chaplain step into the witness box and smiled beneath the black veil. Apparently, her strategy had worked. She would bet her last penny that the chaplain would testify about her visit to the prince.

"Mr. Kingston, you are the Tower chaplain?"

"Yes."

"Did Lady Bradford visit Prince Viktor in the Tower?"

"Yes, she did."

"Please describe what transpired between them," Lowing said.

Chaplain Kingston cleared his throat. "The countess kissed the prince and called him *my love* and *darling.*"

Conversations erupted in the gallery and reporters took notes furiously. The Chief Justice banged his gavel until silence descended once again.

"No further questions."

Percy Howell stood. "No questions, my lord."

"The prosecution rests."

The Chief Justice looked toward the defense table.

"The defense calls Arthur Fenton."

Sitting in the gallery with Pickles and Ginger, Artie stood and walked to the witness box. He swore to tell the truth.

"How do you serve the Bradfords?" Howell asked.

"I drive their coach."

"On the day of the murder," Howell said, "did you drive the prince and the countess to London?"

Artie nodded. "I did."

"Where was the earl?"

"His Lordship and Princess Adele had already left the duke's earlier in the day," Artie answered. "They took the prince's coach so he rode to London with the countess."

"Did you drive the prince to his residence?"

"Prince Viktor went into Bradford House with the countess."

"Did you ever drive the prince home that night?"

"No, sir, I did not."

"No further questions."

"The prosecution has no questions."

"Desmond Pickles," Howell called. When the older man stood in the witness box, he asked, "You are the countess's majordomo?"

"I am."

"Did you see Prince Viktor at Bradford House on the night of the murder?"

"I served His Highness and Lady Bradford a late supper."

"Did you see the prince leave Bradford House?"

"I did not."

"No further questions."

"The prosecution has no questions."

"Ginger Evans," Percy Howell called.

Watching her friend walk to the witness box, Regina bit her bottom lip to keep from laughing. Passing Amadeus Black, Ginger gave the constable a murderous glare.

"Miss Evans, please tell the court what contact you had with Prince Viktor on the night of the murder," Howell said.

"Reggie—I mean, Lady Bradford—introduced us when the prince joined her for supper," Ginger answered. "I saw him breakfasting with her the next morning."

"No further questions."

"The prosecution has no questions."

"Are you ready?" Mikhail whispered.

Regina nodded, but her throat felt parched suddenly. Her legs were jelly beneath her gown, and she prayed she would make it to the witness box without swooning.

Prince Stepan squeezed her hand. "You can do this."

Regina nodded. Now she knew what stage fright was.

Percy Howell faced the standing-room-only crowd in the gallery and paused for a long moment. An expectant hush fell over the spectators, his look more effective than the judge's gavel.

When he opened his mouth, Howell spoke in a loud, clear voice. "I call to the witness box Regina Bradford, the Countess of Langley."

Chapter 9

Dementia lifted her chin in a gesture of proud defiance. "The Duke of Charming and I passed the night at Brentwood House."

Scandalized excitement exploded inside the crowded gallery. Spectators talked loudly, reporters scribbled furiously, and the judge banged his gavel futilely in an attempt to restore order.

Dementia stepped out of the witness box and, with her head held high, walked the length of the courtroom to the door. She had saved her love from the gallows.

Someone opened the courtroom door. Dementia stopped short to stare at the older man blocking her way. "Father, what are you doing here?"

"You brazen slut!" Her father struck her hard, the force of his slap sending her reeling back . . .

A tidal wave of excited murmurs surged through the gallery, sweeping away all semblance of proper decorum. The Chief Justice banged his gavel for silence, the titillated audience slow to obey.

Prince Viktor started to rise from his chair at the defense table, only his brother yanking on his arm seeming to prevent him from challenging his own barrister. Cold fury etched itself across the prince's features.

Regina froze, stage fright gripping her, when she noted the sea of faces turned to the rear of the courtroom. Her hands shook, and her legs trembled beneath her gown. She sent up a prayer of thanks for her black widow's veil.

"You can do this," Prince Stepan whispered.

"Do not look at Viktor until you finish testifying," Prince Mikhail advised.

Regina forced herself to take the first step forward, the spectators falling silent. She walked down the aisle to the witness box. After swearing to tell the truth, Regina stunned her audience by drawing her black veil away from her face, exposing her pale complexion and her shocking red hair.

"There is no need for nervousness, my lady." Percy Howell gave her an encouraging smile. "Please explain to the court your relationship with Charles Bradford."

"We were married."

Her audience chuckled at that. She peeked at the three judges who were also smiling.

Regina realized in a sudden flash of clarity that the men who filled the courtroom believed all women were frivolous, stupid creatures. Grown female children who possessed no intelligent thought and needed a man for protection and survival. Mere accessories to their husbands.

That was their masculine weakness, Regina decided with an inward smile. Her behavior would sway them into believing that she was too stupid to lie. Her simple female's mind would not allow her any deviousness. Unless, of course, she used her wiles to wangle herself a new jewel, gown, or fur.

"I meant, what was the nature of your relationship with the earl," Percy Howell amended, a broad grin slashing across his face.

"I despised Charles," Regina said, her tone pleasant and her smile vague, "and Charles despised me." She heard isolated chuckles from the gallery, a sound that was music to her ears.

"Why did you marry?"

"Charles needed funds, and my father needed a title in the family."

"These are not ancient times," Howell said. "Surely, your father could not force you to marry a man you despised."

"I disappointed my father by being a daughter, not the son he wanted." Regina peeked at Viktor, whose expression softened on her. "I married Charles Bradford to win my father's approval."

"Did you manage to win his approval?"

"No." Regina made a show of taking her handkerchief from her pocket and dabbing at her eyes.

"Did you respect your husband?" Howell asked.

"Drinking, gambling, and womanizing were my husband's only pursuits," Regina answered. "Respecting him proved impossible."

Howell nodded in understanding. "Explain to the court the nature of your alledged threats against the earl."

"Charles threatened to shoot my dog, a perfectly loveable pet," Regina said. "I promised my husband that whatever befell my precious dog would also befall him."

More than a few, isolated chuckles sounded from the gallery this time. The Chief Justice banged his gavel once, silencing the amusement.

"My lady, I apologize in advance," Howell said, "but I must ask you an embarrassingly personal question."

Regina inclined her head. The atmosphere

hushed, everyone straining to hear the barrister's question.

"After the birth of your son, did you and the earl enjoy marital relations?"

"I never enjoyed marital relations with my husband," Regina drawled, sounding like a typical society matron.

The courtroom exploded in shouts of laughter. Even the three justices could not control their mirth.

Regina stole a glance at Viktor. His smile on her was pure warmth, and she sent it back in equal measure.

Percy Howell schooled his features to proper solemnity. "I meant, *engage* in marital relations."

Regina shook her head. "No, we did not."

"Did you know of his liaison with Princess Adele?"

"Everyone in London knew Charles and Adele were lovers."

"Does that mean *yes* or *no*?"

"Yes, I knew of their affair."

Percy Howell put his arms behind his back, looked at the crowded gallery, and then faced her again. "I daresay you felt humiliated, if not hurt."

Regina made no reply. She dropped her gaze and twisted her handkerchief, as if his statement bothered her.

"How *did* you feel about their affair?"

Regina lifted her gaze to him. "I prayed each night for Princess Adele's continued good health."

Again, laughter echoed within the crowded chamber, and newspaper reporters scribbled notes hurriedly. The Chief Justice banged his gavel several times for silence.

By the time she finished testifying, the public would forget there even had been a murder. The prosecutor looked none too happy, but the three justices were enjoying themselves. No doubt, she reminded them of their wives.

"Why did your husband's affair not bother you?" Howell asked.

Regina gave him a rueful smile. "Giving birth to my son was *not* the most fun I'd ever had."

The spectators howled with laughter. Silencing the gallery required more bangs of the gavel.

"Do you believe Prince Viktor murdered his wife and your husband?" Howell asked, once silence had been restored.

"I *know* Prince Viktor did *not* murder anyone."

Howell gave her a purposely puzzled look. "How can you possibly know that, my lady?"

Regina lifted her chin a notch and stared at the barrister, afraid to look at anyone else, especially the prince. At last thankful for her red hair, she managed a pretty pink blush.

"Prince Viktor passed the entire night at Bradford House."

An uproar of noise boomed like a canon from the gallery, scandalized spectators talking all at once. The Chief Justice banged his gavel like a shoemaker.

When the noise faded by slow degrees into silence, Percy Howell turned to the three justices. "No further questions."

Prosecutor Lowing rose from his chair, his cold gaze fixing on her. "Lady Bradford, why didn't you tell Constable Black that the prince and you passed the night together?"

Regina gave him a look that said she'd never heard a more stupid question. "Well, sir, he never asked."

Chuckles again. A single gavel bang.

"Do you understand what perjury is?" Lowing asked.

Regina placed an index finger across her lips in a gesture of trying to think. Then she gave him a vacuous smile. "Perjury is when you promise to tell the truth, but then you break your promise."

"Perjury is more serious than breaking promises," the prosecutor said. "Those who perjure themselves are sent to Newgate."

"Those promise-breakers deserve to be locked up. Why are you telling me this?"

"I'll ask the questions."

"Oh, dear, are you upset with me?"

The spectators laughed while the prosecutor turned to the three justices in a silent appeal for help. The Chief Justice cleared his throat, drawing her attention.

"Lady Bradford, the prosecutor's job is asking questions," the Chief Justice explained, his voice pleasant and his words simple. "Your job is answering the prosecutor's questions."

"I am sorry, my lord," Regina apologized, gazing at the old man through enormous emerald eyes. "Sitting here confuses me."

"I understand, my lady. Do the best you can."

"Does that apology include me?" the prosecutor asked, his tone snide.

"I will not apologize to a rude, spiteful man." Her words elicited chuckles from the gallery.

"Lady Bradford." The Chief Justice drew her attention again. "Mr. Lowing's job is behaving rudely and spitefully to defense witnesses."

"He is *paid* for that behavior?"

"Yes."

"Humph! I would love that job."

More chuckles sounded from the gallery.

"Lady Bradford," the prosecutor raised his voice. "Are you absolutely certain Prince Viktor passed that particular night at Bradford House?"

Regina nodded and gave him her sweetest, most vacuous smile. "I promise he did. Cross my heart and hope to die."

Boisterous laughter sounded in the courtroom. Mr. Lowing threw up his hands in disgusted defeat and returned to the prosecutor's table. "No further questions."

"My dear, you may step down from the witness box," the Chief Justice told her.

"Thank you, my lord. A pleasure to meet you."

"The pleasure has been all mine."

Regina stepped out of the witness box. She peeked at the prince as she passed the defense table. Viktor was staring at her, as if he had never seen her before.

Prince Mikhail and Prince Stepan whisked her out of the courtroom. They led her down a corridor to the side door where their coach waited.

"I want to know what happens," she complained.

"We need to return you as quickly as possible to the protection of Bradford House," Prince Mikhail said.

Prince Stepan grinned and lifted her hand to his lips. "You are too amazing for words, Lady Bradford. An Original."

"Thank you for the praise." Regina felt the world becoming unfocused. The ground rushed up to meet her, and she swooned dead away.

Meanwhile, Percy Howell stood and addressed the three justices. "Since a man cannot be two places at once, my lords, I make a motion to dismiss all charges against Prince Viktor Kazanov."

"In light of the new exculpatory testimony, the court grants the defense motion. All charges are dismissed." The Chief Justice banged his gavel. Then the three justices stood in unison and left the courtroom.

Viktor looked at his barrister. "I am free to go home?"

Percy Howell smiled and nodded.

Viktor hugged Rudolf and then stood to shake his barrister's hand. "Thank you, Percy. You are certainly worth your weight in gold."

Howell gave him a wry smile. "Remember that sentiment when my bill arrives." He glanced around the emptying courtroom. "I suggest we wait until the room clears. While you slip out the side door, I will speak to those hungry reporters."

"My coach is already waiting," Rudolf said.

"I lied to protect Regina's reputation." Viktor shook his head. "She ruined her reputation for nothing since there can be no evidence against an innocent man."

"Lady Bradford believed your life is more precious than her reputation," Howell replied. "The judicial system does not search for truth, only convictions."

Viktor looked from the barrister to his brother. "Regina perjured herself."

"I do not want to hear this," Howell said. "The lady took an oath, and I believe her."

Viktor felt his brother's hand on his shoulder, and then came his question. "You did not pass the night at Bradford House?"

"I *did* pass the night there," Viktor told them, "but I slept in a guest bedchamber, not in the lady's bed."

Percy Howell grinned. "In that case, Lady Bradford did not perjure herself."

"But she misled—"

"Do you want to hang for a crime you did not commit?" Rudolf interrupted.

"No." Viktor shook his head.

"Regina insisted on testifying in your defense," Rudolf said. "She cares deeply for you."

Percy Howell spoke then. "Perhaps Lady Bradford has something to hide."

Regina slept through breakfast, her performance of a lifetime having depleted her of energy. She had crawled into bed, after receiving word of the prince's release, and refused to be roused until morning had aged into a feeble old man.

"Good morning, Pickles." Regina stifled a yawn.

"Good afternoon, my lady." The majordomo rushed to set a plate with baked eggs and ham on the dining table in front of her. He returned to the sideboard and brought her a cup of coffee.

Regina lifted the cup and inhaled its strong steaming scent. She could almost feel her strength returning and, after consuming several cups of coffee, would be ready to start an acting career at Drury Lane.

Pickles cleared his throat, drawing her attention. "May I say, Lady Regina, I admire your bravery."

Regina gave him a rueful smile. "The coward within me swooned directly after my performance."

"And what a masterful performance it was," Pickles gushed. "So wise of you to use their prejudices against them."

Amusement shone from her disarming green eyes. "To what prejudices do you refer?"

"The same prejudices that ruled the late earl's life," he answered. "The mistaken belief that women are frivolous creatures without a thought in their pretty little heads."

"How very perceptive of you."

The majordomo grinned. "The lady who testified in court yesterday bears no resemblance to the woman who has lived here for two years."

"Pickles, you are a treasure."

"Thank you for noticing my finer points of character."

Regina smiled. "Would you pass me *The Times*?"

"Trust me, my lady, you do not want to read today's *Times*."

"Forewarned is forearmed, as they say." Regina held her hand out.

Pickles passed her *The Times* and returned to the sideboard. Regina set the paper flat on the table, staring at the first page as if it had transformed into a poisonous snake. Her outstanding performance had earned her the newpaper's headline. COMMONER COUNTESS SAVES LOVER.

Regina moaned and plopped back against the chair. Closing her eyes against the headline, she dreaded to think what her father would say. This fiasco was worth several years of bickering. And that thought gave her the beginnings of a headache.

"Reginald is climbing out of his coach." The voice belonged to Ginger Evans.

Regina opened her eyes. "Can you get rid of him for me?"

"You will *not* get rid of me so easily." Reginald Smith brushed past her friend and marched across the dining room to confront her.

This was all she needed to make her day complete. The headache formed, the pounding intensifying with her father's each step forward.

Regina stood. "Would you care for coffee?"

"This is no social call," his angry voice boomed.

The pounding in her head grew stronger. And then Regina noted the other two men who had walked into her dining room behind her father, Uncle Forest and Cedric Barrows.

Regina shifted her gaze to Uncle Forest and sent him a questioning look. He grimaced in answer, rolled his eyes, and leveled a sidelong sneer at the Earl of Dover.

"Reginald, I urge you to calm yourself," Uncle Forest advised her father.

"Do *not* tell me to calm myself," Reginald shouted. "My daughter has made me the laughingstock of London." He stepped closer. "You listen to me, missy. The Earl of Dover visited me as soon as the newspaper hit the streets and has devised a plan to salvage your reputation."

Regina shifted her gaze to Cedric. "How interesting."

"At great cost to his own pride," Reginald told her, "the earl has offered to marry you. Then you and Austen will retire to his country estate for a year or two. Cedric will reintroduce you into society by degrees."

"I wouldn't marry Cedric Barrows to save my soul."

"Damn you," Reginald swore, his complexion purple with his unbridled fury. "This is the only way to save face."

"Whose face are you saving?" Regina shouted. "Mine or yours?"

"*Both!*"

Regina took several deep breaths. She glanced

from a horrified Pickles to a frightened Ginger. Thankfully, Austen was upstairs with Nanny Sprig.

"I cannot marry Cedric Barrows," she announced. "I am in mourning."

"You cannot mourn a man you conspired to murder," Reginald countered.

Regina paled, startled that he would even think her capable of harming another person. "I never conspired with anyone to do anything."

"You conspired with that prince to spread your legs and give him what belonged to your husband," her father snapped.

"Reginald, how dare you speak so crudely to your own daughter," Uncle Forest spoke in her defense. "Reggie is not your little girl any longer and is free to make her own decisions."

Regina watched her father struggling to control his anger, surprised that her meek Uncle Forest could exhibit influence over her volatile parent. Her father seemed to regain his composure.

"Marriage to Cedric Barrows and leaving London for a couple of years is the only way to save yourself," Reginald said. "Don't you understand the prosecutor will charge you with murder?"

"Don't be ridiculous," Regina scoffed, her tone insulting. "I have an alibi."

His fury exploded again, the conflagration hotter than before. "Do *not* take that tone with me, you ungrateful harlot."

Several things happened at once. Without warning, her father slapped her, the force of it sending her crashing against the sideboard. Ginger screamed while Pickles and Uncle Forest shouted and moved toward her father.

Beyond reason, Reginald raised his hand to strike again. Walking into the room unexpectedly, Prince

Viktor vaulted across the dining table and grabbed the older man's arm, halting his blow.

"If you touch her again," Viktor warned, "I will make you regret it."

"What will you do?" Reginald sneered, stepping back. "Shoot me on the road to London?"

"Leave my house, *Reginald*." The use of his given name implied that she did not recognize him as her father.

"I will cut you off without a cent," her father threatened.

"I do not need your money." Regina looked at her majordomo. "Pickles, show these unwelcome three to the front door and do not allow them entrance into my home again. If they try to force their way in, send for the authorities, and I will press charges."

"Yes, my lady."

"Mark my words, missy," Reginald blustered. "I will not be London's laughingstock. You will marry Cedric Barrows even if I need to abduct you to Gretna Green."

"I will see Cedric dead before I wed him." Regina cast the Earl of Dover a deadly look. He had engineered this rift between her father and her, and she would not forget it.

Reginald marched out of the dining room, accompanied by Uncle Forest and Cedric. Pickles followed them out, insuring they left the premises. Wearing a shocked expression, Ginger left the room, too.

Viktor drew her into his arms as soon as they were alone. He inspected her cheek, still bearing the reddened imprint of her father's hand.

"Are you in pain?"

Regina shook her head. "I will be fine, especially when my father no longer walks this earth."

"Do not say now what you will regret later," Viktor said. "Wishing your father dead will not solve any problems."

"His demise would solve one problem."

"And what is that?"

"Him."

Viktor smiled at her misplaced wit and planted a chaste kiss on her lips. "I am angry with you," he told her. "I lied to Amadeus Black to protect your reputation. You—"

Regina placed a finger across his chiseled lips. "A merchant's daughter has no reputation to lose."

He kissed her finger. "You ruined my sacrifice by perjuring yourself."

His gentle gesture ignited a tiny flame and a quivering melting sensation in her belly. "I did not lie, merely stretched the truth to fit the circumstances."

Viktor led her to the dining table. He sat in the chair beside hers and held her smaller hand in his. "My brothers told me you swooned outside the courthouse."

"That performance sucked the life out of me," Regina admitted. "I have renewed respect for Drury Lane players." She fell silent for a long moment and then asked, "Who murdered Charles and Adele, though?"

"I believe the crime was a random robbery."

"Amadeus Black testified that the murderer could have taken their valuables to make the crime look like a robbery," Regina reminded him. "I believe that is the case. Other than ourselves, someone was motivated to murder them, and I think I know who that person is."

Viktor looked startled. "Who is it?"

"Cedric Barrows could have done the deed," she answered. "He has been trying to marry my father's money since the funeral."

"You can keep Cedric and his mercenary intentions at bay by marrying me," Viktor said, and lifted her hand to his lips.

"Our marriage would place you in danger." Regina gave him a flirtatious smile, knowing that he was merely teasing her to make her forget about the horrible scene with her father. "I don't think I possess the stamina for another successful rescue."

Viktor smiled but then grew serious. He fixed his dark gaze on hers. "Marry me. Please."

The seriousness of his proposal surprised her. Regina dropped her gaze to their hands and saw her butterfly ring. Too bad she'd fallen in love with the prince. If she married again, she would lose her chance to soar.

"We are in mourning," she reminded him, stalling for time. She did not want to refuse him, but she did not want to lose her dream of soaring, either.

His black eyes gleamed with humor. "We will wear black to the ceremony."

Regina laughed. "Your Highness, you are incorrigible. Let us postpone a discussion of marriage until a less worrisome time."

Viktor inclined his head. "Then accompany me to the opera tomorrow night."

"That would not be wise."

"My brothers and sister-in-law will chaperon us."

"What difference does a chaperon make after yesterday?"

"We need to rehabilitate our reputations for our children's sake," Viktor said, his thinking logical and his tone persuasive. "Being seen together but within the shelter of an acceptable group will begin the healing process."

Regina remained silent for long moments, mulling the idea over in her mind. Finally, she raised her gaze to his.

"Yes, Your Highness, I will accompany your family to the opera." The corners of her mouth turned up in a smile, and her disarming green eyes sparkled with mischief. "We will give society something else to gossip about and, at the same time, help the realm's economy by increasing newspaper circulation."

Chapter 10

Dressed in mourning black, Dementia stepped into the ducal opera box. She smiled at the duke when he assisted her into the chair and then sat beside her.

Her gaze drifted from the man at her side to the other opera-goers. Every aristocratic countenance swiveled in their direction. Every bejeweled lorgnette aimed at the duke and her.

"I want to see you drapped in diamonds and nothing else," the Duke of Charming whispered against her ear. "I yearn to kiss your sweet flesh.

"The Bradford bitch lied," Prosecutor Lowing growled. "I can feel it in my bones."

"I gave you my professional opinion," Amadeus Black reminded him, "but you would not be dissuaded from proceeding."

The two men sat in the prosecutor's office located in the Central Criminal Court Building. Stacks of books and documents cramped the small office, and a thin layer of dust coated bookcase shelves. The window was opened only a crack to prevent unhealthy fevers wafting through the air into the room from disease-infected prisoners.

"I found the prince and the countess breakfasting together that morning," Amadeus continued.

"I had heard rumors about the late earl, and the countess seeking solace in another man's arms is highly likely."

"Regina Bradford is hiding something," Lowing said, ignoring the other man's opinion.

"Are you making this case personal against the countess?" Amadeus cocked brow at the man. "I cannot believe a man with your calibre of talent would do that."

"I do not begrudge the Countess of Langley, nor do I have any personal feelings about her."

Amadeus could not control his smile. "She did make you appear less than reasonable while she won the hearts and minds of the gallery and the bench."

Lowing ignored that remark. He appeared insulted by being upstaged by a merchant's daughter. And Percy Howell, the prosecutor's own nemesis.

"My mistake was placing the prince at the crime scene. A wealthy man would hire others to do the bloody deed." A cold smile touched the prosecutor's lips. "I want you to investigate the possibility of a conspiracy between the prince and the countess."

"That would be a waste of my time," Amadeus said. "Conspiracy is difficult to prove; besides, I do not believe those two conspired to kill their spouses."

"Their illicit affair is the motivation behind disposing of the spouses."

"I might believe that if Charles Bradford and Adele Kazanov were suspected of their spouses' deaths, but I will keep an open mind." Amadeus stood to leave. "If you will excuse me, Lowing, I need to mend fences."

Thirty minutes later, Amadeus arrived at Bradford House. He climbed the stairs and banged on the door, all the while wondering the most expedient way to assauge Ginger's anger.

Desmond Pickles opened the door and looked down his long nose at the constable. "Deliveries in the rear." The majordomo started to close the door again.

Amadeus placed his booted foot in the door jamb to prevent it. "I have no deliveries, as you well know."

Pickles stared at the offending booted foot until the constable retracted it. "How may I help you?"

"I want to speak with Ginger Evans."

"Do you have an appointment?"

Amadeus narrowed his gaze on the old codger, who refused to be intimidated. "Miss Evans invited me to visit today," he lied. "She offered me a late lunch."

Pickles arched a haughty brow in disbelief. "She never mentioned a guest to the cook."

"Miss Evans is preparing a special dish for me. Humble pie."

The majordomo's lips twitched. "I will inform Miss Evans of your arrival."

"Will you allow me entrance?" Amadeus asked, when the man started closing the door.

"People we dislike must use the rear door." Pickles slammed the door in his face and threw the bolt home.

Meanwhile, Regina and Ginger worked in silence in the study. With Hamlet on the floor beside her, Regina sat at the desk in front of the window.

Across the room, Ginger worked on the household ledgers at a table placed in front of another window. She had just begun adding a long column of numbers when her friend's voice broke her concentration.

"If a woman can pretend being a virgin," Regina asked, "do you think a woman could pretend not being a virgin?"

"What kind of a question is that?" Ginger asked. The interruption to answer a stupid question irritated her.

"This is the kind of question that requires an answer."

Ginger set the quill aside and turned in her chair to look at her friend. "Why would a woman pretend not being a virgin?" she asked. "Why are you asking this question?"

Regina stared into space, a faraway look in her eyes. "I need the information for my story."

Ginger knew her friend was hiding something, but what it was eluded her. "Why is that information pertinent to your story?"

"Dementia was married to Bertie," Regina answered, "but they never—*you know*—because Bertie couldn't."

That startled Ginger. She had never heard that a man could not—Good Lord, she did not want to think about this.

Ginger cleared her throat. "Why couldn't he—?"

"Bertie could not you-know because . . ." Her voice trailed off, ". . . just because he could not. I heard that a man cannot for a variety of reasons, none of which I know."

"I never realized men were such delicate creatures," Ginger said, smiling at the idea. "Reggie, the Duke of Charming would be thrilled by her virginity."

Regina shook her head. "The duke wants to make love with Dementia, but he is too much of a gentleman to take her virginity without giving her words of love and a commitment of marriage."

Ginger rolled her eyes. "Then let the duke make a commitment to her."

"I can't do that," Regina exclaimed, sounding frustrated. "I haven't written enough pages for a whole book. Besides, the duke should propose marriage after the murderer is caught."

"Who was murdered?"

"Someone shot her husband, Bertie."

Ginger gave her a worried look. "Perhaps you should revise that part. I mean, Dementia's story hits too close to home."

"Nonsense." Regina smiled then. "I think I'll add another murder. In fact, I will add her husband's cousin's untimely demise after he proposes marriage to Dementia." She laughed at that. "Cedric will be so insulted when my book is published."

Ginger smiled at the thought. "Cedric will certainly know your feelings for him then."

"Cedric knows my opinion of him now," Regina said. "If I did make Dementia pretend not to be a virgin, though, what would she do? Precisely, I mean."

Ginger shrugged. "Hide her fear and follow wherever the duke leads her."

"You are a genius," Regina said. "If she does that, the duke won't notice she isn't a virgin because his love for her makes him too excited to notice."

Regina grabbed her quill, dipped it into the ink, and began writing again. Ginger prayed she could finish the ledgers. Thankfully, her emotions did not rule her, as they did her friend. Simple logic was much easier on a woman's peace of mind.

"Miss Ginger?"

Apparently, she was *not* going to finish the ledgers. She looked over her shoulder. "Yes, Pickles?"

"You have a visitor."

"Who?"

"Constable Amadeus Black."

Ginger stiffened at the gall of the man to show his face here. She had nothing to say to him. "Tell that despicable constable—"

"He looks contrite," Pickles interupted.

"How does *contrite* look?"

"Like the constable."

Both Ginger and Regina burst into laughter. Ginger stood. "Very well, I will—"

"Constable Black is waiting in the garden," Pickles said. "I told him people we dislike need to use the rear entrance, but cook insisted he wait outside."

Again, the two women burst into laughter. Ginger walked to the window and peered into the garden below. The constable was pacing back and forth.

"He doesn't look happy," Regina said.

"He will change that attitude or suffer the consequences." Ginger paused at the door. "Neither of you is to watch from the window."

"We won't," the countess and the majordomo chimed together.

Ginger left the study and hurried downstairs. She stopped at the garden door to smooth her skirt and expression. After pushing a recalcitrant curl behind her ear, she opened the door and stepped outside.

Amadeus Black whirled around. "Thank you for seeing me without an appointment." He gave her a sardonic smile. "Am I unwelcome here?"

"You cannot charge people with murder and expect them to be your friends," Ginger told him.

"*I* did not charge anyone with any crime," Amadeus corrected her, and stepped closer. "Prosecutor Lowing did that."

Ginger tilted her head back to gaze into his blue eyes. "You work for Prosecutor Lowing."

"I argued against arresting the prince."

"You did?"

Amadeus nodded and gestured to a stone bench near a silver birch tree. They crossed the lawn. He sat when she sat.

"How is the countess surviving the public's intense scrutiny?"

Ginger shrugged. "Reggie hasn't left the house but—yesterday was the most horrible day ever. That shocking headline in *The Times* caused problems here."

Amadeus grasped her hand, and his voice gentled. "Tell me about it."

"Reginald Smith stormed into the house in a fury over her testimony," Ginger said. "Uncle Forest tried to calm him down, but Cedric Barrows made the situation worse by offering to marry Reggie to stifle the gossip. Of course, Reggie refused and said she would rather see Cedric dead than wed. Reginald exploded and struck her. Thankfully, Prince Viktor arrived and prevented further violence."

"How was the situation resolved?"

"Reggie banned her father from entering the house ever again. This is all Cedric's fault. I have a mind to kill him myself."

"Didn't her father support the earl and her?" Amadeus asked. "What if he cuts her funds off?"

"A lack of funds would force Reggie to make peace with her father," Ginger said, "but she doesn't need his money. Our investment company is making a huge profit."

"You own a company?" Amadeus asked.

"Reggie and I formed the Evans Smith Company," Ginger answered. "Our investments have paid us well."

"Let me understand this," Amadeus said, looking confused. "Lady Bradford and you have invested money and made a profit?"

Ginger nodded, a smile of pride on her face.

"Who told you which company would be a good risk?"

"Nobody told us anything." Ginger felt insulted that the constable would underestimate their judgment. "I advised Reggie where we should invest our money to best advantage."

"*You?*"

His surprise did not sit well with Ginger. "Constable Black, you are a man of logic. Underestimating the intelligence, the talent, and the logic of women is absurdly illogical."

"Thank you for enlightening me."

Her brown eyes narrowed with suspicion. "You do not believe that."

"I believe it now that you have shown me the error of my ways," Amadeus said, trying to sidestep her anger. "If ever there was a contraption telling if a man lied or not, you would know for a certainty that I am speaking the truth."

Holding her gaze captive, Amadeus dipped his head and pressed his mouth on hers. She felt soft, tasted sweet, and seemed to enjoy his kiss. He drew back and traced a finger down the side of her flushed cheek.

"If I invite you to luncheon tomorrow, will you accept?" he asked. "You could advise me on which investments I should make."

Ginger appeared sultry-eyed, dazed by his kiss. "Yes, I would accept."

"Consider yourself invited." Amadeus ran a

thumb across the crease of her lips and then his lips followed his thumb. "Until tomorrow."

Several hours later, Regina inspected herself in the cheval mirror. She frowned at her reflection and knew she did not appear to be in mourning.

Her high-waisted black silk gown had short puffed sleeves, a rounded neckline, and showed her curves to best advantage. She wore black sandals on her feet and long black gloves.

The problem was her hair. Bold, bright, brazen. How did a woman with a mane of coppery red curls appear in mourning? The fiery color shouted: *I'm so glad the no-good son of a bitch is dead.*

Regina suffered the uncanny feeling that her hair would create a scandal tonight. Why had she agreed to the prince's invitation?

Because you love him, an inner voice answered.

God help her. The merchant's daughter loved the prince. That sounded like the next entry in the Grimm Brothers fairy tales.

Regina hoped hers would be one of their happier tales. Or would society's pigeons pluck her eyes out for daring to reach beyond her station?

"You look lovely."

In the cheval mirror, Regina saw Ginger crossing the bedchamber and whirled around. "Do I look like I am mourning Charles?"

"Celebrating his passing, perhaps." Ginger shook her head. "Do you think accompanying the prince to the opera is wise?"

"No, but I am going anyway. Besides, I am accompanying his whole family."

"Reggie, you testified in court that you and the prince . . . you know," Ginger reminded her. "Appearing by his side in public will only serve to fuel the gossip."

Regina shrugged. "I accepted his invitation and nothing can dissuade me."

"Enjoy the evening, then. Your prince awaits you in the foyer."

Speaking with Pickles in the foyer, Viktor turned around when the majordomo looked toward the stairs. Never had he seen a more lovely woman, though he knew she would prefer being admired for her intellect.

Viktor crossed the foyer, and when she reached the bottom stair, he bowed in courtly manner over her hand. "You are the loveliest woman I have ever seen."

"Thank you, Your Highness, but do not exaggerate," Regina said. "Do I appear to be in mourning?"

His lips twitched. "No."

"It's my damn hair."

"What is the problem with your hair? Though, I do prefer the wild disarray of curls when you wear it down."

Regina stepped down the final stair and tilted her head to meet his dark gaze. "My hair is bold and brazen."

Viktor laughed at that. "No one can blame you for your hair color."

"Society can fault me for attending the opera with my lover while my husband lies in an early grave," Regina said.

He lowered his voice to a husky whisper. "Are you planning to make me your lover tonight?"

Regina blushed a vibrant scarlet. "I did not mean—"

"I am teasing you." Viktor offered his arm. "Shall we go?"

Pickles opened the door. "Enjoy your evening."

Two coaches stood in front of Bradford House. Princess Samantha waved to her from inside one of the coaches. Regina returned the greeting and gave the prince a confused smile.

"Rudolf and Samantha believed you would feel more comfortable if they arrived with us," Viktor explained. "They will be attending a ball after the opera, hence the two coaches. Mikhail and Stepan will join us at the theater." He sat opposite her inside the coach. "You look stunning in black, but the gown needs diamonds as a complement."

"I don't own diamonds," Regina told him. His cavalier reference to priceless gems surprised her.

"I will purchase a diamond necklace," Viktor said. "You will also need a braclet and earrings."

"Your Highness, I urge you to be discreet."

"Discretion is my middle name. Viktor Discretion Kazanov."

Regina smiled at that, but then warned him, "Do not laugh tonight. We are mourning our spouses."

"Do you feel nervous?"

"Yes." Regina sighed. "Cedric and Vanessa gave me the cut direct the last time I attended the opera."

"Do not concern yourself with that." Viktor moved to sit beside her and reached for her hand. "My brothers' plan is giving others the cut first so they cannot do it to us. We will speak to my family only, no one else."

The closer their coach got to the opera, the more nervous Regina felt. She had never been accepted by society, did not possess a voucher for Almack's, had never even sought one.

Regina knew that after tonight she would be a social pariah. After tonight? She was a social pariah already. Society would eventually forgive the prince.

How could they not? He was titled, wealthy, and available for matrimony. Every mama in London would be pushing her daughter in his direction. They would not care if he had actually dispatched his wife.

Regina could scarcely breathe through her fear by the time their coach halted in front of the opera house. Viktor climbed out first and then assisted her.

"Do not look or speak to anyone but my family," Viktor reminded her.

Regina nodded and looped her hand through his arm. She stole a surreptitious peek at their surroundings and noted that the opera-goers were turning to watch the prince and her.

"Reggie, how good to see you," Princess Samantha greeted her warmly. She lowered her voice, adding, "You aren't going to the gallows so smile at me."

Regina instantly smiled at the princess, which made the two Kazanov brothers smile. Rudolf and Viktor walked on either side of the ladies into the grand foyer.

Princes Mikhail and Stepan were waiting inside, holding court to a number of ladies and gentlemen who melted away at their appearance.

"Lady Regina, you look lovely," Mikhail greeted her.

"You have recovered from your swoon," Stepan said.

"I am pleased to see both of you again," Regina said. She could feel a hundred curious gazes watching their small group.

"I do not want to linger here," Rudolf said. "Let us walk upstairs."

"An excellent idea." Viktor reached across his body and touched the hand she had looped through his arm. He leaned close and whispered, "You are doing marvelously. Look at me only."

Regina gave him a wobbly smile. She kept her gaze fixed on him as they climbed the stairs.

Thankfully, Princess Samantha led the way into the opera box. Regina walked behind her, and the four princes came last.

"Sit here," Samantha said, and gently pulled her down on a chair.

Regina felt protected. Viktor and Samantha sat on either side of her while Mikhail and Stepan sat behind her. Rudolf took the chair beside his wife.

"You must bring your son to lunch at my house tomorrow," Samantha invited her. "He can meet my children."

"I would love that," Regina accepted. "Austen will enjoy playmates."

"I will escort you and bring Sally," Viktor said.

Every aristocratic gaze swiveled in the direction of their opera box. A hundred lorgnettes were trained on them.

"Miss Fancy Flambeau will be singing the role of Cherubino tonight," Stepan said, drawing her attention away from interested gazes. "The opera's reigning diva, Patrice Tanner, despises Fancy."

"The fading star is jealous of the rising star," Mikhail said.

"I can understand that," Viktor remarked, "but the woman's hatred borders on obsession."

The overture sounded the beginning of the opera. Regina felt those censorious gazes turn away from her and began to relax. She dreaded the intermission, though, which signaled society to mingle.

Fancy Flambeau was not what Regina expected. Unlike others of her ilk, the young woman was slender and petite but possessed a big, pitch-perfect voice. She did not merely sing a song. She attacked it with her whole being, pouring her heart and soul into the lyrics.

At one point, the young singer turned toward the audience and stood close to the stage's edge. The diva placed a foot in front of her.

Fancy tumbled into the orchestra pit, making the audience gasp in horror. Without missing a note, the rising opera star climbed out of the pit and finished her song.

"Did you see that?" Prince Stepan exclaimed, rising from his chair. "I need to verify that she is uninjured." He left the opera box in a hurry.

Viktor squeezed her hand. "Stepan is a man in love for the first time." He glanced at his brothers, adding, "I cannot wait to see how he handles fatherhood. He will be good for a few laughs."

Regina failed to see the humor in first love. She was a woman in love for the first time and the feeling wasn't pleasant.

And then the moments Regina had dreaded all evening arrived. Intermission, a time to see and be seen. "This has reminded me of the times Uncle Forest and Uncle Bart treated Ginger and me to an evening at the opera," Regina told the prince.

"Who is Uncle Bart?"

"Ginger's father."

Viktor rested his arm across the back of her chair. "What about your own father?"

A sudden sadness shone from her eyes. "Reginald never had time for me."

Viktor touched her hand to offer comfort. "My own father is not the most of loving of parents."

The opera box curtain parted to reveal a man and a woman. Vanessa Stanton and Cedric Barrows entered the box.

"How good to see you out and about," Vanessa said to the prince. She threw the others a smile and then looked at Regina. "I did not expect to see you here tonight."

That Vanessa had not given her the cut surprised Regina. "The Kazanovs invited me to accompany them. To break the monotony of my grieving, I suppose."

"Your appearance here tonight is unseemly," Cedric criticized her.

Viktor opened his mouth to speak, but Regina touched his hand to warn him off. "What is unseemly is your proposal of marriage after your cousin's funeral."

"Reginald approved my suit," Cedric said.

"If you want my father's money," Regina said, "you will need to marry *him.*"

"We will marry sooner or later," Cedric said. "Accustom yourself to that fact."

"I will see you dead first."

"Like Charles?" Vanessa asked.

And then Regina did the unexpected. She turned her back on the sultry brunette, giving her the cut direct.

Cedric and Vanessa made a hurried retreat from the opera box.

"I wish you had let me handle him," Viktor said.

"Cedric does not frighten me," Regina said. "Besides, I like to fight my own battles."

"You inherited your father's temper."

Intermission ended. Stepan returned to the opera box and dropped into his seat.

"Fancy is uninjured." Stepan chuckled softly. "I left her vowing revenge on the diva."

At opera's end, Regina realized that she had enjoyed the evening in spite of the tense circumstances.

She had a feeling that she would enjoy her next toothache if the prince were there to comfort her.

"Rudolf and Samantha are going to the Drummle ball," Viktor said. "Shall we go somewhere for a late supper before we end the evening?"

Regina would love nothing more than extending their time together but knew that would be impossible. "That would be unwise," she said, with obvious reluctance.

"We could sup at my house," he coaxed.

"No," she refused again.

"Will you invite me into Bradford House for a nightcap?"

Regina inclined her head. "Yes, Your Highness, I will invite you inside to share a nightcap."

Chapter 11

The duke dipped his head, his mouth covering hers, his lips warm and firm, his kiss consuming. He lifted her into his arms and carried her to bed, fulfilling her long-denied need and desire . . .

"Lady Dementia?"

With naked limbs entangled, the duke and she roused at the voice. Their now alert gazes darted to the door.

"Oh, my lady!" The maid's expression registered surprise at seeing the lovers entwined so intimately. She averted her gaze. "Constable Green is waiting to speak with you. There's been another murder."

"Here we are." Pickles walked into the drawing room. On a silver tray, the majordomo carried a bottle of champagne and two flutes.

Pickles served the champagne and then sent the prince an arch look. "Enjoy your evening."

"Chilled champagne?" Regina said, confused. "I never ordered it."

"I brought the champagne with me," Viktor said, "and Pickles provided the chill." He smiled. "I knew you would refuse public refreshment."

"Your knowledge impresses me," Regina said. "How did you know I would invite you inside?"

Ignoring her question, Viktor raised his flute in salute. "To our future, my lady."

Viktor and Regina touched flutes and sipped champagne. They sat on the settee and drank their champagne in companionable silence.

"What did you think of our reception tonight?"

"I expected worse." Regina giggled. "These bubbles tickle my nose."

Gently, Viktor turned her face toward him and planted a chaste kiss on her mouth. "You taste sweet."

Regina felt suddenly shy, sitting alone with the prince. Yes, they had stood alone in the gazebo at the duke's, but so much had happened since then. They were no longer polite strangers. Intimate strangers, more accurately.

A disturbing thought popped into her mind. Was the prince's attention an expression of gratitude for her court testimony? While she was falling in love, was he merely considering her a friend?

Even more disturbing, what if he *did* harbor a fondness for her? He seemed to enjoy her kiss. What would she do if he wanted more?

Enjoy the moment with the prince, an inner voice whispered.

Viktor lifted the empty champagne flute out of her hand and set it on the table beside his. "What are you thinking?"

Regina gave him a nervous smile. "I was wondering if Constable Black will ever catch the murderer."

"We will not speak or even think of murder tonight."

"What shall we discuss?" Regina lifted her gaze to his, but he had focused on her lips.

"This." Viktor inched closer until his mouth covered hers in a lingering kiss.

When she sighed in sweet surrender, Viktor wrapped his arms around her, one hand holding the back of her head and the other pressing her against his hard-muscled body. The tip of his tongue caressed the crease of her mouth and persuaded her lips to part. He slipped his tongue inside to taste the sweetness beyond her lips.

Regina trembled, tendrils of delicious sensation fingering her spine. Instinctively, she met his thrusting tongue and sucked on it, feeling a thrill of power when she heard his groan.

Their lips smoldered and their nerves rioted. Like fire kissing gunpowder, their passion exploded and consumed them.

Viktor lifted his mouth from hers, his hand still stroking her silken cheek, his dark gaze noting her dazed expression. Then he stood and offered his hand, as if asking her for a waltz.

Regina looked from the dark intensity of his gaze to his hand outstretched in invitation. Her heartbeat quickened and her breath became shallow gasps.

She knew he wanted her. She wanted him, too.

Regina placed her hand in his. Without a spoken word, they left the parlor and walked down the corridor toward the stairs.

Think experience. Experience. Experience.

Regina repeated that litany over and over in her mind.

It did not work. She felt like a woman on the way to the gallows, not her lover's bed.

"Wait." Regina paused at the base of the stairs, the memory of what she'd written that morning surfacing in her thoughts. "Aren't you going to carry me?"

"If that is your wish." Viktor scooped her into his arms and then pretended to drop her.

Regina gasped and clung to him. She knew he was teasing when he grinned.

Gaining the bedchamber, Viktor used his foot to close the door. Like a man worshipping a rare flower, he inhaled her jasmine and vanilla scent.

"Your dog is sleeping on the settee near the hearth," he whispered against her ear.

"Hamlet does that every night. He won't bother us."

Viktor lowered her to her feet, sliding her down his muscular planes, their bodies touching from chest to thigh. He kissed her. A slow, soul-stealing kiss.

His lips hovered above hers. "Now we will undress each other."

"Undress?" Regina squeaked, his sexy suggestion a dash of cold water to her senses, her panic increasing.

"That is the way lovemaking begins," he said, laughter lurking in his voice. "Does it not?"

Her response was a breathless whisper. "Yes, it begins that way."

Viktor took the pins from her hair, letting her wild red curls cascade around her like a veil of fire. "So exotic, so lovely," he murmured.

His husky compliment pleased Regina. Her prince was even more romantic than Dementia's duke.

"Remove something of mine."

"I should undress *you?*"

Viktor brushed his lips across hers. "I want us to savor each other." His words ignited a flame, a melting sensation in her lower regions, catching her by surprise.

Raising both hands, Regina loosened his cravat

and tossed it away. She pushed his jacket off his broad shoulders and down his arms.

Anticipation gleamed in her emerald eyes. "Your turn, Your Highness."

She pleases me, Viktor thought. Her smile was touchingly sweet, her hands on him almost shy, her come-hither gaze flirtatious.

She would always be a true lady. Until, he pinned her body beneath his. The gleam in her emerald eyes told him she would be no lady between the sheets.

"Kiss me." His lips claimed hers in hot possession.

In the shadows of her mind, Regina knew he had unbuttoned the back of her gown. His hands caressed her smooth skin while his tongue caressed her mouth. The gown dropped to the floor. She wore only her chemise, garters, stockings, and shoes.

Viktor slid his hands down the sides of her body, pleased she had no need of a corset. Her waist was small, her hips curved, her breasts high, her nipples aroused.

"Your turn, my love." He nibbled at the corner of her lips.

With a shyly seductive smile, Regina lifted his right arm and unfastened the sleeve's cuff. She pressed a kiss on the palm of his hand before releasing it and reaching for his left arm. She unfastened that cuff, too, and kissed the palm of his hand.

Regina reached for the buttons on his waistcoat. She inched closer to slide it off his shoulders but paused to kiss the base of his throat.

His growl of pleasure fueled her feminine confidence. The hardness at his groin pressing against her belly excited her.

Regina flicked her tongue out to lick his throat,

her hands busily unfastening his shirt from top to bottom. Then she stared at him, mesmerized by his broad, muscled chest with its light matting of black hair. She had never seen a man's chest, and the wonder of it enticed her fingers to a caress.

"I am glad you like my body."

Regina blushed. "I—I didn't intend to stare."

"You *did* intend to stare." His height overwhelming her, Viktor traced the curve of her collar bone with his tongue. When he stepped back, the frivolous black silk chemise pooled at her feet.

"My turn to stare." His voice sounded choked.

Regina stood before him proudly. She wore only her silk stockings, garters, and shoes.

His gaze fixed on her perfectly rounded breasts. Her nipples were dusky and large, their tips nubs of arousal.

She reminded him of Venus rising from the sea. Sans the unnecessary water.

His hot gaze burned Regina. Her nipples puckered even more, butterflies winged inside her belly, and wetness throbbed between her thighs.

"Like for like, my lady." Viktor glided the palms of his hands across her breasts, marveling at their incredible softness. He cupped each in a hand, as if judging its weight, and slid his thumbs across her nipples. "Simply perfection."

Regina nearly swooned at the sensation of molten fire shooting from her nipples to the moist spot between her thighs, deepening the throb. She had never known such exquisite pleasure existed.

"Your nipples are sensitive." Viktor dipped his head and caught one in his mouth, sucking and licking before giving its mate the same attention.

With her body on fire, Regina soared beyond coherent thought. Instinctively, she held his dark head against her breast and leaned into his mouth.

Viktor heeled his shoes off. Then he reached down to remove his hose.

"My turn." Regina unbuttoned his trousers and pushed them down to reveal black silk drawers with a dramatic bulge at his groin. She inched closer and closer until their bodies touched. Rubbing her breasts back and forth across his chest, she purred at the sensual delight.

With a throaty growl of need, Viktor scooped her into his arms and placed her across the bed. He hovered above her, his mouth claiming hers in a maddening kiss.

Viktor slid his lips down the column of her slender throat and drifted lower. Then he tongued each breast and nipple, satisfied when she moaned and arched her body in an unspoken plea for his possession.

In a gentle assault, Viktor flicked his tongue down her belly. He pressed his face into the juncture between her thighs and inhaled her arousingly distinctive woman's scent.

It was the task of a moment to divest her of garters, stockings, and shoes. She lay naked and vulnerable to his gaze, his mouth, his hands. Unable to resist what she offered, he ran a long finger down and up her moist crevice and smiled when she moaned.

Viktor pushed his own silk drawers off and joined her on the bed. Leaning over her, he kissed her again while his hand traveled lower and his long fingers explored her wet folds of flesh.

Using his leg, Viktor parted her thighs and lay between them. He slid his hands beneath her bottom and lifted her up.

"Look at me." His voice was hoarse.

She opened her disarming emerald eyes. Her expression was dazed.

Viktor entered her with one powerful thrust and then remained motionless, his groin pressed against hers. Regina gasped in surprised pain, her expression clearing of its sensual haze.

Shocked, Viktor stared down at her. He opened his mouth to ask the unthinkable, but she raised her hand to press a finger across his lips.

"Please . . ."

He kissed her finger and began to move inside her. Acting on instinct, she wrapped her legs around his waist and moved with him. Thrust for thrust.

His raw masculinity surrounded and possessed with love, not threat. She succumbed to the primitive urge that made her surrender to the stronger force.

Their hunger became primal frenzy, a fierce mating of two halves to create a whole. Nature reduced them to the elemental, making them bow to the ancient urge to procreate.

His long strokes became shorter, faster, wilder. Her tension built to almost unendurable heights and then she exploded, melting into him. He answered her cry with one of his own and lost himself in her.

Viktor lay panting on top of her for several long moments. Regaining rational thought, he rolled to one side and took her with him. He cuddled her against his side and caressed her back in an unspoken promise of her importance to him beyond the sexual.

"You will now explain how a mother can also be a virgin," Viktor said.

It was a command, not a request.

One word popped into her mind. Deny, deny, deny.

Regina feigned surprise. "I don't know what you—"

Viktor pushed her onto her back and loomed over her. Nose to nose, he said, "I know a virgin when I lay one."

Pretending virginity must be easier than pretending experience. "Can I trust you?"

"Your question insults me," Viktor said. "You perjured yourself for—"

"I did *not* perjure myself."

"You stretched the truth."

"I did *not* stretch the truth."

"Very well, you misled everyone."

"Those men misled themselves."

Viktor inclined his head, giving up an argument he would never win. "Now you will tell me what I want to know. Whatever you confide will remain in confidence for all of eternity." He leaned against the headboard, pulled the coverlet up, and then put his arm around her shoulders to draw her closer.

"As you know, Charles married me for my father's money," Regina began. "To my relief, he declined sexual intimacy on our wedding night and every night after that. He said he needed to bolster himself before he bedded a redheaded commoner."

"Bastard," Viktor muttered.

Regina gave him a sidelong smile. "I was not complaining. To make a long story short, Charles had impregnated a young woman from a village near his country estate. When she died in childbirth, I took the infant. With proper planning, we passed Austen off as our son. Charles got his legitimate heir, my father got his aristocratic grandson, I escaped bedding a repulsive husband, and my son's only blood relative lives secure in the knowledge that his nephew will become an earl."

"Does you father know about this?"

"Reginald believes Austen is his true grandson."

"And the uncle has made no demands, financial or otherwise? He will make no claim on his nephew?"

"I trust his uncle to keep the silence."

Viktor pressed a kiss on her cheek. "You are much too trusting, my dear."

"The uncle watches over the boy every day," Regina said. "He will always receive a salary from the Bradfords, even if he is unable to work."

"The uncle is a member of this household? Who is he?"

"Austen's uncle is Artie, my coachman," Regina answered. "Which is the reason I named my son Austen Arthur Bradford."

Touched by her generous nature, Viktor planted a kiss on her temple. "If Charles had not died, you were prepared to pass your life a virgin?"

"I could not miss what I never had."

"Tomorrow morning I will procure a special license," Viktor told her, "and we will marry as soon as possible."

Regina snapped her head around, her expression stunned. "I will never marry again."

"You will marry me," Viktor insisted. "Even now you may be carrying my child."

"I want to soar, not have my wings clipped."

"I will let you soar within our marriage."

"*Let?*" Regina glared at him. "You will *let* me soar?"

"What angers you?" Viktor asked, sincerely puzzled. "My promise is liberal."

"I do not want any man to *let* me do anything, thereby placing limitations on me."

Viktor smiled at her, a condescending smile that said how adorable she was. "Women need protection and loving limitations."

"I cannot believe—"

"Regina, everyone has limitations." A sterner tone entered his voice.

"I will not live—"

"Live with this." Viktor gently but firmly dragged her to the edge of the bed. He knelt between her spread thighs, pressed his face into her moist folds, and flicked his tongue out to caress her pearl.

"Oh, my God." Regina moaned and clasped his head to keep his tongue and lips on her.

Viktor knew that he had her then. She would struggle and dig her heels in like a donkey, but she would do his bidding in the end. At least, he hoped so.

Amadeus Black crouched beside the motionless lump, stared at the blood-soaked ground, and then raised his sharp gaze to the man's ashen face. He stood and looked toward the east.

He did not need this today. Another of the Quality shot and robbed of valuables. Was one murderer roaming the streets of London? Or two? Was this murder motivated by money or something else?

The summit of Primrose Hill provided a panoramic view of London proper. Not today, though. Heavy mist drizzled down on all. The usual landmarks—St. Paul's Cathedral, Westminster Abbey, The Tower—hid within a shrouding of low-hanging clouds.

"What do you think, Amadeus?"

"I think this man is dead."

Barney rolled his eyes. "I meant—

"I know what you meant." Amadeus smiled at his assistant. "I was making a joke."

"Death is no joking matter," said a voice beside them. Prosecutor Lowing stood there, a most unusual sight. Prosecutors never visited crime scenes this early in a case. The body had not even fully frozen.

Lowing looked at the body. "Miserable day for a murder."

"Especially if one is the victim." Amadeus winked at his assistant.

"I heard another member of the Quality had been attacked," Lowing said. "Imagine, Cedric Barrows had only recently testified in his cousin's case."

"The earl was shot and robbed."

"Like his cousin," Lowing said. "The murderer wants us to believe it's robbery."

"That is one possibility."

"And another would be?"

"It *is* robbery." Amadeus turned to Barney. "Go to the Barrows residence and question his servants about his comings and goings." He looked at the prosecutor. "I will inform his next of kin, the Countess of Tewksbury."

Lowing nodded. "I'll go with you."

Less than an hour later, Amadeus Black and Prosecutor Lowing stood in the Countess of Tewksbury's drawing room. They waited and waited and waited. The countess, they were told, had enjoyed a late night.

Ten minutes stretched to twenty. Which grew to thirty. Forty. Fifty. Sixty.

Finally, Vanessa Stanton breezed into the drawing room. "Gentlemen, how may I help you?"

"My lady, please sit down here." Prosecutor Lowing stepped forward and drew her to the settee. "We carry sad news."

Vanessa looked from one to the other. "Yes?"

"Your brother is dead," Amadeus said baldly.

"Murder," Lowing added.

"Cedric was murdered?" With that, Vanessa swooned dead away.

Amadeus laid her back on the settee. Lowing called a servant to fetch hartshorn and water.

Ten minutes passed before Vanessa opened her eyes, the hartshorn having revived her. Still shaky, she sat on the settee and sipped water from a crystal glass.

"Did you see your brother last night?" Prosecutor Lowing sat beside her and held her hand.

"Cedric and I attended the opera."

"Did you pass the whole evening together or separate after the opera?" Amadeus asked.

"We attended Drummle's ball," Vanessa answered, "but I dropped Cedric at his residence directly afterwards."

"What time was that?"

Vanessa shrugged. "Around midnight."

"Your brother was an outstanding man," Lowing said, "but everyone has enemies. Do you have any opinion about who would want him dead?"

"That Bradford bitch."

Amadeus narrowed his gaze on her. The countess sounded surprisingly strong. He shifted his gaze to the prosecutor, who seemed to have perked up at that.

"Explain yourself."

"That is no proper tone to use on a lady," Lowing chided him.

"I beg your pardon." Amadeus managed a smile. "Explain yourself. Please."

"Regina threatened my brother's life several times," Vanessa answered, her full attention on the more sympathetic prosecutor. "The latest threat came during the opera's intermission last night."

"What about the prince?" Lowing asked.

"Viktor would never harm anyone," Vanessa said. "He is the very soul of kindness. The merchant's daughter is the one to investigate. She passed that weekend at the duke's throwing herself at the prince, who could never show rudeness to anyone. I suppose the chit took his politeness as encouragement because before the weekend ended, Charles and Adele were dead."

"We thank you for your cooperation," Lowing said.

"If I can help you further," she said, "do not hesitate to call upon me."

Amadeus and Lowing left the Countess of Tewksbury's residence. Their next stop would be Bradford House.

"Let's arrest her," Lowing said, heading for their coach.

"I will question Lady Bradford about these alleged death threats," Amadeus told the prosecutor, "but I will not arrest her unless she confesses to the crime."

"You *will* arrest her if I so order."

Amadeus paused before following the other man into the coach, his gaze fixed on the prosecutor. "I will resign the case."

"No matter, Barney will finish the investigation."

"Barney cannot locate yesterday's newspaper." Amadeus grinned at the prospect of his assistant actually finding a murderer. "We play the game my way or not at all."

Lowing acquiesced, but his tone was sullen. "Very well, we will do this your way."

Reaching Bradford House, the two men climbed the stairs. "Let me do the talking," Amadeus said.

Pickles answered their summons. "The hour is too early for visitors."

Amadeus placed his booted foot in the doorway, preventing the majordomo from slamming the door in their faces. "We are conducting official business."

Pickles pursed his lips in displeasure, his gaze cold on the prosecutor. He stepped aside to allow them entrance.

"We want to speak—" Amadeus spied Ginger Evans walking down the stairs.

"Good morning." Ginger glanced at the prosecutor and then sent Amadeus a questioning look.

"I regret the need to cancel our luncheon," he said, "but there has been another murder."

Ginger gasped. Pickles looked appalled.

"I must speak with Lady Bradford."

Ginger hesitated, her curiosity apparent. "Reggie hasn't come down yet. Nothing has happened to Prince Viktor?"

"The matter is urgent."

Ginger inclined her head. "I will wake her."

"Go with her," Lowing whispered, "lest she warn the countess."

Amadeus refused to stand in the foyer and argue with the prosecutor. He knew his relationship with Ginger already cast a shadow over his objectivity since the countess was her dearest friend. He followed Ginger up the stairs.

"This is outrageous." Pickles chased after them. "Constable, you are invading Her Ladyship's privacy. Please wait in the foyer."

Ginger paused outside the third-floor bedchamber and turned to Amadeus. "I will leave the door open for you to listen. Do not embarrass her by entering."

"I would never wish to embarrass the countess."

"Thank you." Ginger opened the door and slipped into the bedchamber. *Oh, my God!*

Amadeus rushed into the bedchamber and stopped short, his startled gaze on the bed. The prince and the countess lay on the disheveled bed, their naked limbs entangled.

"What in God's name?" Viktor looked toward the door.

"Oh, no!" Regina squeaked, and burrowed herself into the prince, unaware her naked backside was exposed.

Amadeus grabbed a stunned Ginger and gently pushed her into the corridor. Averting his gaze, he registered the enormous dog leaping off the settee and dashing past him out the door.

"Dress and come downstairs." Amadeus began to close the door. "There has been another murder."

Chapter 12

Dementia walked into the drawing room and stopped short at the sight of her father and his best friend. She inclined her head to acknowledge Harry Dutton, her father's long-time associate.

"I forgive your bad behavior," her father said. "I have formulated a plan to salvage your reputation."

Dementia suffered the uncanny feeling that his forgiveness and this meeting would not last beyond the next few minutes. "What is this plan?"

"Remarrying and living quietly is the only way to redeem yourself," her father said. "I propose a match between you and Harry."

Dementia shifted her gaze to her father's best friend. Harry Dutton was middle-aged, short, and paunchy. Not the best qualities for attracting a young, nubile bride.

Good Lord, she would kill him in an hour if she agreed. Which, she had no intention of doing.

"I cannot agree to the match," Dementia said. "I love the Duke of Charming."

Her father gave her an exasperated look. "The duke will never marry a merchant's daughter."

Her smile was feline. "His Grace has already proposed marriage . . ."

"We forgot to lock the door." Regina groaned in humiliation and hid her blushing face under the pillow.

The prince's amused chuckles made her feel even worse. She had worried about the embarrassment of seeing the prince this morning. Not only had she needed to face him, but her whole damn household would know what they had been doing. Not to mention the constable. She would probably read about her nocturnal activities in tomorrow's *Times*.

"Reggie, there is no sense weeping about the cow's milk after we left the barn door open." The prince was confusing his proverbs, and there was laughter in his voice. His hand caressed her buttocks. *His wonderfully talented, slow-moving hand.*

Regina lifted her head to look at him, sitting on the edge of the bed. "Are you calling me a cow?"

Viktor laughed. "Lady Heifer or the Countess of Heifer?"

The thought of a second murder suddenly shoved her embarrassment aside. Regina sat up and the coverlet dropped to her waist, exposing her pink-tipped breasts. She touched his arm, unconsciously admiring his muscles, and leaned against him.

He glanced at her. "Are you trying to seduce me?"

Regina raised her worried gaze to his. "There has been another murder, and the constable wants to question me. Does that mean I am suspect?"

Viktor reached across his body and his hand covered hers. "Be calm, Reggie. No one could ever believe you are capable of murder." His dark gaze warmed on her. "Besides, lying naked beneath me gives you an alibi. Are you glad you succumbed to my seduction?"

Her lips twitched into a smile. She rubbed her cheek against the muscles in his upper arm like a half-grown she-cat seeking her mate's comforting strength.

"Oh, Lord." Regina noticed the spots of blood staining the sheets.

Viktor looked over his shoulder. "That is your virgin's blood, Reggie."

"I know what it is." She stared at the tell-tale stains. "How will I explain giving you my virginity when I already have a son?"

"You are the lady of the house," Viktor reminded her. "You explain yourself to no one."

"The maids will see the blood and gossip."

"Ah, I understand." Viktor thought for a moment. "We will remove the sheet, and I will dispose of it."

"You cannot carry my virgin's blood around London."

That made him laugh. "I promise to go directly home."

"I don't care."

He laughed again. "Artie knows the situation. Let him dispose of the sheet."

"No!" Regina gasped, even more mortified by that idea.

"Wrap the sheet in pretty packaging," Viktor said, a tinge of exasperation in his voice. "Artie will deliver the package to me, and I will dispose of it."

Regina mulled that idea over in her mind. She chewed on her bottom lip in indecision.

"You are irritating me, Regina." His voice held a warning note.

"Very well, we will do that." Regina knelt beside him on the bed and gazed into his eyes. "Whenever you become displeased you say *Regina*. Otherwise, you call me Reggie."

"How observant of you," Viktor drawled, and then smiled.

"Some poor soul is murdered, and I am probably suspect," Regina said. "Does that make you happy?"

His smile grew into a grin. "Now that we have been caught in the act," he said, "we will marry without delay in order to prevent further damage to your reputation."

"I will not marry you or any other gentleman."

"You will marry me, Regina, and do my bidding," Viktor insisted. "Make no mistake about that."

With that debate ended, Viktor and Regina stripped the sheet from the bed, folded it into an old shawl, and hid it in her dressing room. Then they dressed hurriedly and left the bedchamber.

On the second-floor landing, they met a blushing Ginger. "I took them to the dining room for breakfast."

Viktor cocked a brow. "Who is *them?*"

"Prosecutor Lowing accompanied Constable Black."

"Damn it, Lowing will never forget you embarrassed him in court," Viktor said to Regina.

She looked at her friend. "Who was murdered?"

"Cedric Barrows was shot and robbed on Primrose Hill last night."

"Why would someone kill Cedric? The man was an ineffectual buffoon."

"Like Charles, Cedric enjoyed his pleasures," Viktor said. "They passed many evenings carousing together."

"Constable Black keeps telling the prosecutor that you alibi each other," Ginger said, nearing the dining room door, "but Lowing has set his heart on a conspiracy theory. I will leave you to it." She disappeared in the direction of the kitchen.

Regina felt nauseous at the prospect of facing another day in court, and the real possibility of hanging for murder left her in a near panic. Her hands and legs shook like the palsey. Viktor paused in the corridor. He lifted her chin and gazed into her eyes, her hysteria close to the surface. "Be calm, Reggie. We have done nothing wrong."

Regina nodded but still looked frightened. Viktor put his arm around her shoulders and escorted her into the dining room.

Like true adversaries, Viktor and Regina sat across the dining table from the constable and the prosecutor. Pickles served them coffee and returned to the sideboard to fetch their breakfast.

"Confess to your crime, Lady Bradford," Lowing said. "We know you threatened the earl's life."

Stunned speechless, Regina stared at the prosecutor. Then she lifted her gaze to the prince, who appeared perfectly relaxed.

"Forget the game playing," Prince Viktor said. "If you have questions about Barrows, we will answer to the best of our ability. If not, leave Bradford House."

"Are you practicing law?" Lowing asked, his tone snide.

Viktor gave the prosecutor a knowing smile and mentioned the other man's personal nemesis. "Percy Howell will defend Lady Bradford, if she requires representation."

"Three people are dead," Amadeus Black spoke up, his gaze on the prosecutor, "and making this personal will not catch the murderer."

"We need look no farther than across the table for the guilty parties," Lowing said.

"I am warning you," Amadeus said. "If need be, I

will ask the magistrates to remove you from both murder cases."

"Whose side are you on?"

"Truth and justice."

"Very commendable."

Amadeus Black ignored the comment and focused his attention on Regina. "Lady Bradford, did Cedric Barrows cause a rife between you and your father by asking for your hand in marriage?"

"Yes, he did."

The next question came from Lowing. "Did you threaten the earl's life?"

Regina gave the prosecutor a disgruntled look. "Wouldn't you threaten him if he was trying to force you into marriage?"

Both Prince Viktor and Amadeus Black smiled. Prosecutor Lowing scowled.

Viktor grasped Regina's hand and lifted it to his lips. "The lady and I passed the night in her bechamber."

Regina blushed and dropped her gaze to her lap.

"I suspect the lady and you conspired to dispatch both earls and the princess," Lowing said, unimpressed with the alibi. "Only third-party verification could sway me from that opinion."

Pickles whirled around. "I can vouch for their whereabouts."

Four startled gazes turned in his direction. Regina knew the majordomo would lie for her. She dropped her gaze to her lap again, trying to keep her face expressionless. How could Pickles convince the prosecutor that she and the prince had passed the entire night in her bedchamber?

"Enlighten us," Amadeus Black said.

"I served His Highness and Her Ladyship champagne when they returned after the opera," Pickles told the constable. "After midnight, I decided to verify that Her Ladyship had bolted the door. I spied Hamlet sleeping in the corridor in front of Her Ladyship's bedchamber, which is unusual because he always sleeps on the settee inside her chamber." Pickles looked pointedly at Regina and blushed at his next words. "I heard ghastly moans emanating from within, worried she was ill, and opened the door. Hamlet rushed inside and then I"—the majordomo cleared his throat—"I saw His Highness and Her Ladyship involved in a certain activity."

"They never knew you were there?" the constable asked.

"Thankfully, no."

The constable looked at the disappointed prosecutor and then stood. "Let's go, Lowing."

"I will escort you to the door." Pickles hurried after the two men.

Viktor looked at Regina. "You inspire great loyalty."

A smile touched her lips. "Pickles should be writing fiction."

Viktor glanced at his pocket watch. "I will return at one o'clock for you and Austen."

"Do you think it's wise to keep our plans with Princess Samantha?"

"Reggie, we have done nothing wrong and will not hide like the guilty," Viktor answered. "Lowing is fixated on us to the exclusion of any other suspect. My brothers and I will need to investigate Charles and Cedric and their vices."

"I will help you."

Viktor slanted an unamused look at her. "You will *not* investigate murders. That is men's work."

"*Men's work?* When my neck is in danger of hanging from the gallows," Regina told him, "I will investigate. *You* will acquiesce to my wishes. That is, if you want any chance of marrying me."

He smiled. "You bitch."

She returned his smile. "I'm a fast learner."

The Royal Rooster Tavern on Friday Street offered patrons a warm welcome on a raw, drizzling spring day. The common room was reasonably spacious, and a fire crackled in the hearth.

Lunch at the tavern was a crowded affair, filled with men mostly. A cacophony of sounds and smells assaulted the senses, from low masculine voices to deep rumbles of laughter and slowly roasting meats to simmering stew to beer and ale.

"What did you learn at the Barrows residence?" Amadeus Black asked Barney.

"I solved the case."

Amadeus stared in surpise at his assistant and set his spoon down in the bowl of beef stew. "Explain yourself."

"Cedric Barrows accompanied his sister to the opera and returned around midnight," Barney told him. "No sooner had the earl walked through the door than his majordomo handed him a note that had been delivered earlier."

"Can the majordomo identify the messenger?"

Barney shook his head. "A man with the bottom half of his face covered by a muffler. *Not* a gentleman. The earl read the note, called for a horse, and went out again. Never to return."

Amadeus looked puzzled. "We found no note on his person."

"The earl left it behind." Barney reached into his pocket, produced a missive, and set it down on the table.

Amadeus reached for the note. "Have you read it?"

Barney grinned and nodded.

Unfolding the parchment, Amadeus scanned the note. It read: *I have a proposition for you and wish to discuss this privately. Meet me on Primrose Hill as soon as possible. Tomorrow will be too late. Regina.*

Amadeus frowned at the message. Something smelled rotten here. This was too neat for belief.

"We closed the case, right?"

"A woman cannot be in two places at the same time."

Barney sipped his ale. "I don't understand."

"Prince Viktor and Lady Regina were closeted in her bedchamber from before midnight until this morning. The Bradford majordomo verified their alibi."

"The lady wrote the note to the earl," Barney speculated, "but she hired an assassin to do the deed."

"We do not know if this is the lady's handwriting," Amadeus said, pocketing the note. "We will keep this a secret from Lowing until I decide otherwise. After all, we would not want the prosecutor to embarrass himself again."

"Are we allowed to keep evidence from him?"

"The note is a lead, not evidence," Amadeus explained, knowing his assistant would believe him. "It becomes evidence when we match the handwriting to the correct person."

"So someone else could be making the countess appear guilty?"

Amadeus smiled at the other man. "You are a fast learner, my friend."

Barney preened at the praise. "What do we do now?"

"I will procure a sample of Lady Bradford's handwriting," Amadeus said. "What comes after that depends on the outcome."

Ginger walked downstairs, intending to brew herself a pot of tea. She reached the foyer in time to see the majordomo opening the front door.

"I must speak with the countess," a familiar voice said.

"I told you yesterday," the majordomo said, blocking the the man's way, "people we dislike—"

"Pickles!" Ginger hurried across the foyer, a horrified giggle bubbling up in her throat. "Let Constable Black inside."

"Against my better judgment," Pickles muttered, and stepped back to allow the other man entrance.

Ginger smiled at the constable. "Good afternoon, Amadeus."

He returned her greeting with a smile of his own. "May I speak with Lady Bradford? The matter is urgent and could clear her of any wrongdoing."

"Reggie has taken her son to visit friends."

Amadeus hesitated. "Perhaps you can help me."

"I will do my best."

Amadeus reached into his pocket for the note. He glanced at the majordomo, who was pretending deafness.

"You may listen to this, Pickles," he told the majordomo, "if you cease slamming doors in my face."

"I apologize," Pickles drawled, "and promise never to do that again."

Amadeus unfolded the note and held it up. "Is this the countess's handwriting?"

"No." Ginger read the note and looked up in surprise. "Whoever wrote this murdered Cedric?"

"I believe so, but Lowing will never accept your

word," Amadeus said. "May I see a sample of her handwriting for comparison?"

"Let's go upstairs," Ginger said, turning away. "I'm certain I can find something."

Ginger led the way to the second-floor parlor. She gestured for him to sit on the settee and then spied the manuscript on the table.

"You can use Reggie's manuscript for comparison," she said, "but you cannot take it."

Amadeus winked at her. "I believe Lowing will trust my word as truth."

"I was intending to brew a pot of tea. Would you care for a cup?"

"I would love tea."

Ginger blushed. "I'll return in a few minutes."

Amadeus unfolded the note and opened the manuscript to the first page. In an instant, he saw the difference in the handwriting. Of course, Lowing could argue that the countess had tried to disguise her handwriting.

Focusing on the manuscript, Amadeus began to read. He smiled at Dementia, her thoroughly obnoxious husband, and the Great Dane, Horatio.

Great Dane? Lady Bradford owned a Great Dane named Hamlet. In the Shakesperean play, Hamlet and Horatio were best friends.

Like the countess, Dementia had red hair, and both women were writing novels. Was the Duke of Charming actually Prince Viktor Kazanov? Good Lord, the heroine's husband was murdered in the same manner as Charles Bradford.

Amadeus skimmed the manuscript, searching for other similiarities between fiction and reality. The duke being arrested for the earl's murder, the countess testifying in court . . .

Though too numerous to ignore, the similarities

did not prove murder. Unless, he could show beyond reasonable doubt that the countess had written these fictional events prior to the real ones.

Lowing would see this complication another way. The prosecutor would not hesitate to arrest the countess.

Still, Amadeus could not believe that Regina Bradford would murder or conspire to murder. He would stake his reputation on that belief. Like the note, he would keep silent about the manuscript and hope his growing fondness for the countess's friend was not coloring his judgment.

Ginger returned carrying a tray laden with the tea and cookies. They passed a pleasant hour speaking of inconsequential matters.

"I must be leaving." Amadeus stood but recognized her disappointed expression. "Thank you."

Ginger gave him a confused smile. "For what?"

"Thank you for missing me." Amadeus pressed his lips to hers in a gentle kiss. "Years have passed since anyone missed me."

"I don't believe that." Ginger looped her hand through the crook of his arm and escorted him to the foyer.

"Will you luncheon with me tomorrow?"

His invitation pleased Ginger. "You do not think our luncheon plans will cause another's untimely death?"

"We *do* jinx people," Amadeus said, referring to the previous dates postponed due to murders. "I promise I won't arrest us."

Ginger stood in the open doorway and watched the constable climb into the coach. Amadeus gave her a last look and lifted his hand to acknowledge her.

Ginger sighed, a dreamy expression on her face.

Amadeus Black was the handsomest man she'd ever seen, but his logic and integrity attracted her most. Though a trifle stern at times, he would learn to relax with the help of a loving wife.

"When is the wedding?" Pickles intruded on her thoughts.

Ginger looked at him. "Amadeus proposed luncheon, not marriage."

His lips twitched. "Constable Black has no chance of escaping your matrimonial intentions."

"I have no intentions," she lied.

"How rewarding to witness that man's downfall at your tiny hands," Pickles said, as if she hadn't spoken.

Ginger laughed and started to shut the door. Then she saw another coach halting in front of the house. "Reginald Smith is here."

"Oh, joyful day." Pickles rolled his eyes. "Shall I send him away?"

She shook her head. "Reginald wants to visit Austen, and I doubt Reggie will be gone much longer."

Ginger escorted Reginald and Uncle Forest upstairs to the family parlor. Pickles went in the other direction to fetch refreshment.

"Regina and Austen were invited to visit Princess Samantha and her children," Ginger told the two men. "Reggie thought Austen would enjoy being with children."

Reginald sat in a high-backed chair and smiled with satisfaction. "Regina is traveling in lofty circles."

Uncle Forest sat on the settee. He pushed his spectacles up and asked, "How are you, Ginger?"

"Quite well."

Forest noticed the manuscript on the table near him. "Do you mind if I peruse this?"

"I am certain Reggie would give you permission."

Ginger watched him open to the first page and begin to read. A slight smile appeared on his face. She glanced at Reginald. He should be the one interested in his daughter's aspirations. Uncle Forest had always been more of a father to Reggie than her own.

After reading snatches of the story, Uncle Forest placed the manuscript on the table again. He stood and wandered to the window that overlooked the street.

Ginger joined him there. Another coach halted in front of the house, and Prince Viktor climbed down. The prince reached inside for Austen and then assisted Regina. Viktor passed her the boy and said something that made her smile.

Uncle Forest placed a finger across his lips in a gesture to be careful in front of Reginald. "Viktor and Regina looked besotted," he whispered.

"She loves him."

Carrying her sleeping son, Regina walked into the parlor. She stopped short, surprised to find her father there.

"Let me hold him," Reginald said, as if there had never been any trouble between them. "Playing with other children tired him out?"

Regina passed her father the boy. She waited for him to mention what had happened between them.

"Lose that sour puss and sit," Reginald said, cuddling his grandson against his chest. "I want to speak with you." When she sat, he said, "Forest and Ginger, leave us please."

"They stay," Regina insisted.

"Very well, Daughter." Her father seemed to compose himself and said, "I can understand that you did not wish to marry Cedric Barrows."

"The point is moot since Cedric was murdered

last night," Regina said, drawing surprised looks from the two men.

"The problem of your reputation remains," Reginald told her.

"My reputation is not your problem."

Reginald ignored her words. "I want you to marry Forest. In name only, of course."

Damn him. Not only did he disregard her feelings but Uncle Forest's as well. Most importantly, her father had put her in the position of hurting a man she considered family.

"I apologize, Uncle Forest," Regina said, "but I do not require a husband."

Uncle Forest glanced at her father and then said, "Take a few days to consider your options."

"The prince will never marry you," Reginald said.

Regina could not suppress the urge to prove her father wrong. "Viktor has already proposed marriage."

Ginger laughed and hugged her. Uncle Forest looked stunned. Reginald grinned in obvious pleasure.

Regina could almost see his mind at work. One grandson was an earl. His other grandchildren would be princes and princesses. Quite a feat for a self-made man.

"When will you marry?" her father asked.

"I haven't accepted him yet," Regina answered. "We will let you know."

"I could not be happier for you," Uncle Forest said.

"Do not let too much time pass," Reginald advised her. "The longer the prince knows you, the more apt he is to change his mind."

"Thank you, Father." Regina turned to Uncle Forest, asking, "May I speak with you privately?"

"Of course, my dear."

Regina led the way into the corridor. "Uncle Forest, I meant no insult to you."

"None taken, my dear." He patted her shoulder. "I only agreed because your father worried about you. In spite of what you think, Reginald loves you."

Regina threw herself into the older man's arms. "Thank you for your understanding, Uncle Forest."

"Finally, this place serves us a decent drink." Viktor quaffed the shot of vodka in one gulp.

Rudolf refilled his brother's glass. "I sent the management a dozen cases of our best vodka."

"That was smart," Prince Mikhail said.

"I am grateful we no longer need to drink whisky," Prince Stepan said, raising his glass in salute to his eldest brother.

"Whisky is for women," Mikhail agreed.

The four Kazanov princes sat together inside the exclusive White's Gentleman's Club. The atmosphere was relaxing with dim lighting, muted voices, and leather chairs as soft as a lady's lap.

"Lowing is focused on Reggie and me to the exclusion of everyone else in England," Viktor told them. "We will need to investigate Cedric's and Charles's vices and debts."

"Stepan and I will scour the wilder gambling establishments," Mikhail offered. "Bearbaiting, cockfighting, and dogfights."

"I cannot go to those places," Stepan told his brother. "You know violence against animals upsets me. I'll do the bawdy houses."

"I will discreetly ask around all the town's gentlemen's clubs," Rudolf said. "Samantha would kill me if I visited a bawdy house."

"Regina insists on accompanying me on my investigation." Viktor grinned at his brothers. "I may take her to a few parties. A masquerade, perhaps."

"That would certainly put the lady in an amorous mood," Stepan said.

"Make sure her face is covered," Rudolf warned, "or her reputation will never recover."

The Kazanov princes stood to leave. They walked past the bow window to the door.

Outside, a heavy fog swirled around their legs like a voluminous cloak. The glow from the gaslights gave the street an otherworldly appearance.

"Where is your coach?" Rudolf asked.

Viktor pointed into the fog. "Across the street."

"Mine is behind yours," Mikhail said.

Viktor and Mikhail stepped into the street. Suddenly, a coach materialized from nowhere and careened down the street. As it neared, the driver changed direction and aimed his horses and coach at them.

Mikhail grabbed Viktor and pulled him back. The two of them went down hard in the mud.

Their brothers were at their side in an instant. Stepan helped Viktor up while Rudolf lifted Mikhail.

"Did you see that?" Stepan exclaimed. "He aimed directly for you."

"That is absurd," Viktor said. "It was a freakish accident caused by the fog."

"Two men with a personal interest in Regina Bradford are dead," Rudolf said. "You nearly became dead man three."

Viktor shook his head. "You cannot think—"

"I think someone wants the lady unmarried," Rudolf interrupted. "I can only wonder at the reason."

Chapter 13

"My lady?"

Dementia looked at her majordomo. "Yes, Desmond?"

"The Countess of Tyngsboro requests an interview."

Dementia chewed on her full bottom lip, a sign of indecision. The countess had previously engaged in an affair with the Duke of Charming. She knew the sultry noblewoman did not intend a social visit.

"Escort the countess here." Dementia sighed. She was in no mood for confrontation.

"Shall I serve refreshment?"

"Good Lord, no. I do not want to prolong her visit."

"Very good, my lady." Desmond left the drawing room.

Veronica Stamford, the Countess of Tyngsboro, walked into the drawing room a moment later. Her gown was the color of midnight with gold embroidery at neckline and hem, its bodice cut entirely too low.

Dementia forced herself to smile and gestured to the settee. "Please sit."

"No, thank you." The other woman's tone and gaze were colder than the bitter north wind. "I won't be staying."

Dementia rose from her high-backed chair. She would not allow this woman to intimidate her.

"I will be blunt," the countess said. "Leave His Grace alone, or you will regret it."

Dementia met her gaze unwaveringly. "You do not frighten me . . ."

"Good evening, Pickles."

"Good evening, Your Highness." The majordomo stepped aside to allow the prince entrance. "Or should I say good morning?"

Viktor looked at the older man's nightshirt, robe, and nightcap. His lips quirked into a smile. "The hour is late, and the household sleeps. How is it that you are still awake?"

"I knew you would be knocking on the door sooner or later." Pickles looked down his long nose at him. "You have passed the previous six nights with Her Ladyship."

"You are observant, my good man."

"No, Your Highness, I am the one who locks the door at night." Pickles reached into his robe's pocket and produced a key. He passed it to the prince, saying, "After tonight, let yourself into the house."

Viktor grinned at the majordomo and lifted the key out of his hand. "Your trust honors me."

"You are unlikely to abscond with the silver," Pickles drawled. "Before you retire, I have a matter of importance to discuss."

"At this hour?"

"You will be gone before dawn."

"True." Viktor sat on the bottom stair and waited for the majordomo to speak.

"In the absence of her father, I want to know your intentions to Her Ladyship." Pickles gave him a meaningful look. "You cannot expect to pass these many nights together and not get her *in the family way.*"

Viktor stared at the older man. He could not credit that a servant was demanding to know his intentions toward Reggie. And then he realized that the woman he loved also inspired love and loyalty in others. Both the majordomo and he had her best interests at heart.

"I have proposed marriage," Viktor admitted, "but the lady refuses. She wants the freedom to soar with independence."

Pickles frowned. "Her father and the late earl have damaged her outlook on men and marriage."

"How do I overcome the handicap of being a man?"

"As I see it, you must convince the lady that she will be as free within marriage as without."

Viktor nodded. "How would I do that precisely?"

"I will ponder the matter," Pickles said, and then shrugged. "Until then, getting her in the family way would be best."

"I won't tell her you said that."

Viktor climbed the stairs to the third-floor bedchamber. Walking into the room, he paused at the inviting sight of her sleeping. The perfume of lilacs wafted into the room through the open window, lending the atmosphere a dreamy quality.

Lying on the settee, Hamlet lifted his head and wagged his tail in greeting. Then the Great Dane returned to his sleep.

Viktor undressed and tossed his evening attire across the back of the settee. He approached the bed and drew the coverlet back.

Good God, he felt like a boy at Christmas unwrapping the toy he'd desired most. Wearing a nightshift sheerer than gossamer wings, Regina slept with a peaceful smile on her face.

Viktor wondered if she was dreaming of him. He

joined her on the bed and pushed her nightshift slowly up her body.

"Viktor?"

"I hope you did not expect another man." Viktor lifted the nightshift over her head, tossed it aside, and went straight for her breasts. His nuzzling, tonguing, and sucking brought a sigh to her lips; and she moaned in protest when he drew back. "You could corrupt a monk, my love."

Their lips met in a desperate, earth-shattering kiss. That melted into another. And then another.

"You taste like whisky."

"You smell like jasmine and vanilla and woman." She sighed. "Please."

He groaned, knowing what she wanted. Using his legs, he spread her thighs and slid his hands beneath her bottom to lift her into better position. He thrust inside her, making her gasp, filling her.

And then Viktor moved. His long seductive strokes became short pumping thrusts.

She wrapped her legs around his waist and took him deep, surrendering herself. She was soft and hot and moist.

Regina cried out and arched her body, melting into him. Viktor groaned and shuddered and spilled his seed.

He fell to one side and pulled her against his body, his chest pillowing her head. She fell asleep in an instant.

Viktor knew the majordomo was correct. If they made love every night, Regina would soon be caught in the family way, and she was too naive to realize it.

He would cease pressuring her for marriage. Instead, he would arrange their lives so she needed to marry him. He would gladly let her soar. Within reasonable bounds, of course.

Awakening later, Viktor looked toward the open window. Night's darkness had lightened into gray, signaling the approaching dawn.

Viktor slipped from the bed to retrieve his clothes from the settee. Then he returned to the edge of the bed and tried to summon enough energy to dress. His coachman would be waiting in the alley behind the garden.

A small hand caressed his back. Moist lips followed the hand.

"Don't leave me." Her voice was a drowsy whisper.

"I must leave," Viktor told her. "My daughter expects to breakfast with me."

"The hour is too early for breakfast."

A smile touched his lips. She sounded like his daughter trying to use logic to get what she wanted from him.

"If I delay my departure, your reputation will suffer even more." Viktor looked over his shoulder at her. "Marry me, Reggie, and we can lie abed until noon and luncheon with our children. Sally and Austen in the beginning, but there will be others."

"If you need to leave," Regina said, ignoring his mention of marriage, "I will not keep you."

"You little minx." Viktor pulled her into his arms and kissed her. "Rest today, love, for we are attending a party tonight."

"We are in mourning. Let's stay home in bed."

"This is no society party," he told her. "Wear something daringly seductive, and bring a black veil to cover your hair. I will provide a mask."

* * *

"Kiss Mama."

Regina smiled at her son and planted a noisy kiss on his cheek, making him laugh. Then she pointed to the floor beside her chair. "Doggy."

Austen pointed at the Great Dane, too. "Kiss doggy."

"No kiss doggy."

"Wak?"

"We can walk." Regina rose from the high-backed chair and set Austen on the floor. Holding his hand, she and her son toddled around the family parlor.

Regina's thoughts wandered to Viktor, the man who had occupied her mind since giving him her virginity. She wished he did not insist on leaving with the dawn. Why should he worry for her reputation if she did not?

"My lady?"

Regina looked at the majordomo, who hurried across the parlor. "Yes, Pickles?"

"Kiss Pik," Austen said.

The majordomo crouched down and planted a kiss on the boy's cheek. Then he stood and announced, "The Countess of Tewksbury is here. Shall I send her away?"

Regina grimaced at the thought of entertaining Vanessa. Then she realized the other woman had lost her brother and could need the comfort of company.

Regina sighed. "Escort her here. Then serve us tea."

"Yes, my lady." Pickles left the parlor.

Regina looked at her son. "Say witch."

"Bitch."

"Very good, Austen." Regina laughed out loud, lifted her son into her arms, and sat on the high-backed chair again.

In a swirl of black silk, Vanessa Stanton walked into the parlor. No dull broadcloth, crepe, or parametta for the Countess of Tewksbury.

"Austen resembles Charles so much," Vanessa said, making herself comfortable on the settee.

"Yes, he does." Avoiding the other woman's gaze, Regina cleared her throat. Good manners required her to mention her brother. "Learning of Cedric's passing saddened me."

"Were you?"

Regina recognized the venom in the other woman's expression. "I wish no one harm." She stood then, unwilling to expose her son to the woman's poison. "Let me return Austen to Nanny Sprig, and then you can say whatever you want."

With her son in her arms, Regina made a hasty exit from the parlor. She stopped short at the stairs and looked down the corridor toward the parlor. Damn, she had left her manuscript on the table near the settee.

Indecision gripped her. Should she return for it? She did not want Vanessa to read her work. On the other hand, she did not want to call undue attention to it lest Vanessa think she was hiding something.

Ten minutes passed before Regina returned to the parlor. Pickles entered on her heels and poured tea. Vanessa had the opened manuscript on her lap.

"I hope you don't mind."

"I *do* mind." Regina reached for the manuscript. "I prefer to finish before allowing others to read it."

"I apologize." Vanessa smiled, a disturbing gesture. "What I read was interesting."

"Thank you." Regina handed the majordomo her manuscript. "Return this to my office."

"Yes, my lady." Pickles left them alone.

"I have a particular reason for visiting you."

Regina looked at her, expecting the worst. "What would that be?"

"Leave Viktor alone," Vanessa warned, "or you will regret it."

"I beg your pardon?" Regina couldn't credit that the other woman was threatening her.

"The prince belongs to me," Vanessa told her. "Leave him alone or I will tell the prosecutor all about you."

"What is there to tell?"

"You threatened Charles, and someone murdered him," Vanessa answered. "Cedric proposed marriage, and he suffered an untimely death."

Regina had the wild idea that Vanessa killed her own brother to make her look guilty. That was too absurd to consider. Wasn't it? How far would she go to win the prince?

"My leaving Viktor alone will not make him love you," Regina said. "Either he does or doesn't."

"If you care for the prince, you will leave him alone," Vanessa said. "Every man interested in you is murdered."

Regina had not considered that. She glanced at her butterfly ring and thought of soaring. She had no intention of rejecting the man she loved but—

"I will never marry the prince," Regina said, her emphatically spoken words ringing true. "I have no desire to marry anyone."

Vanessa smiled in satisfaction and stood. "We understand each other."

Regina stood when she did. "I will not leave him alone, though."

Vanessa did not look pleased, her expression a mask of hatred. "Don't say I didn't warn you."

Regina watched her leave the parlor and then

dropped into her chair. Good Lord, Vanessa Stanton was dangerous. What an idiotic woman to make winning a wealthy, titled husband into a war between them.

Wealthy, titled, and *handsome*. Regina conjured the prince's image in her mind's eye. Definitely handsome.

And virile, too.

"You look a million miles away."

Regina focused on the speaker. Then she smiled and hurried across the parlor to greet Princess Samantha.

"I am so surprised," Regina said. "I never expected—"

"I apologize for intruding."

"You aren't intruding." Regina drew the princess across the parlor to sit on the settee. "I have just suffered a disturbing visit from Vanessa Stanton."

"Oh, Reggie—"

Regina shifted her gaze to the doorway. "Come and join us."

Ginger Evans crossed the parlor and sat beside the princess on the settee.

"Samantha, Ginger Evans is my dearest friend in the whole world," Regina introduced the two women.

Ginger looked embarrassed. "Oh, dear, I should have curtseyed."

"Do *not* dare curtsey to me." Princess Samantha smiled and touched the other woman's hand. "You must be the financial genius my husband and brothers-in-law were discussing."

Ginger blushed. "I hope their comments were complimentary."

"They speak as if you walk on water. Rudolf would

propose marriage if he wasn't already encumbered with me."

"You are too kind."

Samantha looked at Regina. "Someone tried to murder Viktor last night."

Regina paled to a ghastly white, and her heartbeat quickened with her alarm. She was beginning to feel like a jinx.

"What happened?"

"My husband and brothers-in-law were leaving White's," Samantha answered. "Viktor and Mikhail started to cross the street to their coaches when someone tried to run them over. Thankfully, Mikhail pulled Viktor out of the way."

"He never mentioned it last night."

Samantha dropped her mouth open in surprise. Ginger gave her a knowing smile.

Regina looked at her friend. "You knew?"

Ginger nodded. "The whole household knows the prince has been passing his nights here. Pickles gave him his own key last night."

Regina moaned and hid her face in her hands. She never realized how much the titled suffered from an embarrassing lack of privacy. His leaving before dawn had not gone unnoticed.

"That means I won't be the sole female with the Kazanov men." Samantha clapped her hands. "We'll soon be sisters-by-marriage. Stepan intends to marry Fancy Flambeau, if he can win her agreement. Then the three of us will put our heads together to find a bride for Mikhail. The poor man has taken no interest since his wife passed away last year."

Ginger rose from her perch on the settee. "I must be leaving for a luncheon appointment. Meeting you, Your Highness, has been a pleasure."

"Call me Samantha."

"Oh, I couldn't do—"

"I command you to call me Samantha."

Ginger inclined her head. "Samantha, then."

Regina watched her friend leave and then turned to the princess. "I would have thought the opera singer would leap at the chance to marry a prince." Could there possibly be another woman with the same outlook on life?

"Fancy Flambeau harbors a grudge against all aristocrats," Samantha told her. "As a child, her mother fled the Terror, the only one of her aristocratic family to survive."

"But if her mother was—"

"Rumor says Fancy's father is an influential English nobleman who kept her penniless mother."

"Kept?" Regina felt confused. "Where did he keep her?"

Princess Samantha laughed. "I meant, this anonymous nobleman made her mother his mistress. Together, they produced seven daughters, Fancy being the eldest."

"Seven daughters?"

"There were two sets of twins."

Regina decided there were worse things in life than dealing with her own father's blustering. "What happened to Prince Mikhail's wife?"

"Elizabeth died from pneumonia last year and left him with a four-year-old daughter," Samantha answered. "I keep telling him he needs a mother for his daughter and a wife to give him an heir. Mikhail loved Elizabeth dearly so he resists."

"How sad."

"We should begin planning your wedding," Samantha suggested.

"I cannot marry Viktor," Regina said. "A prince

and a merchant's daughter could never enjoy a happy union."

"What about a prince and a pickpocket?"

"I beg your pardon?"

"Before marrying Rudolf, I picked pockets to survive." Samantha smiled at her skeptical expression. "My father was a drunken, bankrupt earl. My aunt, my sisters, and I lived in a cottage on the far side of Primrose Hill.

"The Duke of Inverary had been my father's closest friend. Discovering our whereabouts, His Grace sent for us and gave us a home with him.

"The rest is history, as they say. My aunt married the duke, my sister Angelica married his son, and my sister Victoria married the Earl of Winchester. I met Rudolf at the very first ball I ever attended."

"How romantic," Regina said. "May I use your story in a book?"

"Only if you promise not to use our real names."

Pickles walked into the parlor. The majordomo set a fresh tea tray on the table and began pouring.

Princess Samantha winked at Regina. "Pickles, do you carry money on your person? Or a pocket watch?"

Pickles looked at the princess. If he thought her question odd, his expression did not show it. "A pocket watch, Your Highness."

Samantha crossed the parlor to the doorway. "Walk toward me as if we were passing on the street."

Pickles did as she'd requested. The princess tripped and bumped into him.

"Excuse me, sir," she said, giving him a sweet smile. "Please check your pockets."

Pickles stuck his hands in his jacket pockets and came up empty. Frowning, he checked the inside pocket.

"Are you looking for this?" Samantha swung the pocket watch in front of his face.

Regina burst into appreciative laughter and clapped her hands. Pickles gave the princess a puzzled smile, accepted his watch, and left the room.

"A lady should always have an extra means of income in the event her husband gambles everything away," Samantha said, her eyes sparkling with merriment.

"I have my writing, Ginger has her mathematical ability, and you have your own particular talent."

Princess Samantha sipped her tea and looked at her over the rim of the cup. "The Kazanov brothers are embarking on their own murder investigation."

"What precisely is their plan?" Regina knew the princess would tell her the whole truth, not an edited version like Viktor did.

"Mikhail is making the rounds of the cockfights and other violent arenas of gambling. Stepan is scouring the bawdy houses since extreme cruelty makes him nauseous." Princess Samantha smiled. "My husband wisely preferred to maintain his good health and is visiting all the gentlemen's clubs. Viktor and you are attending a party tonight? I heard it would be wildly risqué."

"Viktor did tell me to wear something seductive and bring a dark veil. He will supply a mask."

"Which brings me to the purpose of my visit," Samantha said. "You must know the basics of self-defense."

"*You* will teach *me* about self-defense?"

Samantha flicked the bottom edge of her skirt up. Attached to the garter strapped on her leg was a small, black leather sheath. The blade it carried appeared about four inches long.

"This is a weapon of last resort," the princess said, pointing to the deadly little dagger.

Regina looked from the dagger to the princess's face and then back to the dagger. She could not believe that a sophisticated, society lady wore a dagger strapped to her leg.

"Old habits die hard, as they say." Samantha reached into her reticule and produced another weapon of last resort, complete with garter and sheath and blade.

Regina pulled the edge of her skirt up and strapped the last resort to her left leg. Then she looked at the princess for further instructions.

"The first goal is getting your last resort unsheathed," Samantha told her, "and the second goal is using it effectively."

The princess stood and faced her. In a flash of movement, she reached down and pulled the last resort from its sheath.

"To reach your last resort, you can do what I did. You can also pretend to trip or swoon."

Regina stood and tried each of the princess's ploys. By far the easiest were pretending to swoon and grabbing the dagger from a sitting position.

"Speed comes with practice," Samantha assured her. "Once the blade is in hand, you must effectively use it. Hold the dagger in a firm but flexible grip up and away from your body, not down. A thrust is faster than a circular cut. With a last resort, you want speed with accuracy."

Regina passed the next thirty minutes practicing unsheathing her last resort in the proper grip. If her situation required a blade, she would not have time to position it correctly. She needed to unsheath in the proper position.

Speed, speed, speed.

Accuracy, accuracy, accuracy.
Speed and accuracy married in one fluid movement.

"You need to strike your adversary where the blade will do the most harm," Samantha said. "Stabbing a throat artery is effective but bloody. Your adversary will instinctively reach for his throat, leaving the rest of him unprotected. You can then thrust the blade into his heart."

Regina closed her eyes at the graphic instructions. Lord, but the thought of thrusting and cutting made her nauseous.

"If you want to get away from an attacker without killing him," Samantha continued, "stabbing his eyes will blind him and give you a chance to escape."

"Maybe I should wear a last resort on each leg," Regina said.

"What an outstanding idea." Princess Samantha unfastened her own last resort and passed it to her. "Don't worry. Rudolf will buy me another. By the way, did you receive my aunt's invitation to her annual ladies luncheon?"

Regina needed a moment to make the unlikely switch in conversation from cutting a man's throat to an innocuous luncheon. "Yes, I did receive the invitation."

"I hope you plan to attend," Samantha said. "The duchess does this every year on the day the gentlemen golf on Pall Mall."

"Yes, I will definitely attend."

"Are you all right?"

Regina gave the princess a wan smile. "Practicing to gut another person has turned my stomach queasy."

"I apologize for that, but—"

"—but I may need that knowledge one day."

* * *

Located in Mayfair between King Street and Pall Mall, Crown Passage hid a seemingly secret world of tiny shops and quiet pubs. Peacefulness pervaded the atmosphere, cutting it off from the area's busiest streets.

Established before the reign of Charles II, the Red Lion Tavern stood between cobbler and ironmonger shops. The tavern's lighting was comfortably dim, the conversations muted. The aromas of roasting beef and frying fish and simmering soup mingled deliciously with ale and beer.

Amadeus pulled out a chair and then sat opposite her. "The Red Lion is one of my favorite places."

Ginger smiled. "Like an oasis of peace in a world of chaos."

A waitress appeared. "What'll it be, folks?"

"Roast beef with horseradish sauce," Amadeus said. "Roasted potatoes. Ale for me and—?" He looked at her.

"Tea," Ginger said.

"Finally, we managed a lunch without someone dying," Amadeus said, once the waitress had gone.

"It wasn't for lack of trying on the villain's part."

Amadeus cocked a dark brow at her. "Explain yourself."

Ginger leaned forward and lowered her voice. "Someone tried to kill Prince Viktor last night." His surprised expression satisfied her. "The culprit tried to run him over."

"A carriage accident is a world away from a shooting," Amadeus said. "If it was deliberate, the prince did not report it."

"Perhaps he doesn't trust you."

lowest common denominator. Once we know who the murderer is, we can get the evidence."

"The lowest common denominator?" Amadeus echoed.

Ginger nodded, emphatic in her belief. *"Lowest common denominator."*

Chapter 14

The coach halted in the main courtyard at the Earl of Swinesford's country estate. Dementia turned an anxious gaze on her escort.

"What you see will shock your sensibilities," the Duke of Charming warned her.

"I am no virgin." Dementia sounded more confident than she felt.

The duke covered her lovely face with a jeweled mask, showing only her eyes, and passed her a red and gold fan. He climbed out of the coach and helped her down.

Dementia placed her hand in his, and together, they walked toward the mansion. Once inside, the duke led her in the direction of the grand ballroom. She heard music, voices, and laughter.

"Oh, my." Dementia stopped short, her gaze riveted on the center of the ballroom. A nearly naked woman poised on her knees on top of the table. A man stood in front of her, and she was—

"She's a professional," the duke whispered.

Dementia looked at him. "What profession?"

"The world's oldest."

"Are you wearing *that?*"

Regina turned slowly in a circle. She wore a strapless, black velvet evening gown, cut daringly low.

Her well turned ankles showed below the gown's hem as did her black kid sandals and her embroidered silk stockings. She wore long black gloves and carried a sheer black veil. Her only splash of color was her vibrant red hair.

"What do you think?"

"That gown is immodest," Ginger answered. "You are in mourning."

"I'm wearing black."

Ginger laughed at that.

"Viktor is giving me a mask so no one will know who I am." Regina sat on the edge of the bed. On her left leg, she strapped a garter with leather sheath and last resort dagger. Then she fastened the second on her right leg.

"Is that necessary?"

"Being prepared never hurts." With the second garter attached to her leg, Regina straightened and a wave of dizziness crashed into her. Rolling queasiness pitched this way and that in the pit of her stomach. She placed one hand on her throat to swallow the nausea and one hand on the mattress to steady herself.

"Are you all right?"

Regina managed a wan smile, but these increasing bouts of nausea worried her. "The thought of the princess's gory instructions leaves me woozy and nauseous."

"Perhaps you should cancel."

"I will be fine," Regina assured her, "if I do not dwell on stabbing eyes and cutting arteries." She stood and looked at her friend. "I feel safer knowing protection is strapped on my leg."

"Those measly daggers will be useless against a pistol."

"If I knew how to use a pistol," Regina said, "Pros-

ecutor Lowing would have locked me in the Tower
for murdering Charles and Cedric."

"I suppose you're right."

Instead of covering her head with the veil, Regina
draped it around her shoulders, hiding her cleavage, and slanted a smile at the other woman, "I do
not want my flesh to startle Pickles. Good heavens,
the man would swoon dead away."

Standing with the majordomo in the foyer,
Prince Viktor stopped talking the moment he saw
her walking down the stairs. Regina appeared sultry, dressed completely in black with that sheer veil
draped around her. Even more enticing was the
love that shone from her disarming green eyes.

Viktor bowed over her hand, her scent of jasmine
and vanilla seducing his senses. "My lady, you look
ravishing."

Regina gave him an ambiguous smile. "Thank
you, Your Highness."

"Have an enjoyable evening," Pickles said, opening the door for them.

Regina inclined her head. "Thank you, Pickles."

Ensconced inside his closed coach, Viktor
grasped one edge of the sheer black veil and pulled
slowly, exposing her bare skin inch by inch. His
black gaze missed nothing, bared shoulders in the
strapless gown, nearly bared breasts in the low-cut
bodice.

"I said daring, not naked." His gaze lingered on
the upper swell of her breasts. "I dislike the thought
of others ogling what belongs to me. Do not wear
that gown in public again."

Regina arched a perfectly shaped copper brow at
him. "These breasts belong to me."

Viktor guided her hand to bulge at his groin. "This
belongs to you, and your breasts belong to me."

"You are crass, Your Highness."

"I am preparing you for the evening's risqué activities."

"How bad can risqué be?"

"You will see sights you never imagined."

"Like what?"

"Like nothing you have ever seen." Viktor reached for something on the opposite leather seat, a black wig with shoulder-length straight hair and bangs. Pieces of hair on the sides had been braided with colorful beads. "I want you to wear this. Your hair color is too recognizable." He set the wig in place on her head. "You look like a different woman."

"The Queen of the Nile?"

"Nobody will recognize you now. The demi-mask will hold the wig securely in place."

"Let me see it."

The black demi-mask covered three-fourths of her face, ending above her mouth. Glittering gold beading outlined its eye openings.

"Ladies will be masked, but the whores will not bother."

"Do many ladies attend?"

Viktor shrugged. "Enough, I suppose."

"Tell me what you expect to learn tonight," Regina said. "Do you believe the murderer will be there?"

"We are going to the home of Edward Shores, Baron Bromley, also known as Crazy Eddie," Viktor said, making her laugh. "Crazy Eddie loans gentlemen money at exorbitant interest rates. I want to look at his books to see if Charles or Cedric owed him."

"Why don't you just ask Crazy Eddie if they owed money?"

"If he is guilty," Viktor answered, "Eddie will not divulge that information."

"Then tell Constable Black to ask him."

"I cannot do that, Reggie. The man's business is illegal."

"If Crazy Eddie murdered his customers," Regina said, "how could he make money?"

"If the punishment for one delinquent debtor is death," Viktor answered, "the others will pay on time."

"That is a definite possibility."

"Reggie, you will see some extreme activities at the party." Viktor put his arm around her shoulders and drew her close, as if to protect her from what she would see. "If you want to remain in the coach, my man will protect you."

"I will not swoon," Regina said, making him smile. "By the way, Vanessa Stanton visited me this morning."

Viktor knew the Countess of Tewksbury had not intended a social visit. "And?"

"Vanessa threatened to accuse me of murder if I didn't leave you alone."

This new threat was not what he needed at the moment. Viktor refused to let Prosecutor Lowing arrest his intended wife. Before he spoke, he knew his next suggestion would upset her.

"I will escort Vanessa to a few social events." Viktor watched for her reaction. "That is, until the murderer is caught."

Regina rounded on him, and there was no mistaking her disgruntled expression. "Vanessa does not frighten me. If you do that, do not visit my bed afterwards."

"I will go home those nights." She opened her mouth to argue, but he added, "We have arrived."

When the coach halted, Viktor checked her wig and mask to verify nothing was out of place. He climbed out and then helped her down.

Taking the prince's offered arm, Regina let him escort her toward the mansion. Other guests emerged from coaches and headed for the mansion, too. There were masked and unmasked women and, good Lord, several gentlemen she recognized from various society events.

"Do not leave my side," Viktor instructed her. "I prefer not to share you."

Regina snapped her gaze to his. "Share me?"

Viktor pulled her off to one side, letting others pass, and drew her into his embrace. "Do you want to wait in the coach?"

"No, I want to go with you." Regina summoned her courage though she felt as if she were about to walk through the gates of hell. A den of iniquity, at the very least.

The muted light from hundreds of candles placed inside red lanterns set an intimate mood. Sounds and scents wafted through the air, beckoning them. Sensuous music provided the background for voices and laughter. Myriad perfumes mingled with the unmistakeable aromas of whisky, ale, and beer.

Regina tightened her grip on the prince's hand. She smiled when he gave it an encouraging squeeze.

"The masked women accompanied by escorts are those gentlemen's mistresses," Viktor said. "The masked females without escort are married and bored and seeking thrills."

Regina paused in the entrance to the ballroom and inched closer to Viktor. He was correct. She would never have envisioned this scene.

Men and women mingled informally in the

crowded ballroom. Drinking and dancing. Talking and touching.

Regina noted the touching straightaway. So proper and formal at society functions, these gentlemen made free with their hands, fondling whoever they wished and whenever they wanted. Scandalously attired in the most daring gowns, the women flirted and allowed the gentlemen shocking liberties.

"Most of the action takes place here." Viktor pressed her close against his side. "A buffet will be set in the dining room, high stakes gambling in the drawing room, and the bedrooms available for any couple's use."

Without warning, Viktor turned her to face him. His lips swooped down and captured hers in a kiss that stole her breath and curled her toes.

"*Kazanov.*"

Breaking the kiss, Viktor pulled her in front of him and held her back against his powerful body. His arousal pressed into her bottom, exciting her even in this public place.

Viktor nodded at the man who had approached them. "Good to see you, Eddie. The evening appears headed for success."

Crazy Eddie was passably good-looking. In his late twenties, he was tall and well-built. Though not quite as tall and handsome as the prince.

"I haven't seen you in eons," Eddie said conversationally, his gaze fixed on her bosom. "Who is this breathtaking Cleopatra?"

"She is the reason no one has seen me in eons," Viktor answered, eliciting a chuckle from the other man. He dropped a hand to cup her breast. "Can you blame me?"

Regina was shocked by his public groping. Her

face flamed beneath the mask, a pretty flush spread across the tops of her breasts, and her breathing came in harsh gasps.

"The lady is panting for you now," Eddie remarked. "Would you consider sharing? I would make your sacrifice worthwhile."

"*No.*" Viktor sounded emphatic and tightened his embrace.

"I didn't expect you would." Eddie looked at her. "When you tire of the Russian, you will find a place with me." He shifted his gaze to the prince. "You know where the bedrooms are located." With that, Crazy Eddie walked away.

Regina rounded on Viktor. "How d-dare you g-grope me in p-public?" she sputtered in an outraged whisper.

"I warned you." Viktor leaned close and nuzzled her neck. "People are watching us, my love."

"I stand corrected." Regina smiled but narrowed her gaze on him. "How do you know where the bedrooms are located?"

Viktor laughed in her face. "You sound like a wife, not a mistress." He drew her against the muscular planes of his body and wrapped her in his embrace. A hand slid down her back to caress her bottom. "Mistresses are subservient and—"

"Subservient, my arse."

"Reggie, you insisted on accompanying me," he reminded her. "Trouble will find us if you do not play your role convincingly."

"Is this convincing enough?" Regina asked, rubbing her body against him. She slid her hand across the muscles of his chest and glided it passed his taut belly to caress the bulge at his groin. "Or that?"

"You are getting into the spirit of the performance." Cupping her buttocks, Viktor lifted her and grinded his arousal against her body.

"Ladies and gentlemen," Crazy Eddie called, standing on an enormous pedestal at the opposite end of the ballroom. "The evening's festivities will soon begin."

Regina turned in the circle of the prince's arms to watch the proceedings. She felt flustered to note the man's gaze on her, knowing he must have seen the prince and her grinding their bodies together.

"I do believe you have made a conquest in Eddie," Viktor murmured.

Crazy Eddie gestured to a woman who was disrobing beside the pedestal. "This naughty lady has agreed to pose for your viewing pleasure on the pedestal. She will, of course, remain masked."

Their host leaped off the pedestal and offered the naked woman his hand. She accepted it without hesitation and allowed him to press a kiss on each breast. Then he lifted her onto the pedestal, and she gifted her audience with a beguiling smile.

Regina could not believe a lady had disrobed in front of all these lechers and placed herself on display. Several gentlemen were already sliding their hands across her more interesting body parts.

"She is one of the lucky ones," Viktor whispered, the warmth of his breath sending deliciously sensual chills through her body. "When a lady cannot settle her debts, Eddie accepts her body as payment."

"He must be exhausted," Regina drawled, and smiled at the prince's chuckle.

"Actually, Eddie finds a man willing to pay to bed the masked lady in one of the upstairs bedchambers," Viktor told her. "You cannot imagine the number of coachmen and grooms willing to trade a year's salary for an hour inside a real lady."

"But that is—"

"Shhh." Viktor nuzzled the side of her throat and slid his lips to her ear. "Anything goes at a private party. Come, Cleopatra. Let us wander to the dining room for a drink." With his arm around her shoulders, he led her away from the ballroom.

"When do we search for the ledgers?"

"Patience is a virtue, my love," he murmured, dropping a hand from her shoulder to her rump. "We do not want to call attention to ourselves."

Gaining the dining room, Regina accepted the offered crystal flute. She sipped champagne and wondered how she could integrate tonight's adventure into her manuscript.

"Your Highness."

Regina shifted her gaze from the prince to the newcomer. He was a stocky, expensively dressed middle-aged man. She knew he was titled but could not place him.

Viktor nodded at him. "Burlington."

"Who is this delightful Queen of the Nile?" Burlington reached to trace his pudgy fingertips across the exposed swell of her breasts.

Viktor caught the hand before it made contact. "This exquisite creature is my private property. Look but do not touch."

"I cannot fault you for that." Burlington chuckled, his gaze riveted on her exposed flesh. "You always did have impeccable taste in women."

All men are pigs, Regina decided, her anger simmering. They were discussing women like horses in their stables. Steering clear of these arrogant, masculine beasts had been sensible. Not one of them viewed women as people, merely toys for their immediate pleasure. The last resorts strapped to her legs itched to be unsheathed.

"So, have you ended your affair with the merchant's daughter?" Burlington asked. "How fortunate to be nesting between the slut's thighs the night—you know. I hope you don't mind me asking."

"I do mind you asking." Regina heard the prince's irritation, but then his tone became conspiratorial. "Lady Bradford will become my wife, and this delectable Cleopatra will remain my mistress."

Lord Burlington made a hasty escape. No doubt, to spread that tasty tidbit of gossip.

"How could you?" Regina whispered. "We'll be reading about ourselves in tomorrow's papers."

"The *Times* will probably carry it the day after tomorrow since the hour is late." Viktor gave her an infuriatingly wolfish smile and slipped a grilled shrimp between her lips. "Women should be seen, not heard."

The high stakes gambling in the drawing room required infinite concentration unlike the frenetic party in the ballroom. Fortunes could be won or lost and, Regina now knew, an unlucky roll of the dice could force a lady to spread her legs in an upstairs bedchamber.

Viktor and Regina wandered in silence from table to table to watch the games in progress. When they had circled the room and reached the door, he pulled her into the corridor.

Regina felt her heartbeat quicken, knowing the moment of snooping had arrived. Her nerves rioted in fear of exposure. No doubt, Crazy Eddie would kill the prince and force her into an upstairs bechamber.

Viktor located the office within minutes, and they slipped inside, silently closing the door behind. The prince stood motionless, his gaze scanning the chamber.

"What's wrong?" Regina whispered.

"I am deciding the most likely place to hide the ledger."

"Try the desk."

"The desk is too obvious," he said. "Eddie would keep it locked."

"Try the desk first."

Viktor rolled his eyes, his expression telling her how dumb she was. Lovely but dumb.

With an air of resignation, Viktor crossed the chamber to the desk. The prince was humoring her instead of wasting time by arguing. He pulled the middle drawer and flashed her a look of surprise. The desk was unlocked.

Regina met his gaze. Her smile told him how dumb he was. Handsome but dumb.

Viktor withdrew a ledger from the drawer. He flipped through the pages, stopped at one, and ran a finger the length of the page.

"They owed nothing substantial." Viktor replaced the ledger and then hurried her to the door.

Voices. Regina stopped short and looked at the prince in alarm. There were voices coming down the corrdior. A deep, masculine voice. A woman's drunken giggle.

"I'll take payment now," Crazy Eddie was saying, "but not in the corridor. Come into my office, pretty lady, and lie across my desk."

"Sorry, love." Viktor grabbed Regina and shoved her back against the wall. He pulled her arms above her head and easily held her wrists in one hand. Then he yanked the strapless gown's bodice down, freeing her breasts, making her gasp.

"Remember, your mask hides your identity." Viktor dropped his head, captured a breast in his mouth, and sucked hard. His tongue flicked across the tip of her nipple.

Regina closed her eyes, a moan rising in her throat as the study door opened. She sensed another's presence and heard a woman's giggle.

"Let's the four of us be naughty together," the woman suggested, her gaze on the prince.

"I would love to indulge you," Eddie said, his gaze on Regina's breasts, "but the prince won't share."

Viktor was in no hurry to stop what he was doing. He cupped each breast and gave each nipple a final suck.

"I shared the view." Viktor drew her bodice up slowly, giving the other man a tantalizingly long look. "When I finish with Cleopatra, I will send her along to you."

With that, Viktor grasped her upper arm and pulled her into the corridor. They hurried downstairs to the foyer and escaped outside.

"Go!" And their coach started down the drive toward the gates.

Only then did Regina let her righteous outrage surface. "I cannot believe that you—"

Viktor kissed her into silence. He pulled her onto his lap, facing him, and yanked her bodice down. Then he rooted on one large, dusky nipple while his fingers tormented the other.

"Wrap your legs around me." His voice was thick and hoarse with desire. When she did, he freed his manhood, lifted and poised her over it.

Regina lowered herself onto his shaft, taking him deep until their groins touched. And then she moved, back and forth, the motion of the coach adding to her exquisite pleasure.

Viktor leaned forward, his lips tugging on a distended nipple. She melted and collapsed against him, his possession sending her over the edge. With her satisfaction assured, he let himself go and followed her into a paradise of sensation.

"Do not move," Viktor ordered, recovering himself. "I want to stay inside you all the way back to London."

Regina trembled, his words rekindling her desire.

"What the bloody hell is pressing into me," Viktor asked, reaching for her legs. He touched the objects strapped to her legs and then shouted with laughter. "My dearest sister-in-law has been tutoring you in the art of self-defense."

London was sleeping by the time the coach halted in front of Bradford House. Viktor climbed out and helped her down.

"Return at dawn," he instructed his driver.

"We made love already," Regina said. "Why didn't you go home?"

Viktor ushered her into the foyer before answering. "I like sleeping with you in my arms."

His romantic sentiment surprised Regina. Her smile could have lit the whole mansion.

There *were* exceptions to the men-are-pigs rule. Prince Viktor was one of those.

"Are you tired?" he asked, putting his arm around her, guiding her up the stairs.

"Only a little."

Gaining the bedchamber, Viktor turned her around to unfasten her gown. He brushed aside the back of the black wig to nuzzle the slender column of her neck.

"The Cleopatra wig makes you look like a different woman," Viktor said, undressing and tossing his evening clothes across the back of the settee.

"That relieves my mind." Regina drew the bed's coverlet down. "I cannot believe those ladies—"

"You should wear the wig sometimes when we make love."

There were no exceptions to the men-are-pigs rule.

Regina rounded on him and pulled the wig off. "I beg your pardon?"

Only a dead man would have missed her disgruntled expression.

"I was joking," Viktor said, climbing into bed. "A very, very poor joke . . ."

The prince had spoken truthfully about liking to sleep beside her. He gathered her into his arms, dropped a kiss on the crown of her head, and promptly fell asleep.

Regina awakened alone in the morning. She had roused herself for a few moments when the prince left at dawn.

Glancing toward the light streaming through the window, Regina realized the hour was later than usual. Austen would be looking for her.

With her son in mind, Regina forced herself out of bed. The nausea struck with sudden impact. She covered her mouth and raced across the chamber. Draped over the pot, she heaved dryly.

"Reggie!" On her way into the bedchamber, Ginger dashed across the room and held her hair away from her face.

When her spasms ended, Regina said, "Fetch me a robe." Naked and exhausted, she sat on the floor and let her friend cover her with the robe.

"I'll help you to bed and send for the physician."

Regina waved that suggestion aside. "Leave me here to die in peace."

"A physician can help you."

"No one can help me," Regina moaned in misery. "I am pregnant."

Ginger paled by several shades. "Did you tell the prince?"

"I cannot do that now."

"Do you have a screw loose?" Ginger stood with her hands on her hips. "You *must* tell the prince immediately. He will want his child born in wedlock."

"If Viktor forces me to the altar," Regina said, "the murderer will shoot him."

"Nobody would dare harm the prince," Ginger insisted. "His brothers would chase the villain through the gates of hell."

"I want to soar," Regina whined, feeling trapped and sorry for herself.

"You should have gone to bed with that aspiration instead of the prince."

"He tricked me by making me desire him."

That made Ginger smile.

"And he told me to wear that damn black wig so I'll look like a different woman in bed."

Ginger laughed in her face. "Reggie, the prince will never forgive your silence."

Regina sighed in defeat. "I will tell him as soon as possible."

"I won't forget to remind you," Ginger said, helping her to bed.

Regina narrowed her gaze on her friend and secretly crossed two fingers at her lie. "I said I'll tell him as soon as possible."

"See that you do." Ginger headed for the door. "I'll bring you tea and toast."

Regina uncrossed her fingers. As soon as possible would be after the murderer had been caught.

Chapter 15

From a distance of ten feet, Dementia studied the two circles painted on the silver birch tree in her garden. One circle had been painted at the approximate neck level of a six-foot man and the other level with his heart.

In one fluid motion, Dementia flipped the bottom edge of her gown and grabbed the last resort daggers strapped on each leg. She aimed the first blade at the neck level, flashed the second dagger into her right hand, and tossed it at the heart circle.

Two direct hits! Too bad she hadn't been born ambidextrous. Moving the dagger from her left hand to her right wasted precious seconds.

"Bravo!"

Dementia whirled around. "Ginnie." She hurried across the garden to embrace her dearest friend.

"You won't use that skill on me?"

"I have been frightened since Bertie died." Dementia took her friend's hand and led her to a stone bench. "How do you manage to visit at the very moment I need a friend?"

Ginnie winked at her. "I'm a witch, of course."

Dementia smiled and then grew serious. "I am carrying the Duke of Charming's child."

"What wonderful news," Ginnie gushed. "His Grace must be ecstatic. When is the wedding?"

"My news is not wonderful," Dementia said. "His Grace doesn't know, and even if he did, he would never marry me."

"The duke adores you."

"His Grace hasn't called upon me recently." Dementia sighed and shook her head. "Rumor says he escorted the Countess of Tyngsboro to the opera."

"Success to our murder investigation." Prince Viktor raised his glass in salute and then downed the shot of vodka in one gulp.

With him were Princes Rudolf, Mikhail, and Stepan. His brothers gulped their vodka, too.

"You should have seen Reggie when the woman disrobed to pose on the pedestal." Viktor chuckled at the memory. "I had hidden her with a mask and a black wig, only her mouth and eyes visible above the neck. She dropped her mouth open in surprise and her eyes nearly popped out of the mask."

The other Kazanov princes laughed at the picture he created. "I understand my wife gave the lady self-defense lessons," Rudolf said.

"And weapons, too." Viktor grinned at his brothers. "Those damn daggers bruised my legs."

His brothers laughed again.

"Did you hear any gossip about Charles or Cedric?" Prince Mikhail asked.

Viktor shook his head. "Protecting Reggie from would-be lovers kept me busy. Burlington called her the Queen of the Nile, and even jaded Crazy Eddie wanted me to share her."

Prince Stepan refilled the four vodka glasses. "The lady must have looked good in the black wig."

"Nobody was looking above her neck, Brother," Viktor said, slanting an amused glance at him. "Reggie wore a low-cut, strapless gown which, I assure you, she will never wear in public again." He leaned back in his chair and sipped the vodka. "Crazy Eddie almost caught us with his gambling ledger."

"What happened?" Rudolf asked.

"We were leaving the room when voices sounded in the corridor," Viktor answered. "I recognized Crazy Eddie's voice."

"Did Eddie walk past the room?" Mikhail asked. "How did you escape detection?"

Viktor opened his mouth to answer but then shut it. "I should not repeat what happened. Reggie would be mortified if she knew I told you."

"Come on, Viktor." Prince Stepan leaned close to his older brother. "You know you want to tell us."

"We will never reveal what we know," Prince Mikhail coaxed him.

"If you do not hurry," Prince Rudolf added, "Ginger Evans will arrive, and you will not relate the story then."

"You remind me of when we were boys." Viktor grinned and lowered his voice. "I pushed Reggie against the wall, yanked her bodice down, and sucked on a nipple."

His three brothers shouted with laughter. The youngest refilled their glasses and raised his in salute.

"I honor your creative thinking." After gulping his vodka, Stepan set the empty glass on the carpet and shattered it with the heel of his boot.

"Her tits mesmerized Eddie into inaction," Viktor added, eliciting more laughter.

"I salute you." Rudolf gulped his vodka and slammed his boot down to break the glass.

"Then the woman with Eddie suggested a foursome," Viktor finished.

"I salute you, too." Mikhail gulped his vodka and tossed his glass into the darkened hearth.

"I daresay, Lady Regina was not singing your praises," Rudolf said. "By the way, I had no luck at the gentlemen's clubs."

"I visited every brothel in London," Stepan reported. "No luck."

"Are you complaining?" Viktor asked.

Stepan shrugged. "Too many whores are like too many sweets."

"And I am sick unto death with the bloodletting of bears, cocks, and dogs," Mikhail complained. "The Lord Mayor should shut those places down."

"Charles and Cedric owed Eddie no substantial debt," Viktor said. "That troubles me because I do not believe either of the murders was random."

Someone tapped on the door, drawing their attention. Godfrey, the prince's majordomo, stepped into the study. "Miss Evans has arrived."

Prince Viktor crossed to the door and smiled at the young woman waiting in the corridor. "Come in," he said, drawing her forward. "We saved you the seat of honor."

Looking prim as a governess, Ginger Evans sat in the chair in front of the desk. She turned to Prince Rudolf, saying, "I had the pleasure of meeting your wife."

"Samantha mentioned that she visited Lady Regina to share her knowledge of daggers," Rudolf said.

"Reggie startled me last night when she fastened those daggers to her legs." Ginger looked at Viktor. "When I left Bradford House, she was ordering Artie to paint circles on one of the trees in the garden."

"Painting circles on trees?" he echoed in puzzled amusement.

Ginger nodded. "Reggie had Artie measuring where the neck and the heart would be located if

the tree was a six-foot man." The four Kazanov
princes laughed at that. "She swears she'll practice
tossing the daggers every day until she gets a direct
hit each time she throws."

Viktor smiled at his beloved's persistence, just
one of her many remarkable attributes. Regina,
Ginger, and Samantha refused to behave like most
women. Writing books, investing money, and even
picking pockets fell into the realm of men's work;
apparently, no one had told them, and each was
more interesting because of that.

"What is all this broken glass?" Ginger asked,
making the princes laugh. She looked at each and
then said, "Shall we begin?"

Prince Rudolf retrieved his papers. While his
brothers lounged in their chairs, he spoke about
percentage of profits and projections for the next
quarter.

When he finished, Ginger asked, "Have you considered investing in grain farms to create a beer
and ale cartel?"

Prince Stepan laughed, earning a censorious
stare from his brothers. "I cannot help it," he defended himself. "Listening to a female speak about
business is like hearing a dog singing an opera."

Ginger rounded on the youngest prince. "I beg
your pardon?"

"I—I—I meant no insult," Stepan said. "Please accept my apology."

She didn't. Which made Viktor smile. Lord, but
Ginger's attitude reminded him of Reggie. He wondered who had infected whom.

"I promise never to say anything—ah, stupid—
again," Stepan continued making amends.

"Perhaps you shouldn't speak at all," Ginger
said, eliciting chuckles from the other princes.

She passed papers to all the princes. "I calculated the financial viability of such an undertaking, and my agents are investigating farms for sale. We should offer the farmers who become our employees an assured salary, bonuses for production above a certain amount, and one percent of the profits."

"Why do you suggest that?" Viktor asked.

"People who work for themselves work harder," Ginger answered. "We would assume the financial burden and risk but provide an incentive for hard work. A limited franchise, in a manner of speaking."

"What do you mean by limited?" Prince Stepan asked.

Viktor struggled against laughter when Ginger informed his brother, "*Limited* means restricted."

Stepan flushed but remained impeccably polite. "Thank you."

"You are welcome." Ginger looked at the other princes. "As long as the farmer works the land for us, he—"

"Or she," Prince Stepan interrupted.

Ginger gave him a grudging smile. "Your Highness, I do believe you are not entirely beyond redemption. The farmer would be entitled to one percent profit while employed by us."

"I like this idea," Rudolf said.

"So do I," Mikhail agreed.

"I like it, too," Viktor said.

Ginger looked at Stepan. He winked at her and nodded.

"Give me a week to study these calculations," Rudolf said.

"Of course." Ginger turned to Viktor and lowered her voice. "We need to discuss a situation developing with Reggie."

Her words caught him by surprise. Viktor nodded, everyone's attention on him. "I have no secrets from my brothers. You can speak freely in their presence."

"Reggie is pregnant."

"What?" Viktor bolted out of his chair, making his brothers laugh. "I must go to her."

"No!" When he looked at her, Ginger said, "You aren't supposed to know until Reggie tells you."

"Then I will visit her," Viktor said, "and she will tell me."

"You know Reggie, Your Highness. She will not accept the most expedient solution to the problem. Reggie fears marrying you will endanger your life."

"That is ridiculous."

"Reggie wants to soar, whatever that means." Ginger shook her head in disapproval. "She believes you tricked her by making her feel desire, and now you will stifle her with marriage."

Viktor ran a hand through his black hair in frustration and tried to ignore his brothers' smiles. "Regina should consider the baby, not her selfish aspirations."

"She should have bedded those aspirations instead of you," Ginger agreed.

Princes Rudolf, Mikhail, and Stepan laughed at that. Even Viktor smiled in spite of his irritation.

"I made her promise to tell you as soon as possible," Ginger said, "but she crossed her fingers at the lie. She must really think I'm a blind fool."

"Lady Regina crossed what?" Rudolf asked.

"She crossed her fingers. One can lie with impunity if one crosses her fingers."

Three Kazanov princes burst into laughter at

such female foolishness. Only Prince Stepan spoke up, "That sounds logical to me."

"Do not overdo it," Ginger drawled. "Reggie crossed her fingers the day she testified in court. Pickles and I—"

"The majordomo and you discussed this?" Viktor could not believe what he was hearing.

"Yes." Ginger flicked a glance at his smiling brothers. "Do you want to observe propriety or marry Regina?"

A servant and a slip of a girl advising him on women? This was getting out of hand. "Are you and that majordomo giving me advice?"

"We believe a bit of old-fashioned jealousy could work a miracle," Ginger said. "Reggie is as jealous of Vanessa Stanton as Vanessa is of her. We suggest you ignore Reggie for a few days and squire Vanessa around town. The *Times* will probably mention your social activities."

Prince Viktor was silent for a long moment. Jealousy was not an original idea, nor was it a bad one. He looked at his brothers. "Vanessa threatened Reggie with an accusation of murder if she didn't get out of my life."

Prince Rudolf raised his brows. "I suppose hell hath no fury."

Viktor looked at Ginger. "Reggie cannot be too far along. I can spare a few days for playacting before I drag her to the altar."

Regina awakened late the next morning. Had Viktor come to her bed last night and gone at dawn without her waking? She rolled toward his side of the bed. The pillow showed no sign of use.

In an attempt to keep nausea at bay, Regina

moved slowly until she sat on the edge of the bed. She closed her eyes and took deep breaths.

Morning sickness is a state of mind, Regina told herself.

It didn't work.

She bolted across the bedchamber to the pot. An empty stomach did not lessen the violence of her spasms.

Regina wished her mother had never died. She needed to consult a woman experienced in childbearing. There could be a way to alleviate this horrible nausea. How would she ever finish her manuscript if she was sick?

After resting on the bed for another fifteen minutes, Regina felt better. She dressed and went downstairs to breakfast.

"Good morning," Regina called, walking into the dining room.

Pickles stood at the sideboard. Regina sat across the table from Ginger.

"How do you feel this morning?"

"I—" Regina looked down at the cup of coffee the majordomo placed in front of her. "I want tea."

"You always start the day with coffee," Pickles said.

"Today I want black tea, dry toast, and a scrambled egg," Regina said.

"You always eat boiled."

"I need variety in my life."

"Scrambled eggs and black tea constitute variety?"

Irritated, Regina met the majordomo's gaze. "Do you harbor a grudge against black tea and scrambled eggs?"

"I will serve you immediately, my lady. Do you want the eggs runny or dry?"

Regina placed a hand in front of her mouth, nauseous again. "Forget the eggs." She looked at her friend. "What is your schedule today?"

"I am meeting with the agents searching for likely farms for sale," Ginger answered.

"Did you meet with the Kazanovs yesterday?'

"Yes, I did."

"Was Viktor there?"

"Yes."

"Did he mention me?"

"No."

Regina caught the majordomo's eyes. *"The Times?"*

Pickles served her black tea and dry toast. Then he delivered the morning paper.

Sipping her tea, Regina read the headlines and browsed the first page before turning to society gossip on page three. And then she saw it.

Attending the opera for the first time in weeks, Prince Viktor Kazanov engaged in an intimate conversation with the Countess of Tewksbury.

Her queasiness returned. Viktor had attended the opera, spoken with Vanessa, but never arrived at Bradford House. There had to be a reasonable explanation for his behavior. He would send her a note or call upon her today. That thought did not make her feel better.

Setting her napkin on the table, Regina closed the newspaper and stood. Without a word, she walked toward the door.

"My lady, what about your breakfast?" Pickles called.

"Give it to Hamlet." She left the dining room, never seeing her friend and her majordomo exchanging satisfied smiles.

The day dragged for Regina. She passed time with Austen, worked on her manuscript, and practiced tossing her daggers. No note arrived from Viktor. Nor did he visit.

When she awakened the following morning, Regina rolled over. The other pillow bore no indentation, and her heart ached with loss.

Regina surrendered to her pregnancy by sitting beside the chamber pot to await the nausea. Nothing happened. She moved to the edge of the bed and drank a glass of water. Within seconds, the water came back up. She groaned in misery and lay back on the bed.

Later, Regina dressed and went downstairs to breakfast. Like the previous day, she sat opposite her friend.

Pickles appeared at her side and set a cup of coffee on the table. "What kind of eggs this morning, my lady?"

Regina lifted her gaze from the coffee to the majordomo. "I prefer tea."

"You drank tea yesterday."

"Is there a problem with drinking tea two days?"

"No, my lady." Pickles returned with her tea and set a plate of fried kippers near her.

Her hand flew to her throat, trying to hold back the nausea. "I want dry toast."

"Cook made these delicious kippers especially for you."

"Take it away," Regina snapped. Only bloaters would be worse. Oh, Lord, she wished she hadn't thought of revolting bloaters.

Regina didn't bother to pretend to read the *Times.* She opened to the page three gossip column.

Among the guests at Lord Burlington's annual gala, Prince Viktor Kazanov disappointed dozens of ladies when he danced only with the Countess of Tewksbury.

Her nausea returned, and her heart ached with

emotional pain. How dare the prince make love to her, get her pregnant, and then ignore her.

Regina took a sip of tea and stood, heading for the door. "Forget the toast, Pickles."

"Where are you going?" Ginger called.

"I need to practice tossing my daggers." Regina paused, as if remembering something, and then turned around. "Pickles, I want a locksmith to change the locks. *Today.*"

Pickles smiled at Ginger and drawled, "By tomorrow, the word *Viktor* will be painted on that poor tree."

That day was even worse than the previous one. The thought of another lonely evening and night filled Regina with dread. Being alone had never bothered her until love walked into her life. How could she live without it? Even worse, her child would bear the stigma of bastardy. She would never forgive herself for refusing the prince's proposal.

After her usual bout of nausea the next morning, Regina went to breakfast. She fixed a wan smile on her face and called, "Good morning, Ginger. Pickles, bring tea and the *Times.*"

"Tea?" the majordomo echoed. "Again?"

"Have the colonials dumped our tea in the Thames?"

"No, my lady."

Pickles brought her a pot of black tea and the morning *Times.* "What may I serve you?"

"Nothing." Regina opened the newspaper to the society gossip column.

A society romance is blooming like the flowers in Hyde Park where Prince Viktor Kazanov and the Countess of Tewksbury were seen riding together.

With a cry of pain, Regina stared at the newspaper. Finally, she stood and headed for the door.

"Reggie?" Ginger called.

"Leave me alone," Regina sobbed, and disappeared out the door.

Pickles looked at Ginger and raised his brows. "When the prince returns, I do hope Her Ladyship doesn't meet him at the door with those infernal daggers drawn."

"Are you here again?"

"No, I am a figment of your imagination."

Before the majordomo could shut the door in his face, Amadeus Black grabbed it and stepped into the foyer.

"I didn't realize you had a sense of humor," Pickles drawled.

"I must speak with Miss Evans." Amadeus gave the majordomo his most frigid frown to discourage argument.

"Follow me." Pickles led the way upstairs.

Amadeus brushed past the majordomo into the study. His piercing blue gaze challenged the older man to protest.

Ginger sat at the desk overlooking the garden. Several ledgers and documents were spread across the desk.

She smiled. "Amadeus."

He sat in the chair beside the desk. "I'm sorry to interrupt."

"Damn, damn, damn."

"I'll stand behind you, my lady."

"I doubt you'll be safe there either."

Amadeus stood and looked out the open window at the Countess of Langley and her coachman. "What is happening?"

"Reggie is practicing tossing daggers," Ginger answered. "Poor Artie is dodging the daggers and fetching the ones that miss the tree."

"Why is she doing that?"

"Self-defense."

In one fluid movement, the Countess of Langley flicked the bottom edge of her gown and pulled a dagger from her sheath strapped to her leg. Then she took aim and tossed the blade at the silver white birch tree. Without pausing, the countess pulled a dagger from the sheath strapped to her other leg and tossed that, too.

Only then did Regina Bradford inspect her work. The first blade had hit the top circle dead center and the other inside the lower circle.

"I did it, Artie."

"Aye, my lady, you did."

Amadeus turned away from the window, asking, "What do the circles signify?"

"The top circle is where the neck of a six-foot man would be located," Ginger answered. "The lower circle is his heart."

"What is the *V*?"

"The *V* represents Viktor."

"Is the countess planning bodily harm on the prince?"

Ginger grinned and nodded. "At first opportunity."

His lips twitched. "I suppose the reason is the gossip column in the *Times*?"

"Reggie doesn't know the prince is purposely making her jealous," Ginger told him. "She has been resisting his marriage proposal."

"Ah, I understand." Amadeus sat in the chair again. "Prosecutor Lowing will be disappointed if they marry. He hopes to arrest Lady Bradford for murder and wants the prince to testify."

"Reggie never harmed anyone in her life," Ginger said, "and even if she had, the prince would never say a single word against her. Why doesn't Lowing arrest the real murderer?"

"Lowing believes either the prince or the countess or both did the deed."

"He will not change his mind unless you catch the murderer."

Amadeus inclined his head in agreement. "I admire your logical mind and want to discuss your theory about victims and motivations."

His compliment pleased Ginger. "I admire your own logic and objectivity."

"Do you agree that Adele Kazanov was not the target?"

"Yes."

"The targets in the first scenario are Charles, Cedric, and Viktor," Amadeus said. "Do you think the motivation is gambling debts or a desire to keep Regina Bradford unmarried?"

"Gambling debts is not the motivation," Ginger answered. "Prince Viktor is wealthy. Charles and Cedric owed nothing substantial, at least not enough to get them killed."

"How do you know?"

"The Kazanov brothers investigated that."

Amadeus frowned, clearly unhappy. Investigating murders was his job, not the work for amateurs. Though, he could not fault the brothers for obstructing his own investigation or looking into that aspect. After all, the princes had entrance into places where he would not be welcomed.

"So, you believe keeping the countess unmarried is the motivation?"

"All three had a marital or romantic interest in Reggie."

"Why would someone want to keep her unmarried?"

"That is unimportant. Keeping her unmarried is the important part."

"The second scenario would include your father on the target list."

"Money is the only motivation that fits," Ginger said, "but I don't understand how money is involved."

"Charles and Cedric squandered money to the point of debt," Amadeus said, "but Viktor has more money than he could spend in a lifetime. Where would your father fit?"

Ginger shook her head. "I have a feeling the amount of money, too much or too little, did not make them targets."

Amadeus ran a hand through his hair in frustration. "Then what is the significance of the money?"

"I wish I knew." Ginger sighed. "Two targets had too little money, one has too much, and my father earned a good salary which he did not squander."

"Tell me again your father's job for Reginald Smith."

"Father did the financial ledgers mostly," Ginger told him. "I'll speak to Reggie about asking to see her father's ledgers."

"How would Reginald's ledgers affect Charles, Cedric, and Viktor?"

"I don't know," Ginger answered, "but we'll know it when we see it. Inspecting those ledgers can do no harm."

Amadeus stood and took her hand in his. He gazed into her velvet brown eyes for a long moment and then pressed his lips to her hand. "Whom do I ask permission to court you officially?"

"You ask me."

Amadeus smiled, his blue eyes filled with warmth. "Consider yourself asked."

Chapter 16

The man I love doesn't love me . . .

Dementia paced back and forth in the drawing room and pondered her dilemma. The society gossip column had reported the Duke of Charming and the Countess of Tyngsboro conversing at the opera, dancing at a ball, and riding in the park.

There was no chance the duke loved her. Now she would keep her own counsel, never telling him of the child she carried or listening to his self-serving lies.

Intending to make herself a pot of tea, Dementia walked downstairs. She reached the foyer just as her majordomo opened the front door.

The Duke of Charming stepped into the foyer and smiled when he saw her. "How pleased I am to see you, my love."

Dementia arched a copper brow at him. "Are you?"

His smile faltered at the coldness in her voice. "I missed you."

"Did you?"

"I wanted to see you," the duke said, "but certain matters required my attention."

Dementia lifted her chin a notch, determined to retain her pride. "Would these certain matters have anything to do with operas, balls, and parks?"

"Darling, that was business, not pleasure."

"I do hope your business was profitable." Dementia managed a smile. *"You may leave now."*

"I don't understand, sweetheart."

"Let me say this, Your Grace. Get the hell out of my house!"

I hope he tries to use his key tonight. That no-good, royal bastard will receive the surprise of his life.

Unable to sleep, Regina brooded in her bedchamber. She sat on the settee in front of the dark hearth and inhaled deeply of early summer's mingling fragrances wafting on a breeze through the open window. Hamlet lay beside her with his head on her lap.

The words *royal bastard* slapped her senses, her conscience, her heart. She would forget about the prince and pass her unborn child off as her late husband's second child. In view of her testimony at the prince's trial, people would gossip, but no one would question her openly. Only Viktor would know the child was his, and by then a vow of love and proposal of marriage would come too late.

What she needed was tea and toast. "Hamlet, let's eat."

The Great Dane needed no second invitation. The word *eat* propelled him off the settee to the door.

With the dog leading the way, Regina walked downstairs. After more than two years, she was tired of people waiting on her and wanted to putter around the kitchen making her own tea and toast.

Regina reached the ground floor in time to see her majordomo walking across the foyer. "What is it, Pickles?"

"Someone banged on the door."

"I will take care of this." Regina marched toward the door like Napoleon crossing Europe. She knew who it was and almost looked forward to the coming confrontation.

"Who's there?"

"Viktor."

Regina smiled at the door. "What do you want, Your Highness?"

"I want you to open the door. The damn key will not work."

"I changed the lock." Regina hoped her tone was suitably frigid but suspected her enjoyment at thwarting his wishes seeped into her voice. "Go away."

"Why did you not attend the Duchess of Inverary's annual luncheon?"

"What I do is no business of yours."

"Humor me," Viktor snapped. "I worried for your health."

"I thank you for your concern, Your Highness." There was no mistaking the sarcasm in her voice. "I am perfectly well."

"Open this door," he ordered. "I want to see you."

"You may call at Bradford House tomorrow," she told him. "Leave Pickles your card."

Regina turned around at the sound of the majordomo chuckling. She dropped her gaze to her dog, his tail wagging as if he were enjoying this, too.

"Other matters required my attention, Regina."

She smiled at the door again. The prince's use of her full name meant he was angry.

"Would those matters be the opera, the ball, and the park?"

"Damn," she heard the prince mutter.

"Regina, how long do you intend to punish me?"

"Until there's a snowball fight in hell."

"I was protecting you from Vanessa's threats."

Regina remained silent and stared at the door. The prince was considering her welfare by passing time with Vanessa? He insulted her intelligence by thinking she would believe him.

"Are you still there?"

"Yes."

"What do you say, my love." His voice was husky with intimacy.

Regina wasn't fooled. She knew the prince was furious to be treated like a beggar at her door.

"I sent my driver away, Regina."

"Enjoy your walk home. Good night, Your Highness."

"Regina!"

Ignoring his call, Regina turned away from the door, her gaze falling on the majordomo. "Do not open this door to the prince upon peril of your employment. Do you understand?"

"Yes, my lady. Perfectly."

The infuriating minx had refused him entrance to Bradford House and forced him to walk home. Prince Viktor leaned back on the soft leather seat in his coach and smiled at the thought of his beloved defying him from the other side of the door. If they had already been married, she would probably have attacked him with a frying pan.

Regina Bradford was an amazing woman, proper when necessary but otherwise not. She was carrying his child, possibly his heir. He wanted her calm and happy, at least until she delivered the babe.

To that end, Viktor had risen early. After breakfasting with his daughter, he had instructed his driver to take him to the West India Docks on the Isle of Dogs.

After passing the Tower, the coach wended its way from Commerical Road to the India Dock Road. The mingling scents of spices, grains, and lumber wafted on the air like an unseen fog.

Dock noises reached him and grew louder. Cargoes loaded and unloaded, and masculine voices shouted greetings to friends.

"Stop here," Viktor called to his driver.

When the coach halted near a row of merchant offices, Viktor climbed down and entered one of the buildings. The scent of ink permeated the atmosphere inside the business office.

"Your Highness?"

Viktor turned toward the voice. Forest Fredericks, Reginald Smith's nondescript business associate, rose from his chair and hurried across the room.

"I hope Reginald is here," Viktor said.

"Oh, yes." Fredericks pushed his glasses up with an index finger. "I'll fetch him."

Watching the man hurry away, Viktor wondered idly what kind of life a man like that led. Fredericks was an employee so he could not be wealthy, and he was a bachelor. The man seemed older than his forty-odd years. A balding, potbellied physique did not help his appearance, nor did the slipping spectacles.

Reginald Smith appeared, followed by Forest Fredericks. "To what do I owe this honor, Your Highness?"

"I want to discuss your daughter."

Reginald raised his brows. "Come, Your Highness, sit in my chair. Forest, bring us coffee."

"None for me, thank you." Viktor sat in the offered chair, a good quality leather, while Smith brought another chair to place beside his desk.

Reginald glanced at his associate and then asked, "Do you require privacy?"

"Regina considers Forest an unofficial uncle," Viktor answered. "There is no reason for him to leave when he will hear the news sooner rather than later."

Reginald Smith inclined his head. "What has Regina done now, Your Highness?"

Viktor surprised both men. "I would like permission to marry your daughter. I ask as a courtesy only and will marry her no matter your answer."

"Do you love Regina?"

"Does it matter?"

"I should never have forced my daughter into that marriage." Reginald gave his associate a sidelong glance. "Forest believes Regina should choose her own husband. Or none at all, if she so desires."

Viktor turned to Fredericks. "Thank you for lending my intended wife your moral support." He looked at her father again. "Reggie and I have fallen in love, though she fears being trapped in a stifling marriage."

Reginald shook his head in disapproval. "The Lord intended woman to serve and obey her husband and bear his children."

"Unless you want to meet your Maker, do not repeat those words to Reggie," Viktor said dryly. "She is carrying my baby prince or princess."

Both Smith and Fredericks stared at him in appalled surprise. Reginald stood, saying, "Wait until I—"

Viktor stood when the older man did. "You will sit and listen to me. *Now.*"

Reginald Smith dropped into his chair. "Can you change her mind about marriage?"

"Your question offends me, Smith. Reggie will

marry me whenever I say," Viktor told him. "However, I know nothing about her pregnancy officially. Ginger informed me of my impending fatherhood."

"At least, Ginger Evans has common sense."

"Ginger has a head for numbers, too," Forest interjected, his spectacles slipping down his long nose.

"At the moment, Reggie is angry because of the gossip linking me to Vanessa Stanton," Viktor said, and then smiled. "Reggie refused to open the door last night, and I did not force the issue because she has been practicing to throw a small dagger."

"What?" Reginald shook his head in disapproval again. "My daughter is even more headstrong than her mother was."

Forest Fredericks laughed at that, drawing their attention. "Regina, looks like her mother, but *your* personality lies beneath. Both of you are strong-willed and stubborn, which is the reason you bicker so much."

"Do you love Regina?" Viktor asked his future father-in-law.

Reginald appeared startled by the question. "She's my daughter. Of course, I love her."

"She does not believe you love her. Did you ever tell her?"

"I must have told her. Though, I do admit I cannot remember when."

"The mother of my unborn child deserves to feel secure and loved," Viktor said. "You will make peace with her today."

Reginald Smith nodded. "I had no idea that Regina—" He shrugged.

"Do not mention pregnancy, marriage, or my visit to you," Viktor warned.

"I understand, Your Highness."

"Call me, Viktor."

"Forest, bring whisky and glasses," Reginald ordered. "We'll toast Regina's forthcoming marriage and baby."

Forest Fredericks hurried to do his employer's bidding. He returned with three glasses and poured the whisky.

"To Regina." Viktor raised his glass, and the other two joined him.

"I'll need to make changes in my will to provide for my new grandchild," Reginald said. "About the dowry—"

"The child Reggie carries is dowry enough for me," Viktor interrupted. "Do not change your will. Austen will receive the Smith fortune."

"I will appoint you executor," Reginald said, and glanced at Forest. "You don't mind, do you?"

"Prince Viktor is welcome to the job which, I hope, lies far in the future," Fredericks said. "I'll send a note to the solicitor. I hope there is no rush. I did tell you I was going out of town today." He looked at Viktor. "My nephew's wedding."

"That slipped my mind. How long will you be gone?"

"One or two days."

"It is settled, then." Viktor stood and shook his future father-in-law's hand. "You will make peace with Reggie today."

"Want to go to London? Want to go to town? Better watch out that you don't fall down." Singing those words, Regina bounced her son up and down on her lap. At the word *down,* she pretended to let him slip.

Austen laughed, delighted with the game. He touched her cheek, ordering, "More."

"Want to go to London? Want to go to town? Better watch out that you don't fall down." Regina pretended to let him slip on the word *down.*

Again, Austen laughed uproariously. "More."

"No more," Regina said. "Mama is tired."

Austen pointed at Hamlet, snoozing near them. "Dog."

"Very good, Austen. Hamlet is a dog."

"Kiss dog."

Regina smiled. "No kissing dogs."

"How about kissing Grandpa?"

At the sound of her father's voice, Regina looked over her shoulder and watched him crossing the family parlor. This was all she needed today. Viktor's defection to Vanessa Stanton, a bout of morning sickness, and her father. How much worse could the day get?

"Gapa," Austen said, holding his arms out.

Reginald sat beside Regina on the settee and lifted the boy out of his mother's arms. Then he planted a kiss on his grandson's cheek.

"Where is Uncle Forest?" Regina asked, telling herself to remain calm. Bickering with her father would not be good for her unborn child.

"Forest went out of town to his nephew's wedding."

"Would you prefer tea in the formal drawing room?"

"No, Daughter. The family parlor will suit."

Regina wondered if her father was ill. What other reason could there be for his pleasantness?

She stood, saying, "Come, Hamlet."

"Let the dog stay."

Regina sat again, but narrowed her gaze on her father. Something was definitely wrong, but she would wait and let him tell her.

"Dog," Austen chirped. "Kiss dog."

Reginald chuckled. "People kiss people," he told his grandson. "Dogs kiss dogs."

"Nose," Austen said, and pulled his grandfather's nose.

"Only naughty boys pull noses," Regina said.

Austen pointed at her. "Mama." Then he rested his head on his grandfather's shoulder and fell asleep.

Reginald chuckled. "I can't count the number of years it's been since I held a little one like this. I believe it was you."

"Let me take him upstairs," Regina said, lifting Austen into her arms. "He'll sleep for an hour, and you can play with him before you leave."

When she returned to the parlor, Pickles had served tea, and her father was reading her manuscript. He set it aside and patted the settee, saying, "Sit here."

Regina sat beside him. She didn't know if she should ask if he was ill or brace herself for his criticism of her work.

"You are a talented writer," Reginald praised her.

Her father was terminally ill. His praise shocked her. She couldn't remember the last time he had complimented her or smiled at her like he did now.

Tears welled up in her eyes. "Do you really think so?"

"I wouldn't say it if I didn't mean it." Reginald cupped her chin and studied her face, saying, "You were made in your mother's image." He wiped a solitary teardrop from her cheek with a fingertip. "Do you know why I never remarried?"

Regina shook her head. "You worried that a gold-digger wanted your money?"

Reginald smiled at that. "I loved your mother so

much I could never bear another woman replacing her."

"You loved her so much?"

"And I love you as much as I loved her. Maybe more."

"Oh, Papa, I love you, too." Regina bowed her head and wept, unable to control her emotions. She felt her father's arms around her, pulling her closer, and rested her head against his shoulder.

"If I didn't love you, would I have considered Uncle Forest's ridiculous idea to marry you in name only? I feared you would be blamed for Cedric's death."

Regina looked up at her father through eyes blurred with her tears. "Are you telling me this because you're going to die?"

"I am as hail and hearty as ever." He passed her a handkerchief.

Regina wiped her tears. "Papa, I am pregnant with the prince's child."

"These things happen sometimes," Reginald said, his tone soothing, keeping her within the warmth of his protective embrace. "You will marry the prince. I know you believe the baby's welfare must come before your personal ambitions. Marriage to the right man will not stifle you, and the prince seems a decent man."

"I don't think the prince cares for me," Regina said. "He has been seen with the Countess of Tewksbury."

"That proves he loves you."

"It does?" Regina couldn't credit that.

"Prince Viktor denies his deep emotions by flirting with another woman," Reginald explained. "Men do stupid things sometimes. The prince will soon return to your side, and when he does, he will never leave you again."

"What if he doesn't?"

"Trust me, Regina. He will return."

"But what if—?"

"In that unlikely event," Reginald said, "I will take my pistol and force him to the altar."

Regina smiled at the image. She didn't believe anyone could force the prince to do anything.

"Papa, could I borrow your financial ledgers for the previous two years?"

Reginald smiled at her question. Her inability to understand such things danced on the tip of his tongue. Recalling the prince's warning, he controlled himself.

"Why do you want those?"

"Ginger wants to inspect them. She thinks a motive for murder could be contained in them."

Reginald frowned. "What is she searching for?"

"Ginger doesn't know, but Constable Black agrees that she should inspect them."

"When I leave, send your coachman to follow me to the office," Reginald agreed. "I'll give him the ledgers. Do you think Ginger will understand all those numbers?"

Regina laughed at the doubt in his voice. "Ginger and I own the Evans Smith Company," she told him. "We have made thousands of pounds investing in other companies. At the moment, Ginger and the Kazanov brothers are forming a beer and ale cartel. Ginger is a financial wizard. Or should I say witch?"

Reginald grinned. "Would you and Ginger consider allowing me to invest in the cartel?"

Regina threw herself into his arms and planted a kiss on his cheek. "I love you, Papa."

* * *

In spite of her daily struggle with nausea, Regina felt almost lighthearted the next morning. She still faced the problem of the prince and the pregnancy, but her father loved and valued her, a heady realization after living with his criticism for so many years.

As promised, her father had given Artie the financial ledgers. Regina wondered if Ginger had begun studying them. She hoped her friend would discover the murderer's identity. Perhaps the villain was a disgruntled customer of her father's, his twisted mind bent on revenge.

"Good morning," Regina called, walking into the dining room.

Missing the look that passed between her friend and the majordomo, Regina headed straight for the sideboard. For the first time in days, she had an appetite. Finding approbation in her father's eyes had improved her state of mind which, in turn, helped her appetite.

Regina scooped scrambled eggs onto a plate with ham and toast. She sat across the table from her friend and smiled when the majordomo set a pot of tea beside her plate.

"Thank you, Pickles. Bring me *The Times*." Regina looked at Ginger. "Have you started on those ledgers?"

Ginger nodded. "I began with the ledgers from two years ago and will work my way to the present."

Regina read *The Times* headline and glanced at the front page articles. Then she turned to page two and, finally, the society gossip column on page three. Nearing the bottom, her own name caught her eye.

Prince Viktor Kazanov announces his betrothal to Lady Regina Bradford, the Countess of Langley. The couple will marry quietly surrounded only by family and close friends.

"No-good, son of a bitch." Regina bolted out of her chair and stared at the newspaper as if it were a poisonous snake. "I'd like to know which of those two did this."

Ginger looked at her. "What are you talking about?"

"That!" Regina pointed at the paper. "The society reporter announces my betrothal to Viktor."

"What wonderful news," Ginger gushed.

"May I express my best wishes," Pickles said.

"I never agreed to marry him." Regina pressed the palm of her hand to her forehead as if it pained her. "Either Viktor, my father, or both planted that tidbit. Pickles, tell Artie to bring the coach around."

"Where are you going?" Ginger asked.

"I cannot trust Viktor to speak truthfully," Regina said. "I will question my father first."

Ginger stood. "Only yesterday, you reconciled with Reginald. I am going with you to prevent another war."

"You are welcome to come." Regina marched toward the door. "If my father is innocent, you can prevent me from murdering the prince."

Waiting beside the coach, Artie opened its door and helped the two women inside. Then he climbed into the driver's seat. "Take us to West India Docks," Regina instructed him.

"Wait!" Prince Viktor materialized beside the coach. "Where are you going so early?"

"I do not answer to you," Regina told him. "Let's go, Artie." The coach lurched forward into the street before the prince could open the door and jump inside.

"What is he doing?" Regina asked, refusing to give the prince the satisfaction of seeing her turn around.

"He's returning to his coach."

"I guarantee he'll follow us."

"Why didn't you ask the prince if he announced your betrothal?" Ginger asked.

"I trust my father to tell me the truth. I want to speak with him before Viktor gets there."

Being trapped into marriage infuriated Regina. True, she loved the prince and would accept his marriage proposal, but she deserved the courtesy of accepting before anyone made a public announcement.

Coaches and carts and people clogged London's streets on this business day. The scents of spices and grains, as well as humanity and the river, drifted through the air.

Regina watched the hustle and bustle outside her coach. "I never realized the number of people up and about at this hour of the day." She looked at her friend. "Can you see his coach?"

Ginger shook her head. "The prince is caught in traffic somewhere behind us."

"Thankfully, I sent Artie for those ledgers yesterday," Regina said. "My father might not have handed them over today."

"You are carrying the prince's child," Ginger said, "and you plan to accept his marriage proposal. Why are you reacting so furiously to the betrothal announcement?"

"Viktor doesn't know I carry his child."

"The prince knows about the baby."

Regina felt confused. How could the prince know what she hadn't told him? And then she knew. Her father had contacted the prince yesterday.

"I told Viktor," Ginger admitted. "The prince worried about you, Reggie. He loves you."

"You told the prince?"

"Please don't be angry with me."

"I—I . . ." Regina pressed the palm of her hand to her forehead. Tears welled up in her eyes and rolled down her cheeks. "Something foreign has possession of my body and my emotions, and I am powerless to control myself."

"The baby is affecting your moods." Ginger reached over and patted her hand. "Shall we tell Artie to turn around and go home?"

Regina shook her head. "We'll visit my father. Viktor and I will share our wedding plans, whatever they are."

Artie halted the coach beside the row of merchant offices. He opened its door and helped the two women down.

"The prince cannot be far behind us," Ginger said. "Shall we wait for him?"

"No, my father has probably read *The Times* already," Regina answered. "I guarantee he can't wait to speak to me."

Ginger smiled. "Lead the way."

Regina stepped into the deserted office. "My father is lurking around somewhere." She walked in the direction of his desk, calling, "Papa?"

"Oh, God!" Regina dropped to her knees beside her father, his gaze unseeing, a dagger protruding from his chest.

And then she screamed.

Chapter 17

To tell or not to tell His Grace about the baby? Answering that question was her own moral dilemma.

Certainly, he had the right to know about his impending fatherhood. She did not want him to propose marriage out of duty to her or their child.

Dementia sat on the settee in her drawing room and knitted a blue baby blanket. The more she thought, the more confused she became.

"My lady?"

"Don't bother to announce me." The Duke of Charming brushed past the majordomo and marched across the room to tower over her. "Listen to me, Lady Merlot."

Dementia gave him a sullen look and then gestured her majordomo out. She avoided looking at the duke by giving her attention to her knitting.

"Are you ready to listen?" He sounded irritated.

Reluctantly, she lifted her gaze to his. There was no mistaking the unhappiness mirrored in her fabulous green eyes.

The Duke of Charming ran a hand through his black hair, his frustration all too apparent. "I flirted with the Countess of Tyngsboro because of her threats against you. I apologize if that upsets you."

Dementia gave him a frosty look. "With whom you flirt is no concern of mine."

"Lovely liar." The Duke of Charming grinned, amused by her cool attitude. *"Dementia, I will not allow you to bear my child out of wedlock."*

His words surprised her. *"You know?"*

Ignoring her question, the duke knelt on one bended knee and lifted her hands to his lips. *"Prepare to become my duchess."* He stood then and helped her off the settee. *"Come, love, we'll visit your father and share our news."*

"Lady Brentwood?"

Dementia and the duke turned toward the voice. What bad news did the constable carry?

Constable Green narrowed his gaze on her. *"So, now you've murdered your own father."*

Dementia swooned dead away . . .

"Tell Artie to get Amadeus Black," Viktor instructed Ginger. "Send my man for Rudolf."

Viktor knelt beside Regina in the pool of blood on the floor. He put his arm around her shoulders and drew her against the side of his body, her uncontrollable weeping wrenching his heart.

"Reggie, come away."

"I've killed him," she sobbed. "That madman is slaughtering men because of me, even my own father."

"You had nothing to do with this." He glanced at the small dagger protruding from his chest. "Come away, love."

"I can't leave him like this."

Viktor tightened his hold on her. "We will guard him until the authorities arrive."

They knelt beside her father's body, the only sounds her quiet sobbing. Ten minutes passed and then another ten.

"Your Highness?"

Viktor turned his head to see Amadeus Black and another man. Beyond them, Ginger and Artie poised near the doorway.

"Lady Bradford, I am sorry for your loss," Amadeus Black said, "but I will need to inspect the crime scene. Please, step away from the body."

Regina looked at him, her eyes swollen from weeping. "He's my father, not a body."

Viktor rubbed her back. "Reggie, the constable needs—"

"My father is not a body!"

Amadeus Black crouched down beside her and spoke in a soft tone. "Lady Bradford, I know from experience how difficult losing a loved one is. I want to find the man who did this to your father, and so do you. In order to find the villain, I need to inspect the scene for possible clues. You want me to do my job, don't you?"

Regina nodded.

Viktor helped her stand. "Let me take you home."

"No." The constable shook his head. "I need to question everyone once I inspect the scene."

Viktor shifted his gaze to Regina. "May I take her outside to wait?"

"Yes." Black turned to his assistant. "Barney, drag chairs outside for the ladies."

The Kazanov princes were standing outside. Viktor nodded at his brothers and helped Regina into a chair.

"Stay with her," Viktor instructed Ginger. "Reggie, I will leave you for two minutes to speak to my brothers." He studied her face for a moment, her eyes red and almost swollen shut.

Leaving her side, Viktor spoke in a low voice

to his brothers, "Someone murdered Reginald Smith."

"Was he shot like the others?" Mikhail asked.

"Smith has a last resort dagger in his heart."

Rudolf raised his brows. "Whoever did this knew Regina was practicing the use of a blade."

"The murderer is known to all of us?" Stepan asked.

"I believe so." The four brothers fell silent.

"I am wet with blood," Regina was murmuring in distress. "My hands are bloody, too."

Viktor hurried to her side and crouched beside her chair. He stroked her back, trying to soothe her. "Only a few more minutes, love. I promise."

What the hell was keeping the constable? Reginald Smith could wait, but his daughter needed care.

Regina lifted her hand to her throat, staining it with blood, her expression a mask of misery. "I feel sick."

Putting his arm around her, Viktor helped her out of the chair and walked her several paces away. He held her head while she gagged dryly. "Do you want to sit inside the coach?"

"I want to go home." She began weeping again.

Viktor sat her down and crouched beside the chair again. "Rudolf, can you get the constable to come outside now?"

Prince Rudolf disappeared inside the office. A moment later, the constable appeared with the prince.

"Your Highness, I apologize for keeping you waiting," Amadeus Black said, "but my method is inspecting the scene thoroughly before I ask questions."

"Change your method." Viktor stood, ready to

argue. "Lady Bradford is with child and ill. I refuse to endanger my heir or his mother."

Amadeus Black looked from him to Regina and then inclined his head. He squatted in front of her. "When you arrived today, Lady Bradford, did you touch anything?"

"I touched my father."

"Did you touch the dagger?"

She shuddered. "No."

"When did you last see your father?"

"Yesterday, he visited me at home."

"Did you discuss anything of importance?"

Regina nodded. "Papa said he loved me. He never told me that before."

"I am glad you had that time together." Amadeus Black stood and told Viktor, "I will delay questioning her for a few days. Do you know where Mr. Smith's business associate lives?"

"Forest Fredericks traveled out of town yesterday to attend his nephew's wedding," Viktor answered. "He will return tomorrow."

"Your Highness?"

Viktor looked beyond the constable. "Yes?"

"I saw Mr. Smith yesterday evening," Artie said. "Lady Bradford sent me here to fetch something home. That was about seven o'clock."

Amadeus narrowed his gaze on the coachman. "What did you deliver to Lady Bradford?"

"Artie brought me those ledgers I want to examine," Ginger spoke up, drawing their attention. "Reginald stayed for tea, and then Artie followed him to the office to collect them."

Amadeus turned to Viktor again. "I assume you will want to be present when I speak with the lady about her father. I'll send you a warning before I do."

"Thank you."

"Damn it," the constable muttered, his gaze fixed on something beyond the prince.

Viktor looked over his shoulder to see another coach coming down the road. He helped Regina stand, saying, "Let me take you home now."

"I can't leave my father."

Rudolf stepped forward. "My brothers and I will take care of everything."

"You won't leave him alone?"

"We will take good care of your father," Rudolf promised. "Go with Viktor."

A coach halted behind the others. The door opened, and Prosecutor Lowing climbed down.

"What are you doing here?" Amadeus Black asked.

"I heard the news of another murder," Lowing answered, and then rounded on Regina. "So, now you've murdered your own father."

"Insensitive bastard." Viktor lifted Regina into his arms when she fainted. "I could kill you myself."

". . . *the love of God, and the fellowship of the Holy Ghost, be with us all evermore . . .*"

"Amen."

Covered in black from head to toe, Regina turned away from her father's grave. She looked at the prince when his arm went around her to give support.

Her father rested bedside her mother again. She was glad he had told her how much he loved her mother. And her. The only regret was how long it had taken for them to understand each other. If ˋe delivered a boy, she would name him in honor ˋer father.

ˋn their return from the cemetary, Regina

brought her guests into the dining room for a light luncheon. She gave the seat of honor at the head of the table to the Duke of Inverary. On either side of the duke sat his duchess and Percy Howell, his barrister. Ginger, Uncle Forest, and Viktor's family sat on both sides of the table. Pickles supervised the serving of the luncheon the cook had prepared.

Unexpectedly, Prosecutor Lowing walked into the dining room. With him was Constable Black. Did they think to question everyone on the day she buried her father?

Regina rose from her chair. "Mr. Lowing, you are not welcome in my home. Please leave."

"I intend to leave shortly," Lowing said. "Percy Howell, my friend, I will present these warrants to you." The prosecutor pulled two documents from his pocket and handed them to the barrister.

"I have obtained a search warrant for Lady Bradford's manuscript," Lowing announced, and then paused for effect. "The other is an arrest warrant for Regina Bradford for four charges of murder and one charge of attempted murder."

Several things happened simultaneously.

"My baby," Regina cried, dropping into the chair. Her hands moved to her belly to protect her child.

"Bastard!" Viktor leaped out of his chair and lunged for the prosecutor. His brothers moved when he did and held him back.

"Amadeus?" Ginger gasped. "How can you do this?"

Clearly unhappy, Constable Black shook his head. "Fetch the countess's manuscript, Ginger."

"I won't."

"Miss Evans, get the manuscript," Percy Howell instructed. "Pack a few necessities in a bag for the countess, too."

Ginger stood to leave the room. "Never speak to me again," she said, passing the constable on the way out.

Prosecutor Lowing turned a triumphant smile on Regina. "Come, Lady Bradford. Newgate awaits you."

The Duke of Inverary banged his fist on the table and rose from his chair. "The Countess of Langley will be housed in the Tower. Unless, you want an abrupt end to your misbegotten career?"

"I am sorry, my lady," Amadeus Black said. "You will need to accompany us now."

Regina shrank back in fear. She looked at Viktor who said, "I will go with her."

"No visitors," Lowing said.

"Lady Bradford is entitled to have her barrister in attendance," Percy Howell told the prosecutor.

"I will go, too," the Duke of Inverary said, his gaze challenging the prosecutor. "Prince Viktor will escort his lady, or I will dine on your innards."

The prosecutor nodded, albeit with reluctance. "I want him to keep his distance from me."

Ginger returned and shoved the manuscript into the constable's hands. She carried two bags and announced, "I will stay in the Tower with Reggie."

"You are going nowhere," Lowing told her.

Ginger rounded on the prosecutor, her hands on her hips. "Regina is with child and needs a woman with her."

"I want you to stay with Austen," Regina said. "Please. My absence will confuse him."

Viktor wrapped Regina in a cashmere shawl. He slipped his arm around her shoulders and carried the bag in his free hand.

Outside, Viktor helped Regina into the constable's coach and climbed inside beside her. Prosecutor

Lowing and Amadeus Black sat on the opposite seat. The duke and his barrister rode in another coach.

Regina huddled into Viktor. She rested her head against his chest and wondered if she would ever see him again. What would happen to her baby if she was convicted?

"His Grace will send his cook," Viktor told her, "and I will supply the food. You will be free after the evidentiary hearing."

Regina trembled at the sight of the Tower's pepper-pot turrets and forbidding stone walls. God was punishing her for her sins.

She had failed as a daughter. She had failed as a wife. She had failed as a mother for Austen and the baby she carried.

Their coach halted at the Middle Tower. Viktor climbed down and lifted her out of the coach.

Constable Black and Prosecutor Lowing led the way through the Lieutenant's Lodging to the grassy inner courtyard. Behind them walked the duke and the barrister.

The Chapel of St. Peter ad Vincula stood on the far side of the green. There was the scaffold and the simple cobbled square where two queens had lost their heads.

Indeed, the Tower Green with its stained cobblestones was the saddest place on earth. The hushed atmosphere could not silence the anguished cries of misery that had echoed within these walls for hundreds of years.

Two men stood near the Beauchamp Tower, the Tower constable and the Tower chaplain. The Duke of Inverary shook hands with both men.

"We always eat well when one of your friends visits," the Tower constable said.

"Is the prince our visitor again?" the chaplain asked.

"The Countess of Langley will be staying here until we hang her for murder," Lowing said.

Regina gasped at his words. She threw her arms around the prince and clung to him.

"I am warning you, Lowing," the Duke of Inverary said. "Keep your mouth shut, or I will shut it permanently. At least, in a court of law."

The Tower chaplain gave Regina a kindly smile. "I am certain this is only a misunderstanding, my lady. You will reside in Beauchamp Tower while you visit. Do you know any card games to pass the hours?"

Regina nodded. "Uncle Forest taught me hazard and other games of chance. He loves to gamble but always loses."

"I would like to meet this uncle very much."

Viktor ushered her inside Beauchamp Tower. Regina climbed the stairs slowly, dreading what she would find at the top.

Only a room! The chamber contained a table and chairs set in the middle and a hearth along one wall. A spiral staircase led to an upper level.

"Where shall I sleep?" she asked.

"The upper level is a bedchamber," the prince told her.

"These stone walls keep the place cool." The Tower constable started a fire in the hearth and headed for the staircase. "We don't want you catching a chill."

"I am holding you personally responsible for her health," Viktor said, rounding on the prosecutor. "If she sickens and loses the baby, I will kill you, and the hangman be damned."

The chaplain whirled toward the prosecutor. "You have arrested a pregnant lady?"

Lowing turned his back on the chaplain. He found himself facing Percy Howell, his personal nemesis.

"You will not question my client unless I am present," the barrister told the prosecutor. "My lady, answer no questions."

The Tower constable walked down the spiral staircase. "I've got a nice fire warming the room."

"I will take you upstairs." Viktor lifted her bag and followed Regina up the staircase.

The chamber was large and airy. A cheery fire blazed in the hearth, and a bed stood on one side of the room.

"I wish I could change places with you," Viktor said, pulling her close. "You will be safe and relatively comfortable."

"Why does Lowing hate me?"

"You made him look foolish in court." Viktor planted a kiss on her lips and dropped his hand to her belly. "Take care of our baby."

Regina wrapped her arms around his neck and pressed herself against his solid, comforting strength. "I love you."

Viktor lifted her chin and stared into her disarming green eyes. "I love you, my future princess."

Chapter 18

Frightened and bereft of friends, Dementia sat beside her barrister at the defense table. Her heartbeat quickened when the prosecutor stood to address the three judges sitting at the high bench.

"I intend to prove beyond a reasonable doubt that Dementia Merlot conspired to murder three people," the prosecutor announced in a loud, clear voice. "She did, in fact, murder her own father."

Her defense barrister stood to address the court. "I intend to prove that Dementia Merlot is an innocent woman."

Then the parade began. Enemies and even friends pushed her closer and closer to the hangman.

"She threatened the earl and his cousin," her late husband's valet testified.

"She wrote about the murders in her manuscript," her rival for the duke's affection said.

"Dementia and Bertie were never in accord," her best friend told the court.

"Her Ladyship practiced tossing daggers at a tree in her garden," stated her coachman.

"I cannot confirm or deny that Her Ladyship passed the entire night in her bedchamber," came her majordomo's damning testimony.

"Her father either ignored or criticized her," her uncle said.

And then came the ultimate betrayal. The Duke of Charming stood in the witness box, sent her a look of regret, and announced, "I cannot vouch for the whereabouts of the lady on the night of her father's murder . . ."

Where was Viktor? On orders from the prosecutor, Regina had not seen him in several weeks but had assumed he would show in court today.

Regina sat at the defense table in front of the standing-room-only, crowded courtroom. Percy Howell sat on her right. In a powerful demonstration of support, the influential Duke of Inverary sat on her left.

Shock at her father's murder had subsided. Anger had replaced her listlessness. If she ever got her hands on the murderer, she would kill him with her bare hands and then turn her murderous fury on the vindictive prosecutor. How dare he condemn her unborn prince or princess to an ignominious beginning in prison.

"Do not worry," Percy Howell said, leaning close to her. "Lowing has no proof against you, only a theory based on his dislike of you."

"The judges are personal friends who owe me favors," the Duke of Inverary added. "My presence beside you will remind them of those favors and tell them which way the wind blows."

"Thank you, Your Grace. Where is Viktor?"

"The prince is standing in the back of the courtroom."

"We ordered him to stay there," Percy Howell told her, "because I feared he would misbehave. Unbeknownst to him, his brothers are actually guarding him and will shove him out the door if his anger gets the best of him."

Regina glanced over her shoulder and spied the prince standing near the door. She took strength from his presence, her gaze drinking his presence, making her feel light-headed.

"Why are all these people here?" she asked. "Are they witnesses?"

"Your hearing is open to the public," the barrister answered. "Reporters and commoners take special interest when a countess is charged with murder." He patted her hand. "Trust me, Reggie. I intend to roast Lowing, and you will walk away from this courtroom a free woman."

The Duke of Inverary smiled at her. "You can go home and concentrate on your baby."

Regina returned his smile in spite of her fear. "I have been missing Austen, too."

"All rise," the clerk of court called.

Everyone stood. Three judges marched into the courtroom and took their seats at the bench. They were the same justices who had presided at Viktor's hearing.

"Proceed, Mr. Lowing," the Chief Justice said.

The prosecutor stood. "I call Louis deVere to the witness box."

Regina watched her late husband's valet step into the box and swear to tell the truth. Apparently, Ginger was right when she said that Louis would get even with her.

"Mr. deVere, you held the position of valet to Charles Bradford?" Lowing said.

Louis lifted his chin, his tone haughty. "I was His Lordship's valet."

"At an earlier hearing, you testified under oath that the Earl and Countess of Langley despised each other," Lowing said. "The countess had threatened the earl's life. Do you stand by that testimony?"

"Yes, I do."

"After Bradford's murder, the countess terminated your employment," Lowing continued. "Where did you go?"

"I found employment with Cedric Barrows, the Earl of Dover," Louis answered.

"Did Barrows ever mention Regina Bradford?"

"Yes."

"What did he tell you?"

"The earl had offered for Lady Bradford," Louis answered. "Although her father had accepted the offer, the lady had rejected him."

"Anything else?"

Louis sent her a look of pure hatred. "She terminated my employment a second time by terminating the Earl of Dover."

The spectators in the gallery laughed at that.

"I object," Percy Howell called.

"Objection sustained."

Lowing turned to the judges. "No further questions."

Percy Howell stood and crossed to the witness box. "Good to see you again, Mr. deVere."

Louis said nothing.

"Do you like Regina Bradford personally?" Howell asked.

Louis flicked a cold glance at her. "No."

"Do you hold her responsible for your loss of employment?"

"Yes, I do."

"When Lady Bradford threatened her late husband," Howell asked, "hadn't the earl threatened to shoot her dog?"

"Yes."

"When Cedric Barrows proposed marriage to the

countess," Howell said, "wasn't it the day after her husband's funeral?"

"I don't know."

"Cedric Barrows testified under oath in a previous hearing that it was a day or two after his cousin's funeral."

Louis met the barrister's gaze. "If you say so."

"Isn't the lady's grief for her husband's passing—"

"Regina Bradford was glad to be rid of her husband," Louis interrupted. "She never knew a moment of grief."

Percy Howell paused after the valet's outburst. "Do you have special talents?"

"I—I don't understand."

"Unless you read minds, how can you possibly know Regina Bradford's thoughts? What am I thinking at this moment?"

Regina heard muffled chuckles from the gallery. Louis said nothing.

Percy Howell turned to the judges. "Since Mr. deVere refuses to read my thoughts, I have no further questions."

The chuckles in the gallery were not quite so muffled.

Prosecutor Lowing stood. "Vanessa Stanton, the Countess of Tewksbury."

Dressed in a stylish midnight blue gown with modestly high neckline, Vanessa Stanton glided to the witness box. She wore a matching hat with sheer netting to shield her face.

"What did your brother, Cedric Barrows, tell you about Regina Bradford?" Lowing asked.

"Cedric told me that Regina threatened not only his life but also her father's," Vanessa answered.

"Objection," Percy Howell called. "Hearsay."

"Overruled."

"Recently, you visited Regina Bradford," Lowing said. "What was the purpose of your visit?"

"I warned her to stop bothering Prince Viktor," Vanessa answered. "If she didn't leave the prince alone, I would tell the authorities all I knew about the murders."

"What happened?"

Vanessa gave the prosecutor a triumphant smile. "Regina Bradford stopped bothering the prince."

"Why do you think she—"

"Objection," Howell called. "The Countess of Tewksbury cannot possibly know my client's thoughts unless, of course, she has been consulting with Louis deVere."

Laughter erupted from the gallery. Even the judges smiled.

"Objection sustained."

"What did you discover the day you visited Lady Bradford?" the prosecutor asked.

"When Regina left the room," Vanessa answered, "I noticed the manuscript she is writing. I read a few pages and realized in horror that she had written about the murders."

Regina heard shocked gasps emanating from the gallery. Pockets of conversation erupted here and there.

The Chief Justice banged his gavel, restoring silence to the room. "Do you have that manuscript?"

"Yes, my lord." Lowing retrieved it from the table and handed it to the Chief Justice. "No further questions."

Percy Howell walked to the witness box. "Do you ususally read other people's private property, my lady?"

"I object," Lowing called.

"Sustained." The Chief Justice admonished Howell, "There is no need for rudeness."

"I apologize, my lord." Percy Howell looked at Vanessa Stanton but did not apologize to her. "Did you hear Regina Bradford threaten anyone?"

"Well, Cedric said—"

"Answer the question. Did *you* hear any threats?"

Vanessa gave the barrister a sullen stare. "No."

"Why did you warn Lady Bradford away from Prince Viktor Kazanov?"

"Regina bothered him."

"Did Prince Viktor tell you this?"

"No."

"Did Regina Bradford tell you she was bothering the prince?"

"No."

"Have you ever had romantic designs on the prince?"

Vanessa blushed. "I do not see the relevance—"

"I did not ask your opinion," Howell interrupted. "Answer the question."

"Prince Viktor and I were romantically involved at one point," Vanessa admitted.

Howell nodded. "Did he leave you for Regina Bradford?"

"I suppose she played a small part."

"Is that yes or no?"

Vanessa appeared uncomfortable. "Yes."

Regina could scarcely believe the other woman would see her hanged in order to win her man.

"When were you involved with Prince Viktor?"

Vanessa looked confused. "When?"

"How long ago?"

"Until recently, Viktor and I enjoyed a close friendship."

"How recently?"

"May."

"You were romantically involved with the prince while he was married to another woman?"

Vanessa blushed a vibrant scarlet. "Yes, but Princess Adele was engaged in an affair with Charles Bradford."

A loud, collective gasp sounded in the gallery. Muffled chuckles followed that. The judge banged his gavel for order.

Percy Howell smiled at the countess and then turned to the judges. "No further questions."

Prosecutor Lowing stood and called, "Ginger Evans."

Regina looked over her shoulder and smiled at Ginger as she passed the defense table. Here, at least, was someone who liked her.

"Miss Evans, what is your relationship with the defendant?" Lowing asked.

Ginger smiled at her. "Regina and I are the best of friends."

"Please tell the court—"

"You could never find a more loyal friend than Regina," Ginger added.

"How nice for you. Please tell the court—"

"Even if you searched for a thousand years," Ginger interrupted, making the spectators chuckle.

"Enough," Lowing said. "Tell the court the relationship Lady Bradford had with her husband."

"Regina and Charles were not in accord," Ginger answered.

Lowing smiled, pleased with her answer. "Did you ever witness their discord?"

Ginger nodded. "At times, the whole household heard their discord. Charles was a nasty man and constantly started arguments with Regina. The world is a better place without him."

"What about her relationship with Cedric Barrows?"

"She had no relationship with Cedric Barrows."

"The earl offered for her, did he not?"

"Cedric Barrows wanted to marry her father's money, not Regina."

"Did she have a warm relationship with her father?"

"Let me explain their relationship like this," Ginger said. "The day before he died, Reginald held her in his arms and told her how proud he was of her and how much he loved her. She returned his affection in equal measure."

Tears slid down Regina's face. If only she and her father had had more time together. They had wasted so many years bickering.

Lowing appeared disappointed. "No further questions."

Percy Howell grinned. "No questions."

Lowing called, "Arthur Fenton."

Appearing nervous, Artie stood in the witness box. He glanced once at Regina and then gave his full attention to the prosecutor.

"Mr. Fenton, you work for Lady Bradford?"

"I do."

"Besides driving her coach, what other duties have you performed in recent days?"

Artie looked confused.

"In other words, what task have you been assigned to do in her garden?"

The coachman's expression cleared. "Do you mean when Her Ladyship practices tossing her daggers at the tree?"

"Her Ladyship practices her aim with daggers?"

Artie grinned. "My job is to fetch the throws that miss. I think I lost a stone those two weeks. Gawd, she is the absolute worst. Poor hand and eye coordination."

Lowing rolled his eyes. "No more questions."

Percy Howell walked to the witness box. "Mr. Fenton—"

"Call me Artie."

The barrister smiled at that. "Artie, did you drive Lady Bradford to her father's the night before his body was found?"

"No."

"Can Lady Bradford drive a coach?"

"I don't think so. At least, I never saw her do it."

"Thank you, Artie. No further questions."

"Desmond Pickles," the prosecutor called.

Pickles came forward. He stood in the witness box and smiled at Regina.

"Did Lady Bradford go out on the nights in question?" Lowing asked.

"What nights would those be?" Pickles drawled.

"The nights of the three murders."

"I hesitate to answer this question."

"I understand," Lowing said, "but the court needs to know the answer."

"Prince Viktor and Lady Regina passed those nights together in bed," Pickles answered.

Excited whispers sounded in the gallery. The Chief Justice banged his gavel for silence.

"You actually saw them in bed?"

Pickles nodded. "Constable Black saw them, too."

"Did they charge admission?"

Howls of laughter echoed in the gallery, and reporters wrote their notes in a frenzy. Humiliated, Regina covered her face with her hands. The Duke of Inverary put his arm around her shoulders to offer comfort, a gesture not lost on the three justices.

"I object," Percy Howell called.

"Sustained." The Chief Justice looked at the prosecutor. "Mr. Lowing, if you want to perform, go into private practice like Mr. Howell. The pay is better."

"I apologize, my lord." Lowing returned his attention to the majordomo. "You saw them in bed on the three nights in question?"

"No, I saw them only on the first two nights," Pickles answered. "I know nothing about the third night except Her Ladyship remained at home for the evening. She hasn't been feeling well lately."

"What is her complaint?"

Pickles looked down his long nose at the prosecutor. "You will need to ask her."

"I intend to do that if she has the courage to take the stand." Lowing turned to the judges. "I have no more questions."

Percy Howell crossed the courtroom. "When did Lady Bradford threaten her husband?"

"She threatened him when he threatened her," Pickles answered.

"What did Lady Bradford say or do when Cedric Barrows offered for her?"

"She told him to leave and never return. I never cared much for him, either. Nastiness runs in that family."

"Objection."

"Sustained." The Chief Justice turned the majordomo, saying, "Only answer the question asked."

"I apologize for telling the truth."

"My lord," Lowing whined.

"Let it go," the Chief Justice said. "Continue, Mr. Howell."

"You testified to having seen the prince and the countess in bed together on two of the three nights

in question," Howell said. "Why don't you know if
the lady had company the third night?"

"Prince Viktor prowled around Bradford House
like a tomcat," Pickles drawled, eliciting laughter
from the gallery. "No matter where he passed an
evening, the prince returned to Bradford House
like a homing pigeon. Having my sleep interrupted
to allow him entrance exhausted me. I gave him his
own key."

"Since the prince had his own key," Howell said,
"could he have arrived and gone upstairs without
your knowledge?"

"Yes."

"No more questions."

Prosecutor Lowing called, "Forest Fredericks."

Uncle Forest smiled at Regina as he passed her.
She returned his smile. He and Ginger were the
only loved ones left from her childhood. She had
never expected to lose her father or Bart Evans
so soon.

"Mr. Fredericks, you were Reginald Smith's business associate?"

"Yes, I was."

"Where were you on the night Reginald Smith
was murdered?"

"I had gone out of town to my nephew's wedding."

"Please tell the court about the relationship between Reginald Smith and his daughter."

Uncle Forest sent her a look of apology and
pushed his spectacles up. "Unfortunately, Reginald
was either critical of Regina or ignored her. I tried
to play the peacemaker whenever I could."

Lowing smiled at the older man. "No further
questions."

"You were very close to both Reginald and

Regina," Percy Howell said, walking toward the witness box.

"Like family, I hope."

"You were so close that when Reginald was distraught about his daughter's reputation after Cedric Barrows's murder," Howell said, "you agreed to his scheme to marry Regina in order to shield her from censure."

The spectacles slipped. "That is correct."

"And you were not murdered?"

The spectators in the gallery laughed. One bang of the gavel quieted them.

Forest Fredericks pushed his spectacles up. "I may be old, but I'm not dead yet."

More laughter. One gavel bang.

"No more questions."

Prosecutor Lowing stood. "Princess Samantha Kazanov."

Regina whirled around. She could not imagine the reason the princess would be called to testify. What did she have to do with any of this?

"Princess Samantha, do you have knowledge in the use of daggers?"

"Yes, I do."

"Did you share this knowledge with Regina Bradford?"

Samantha sent her an apologetic look. "Yes, I did."

"Did you give her two small daggers?"

"Yes, I did."

"No further questions."

Percy Howell stood. "Princess Samantha, do you own several daggers?"

"Yes, I do."

"Have you ever murdered anyone?"

Chuckles in the gallery. One bang of the gavel.

Samantha smiled. "I have never murdered anyone, but I have threatened my husband a few times."

"No further questions."

Prosecutor Lowing stood and paused to send Regina a chillingly frightening smile. "I call Prince Viktor Kazanov to the witness stand."

Stunned by this unexpected turn, Regina watched Viktor walk from the rear of the courtroom to the witness box. Her heart ached with love and yearning. She knew her prince had come to rescue her from the hangman and the prosecutor.

After taking the oath, Viktor looked at Regina. His love for her shone from his dark gaze, and she gave him a smile meant to encourage.

"Your Highness, please tell this court the whereabouts of Regina Bradford on the night of her father's murder," Lowing said.

Viktor flicked a glance toward the defense table. "I cannot say."

His words pierced Regina's heart sharper than any dagger. He knew she could never hurt anyone but refused to stretch the truth. *As she had done for him.*

"Cannot say or will not say?" Lowing asked.

"I do not know the lady's whereabouts on the night of her father's murder."

A collective gasp from the gallery echoed in the courtroom. Loud murmurings erupted, and reporters scribbled their notes.

Viktor looked at her, his expression asking for her understanding. Regina turned her whole body away from his entreating gaze.

"No further questions."

Percy Howell rose from his chair. "Your Highness, do you believe—?"

"I object," Lowing protested. "The prince's belief calls for a conclusion."

"Sustained."

Percy Howell looked unhappy. "No questions."

Prince Viktor left the witness box. He paused at the defense table, but she refused to acknowledge him.

"Reggie, please look at me."

Regina whirled around and leveled an expression of hatred on him. "Do not speak to me again. Ever."

For once, the gallery was completely silent, all interest on the confrontation between the lovers. The Chief Justice banged his gavel to get the prince's attention.

Viktor ignored him. "Please, Reggie, try to—"

Regina bolted out of her chair to confront him, shrugging off her barrister's restraining hand. "Spare me your presence at my hanging, Judas traitor."

The Chief Justice banged his gavel again. Percy Howell managed to get Regina seated, but Viktor refused to walk away.

"Your Highness," the Chief Justice called.

Viktor glanced at the judges. He gave her a silent appeal, which went unanswered, and returned to his place at the rear of the courtroom.

"Amadeus Black," Lowing called.

The constable stood in the witness box, his attention on the prosecutor.

"Constable Black, please tell the court what killed Reginald Smith."

"When I arrived on the scene, the victim had a small dagger protruding from his chest."

"Did you read Regina Bradford's manuscript?"

"Yes, I did."

"Had she written accurately about the murders?"

"In the countess's manuscript, the heroine's father was killed with a pistol," Amadeus answered, "but the other murders were the same."

"Do you have a personal opinion about the discrepancy?"

"I would say the fictional father's death was written before Reginald Smith died. I cannot speculate when the other fictional murders were written, before or after the real ones."

"So, it is possible that the fictional murders were written before the real ones?" Lowing asked.

"Anything is possible."

"No further questions."

Percy Howell left the defense table and advanced on the witness box. "So, constable, we have no accurate way of knowing when Lady Bradford wrote the fictional murders."

"That is what I said."

Percy Howell paced back and forth in front of the witness box, his brow furrowed as if in deep thought. Abruptly, he turned to the constable.

"Are you generally considered a master crime investigator?"

Amadeus Black shrugged. "I suppose so."

"Do you usually recommend whom the prosecutor should arrest?" Howell asked.

"I collect evidence, question people, and listen to what my instincts are saying," Amadeus answered. "Then I inform the prosecutor what the evidence is and who seems guilty."

"Did you follow that procedure in this case?"

"Not precisely."

Howell looked at him. "What did you do in this case?"

"I did everything except tell the prosecutor who seemed guilty."

"Didn't the evidence, the people questioned, and your instincts point to Regina Bradford as the murderer?" Howell asked.

"Objection," Lowing called. "Mr. Howell is asking the witness to reach a conclusion."

"My lords, the esteemed prosecutor asked the constable for an opinion," Howell said. "Will the defense be held to a different standard? Mr. Lowing brought the constable's expert opinion into this hearing. I am merely delving deeper into that opinion."

"Objection overruled. Answer the question, Constable Black."

"I advised Mr. Lowing *not* to bring charges against Regina Bradford," Amadeus answered. "I believe the evidence is insufficient and the lady is incapable of harming another person except, perhaps, in defense of her child or herself."

"Thank you, Constable Black. No further questions."

Prosecutor Lowing stood. "The prosecution rests."

"Mr. Howell?"

Percy Howell faced the courtroom. "I call Regina Bradford, the Countess of Langley."

Chapter 19

"My lords." Her barrister stood to petition the judges. *"I make a motion to dismiss all charges for lack of evidence."*

"Motion granted. I dismiss all charges against Dementia Merlot." The Chief Justice banged his gavel once, ending the proceedings.

Dementia breathed a sigh of relief, her date with the hangman canceled. She hugged her barrister, telling him, *"I owe you my life."*

The Duke of Charming rushed to her side. *"Darling Dementia, we can go home now and begin our lives together."*

"You go home, Your Grace." Dementia gave him her most engaging smile. *"Begin that new life without me."*

The duke looked surprised. *"I am an honorable man, my love, and swore to tell the truth. Only a man without integrity would perjure himself."*

"Cherish your honor, my love." Her gaze on him smoldered with passion, so at odds with her words. *"I do hope your integrity keeps you warm tonight."*

"But Dementia—"

She showed him her back and walked away.

Regina stood, her shoulders straight and her head held high. She accepted her barrister's arm like a young queen and allowed him to escort her to the witness box.

Her simple black gown accentuated her frailty, her starkly pale complexion contrasting with the sombre color. Her riotous red hair was the only splash of color, her unruly curls pulled away from her face and fastened with a black ribbon at the nape of her neck. Softening the look, a few recalcitrant wisps of red escaped to frame her wan face.

"My lady, do you need a chair?" Percy Howell asked.

"No, thank you." Her voice was soft, forcing her audience to strain to hear her words.

"If at any time you want a chair," Howell said, "the court will oblige your need."

"Thank you." She gave him a wobbly smile.

"Lady Bradford, please describe your relationship with your late husband."

"We despised each other."

Muted, almost nervous chuckles emanated from the spectators. When she glanced in the direction of the gallery, silence broke out.

"Then why did you marry the earl?"

"Charles Bradford wanted my father's money," Regina answered, "and my father wanted a title in the family."

"We do not live in olden times when women married where they were told." Percy Howell gave her a long look. "What did *you* want?"

Regina lifted her gaze to the Chief Justice as her barrister had instructed. "I wanted to win my father's love and approval."

"And did you?"

"No."

"I am sorry for that," Percy Howell said. "Please

tell the court about your relationship with Cedric Barrows."

"I had no relationship with Cedric Barrows," Regina said. "With Charles dead, Cedric saw his chance to marry my father's money, but I would never again marry to win my father's approval."

"Tell us about Prince Viktor Kazanov."

"I met the prince at the Duke of Inverary's country party," Regina said. "The prince and I shared the knowledge that our spouses were engaged in an illicit affair, and he protected me from my husband's violence."

"Anything else?"

"We became lovers."

"Thank you, my lady, for your honesty." Percy Howell gave her an encouraging smile. "Please tell the court about your relationship with your father."

"My mother died when I was very young," Regina began, "and my father never remarried. I always seemed to be at odds with him. He ignored or criticized me, and I resented his wishing I had been born a boy. I resemble my mother, but I am my father's daughter. We bickered about everything because we shared similar traits such as extreme stubborness.

"My father visited me the day before he died and said he loved me," she continued, "and I told him I had always loved him. We were looking forward to a closer relationship."

"My lords, I object." Prosecutor Lowing stood. "This is exceedingly touching but irrelevant to the court's proceedings."

"Sit, Lowing, and keep quiet." The Chief Justice looked at Regina. "You may continue, my dear."

"Thank you, my lords," Percy Howell spoke up.

"Tell the court about your manuscript, Lady Bradford."

"I admire Miss Jane Austen greatly," Regina answered. "I decided to try my hand at penning a novel. In the process of creating a story, I borrowed people and events from my own life."

"Have you written me into your story?" the Chief Justice teased her, eliciting chuckles from the gallery.

Regina gave him a shy smile. "My lord, you are the hero of chapter eight."

"Lady Bradford, did you murder or conspire to murder Charles Bradford?" Howell asked.

"No."

"Did you murder or conspire to murder Adele Kazanov?"

"No."

"Did you murder or conspire to murder Cedric Barrows?"

"No."

"Did you murder or conspire to murder Reginald Smith?"

"No."

Percy Howell turned to the bench. "No more questions, my lords."

Prosecutor Lowing stood and advanced on the witness box. "Lady Bradford, do you know what perjury is?"

"Yes."

"Please explain perjury."

Regina stared at him a long moment. "Don't *you* know?"

Laughter rang out in the crowded courtroom. Even the judges could not contain their mirth.

The prosecutor waited until the room quieted. The merriment died a slow death.

"Isn't it true that on the night of your father's murder, you left your house in secret and found your way to his offices?" Lowing asked.

Regina shook her head. "No."

"And when you reached your father's office," the prosecutor continued, "you drove a blade into his heart."

"I could never harm my own father or anyone else. Besides, remaining awake so late at night would be impossible for me."

"Impossible?" Lowing's tone screamed disbelief.

"Recently, I have spent a great many hours sleeping," Regina said. "Pregnant women tend to sleep more often and dread the mornings."

Shocked silence gripped the gallery.

"Ah, yes . . ." The prosecutor's tone was snide. "You carry the prince's bastard."

"I will slay you," Viktor shouted at the prosecutor, and pandemonium exploded in the gallery.

Viktor started forward to confront the prosecutor, but his three brothers grabbed him. They struggled to hold him back.

"Release the prince," one spectator shouted.

"Lowing needs a good thrashing," another called.

The Chief Justice banged his gavel like a shoemaker at work. The three Kazanov princes managed to subdue their brother. When the prince calmed, the spectators quieted, too.

Lowing turned to the bench. "No further questions."

"My lady, you may step down," the Chief Justice said.

Percy Howell helped her out of the witness box and escorted her to the defense table. When she sat, the Duke of Inverary rested his arm on the back of her chair in a protective gesture.

"My lords." Percy Howell addressed the three justices. "I make a motion to dismiss all charges against Regina Bradford for insufficient evidence."

"Motion granted." The Chief Justice banged his gavel, ending the proceedings.

"Thank you." Regina hugged Percy Howell and then the Duke of Inverary.

"Regina." Viktor rushed forward through the departing crowd like a salmon swimming upstream. He pulled her into his embrace, holding her close for the first time in several weeks.

She stood stiffly in his arms. "Release me, Your Highness."

His hands dropped away. "What is wrong?"

"You don't know?"

Viktor ran a hand through his black hair in obvious frustration. He glanced at the witness box and then at her. "I am a man of integrity, Reggie, and had sworn to tell the truth."

"I hope your integrity keeps you warm tonight." Regina showed him her back, ignoring his brothers' chuckles. "Your Grace, will you escort me to Bradford House?"

"I would be honored," the duke answered.

"I will take you home," Viktor said.

Regina turned to face him. "I want nothing more to do with you, nor will I ever be used by another man again."

"You are carrying my child."

"No, Your Highness, I am carrying *my* child." She smiled at the Duke of Inverary. "Your Grace? I am anxious to see my son."

An hour later, the Duke of Inverary escorted her through the throng of reporters and the simply curious who stood outside Bradford House. The duke

ushered her into the foyer where her friend and retainers waited to welcome her.

"Don't worry about those reporters outside,"
the duke told her. "I will send my agents to break
them up."

"Thank you, Your Grace." Regina hugged him
and planted a kiss on his cheek. "I appreciate all
you have done for me."

When the duke slipped outside, Regina bolted
the door behind him. She lifted her son out of the
nanny's arms and held him close while the others
watched in tearful silence.

"Kiss Mama," Austen said.

Regina planted dozens of kisses across his face,
making him laugh. Then she turned to the others.

"Allow no men into this house, not even Uncle
Forest," Regina instructed her majordomo. "If
Uncle Forest stops by, tell him to carry on with the
business as usual. Artie, I want you to stand guard
in the foyer with Pickles in the event someone gets
surly. Set a couple of footmen in the garden to keep
it clear of reporters and other undesirables."

"Yes, my lady. Who are other undesirables?"

"Prince Viktor." Regina looked at Ginger. "Have
you finished with those ledgers?"

"No, I've been too worried to concentrate," Ginger answered. "I will return to them now that
you're home."

Someone outside banged the door knocker.

"Who is it?" Pickles called, without opening the
door.

"Viktor Kazanov."

"I am sorry, Your Highness," Pickles said. "Her
Ladyship is receiving no visitors."

"This is Amadeus Black," another voice called. "I
want to speak with Ginger Evans."

"I will send you a note," Ginger told him through the door. "For now, I will use every available moment to finish inspecting those ledgers."

"Contact me as soon as possible," the constable said. "Please tell the countess that I will retrieve her manuscript and return it to her."

"Yes, I'll tell her."

Carrying Austen, Regina walked upstairs. She passed a wonderfully peaceful afternoon and evening in the company of her son.

After her bout with nausea the next morning, Regina went to the dining room for breakfast. "Good morning," she called, and then sat opposite her friend at the table.

"Good morning."

Pickles brought her a pot of tea and a plate of scrambled eggs with toast. Then he set the morning paper on the table beside her.

Regina stared at the headlines: PRINCE LOVES COMMONER. Then she read the front page article, which included quotes from several people.

"I never believed the countess was capable of murder," Amadeus Black remarked.

"Lack of evidence does not mean innocent," Prosecutor Lowing said. *"London's most famous constable is not infallible."*

"I intend to marry Lady Bradford as soon as possible," Prince Viktor Kazanov said.

"Lady Bradford has no comment," insisted Desmond Pickles, the countess's majordomo.

Regina looked up. "You made the papers, Pickles. I hope this doesn't mean you will want a raise."

"Oh, drat," he said, and returned to the sideboard.

Artie walked into the dining room. "Prince Viktor and Constable Black are standing outside the front door and demanding admittance. What shall I tell them?"

"Go away," both women said simultaneously, and then smiled at each other.

"Wait." Regina looked at her friend. "The constable redeemed himself in court yesterday. Speak to him."

Ginger nodded. "Tell Amadeus to meet me in the garden."

Banishing the urge to think about the prince standing on her doorstep, Regina gave her attention to her breakfast and the morning paper. She was sipping her second cup of tea when Ginger returned.

The other woman set the manuscript on the dining table. "Amadeus wanted to return this."

Regina stared at the manuscript. Finishing held no appeal for her at the moment.

"He asked me to marry him," Ginger said.

Regina smiled. "We'll have the ceremony and reception here."

"I told him I would marry him after your life is settled."

Regina rolled her eyes. "Ginger, my life *is* settled. Accept the man's proposal."

"Amadeus and the Kazanov brothers will continue to search for the murderer," Ginger told her.

"I wish them luck, but that has nothing to do with me."

Later that afternoon, Regina sat in the family parlor and knitted a blanket for her baby. With her were Nanny Sprig, Austen, and Hamlet.

"Mama look," Austen called.

With Nanny Sprig holding his hand, Austen walked toward her. He kept walking with his arms outstretched for balance when the nanny released his hand. Like a silent sentinel, Hamlet walked beside her son.

Laughing, Regina grabbed her son and kissed him. "What a good boy," she exclaimed. "You can walk."

"We'll need to tie everything down now," Nanny Sprig said, making her smile.

Austen squirmed out of his mother's arms, looked at the nanny, and held his arm out. "Wak, Na-na."

Pickles walked into the parlor. "Princess Samantha requests an interview."

"Escort the princess here." Regina knew Samantha had come to plead the prince's case. "Nanny Sprig, take Austen upstairs."

"Yes, my lady."

A moment later, Princess Samantha walked into the parlor and sat on the settee. "You look wonderful." She dropped her gaze to the table where two last resort daggers lay.

Regina followed the other woman's gaze. "The murderer has not been caught, and I plan to practice every day until he sits in Newgate."

"Reggie—"

"Are you here to plead for Viktor?"

"I have come as your friend," Samantha said. "Viktor loves you and is worrying himself sick."

"Viktor enjoys a stronger constitution than that," Regina said with a smile.

"The prosecutor would not let him visit you."

"Viktor refused to give me an alibi as I did for him," Regina said. "If Percy Howell wasn't so talented, I would be meeting the executioner."

"Didn't Viktor pass the night of Adele's murder here?"

Regina nodded. "He passed the night here, but

not in my bed. I knew the court would misinterpret my meaning; nevertheless, I would have lied for him anyway."

"Reggie—" Ginger Evans hurried into the parlor, sat on the settee, and looked at the princess. "Nice to see you again, Your—"

"Samantha," the princess corrected her.

Ginger inclined her head. "Reggie, there's a problem with the ledgers. I think Uncle Forest's fondness for gambling has got the better of him."

"What do you mean?"

"Uncle Forest has been stealing from your father's business and trying to doctor the figures."

Regina could not believe what she was hearing. His stealing to pay gambling debts was possible. But that would mean—

"Uncle Forest would never murder anyone, especially my father. Would he?"

The three women sat in silence.

Regina tried to reconcile the man she had always considered an unofficial uncle with the idea of him murdering in cold blood. And then she recalled something that settled the matter for her.

"Uncle Forest told me and Percy Howell that my father had asked him to marry me to save my reputation," Regina reminded them. "My father told me he had agreed to Uncle Forest's suggestion to marry me to save my reputation."

"The motive for murder was money," Ginger said. "Forest murdered Charles because, if something happened to your father, he would have discovered the theft."

"Adele was in the wrong place at the wrong time," Samantha said.

"Cedric had won my father's approval to marry me and died for the same reason as Charles,"

Regina added. "Forest tried to murder Viktor for the same reason. Why did he kill my father?"

"Viktor visited your father and received his permission to marry you," Samantha told her.

"When did this happen?"

"The day before your father died."

"Perhaps Forest feared Reginald would make changes in his will," Ginger said. "My father must have discovered the theft. But, how did Forest make the murder appear a suicide?"

"I know how he did it." Regina reached for her last resort daggers and began strapping them to her legs. "You told me a straight line around the neck meant murder, but an inverted *V* meant suicide."

Ginger nodded. "Amadeus said that."

"Forest knocked your father unconscious and then hanged him, which made it appear a suicide." Regina stood, saying, "I am going to speak with Uncle Forest."

Ginger stood when she did. "We should send for Amadeus."

"And Viktor." Samantha rose from the settee. "My brothers-in-law are meeting at my house."

"Go home and tell them to meet at my father's office." Regina looked at Ginger. "Artie is off today. Drop me at my father's office and then fetch Amadeus."

"We don't know how to drive," Ginger protested.

Regina smiled with confidence. "How difficult can it be?"

After several near crashes with the coach, Ginger halted it near the Smith offices. The twenty minute ride felt more like twenty years.

"Get Amadeus." Regina climbed down.

"Wait for the Kazanovs."

"Don't be silly. Uncle Forest won't shoot me."

Regina watched Ginger turn the coach around and drive down West India Road. Then she headed for her father's office.

Aim for the neck first. When he lifts his arms to clutch his neck, aim the second dagger at his heart.

"Uncle Forest?" Regina called, stepping inside.

Forest Fredericks appeared from the back room and smiled when he saw her. "You are recovered from your ordeal. I could have come to Bradford House to discuss your father's will and business."

"I could never welcome my father's murderer into my home," Regina said.

He appeared surprised, but his guilty gaze skittered away from hers. "Reggie, I don't understand."

"Uncle Forest, you should have told my father your gambling was out of control," Regina said, her voice filling with aching regret. "He would have been understanding. You know, he considered you and Bart Evans the brothers he never had."

Forest dropped into his chair. "In hindsight, I see you are correct, but once I—" He shrugged.

"You murdered Uncle Bart and made it appear a suicide," Regina said. "Then you murdered Charles, Adele, and Cedric. Why did you kill my father?"

"I regretted that one," Forest told her. "Reginald was going to make Prince Viktor his executor, and the prince's accountants would have discovered the theft."

"Ginger discovered the theft."

"I knew she had inherited her father's genius with numbers." Forest opened his desk drawer and withdrew his pistol. "Shooting you makes me feel like I'm dispatching my own daughter."

"Shooting me will not solve your problem," Regina said. "Ginger has those ledgers and is fetching Amadeus Black."

"Reggie!"

The door crashed open, startling them. Prince Viktor rushed into the office.

Forest bolted out of his chair. He shifted the pistol away from Regina and aimed for Viktor.

"Don't shoot my prince!"

In a flash of movement, Regina drew her last resort dagger and aimed for his neck. Uncle Forest clutched his neck, and she tossed the second dagger, hitting his heart.

Fredericks went down, blood spurting from both wounds, forming a pool beside his body.

Viktor dashed across the office. Regina looked from the body to the blood to the prince, and she then fainted.

"Reggie, wake up now."

From a far distance, Regina heard her prince recalling her to consciousness. She opened her eyes slowly. He held her in his arms, but other faces hovered above her. Rudolf, Mikhail, Stepan, Ginger, Amadeus.

Regina shifted her gaze from the others to the prince. "I still don't forgive you."

"Why did you save my life?" Viktor asked, amusement lighting his eyes.

"You have not suffered enough."

Viktor laughed in her face. "If you forgive me, I promise to tell you a lie every day for the rest of my life."

"No lies."

"Dementia, I love you." The Duke of Charming marched across the drawing room.

Though she had one last line to write, Dementia set her manuscript aside. She walked toward him, meeting him in the middle of the room.

"I love you, too."

The Duke of Charming smiled. "You will marry me?"

Dementia slid her hands up his chest, reveling in the masculine feel of him. "Yes, I will marry you and promise always to love and to honor you."

"What about obey?"

"No."

Regina sat alone in the parlor the following afternoon and wrote the final chapter of her story. She enjoyed the silence in the room, especially after yesterday's excitement.

Ginger and Amadeus had gone to lunch to discuss plans for their wedding. Walking had tired Austen, who had been put down for a nap. Hamlet had elected to nap in her son's room.

Feeling another's presence, Regina glanced toward the doorway. Viktor stood there, watching her, and then sauntered across the parlor. He was so heartbreakingly handsome.

"May I sit?"

Regina inclined her head, giving him permission.

"I have gifts for you." Viktor sat beside her on the settee. "Will you accept them?"

She shrugged and set her manuscript on the table. He placed a rolled parchment, tied with a red ribbon, in the palm of her hand.

Regina pulled the ribbon off, opened the parchment, and read. She snapped her gaze to his. "You bought a publishing company?"

"If you write books and I publish them," Viktor said, "we will not need to pay a middle man. A book cartel, in a manner of speaking."

Her lips twitched into a grudging smile. "You must be desperate for my forgiveness."

"I do not enjoy suffering." Viktor offered her a small velvet box.

Regina stared at it. She knew it was an engagement ring.

"Open it."

Regina lifted the box from his hand. On a bed of black velvet lay an exquisite diamond brooch fashioned in the shape of butterfly wings.

Pushing the table back, Viktor knelt on one bended knee in front of her and took her hands in his. "Lady Regina, will you do me the honor of soaring with me?"

A soft smile touched her lips. "Yes, I will soar with you."

Viktor kissed her hands and then reached into his pocket for another box. Inside was a diamond ring, shaped like a butterfly. He slipped it onto her finger.

"I love you." Regina wrapped her arms around his neck and pressed her lips to his. She poured all her love into that single, stirring kiss.

"I love you more," Viktor said, his voice husky with emotion. "I bought you a necklace and a bracelet, too."

"No earrings?"

Viktor laughed and crushed her against his body. Their lips met in a kiss that promised eternal passion. Regina closed her eyes and slid her hand down his chest to his groin.

"What are you doing, my love?"

"Seducing the prince."

And they lived happily ever after.

Please turn the page for an exciting sneak peek of
Patricia Grasso's
next historical romance
PLEASURING THE PRINCE
coming in April 2006!

Chapter 1

London, 1821

"Loves me, loves me not . . ."

A tall gentleman, dressed in formal evening attire, stood on the summit of Primrose Hill in the predawn gray of a mist-shrouded morning. Carried on the wind, the unmistakeable smell of the Thames tainted the early spring air, and a raw clamminess permeated his exposed skin.

The man smiled almost lovingly at the woman, beautiful in death, giving proof to the peacefulness of her passing. He dug into his leather pouch, clutched a handful of rose petals, and sprinkled them one-by-one the length her body from head to feet.

"A waste of true beauty," said a hoarse voice.

The gentleman looked at the short, plump woman standing beside him. "Return to the coach." Knowing she would obey without argument, he took another handful of rose petals from his pouch.

"Loves me, loves me not . . ."

Royal Opera House

I refuse to become my mother.

Fancy Flambeau sat on a stool in a pigeonhole dressing room and prepared for her operatic debut. Pots of theater makeup cluttered the tiny table in front of her, and a miniscule mirror hung on the wall over the table.

She had dressed for the role of the adolescent Cherubino in *The Marriage of Figaro*. Her costume consisted of black breeches, white shirt, and red jerkin.

Beyond normal nervousness, her debut did not frighten her. Fancy had more important worries such as aristocratic males who preyed upon singers, dancers, and actresses. Long ago, she had resolved never to love an aristocrat or let herself become love's victim. Like her mother.

Keeping that resolve had been easy until today. Once Fancy stepped on the stage, every wealthy male in London would set their gazes on her for the first time and target her for their next conquest. Men of the aristocratic ilk considered women like her their quarry, living toys to be used and discarded on a whim.

After wiping her hands on a linen, Fancy peered in the mirror at her six younger sisters crowding the dressing room. She turned around and gave them her most confident smile. "By this time tomorrow, I will have become London's most famous diva."

Belle, Blaze, Bliss, Rouge, Solange, and Raven laughed at her feigned bravado. Her sisters ranged in age from sixteen to nineteen, with two sets of twins. The only missing family members were Nanny Smudge and her mother, Gabrielle Flambeau.

Fancy wished her mother and her nanny had lived to see this day. She sighed, thinking she had many unattainable dreams. More dreams than money.

"We should go to our seats." Nineteen-year-old

Belle opened the door and gasped in surprise when something small and hairy ran passed her into the room.

A monkey climbed onto Fancy's lap. The animal covered its ears with its hands, then its eyes, and finally its mouth.

"A Capuchin monkey." Eighteen-year-old Blaze crouched beside her sister's stool. She imitated the monkey's actions and then lifted it into her arms, cradling it against her shoulder like a baby.

"Giggles, there you are." With an apologetic smile, a stocky man stepped into the dressing room and carried the monkey away.

"Who is that?" asked Raven, the youngest.

"Sebastian Tanner is the diva's husband," Fancy answered, "and Giggles is her pet."

"Giggles hates the Tanners," Blaze said. "I saw it in his eyes."

"The monkey has good taste," Fancy said, making them smile.

Her sisters filed out of the dressing room to find their seats in the audience. Only Raven lingered behind.

Fancy produced a fine white linen handkerchief, two of its corners embroidered with the initials MC and the other two with a tiny boar's head. She passed the handkerchief to her sister.

"Is he in the audience?"

Raven held the handkerchief in both hands and closed her eyes. "I feel him close."

"Seeing his oldest bastard on stage should surprise him." Fancy lifted the handkerchief out of her sister's hand. "I hope he suffers agonizing pangs of conscience."

"Why do you persist in nursing a grudge against

the man who sired us?" Raven asked. "Bitterness
hurts you more than him."

"Our father put Mama in an early grave."

"Mama was responsible for her own fate."

"He never loved us," Fancy continued, as if her
sister had not spoken.

"You cannot see what dwells in another's heart,"
Raven said. "His money has supported us through
the years, and he sent Nanny Smudge to care for us."

"Stop being so damned philosophical about a father you would not recognize if you passed him on
the street." Fancy sighed, knowing her sister was
right. "And Nanny Smudge has joined Mama."

"Nanny Smudge has gone nowhere." Raven
touched her hand. "You know she protects us still."

Hearing the orchestra begin the opera's overture, Fancy reached for her hairbrush. "We'll meet
outside after the show."

After her sister had gone, Fancy looked into the
mirror. She brushed her black hair away from her
face and weaved it into a knot at the nape of her
neck.

Without warning, stage fright caught her.

Fancy gagged dryly over the small pot beside the
table. She grabbed a cup off the table, swished
water around her mouth, and spit it into the pot.

"Wish me luck, Nanny Smudge," she murmured.

The aroma of cinnamon scented the air inside
the pigeonhole dressing room, making her smile.
Her nanny's scent.

Fancy grabbed the costume's hat and, leaving the
dressing room, hurried toward the stage to await
her cue. In keeping with her role of Cherubino,
she donned the boy's cap and smiled at Gracie
Stover, the woman playing the role of Barbarina.

"Did you hear about that ballet dancer?" Gracie whispered.

Fancy shook her head. "What happened?"

"The rose-petal murderer got her." Gracie heard her cue and hurried on stage.

Fancy banished this murdered dancer from her mind. *Think adolescent boy,* she told herself. *A charming scamp who loves all women and worships the countess. Eager and randy.*

Stepping onto the stage, Fancy focused on the music and lyrics. A petite woman with a powerful voice, Fancy attacked the song and immersed herself in it. Emotionally involved, she forced the audience to follow wherever she led them.

The power in her voice could break their hearts. Or mend them.

During Cherubino's plea to the countess, Fancy turned downstage center close to the edge of the stage. Patrice Tanner, playing the countess, stuck her foot out.

Unable to stop her forward momentum, Fancy tumbled off the stage and flew into the orchestra pit. She heard the audience's collective gasp but kept singing. Several musicians caught her and lifted her onto the stage.

Fancy narrowed her gaze on the diva in an unspoken declaration of war. She threw her arms out in a sweeping gesture and struck the diva with a backhanded slap.

The audience loved it and roared with laughter. Fancy glanced sidelong at the audience and gave them an exaggerated wink, making them laugh even more.

Both women exited the stage. Wearing a long-suffering expression, Director Bishop waited in the wings.

"The twit struck me," the diva complained. "Get rid of her."

"I cannot do that," the director said. "The audience loved her. Slapping you was an accident, and she's sorry. Aren't you, Fancy?"

"I am not sorry."

Patrice Tanner gave her a murderous glare and stalked off. Loitering near them, her husband followed her.

"Prince Stepan Kazanov requests an introduction during intermission." Director Bishop smiled at her. "The prince wants to gain the advantage over the other young swains."

A passing stagehand gave Fancy a cup of water. She swished the liquid around in her mouth, turned her head, and spit it out. The water splashed the director's shoes.

Fancy lifted her violet gaze to his. "Sorry."

"About the prince?"

"No."

"I cannot tell Prince Stepan you refuse to meet him," the director said. "His Highness is the opera's most generous patron."

"I am not for sale."

"Meeting the prince is part of your job," he told her. "You do want to keep your job, don't you?"

"You may introduce Prince Stepan after the show," Fancy agreed, reluctance etched across her expression. "Tell the prince I refuse to become his mistress."

"Tell him yourself."

"There she is."

Sitting with his three brothers in an opera box, Prince Stepan Kazanov stretched his long legs out and relaxed in his chair. He fixed his dark gaze on the woman making her operatic debut, following her every movement.

Miss Fancy Flambeau stood a mere two inches over five feet, a slight woman with a full-bodied voice. She had attracted his attention the afternoon he had stopped at the opera house to speak with the director. Stepan had listened to her singing and had known he would claim her for himself.

"That is the object of your interest?" Prince Viktor asked.

"She is dressed like a boy," Prince Mikhail remarked.

"Is my baby brother hiding a shockingly sinful secret?" Prince Rudolf asked.

"Miss Flambeau is playing Cherubino." Irritation raised Prince Stepan's voice. "Hence, the boy's attire."

"Shush."

The four Russian princes looked toward the opera box on their right. Lady Althorpe sat with the Duke and Duchess of Inverary, Rudolf's in-laws. The older woman glared at the four brothers.

Sitting closest to the lady, Rudolf gave her his most charming smile. "We apologize for the unnecessary noise, Lady Althorpe."

Stepan returned his attention to the stage. Fancy Flambeau, in the middle of Cherubino's plea to the countess, tripped over the diva's foot and tumbled off the stage.

The audience gasped and leaned forward in their seats. Luckily, several musicians caught her and lifted her onto the stage. The singer missed no lyrics. She took revenge by stepping close to the diva at the moment of an arm-sweeping gesture that struck the other woman.

Stepan chuckled with amusement. When the opera singer winked at the audience, he roared with laughter as did everyone else in the theater.

"I cannot believe those two did that on stage," Prince Viktor said.

"The reigning diva resents the rising star," Prince Mikhail said.

"Miss Flambeau seems strong-willed," Prince Rudolf said. "Her spirit will keep you in tow, baby brother."

"*Shush.*"

Prince Rudolf glanced at Lady Althorpe. "Sorry for the interruption, but my baby brother is misbehaving."

"Then take a paddle to his backside," the lady drawled.

The three oldest Kazanov princes burst into laughter.

"*Shush.*"

Stepan ignored his brothers' jibes. Being the youngest in the family, he had learned to disregard their teasing criticisms. Which, as he saw it, was the only drawback to being the youngest. His older brothers would always accept responsibility for his livelihood, whether he worked in the family business or not. Life was one continuous country house party.

"Your Highness?"

Stepan looked at the opera director. "Yes?"

"Your Highness, Miss Flambeau begs your indulgence," the man whispered, "but prefers to meet you after the show."

"Thank you." Stepan inclined his head and mentally rubbed his hands together. How many evenings would making her his mistress take?

Intermission began, the time when society mingled. Usually, Stepan left the Kazanov opera box and circulated among his many friends, speaking with the males and flirting with the females.

Tonight was different, though. Stepan stood to stretch his legs and sat down again, surprising his brothers.

"If you do not visit the Clarke box," Viktor said, "you will disappoint Lady Cynthia and her mother."

"Mother and daughter are trying to trap me into marriage," Stepan said. "The thought of passing my life with Cynthia Clarke gives me the hives."

"What about the merry widow?" Mikhail asked.

"Lady Veronica would be happier with you," Stepan said, "and you do need a stepmother for your daughter."

Prince Mikhail smiled. "Veronica Winthrop is decidedly unmotherly."

"If you direct your attention across the hall," Rudolf said, leaning close, "you will see Lady Drummond sending longing looks over here."

"Elizabeth Drummond is married." Stepan glanced at his oldest brother. "I am meeting Miss Flambeau after the show."

"The girl looks awfully young," Viktor said, drawing Stepan's attention.

"Once taken, her innocence can never be returned," Mikhail reminded him.

"You assume I plan to make her my mistress," Stepan said. "Who knows? I may propose marriage."

"Give over, baby brother." Rudolf eyed him with amusement. "The prince and the opera singer?"

"I would never corrupt an innocent." Stepan winked at his oldest brother. "Unless, of course, the innocent wanted corruption."

* * *

Fancy felt exhilarated. She stood in the wings and waited her turn to cross the stage and take a bow.

The director had sent the male leads out first and then Patrice Tanner. And now her turn had arrived.

Fancy stepped into the audience's view. Thunderous applause erupted, the deafening sound music to her ears.

In keeping with her role of Cherubino, Fancy swaggered like an adolescent boy and, making a show of her bow, swept the hat off. Her heavy mane of ebony cascaded around her, almost to her waist.

Someone in the audience tossed a rose at her feet. Another followed that. And then another.

"Encore," someone shouted.

And the audience took up the chant. "Encore, encore, encore."

Fancy looked around in confusion. She saw the fury etched across the diva's face, and then the director walked on stage.

"Sing something else." When she nodded, he ushered the others off stage.

Fancy had never felt so alone. She stood in silence for a long moment, wondering what to sing, and the audience quieted.

Somewhere in this theater sat the aristocrat who had killed her mother with emotional neglect. Thrusting a symbolic dagger into his heart appealed to her, and she seized the chance to let him know the damage he had done.

"As a child, I always begged my father for a ride in his coach," Fancy told the silent audience. "He said we needed to wait for a sunny day. When I grew older, I realized my father visited on rainy days only." She heard the audience chuckling. "I never did get that coach ride, but I did write a song about a magical land beyond the horizon where the sun shone every day. From dawn to dusk, raindrops were strictly forbidden."

Without musical accompaniment, Fancy began singing about the land of sunshine beyond the horizon. Her perfect voice and bittersweet words transported the audience through time and space back to their own pasts. Her lyrics recalled long-forgotten dreams and heart-tugging disappointments.

When the last word slipped from her lips, Fancy walked off stage and ignored the wild applause. Tears rolled down her face, leaving her stage makeup streaked.

"How touching." The voice belonged to Patrice Tanner. "Did you really believe an aristocrat would take his bastard into society?"

Reaching her dressing room, Fancy shut the door and leaned back against it. She needed a few minutes of privacy after baring her soul to those strangers.

What had her father thought of her song? She hoped . . .

What did she hope? Her father would beg her forgiveness for his neglect? Would remorse return her mother to life? A man she hadn't seen in fifteen years would feel nothing for her or her sisters.

And the damn prince expected to meet her. Bed her, more likely. How much of a royal pain in the arse would His Highness become?

Fancy caught a faint whiff of cinnamon. She thought of her beloved nanny and knew her advice.

Listen to your head, child, but follow your heart.

Her mother had followed her heart and paid the price.

Seven daughters.

No husband. No love. No prospects.

From outside the dressing room door came the unmistakeable sounds of relief. Performers and stagehands joked and laughed as they went about the business of closing shop for the night.

On this side of the door, traces of cinnamon lingered in the air. The spicy scent mingled with the fragrant theater makeup and musty wood smell from the floorboards.

Fancy knew only she could detect the cinnamon scent. Of all seven Flambeau sisters, she was the one physically sensitive to the unseen. She saw, heard, smelled, and sensed what others could not.

Fancy practiced caution regarding her unworldly gift. She had no wish to be locked in Bedlam.

Her sisters possessed their own special talents. Which she admired, more than her own at times.

Fancy pushed away from the door. Moments were ticking by, and she did not want the prince to catch her undressed.

Growing anxiety urged her to hurry. She scrubbed her face, leaving her complexion flushed.

Fancy stripped the boy's clothing off and donned her simple gown, its violet color matching her eyes. She grabbed her black shawl at the same moment someone rapped on the door.

Whirling around, Fancy stared at the door. She needed to reject the prince without insulting his pride or risk losing her job. How could she do the impossible?

Men were incredibly proud but stupid creatures. The fatter the purse, the bigger the pride, the emptier the head.

Another knock on the door.

Her heartbeat quickened. Her only experience

with men was Alexander Blake, a lifelong friend. What the blue blazes could she say to a prince?

"Fancy?" the opera director called.

She took a fortifying breath. "You may enter now."

The door swung open. Director Bishop stepped aside.

Temptation walked into the dressing room in the shape of a Russian prince, more beautiful than Lucifer before his fall from grace.

Prince Stepan Kazanov stood a couple of inches over six feet, his imposing presence filling the tiny dressing room. The prince possessed the dark good looks that women found intriguing. Broad shoulders, lean hips, and solid muscles showed to best advantage in his evening attire.

His arrestingly handsome face caught Fancy by surprise, igniting a flame in the pit of her stomach. Jet-black hair framed an angular, high cheekboned face. A dark intensity burned in his black eyes, fringed with sinfully long lashes and straight brows. His nose was long and straight and his lips thin but perfectly shaped.

Unexpected humor gleamed at her from his black eyes. His lips quirked into a boyish smile that said he did not take himself too seriously.

Uh-oh. Fancy knew she was in trouble. She needed to reject this disturbingly attractive aristocrat. She wished the prince was a common laborer because she did not want to send him away.

Having seen her from a distance only, Stepan was no less surprised by Fancy. Disarming violet eyes, generous lips, and a heart-shaped face gave her an air of sultry vulnerability.

Uh-oh. Stepan knew he was in trouble. He wanted to ravish the petite beauty, but her innocence screamed emotional commitment. Or even worse, marriage. Every instinct shouted at him to bolt out the door, but a stronger force refused to let him turn away.

Stepan stepped farther into the room. Fancy shrank back against the table.

"I do not bite, Miss Flambeau."

Fancy gave him a wobbly, embarrassed smile.

"Your Highness," Director Bishop said, "I present Fancy Flambeau."

The prince caught her hand and bowed over it in courtly manner, surprising her. "I am pleased to make your acquaintance, Fancy."

She found her voice. "Please call me Miss Flambeau."

Prince Stepan raised his brows at that. Director Bishop coughed. Fancy shifted her gaze from the prince to the director.

Stepan glanced over his shoulder at the director. "You may leave, Bishop. Fancy will not insult me into withdrawing my financial support." He looked at her again. "I find her prim formality refreshingly sweet."

"Leave the door open on your way out," Fancy ordered, making the prince smile. "I mean no insult, Your Highness."

"Call me Stepan."

Fancy considered refusing the familiarity but then inclined her head. "As you wish, Stepan."

"Your voice amazes me." He inched closer, staring at her upturned face. "Your eyes are exquisite Persian violets, and your beauty steals my breath."

Fancy was not buying what this aristocrat was selling. "I would not wish to cause your death. Perhaps you should leave?"

Stepan gave her his boyish smile. "A sharp-witted

woman is an exquisite rose with layers of petals to peel away."

Fancy laughed in his face. "You have too much leisure time, Stepan. Instead of wasting your days creating outrageous compliments, try getting a job."

The prince grinned at her insult. He looked like a boy caught in a prank.

Fancy felt her heart twist at the beauty of his smile. She needed to get rid of this charming aristocrat, but her lips refused to speak words of rejection. Had her mother felt like this when faced with her father? Gawd, she hoped not.

"You will not get rid of me with your biting wit," Stepan told her. "I have developed a thick skin from suffering years of my brothers' teasing."

Fancy had never considered princes would behave like commoners, teasing each other. She gave him an unconsciously flirtatious smile. "Oh, drat."

"You should use your lovely smile more often," the prince said. "I mean that sincerely, and your eyes do remind me of Persian violets."

"Thank you."

"I would like to celebrate your success with supper," Stepan invited her.

"My sisters are waiting for me outside," Fancy said, refusing him.

"Do you have your own coach?"

"No, I have my own legs."

Surprise registered on his expression. "You and your sisters cannot walk home at this hour. We will escort your sisters home and then go to supper."

"I don't want to sup with you."

The prince looked perplexed. Apparently, his aristocratic mind could not comprehend any woman refusing him.

"I met you in order to keep my job," Fancy told him. "Otherwise, I would not speak with you."

"Do you dislike Russians?"

"No."

"Do you dislike foreigners?"

"My mother was a foreigner."

"Do you dislike me?"

"I do not dislike you personally," Fancy tried to explain. "You are an . . . *aristocrat.*"

"Your lips say aristocrat, but your tone says leper." Stepan cocked a dark brow at her. "Before tonight, I have never felt inferior because of my wealth and title."

"I am honored to add to your life experience," Fancy said, willing him to leave before she changed her mind.

He lowered his voice to a seductive tone. "I know more pleasant ways to increase my life experience."

His remark shocked her. Her back stiffened at the insulting suggestion. He would never make a risqué comment to a society lady.

"I should have expected no respect from an aristocrat."

"Aristocrat is not the name of a fatal disease."

Fancy lifted her chin a notch, her gaze cold on his. "I have experience with the aristocracy."

"You are referring to your father." Stepan inclined his head in understanding. "Like commoners, aristocrats are not all the same. Please consider my supper invitation for tomorrow evening. We may have more in common than you realize."

"I doubt that."

"Come." Prince Stepan held out his hand as if asking her to dance.

Fancy wanted to place her hand in his, but her distrust proved too strong. She would allow no man to do to her what her father had done to her mother.

"I will escort you and your sisters home." Stepan took her hand in his. "Otherwise, I will worry for your safety even though you dislike me."

His words made Fancy feel like the meanest creature on earth. The prince seemed like a good man, and she had insulted him.

"I will sup with you tomorrow evening," Fancy relented, "but I refuse to become your mistress."

Amusement gleamed at her from the black depths of his eyes. "I did not ask you to become my mistress."

Fancy blushed, embarrassed by her presumption. What other reason could he have for wanting her company? She was the product of an illicit liaison between a duke and an opera singer, albeit an impovished French aristocrat, the sole surviving member of the Flambeau family after the Terror.

"Trust me." Stepan lifted her hand to his lips. "I would never seduce a reluctant innocent."

Fancy inclined her head. She wondered if the prince could be trusted to keep his word.

"Shall we?" Stepan gestured to the door.

With her hand locked in his, Fancy walked in silence through the deserted theater to the lobby. She felt self-conscious, her mind blanking at a topic for conversation. Gawd, tomorrow evening's supper promised a veritable dumb show.

They stepped outside the theater onto Bow Street, which should have been nearly deserted. Instead, coaches lined both sides of the street.

Fancy looked at him in confusion and tightened her grip on his hand. "What is happening?"

His lips parted into a boyish smile. "Your admirers are offering you the coach ride you never had."

ABOUT THE AUTHOR

Patricia Grasso lives in Massachusetts. She is the author of fourteen historical romances and is currently working on her next, which will be published by Zebra Books in 2006. Pat loves hearing from readers and you may write to her c/o Zebra Books. Please include a self-addressed stamped envelope if you wish a response. Readers can visit her website at www.patriciagrasso.com